AMERICAN GOSPEL

Also by Lin Enger

Undiscovered Country
The High Divide

AMERICAN GOSPEL

A NOVEL

Lin Enger

University of Minnesota Press

Minneapolis

Published by the University of Minnesota Press
111 Third Avenue South, Suite 290
Minneapolis, MN 55401-2520
http://www.upress.umn.edu

LIBRARY OF CONGRESS CATALOGING-IN-PUBLICATION DATA
Enger, Lin, author.
American gospel : a novel / Lin Enger.
Minneapolis : University of Minnesota Press, [2020]
Identifiers: LCCN 2020022377 (print) | ISBN 978-1-5179-1054-9 (hc)
Classification: LCC PS3555.N4224 A85 2020 (print) | DDC 813/.54—dc23
LC record available at https://lccn.loc.gov/2020022377

Printed in the United States of America on acid-free paper

The University of Minnesota is an equal-opportunity educator and employer.

25 24 23 22 21   10 9 8 7 6 5 4 3 2 1

To Kathy, whose wisdom and beauty light my way

AUGUST 6—TUESDAY

Turn, if you will, back to 1974 and the cathartic end of that long summer—a pivot in time that requires only the smallest adjustment. Now rise to an altitude that offers a view of the whole continent, the entire span of desert, mountain, lake, fruited field, towered city, ocean shore. From this height look down and pick them out, these ordinary, remarkable people, three of them, flesh of your flesh: a man, a woman, another man.

Bring them into focus. Squint, if you need to.

There, on a small farm beside a lavender-blue lake in the center of the northern forest, the first man is getting dressed in his upstairs room—worn denim shirt, lace-up boots—awake before the sun, as always. Tall and straight and bone-thin, white hair unshorn, he is simple in appearance only, this self-appointed prophet. Watch him as he descends the narrow staircase of his turn-of-the-century farmhouse, anticipating his coffee, unaware that he is just minutes away from dying.

The woman, way off in the California desert, is still young, barely thirty, asleep this morning in her waterbed, palm trees outside her window, three hours from waking to the life she once believed was charmed—and which still might be. She is lovely, an actress, with hair like the August wheat of the great Midwest. Her face is one that absorbs desire and sends back love. Not long ago she was a child in the hands of Goddess-makers, celebrated and pampered, lusted after. Was she happy? She might have believed so, but now she feels only pain, the kind that calls for routine numbing.

And finally, to the other coast and its city of high towers, New York, where the other man—son of the prophet—has stayed up all night, writing, talking, and drinking. He often jogs the seven blocks west from the all-night tavern that he favors to his third-floor walk-up in the Village, anxious to spend a little time in bed with his girlfriend before she leaves for work. This morning, though, he is in no hurry and even stops to sit on a bench in Washington Square, have a smoke. The sun is just up, light coming in from that low angle that scrubs the world, making everything look cleaner than it is—the sooty bricks, the street, the yellow cabs—and he thinks of the twenty thousand indigent souls that lie beneath his feet, buried here when this place was a potter's field. He can't help an irrational stitch of guilt for the good fortune about to befall him.

But I've earned it, he thinks.

Like his father, like the actress, like all of us, he is unable to see the disappointments and reversals and confounding victories to come. He knows only what he knows, which is far less than he imagines.

Twenty paces away, a sleeper lies curled in a garbage bag, his back hunched against the base of the big marble arch, fingers woven into a bunch of bananas. The man lifts a hand and waves it in Peter's direction, calling out, "Spare change," as if Peter is supposed to jump right up and walk over. Shaking out the *Times* he bought from the vendor at Mercer and Eighth, Peter smiles at the front-page headline: "Nixon Admits Order to Halt Inquiry on Watergate; Expects Impeachment." He reads it aloud for the satisfaction then clenches a fist and makes a victory stab in the air. Freddy was right, what he said last night, and here is the smoking gun to prove it, Nixon all but finished.

At thirty-two Peter has lived in the city for a couple of years with little to show for it: the baseball memoir that he poured himself into but can't sell, a few stories and reviews in the quarterlies that pay only in copies. And finally, earlier this summer, a profile of Joe Namath well placed in *Rooster*, the magazine he's had his sights on. Genuine money for this one, but no byline. Peter's much-published collaborator Freddy D'Amico, whose cousin was Namath's pal in high school, claimed their editor would not allow it. Now, though, Freddy's handing over a political contact—an old college roommate this time—whose access to Alexander Haig, Nixon's chief of staff, is going to be Peter's ticket. It turns out that Haig's assistant, the former roommate, is looking for a writer to document the last days, hold up a mirror, create a neutral record.

The plan is for Freddy to wait for his old friend to call, once Nixon sees what's coming and starts making plans to cash it in. Then Peter will take the train to Washington, and from there he'll be off and running, slamming through doors, nailing interviews, and watching himself multiply, proving everybody wrong who's told him what he's good for and what he's not. At least that's the idea. He gets up and walks to the sleeping man whose shoes are tipped over next to him, drops a dollar bill on his chest then heads west, jumping ahead in his mind to what Joanie will think. For two years she has tried to convince him of his talent. She has been his champion and his muse—though apparently, after the latest round of rejections, she is starting to have her doubts, something Peter has expected all along. "It's all about your ego, not about the craft," she said yesterday, parroting his own fears. "You think it's supposed to happen overnight."

In his previous life, which lasted well into his twenties, he paid his dues in a hundred ramshackle minor-league ballparks, honing the craft long after his hopes were dead. Then four years studying journalism at the University of Minnesota, an old man among kids. So yes, he *is* in a hurry, a big hurry. And now it's happening—not with the memoir, but a huge break nonetheless, and all because of his nights at the Bird, writing what he pleases, drinking with Freddy, and generally keeping his ear to the ground. Then sleeping all day while Joanie with her job at Knopf handles publicity for the writers Peter envies and also pays the rent, God love her.

He runs the final two blocks and sprints up six flights of stairs. In their tiny kitchen, she's transferring dishes from the drying rack into the cupboards, working one-handed as she sips from a pottery mug of coffee. Her dark hair is parted in the middle and falls across her cheeks and down past her shoulders, leaving barely enough space for the brown eyes he can't look into without absorbing a subtle hit against the inner gyroscope that keeps him upright on earth. The freckles on her nose make her look younger than she is, and also less cynical. He has tried to convince himself that they love each other.

"You're out of breath," she says. "What's he promised you now?" She's met Freddy a couple of times and doesn't pretend to like him.

Peter glances toward the small table in the corner. "Let's sit down and talk."

"Five minutes. I have to go."

He touches her elbow, and she backs into a kitchen chair then crosses her legs, watching as he unfolds the *Times* in front of her. She leans forward to read. "And it gets better," Peter says. "Freddy's got an old friend in D.C. who works for Alexander Haig. He's the general's personal aide, lines up all his shit, and he wants somebody embedded with Haig during Nixon's last few days—when it comes to that."

"Haig wants this? Or Freddy's friend?"

"Haig does. He wants the story out as soon as Nixon's gone. He wants the world to know what he's been doing—he's de facto president, for God's sake. But it has to come from somebody who's not invested. Someone without baggage. A political virgin."

"You?"

Peter recalls his own disbelief when Freddy broke the idea. "Me. They're doing the clearance check now. It's a matter of waiting till the endgame starts. A few more days."

Joanie crosses her arms, a gesture that somehow throws the whole plan into doubt.

"All you have to do is say, 'Go after it.' Would that kill you?"

She finishes her coffee then stands and sets her palms on the table and leans toward him. Her face softens, but her eyes are depthless. "That's what I'll say after you've gotten the call and you're on your way to D.C." She circles around to the sink, where she rinses out her coffee mug, then breezes past him on her way to the door, folding her fingers into her hair and lifting it the full length of her arm before letting it fall. "Lock the door behind me," she says—and just then the phone rings on the wall next to her. She looks sharply at Peter, still sitting at the kitchen table.

He gets there on the second ring and hears only the sound of distance on the wires, white noise and metallic chirping. "Hello?" he says. "Hello?"

Finally, a long, drawn-in breath, followed by a voice Peter can't mistake, high in pitch and lacking in affect, as if machine-generated: "Anybody there?"

"Victor? What's going on? Is Dad all right?"

"Ambulance crew had to use those paddles on him. He fell down next to the buckeye tree."

The rush of blood in Peter's stomach is not concern or fear. It is the hot fist of rage. "Is he alive?" he says.

"What is it?" Joanie asks. She's gone up on her tiptoes, which strikes Peter as ludicrous—standing there like a small child trying to see out a high window.

"I have to go," Victor says. "Gotta drive to the hospital."

"They took him away just now? What? Was he breathing? Victor, tell me something."

"Pray," Victor says, and he hangs up.

Next thing Peter knows, he has crossed the small room and smashed the living room wall with his fist, a blow that makes plaster rain down inside. "Damn it," he says, but he's already calming himself, gaining control, planning what needs to be done as he shakes out his hand.

Joanie says, "Is he dead?"

"Probably. Great timing, right to the end." As he crosses toward the bedroom, trying to recall if he has any decent white shirts, Joanie blocks the door, her hands flat against both jambs.

"Please, you can't go," she says. "Stay here and do what you have to do."

"I'm his son, for God's sake. I'll have to plan the funeral. If he's alive, I need to see him."

Joanie doesn't give up. "It might be a ruse, have you thought of that? Your dad's still running that nuthouse, isn't he? Peter?"

"Yeah." Years ago, Enoch turned his farm into a commune of sorts, a captive congregation for his self-taught preaching. And yes, Peter has thought of that.

"Ring up the hospital out there and see what you can learn. Please."

It takes twenty minutes and several tries, but he finally gets through to a doctor whose verdict is on the pessimistic side of hedging. "Your father has experienced a ventricular fibrillation, a deadly arrhythmia," he says. "His heart is stunned and his vital signs are weak. He may not recover, and if he does, it's hard to say what he'll be like. His brain, I mean—oxygen deprivation. If I were you, I'd get here as soon as possible."

"Can you say that last part again?" Peter holds out the receiver for Joanie to hear, but she's heard it already and turns away, throwing her hands in the air.

Forty minutes later, a taxi drops him at LaGuardia. Half an hour after that, he boards a flight for Minneapolis. By 12:30 p.m. Central Time, having gained an hour, he's driving northwest on I-94 through rolling fields of tasseling corn and newly shorn wheat, past white silos and red barns and four-legged water towers perched like moon-landing vehicles above the rural towns. At 2:15 he strikes off due north on a state highway that cuts through scrubland and rocky pastures before giving way to the glorious pine and birch forests his dad always called the North Woods, trees growing so thick and close to the road they block out the sun. Lakes appear and disappear, gashes in the earth filled with aquamarine or summer sky. As he nears home, he tries to decide whether he ought to be sensing his dad's absence from the world—if, in fact, the old man has died—and though Peter wishes he could pray, that's not something he is able to do any longer.

He drives past the sign that says BATTLEPOINT, MINNESOTA, POPULATION 4,456 and turns in at the old brick hospital. Inside, Victor Stubblefield is standing in profile before a window, index finger exploring the inside of his ear. Victor was an early disciple, one of the first to move in when Enoch established Last Lake Ranch in the mid-sixties.

Peter clears his throat. "Hey."

Victor looks up. He's a few years older than Peter, with a round, potato nose and appleseed eyes that regard the world with suspicion, as if certain that some great secret is being kept from him. Without speaking, he leads the way past the front desk, moving with a slight hitch, arms hanging straight to his sides and glancing back every few steps.

The bed stands in the light of a window facing west, where the sun is still high. It's only four o'clock. Enoch, very much alive, is propped upright, knotty forearms crossed in front of him. Against the bleached pillows his long white hair has a yellowish tint, but his eyes, sapphire blue, possess their usual otherworldly glitter. Aside from the sprouting wires, there's nothing about him that looks frail. He leans forward and hooks Peter's forearm with a big paw and pulls him into a hug. He smells like antiseptic soap, his oily hair is pungent. Victor moves into a corner and stands there, watching.

"What's going on, Dad?"

"What's going on is, I died!" His voice booms.

"He's our miracle man." A nurse kneels bedside, fiddling with his catheter bag.

"What happened? Heart attack?"

"No, no, I'm fine." Then, to the nurse, standing over him now and tugging at the neck of his yellow gown: "What in heaven's name are you doing?"

She lays the fabric aside to expose the electrodes on his clean-shaven chest. Chin tucked into his neck, Enoch watches her fingers pick and tug, his face scrunched in disapproval. "Stop your fussing," she says, then leaves the room just as a doctor walks in.

"Electrical misfire," Enoch says. "Right, Doc?"

He's a young guy with styled hair that rests on the collar of the chambray shirt he wears beneath his white coat. He nods and introduces himself. "Your father experienced what we call sudden cardiac death. This kind of thing, there's a survival rate of maybe 2 or 3 percent."

"Ancient of Days!" Enoch points at the ceiling.

The doctor ignores him. "He was revived by EMTs on site, using the paddles, and then once more in the ambulance on the way in. He would not be alive if not for the man who performed CPR before the crew arrived. He was at it for ten minutes."

Enoch says, "Angel, you mean. And he thumped me good. It feels like he jumped up and down on my chest with his boots on. He was driving past when I went down, and apparently he just stopped and hopped out of his car. Told Victor to call for the ambulance. Nobody knows who he was. Right, Victor?"

"Right," Victor says.

"Not even Billy Halvorsen, the ambulance driver. You remember

Billy. He knows everybody. Billy said the guy was driving a foreign car. Nobody drives foreign cars. And nobody saw him leave. He just disappeared. Angel."

"Catheterization revealed no artery blockage," the doctor says, "and the heart muscle appears undamaged. The brain too. That's the good news."

Enoch says, "I forgive you, Doc."

"Excuse me?"

"You're a scientist, you can't help it. Truth is, if God wants me, he'll take me."

"I was going to add," the doctor says, "most V-Fib victims experience another episode within six months."

"What treatments are there?" Peter asks.

"That requires more testing. We'll be referring him on to a larger hospital."

"I'm not going to another hospital," Enoch says, and Peter has half a mind to grab a swatch of the hospital blanket and stuff it in his dad's mouth.

"In the meantime, I'll prescribe a blood pressure drug to ease the heart's workload. Naturally we'll keep him here for a day or two, make sure he's stable while I make arrangements with the U of M. Or with Mayo. Then I'll order a medical van. We'll take every precaution."

Enoch says, "Just so you know, I'm checking out of here tomorrow. I've got things to do."

"Tell you what, Mr. Bywater." The doctor finally turns and looks at him. "I'm going to finish my rounds while your son talks sense into you. I will see you in the morning." He gives Peter a sidelong glance and heads to the door.

"Oh, Doc," Enoch shouts. "Please tell the nurse to come back and remove my catheter. I have to urinate, and I mean to do so like a man, standing on my own two feet."

Once the doctor's gone, Enoch deflates. His face goes slack—his jowls, the skin beneath his eyes—and when he speaks, his voice is softer. "My wallet's in that drawer," he says to Victor. "Take a twenty and go buy yourself a steak dinner at the Valhalla. The filet mignon. Harold does that one well. Ages the beef for two weeks."

When Victor is gone, Peter pulls a chair up next to the bed. Although his old man has a planetary draw and to be within his orbit is to be lured by a feeling of sanctuary, Peter is no longer tempted by the anesthetic of certainty offered by his dad's variety of faith. No, he is ready for this to be over, his mind turning to Freddy and whether his friend has been trying to call. He reaches out and lays a hand on his dad's forearm, still muscular and taut. "I have to head back tomorrow," he says. "I'm so glad you're all right."

Enoch looks at him straight on. His big face is open, vulnerable suddenly, his eyes moist. He wets his lips with his tongue. "You can't leave, not after what God showed me."

The trouble begins in the region of Peter's heart, panic at having to oppose his dad's tremendous will. A rhythm starts inside his head, a little two-bar, syncopated beat that moves to the fingers of his right hand, which drum soundlessly on his leg. "You're such a pain in the ass, Dad," he says. "Do you know that?"

"There, right there." Enoch stabs a finger at his son's face. "The way you can just shrug off the things that matter most."

"And the way you're so sure that you speak for God."

"I simply listen. Same as you could, if you tried. And this time I had no choice."

Peter sits back and lifts an ankle to rest on his knee, showing nonchalance even as he fortifies himself. He's been through these before, his dad's premonitions, but he wishes he had time to put this one off for an hour, go out and have a couple of drinks first. Before Peter moved out to New York, Enoch dreamed his son was falling from the top of a skyscraper, down toward a sea of writhing demons, the vision so real to him that he nearly wept as he told it.

Enoch takes a breath, his face an emblem of weariness. "He took my life today and then gave it back to me for a purpose. I won't go into the details now, but here's the thing. He allowed me to witness the close of history as we know it."

"Ah," Peter says. "The end of the world." Every self-respecting fundamentalist preacher Peter has ever heard, every TV evangelist, Billy Graham himself, they all have this forecast in their repertoire.

"Not exactly, no. Christ's *first* return. His rescue of those who believe.

9

The Rapture. He showed it to me. Or I should say, she did, the messenger he sent."

"Another angel, and a female to boot. Nice wrinkle, Dad."

Enoch shrugs. "He's coming, Peter, I saw it all. And you were there next to me, in the pasture behind our house. We rose together, you and I."

"We did?" Peter's fingers, still tapping a rhythm against his leg, pause now. He loves his dad for saying this—the two of them rising together. How nice if he were able to believe it. When Peter was a boy, Enoch always prayed for him at bedtime, his words a comforting drone, his hand resting lightly on Peter's head, the force of his presence a shield against every fear.

"And there's something else, too," Enoch says. "He showed me when it'll happen."

Shit.

"Two weeks from now, on August 19th. It couldn't be clearer. That's why you need to stay, no matter what you've got going on back there."

"And you're going to talk about this? Tell people?"

Enoch nods, gravely. "Everyone with ears to hear."

At the sound of quick light steps, they both look up, and the nurse breezes into the room. She glances at Peter, dismissing him, and then with a sweep of her arm encloses Enoch's bed inside a wall of white curtains. Peter goes out to the lobby pay phone and tries Freddy's number, without luck. Then Joanie's. Nothing there either. *Damn it, where is everybody?*

In the gift shop, he buys a Snickers bar and a carton of milk, then sits down in a waiting room chair and lets his gaze rest on the line of Norway pines across the road, the sun standing two hands above them. He will sleep at the farm tonight, he decides, then drive back to Minneapolis first thing tomorrow and board a plane for New York. There is nothing he can do here. His dad is fine. No reason to stay.

August 19th. Peter can't help laughing out loud. *Unbelievable.*

Another half-hour at the hospital, barely tolerating his old man's grandiosity, and then Peter cuts himself loose, heading north to the place he grew up, the last couple of miles a tunnel through trees before the road crests a long rise and the view opens. One can never be quite prepared for the dazzling, lavender sheen of Last Lake, and sure enough, turning west on the township road, farm on the right and lake beyond, he is struck again by its beauty—but also by the memory it rouses of the girl he loved and the color of her eyes. It's all too long ago to matter, of course, but sometimes, as now, the image of her face catches like a tune in his head and sticks there.

She's lying on her back in the deep end, slathered with sunscreen, teardrop glasses shading her eyes, legs extended past the end of the air mattress. Her salmon-pink bikini is textured with a pattern of gold stitching that gleams in the hard sun. She looks up at the brown rise of the San Jacintos, the nearest peak centered between the pair of old palm trees at the back of the property, then squints at the fuzz below her navel, at the fine blonde hair on her arm. The heat presses against her skin. She rarely thinks anymore about her first love, can barely remember what it's like to be looked at in the way he looked at her, greedy to know her instead of merely greedy to have her. This morning, though, her first thoughts on waking were of Minnesota—Last Lake, the green cover of the trees, and of course Peter, too—as if some part of her knew that her past was not going to remain much longer in the past. The top of her spine, where it joins to her skull, begins to beat in time with her heart, each pulse a tick of pain.

"It's time, dear. Come on, now." Her mother's shadow falls across her face.

Melanie flicks both hands in lazy, fishlike strokes, propelling herself away. "I'll get out and make myself perfect—but only if I can have another Perc. Just one, Mom—my back hurts again."

"I'm sorry, no. Come out, and I'll give you a tiny little G and T. Lots of ice."

Melanie imagines the soothing chill in her mouth and throat, the calming gin. She says, "Adam is a shithead." Then feels immediately guilty for saying it.

"Well, he's doing us a favor today. You agreed to the cameras, and you agreed to doing it *at* the studio. And now they're coming to us, thanks to Adam. We really should've stayed home."

The word *home* kicks up the pulse in Melanie's brain, and she imagines the seven-foot wall of white concrete that surrounds their sprinkler-green yard in Brentwood, the beeping of the gate when anyone comes or goes. And Morris swimming laps in the pool, or lying sprawled like a lion in their king-size bed. But he's gone, of course. She sees him shirtless on the day last spring when he acknowledged to her what she had known for months about the girl with the white-blonde hair and plenitude of teeth, the one who stars alongside Morris in the sitcom he loves to babble on about, using words like *quintessential* and *zeitgeist*. He couldn't help but smile as he made his confession, and that's what made it feel so final—not that everything hadn't gone to ruin already: her last two films, the accident, her miserable weeks in the hospital. She and Morris have been separated for months now. The divorce, top secret, is all but settled.

Her mom catches hold of her by an arm and manages to pull her up close against the side. "Morris will be here too," she says. "Adam thinks it'll be good for the film. He's in it, after all."

Melanie opens her mouth and screams, "I can't do this anymore!" causing her mom to let go of her arm and fall backward on the concrete. She pops right back up in time to say, "Adam's here."

And so he is, strolling toward them in white bell-bottom trousers and boots with two-inch heels that make him walk like a man not sure of his own legs. He calls out, "There's my two girls!"

Her agent and her mother converge on each other like lovers. Melanie pulls herself from the water. Stern-faced, Adam taps his giant wristwatch with an index finger.

"I'm on my way," she says and brushes past him, first to the kitchen, where she makes the drink herself, three fingers of Tanqueray, and then to her bedroom, where her mom has laid out the dress, identical in color to her pinkish-tan flesh. She turns on the shower and sets her gin and tonic on the top edge of the glass-brick surround. Taking periodic swallows as the water beats against her, she soon feels minimally composed, the prospect of inane questions and flashing cameras less onerous. She blow-dries her hair, parts it down the left side, and squeezes into the dress.

In the living room Adam and her mom pretend to be stunned as she walks in. "Oh, God!" Adam removes his glasses and rubs his eyes. "Perfect, you're perfect. Everyone—and I'm not being hyperbolic, I swear—everyone's going to fall in love."

Her mom produces the small, kitten-like sound that seems to work well with people out here, dabs her eyes with a Kleenex, things she never did back in Minnesota.

"Morris will be here any second," Adam says. "But no worries, I've briefed him. No ad-libbing. Just rock-solid Morris, right there behind his lovely wife. He'll defer all questions to you. And Mel?" Adam cocks his head and sets the knuckle of his index finger against his teeth, meaning, *Listen.* "You know your talking points, yes? Dottie tells me you've been practicing."

Melanie escapes to the kitchen for another gin and tonic. Minutes later she allows herself to be pushed into a corner and seated on a stool in the glare of a hot lamp.

"Here, honey." The makeup girl is kind, someone she's had before, Russian, or maybe Czech, and it's not difficult to give in to her ministrations, the brushing and murmuring, the tender nudging, the little tugs. Melanie's shoulders relax, also her stomach and her jaw. Her hands lie palms up on her thighs in capitulation, time flowing in a parallel stream beside her. And when the lamp clicks off, she stands and follows Adam outside where Morris waits beneath the clutch of royal palms. He's beautiful, of course—that torpedo body of his, the straight nose and pouty lips, dark curls touching his shoulders. Beyond him, on the other side of the rope line Adam has fashioned, they're awaiting her. The sun is merciless.

Sweat trickles from underneath her arms as she takes her place between Charlie Widmer, one of the producers, and Morris. If she had stayed in the city and shown up at the press conference at the studio, as agreed, it would have been a larger group, including insufferable genius-director Will Sellerman. She looks out at the handful of reporters, two camera crews, and the half-dozen or so jackals. *It won't be so bad,* she thinks. Then stiffens at the touch of Morris's steel fingers on her waist.

"Miss Magnus, what's it like for you, reprising this role?" The question comes from the *Snapshot* writer who once described Melanie as a "Scandinavian nymph-child."

"I loved stepping into Mandy's shoes again."

Someone ducks beneath the rope, scoots forward in a crouching half-run, and shoots from his knees, prompting Adam to step in, hands raised. "Please! Until she's had a chance to answer some questions." He points at the trespasser. "Stay behind the rope!"

As Adam steps away, the guy from *Variety* says, "Early screeners think the sequel appeals to a new demographic. They're saying the politics have changed."

Melanie adjusts her sunglasses. "Mandy has changed, naturally. The country has, too."

"It's a story about the apocalypse, isn't it? Does it end well, or should we all be worried?"

"You'll have to wait and see."

"Would you call it an antiwar film, Miss Magnus?"

"I think it reflects the country's mood."

"Is it a repudiation of the first one? Are you still proud of *Boy and Girl*?"

Melanie glances at her mom, standing off to the side and wearing too much lipstick. "Of course I'm proud of it. Repudiation? No. It's a matter of—evolution."

The next couple of questions, which Melanie deflects, are about Sellerman's *Rolling Stone* interview, in which he acknowledged bending to political pressures when making the earlier film, admitted his naive attitude toward the war at the time. Melanie's turn as the girl who marries a wheelchair-bound veteran had been lauded, and she received an Oscar at twenty-three.

"You're telling us you didn't read the interview?"

She shakes her head and offers a dumb half-smile, trying her best to follow Adam's directive, and her mom's: no politics. "Don't wreck your career—think Jane Fonda," they've been telling her. As if Jane Fonda hasn't been right all along.

After Adam steps in to say, "Two more questions," a woman Melanie hasn't noticed until now—a tabloid writer—pops up from behind a sweating cameraman. Her skewed smile gives her away, not to mention her eyes, which are focused to the left of Melanie, on Morris. *Here it comes.*

"Mr. Gage, what was it like, working with your wife? It's the first time you have appeared together in a film, isn't it?"

"It is," Morris says, his voice too hale. "Of course, my part is a cameo. Careful not to blink." He issues a pathetic laugh, made to sound like it comes from his belly.

"It's been reported that your original role was cut way back. Why is that?"

Melanie imagines her husband's wrinkled forehead, his eyes searching the ground at his feet.

"And is it true the two of you are separated?" the writer asks.

Morris's fingers press against her waist, passing the question on to her, and she says, "You ought to find better sources."

But the woman holds her ground. "Are you saying you're *not* separated?"

Melanie doesn't even try to smile. The anger in her face will show up in the papers tomorrow, as well as in the clip that plays on the entertainment news. "That's right," she says.

Within minutes Adam has scattered them, the entire pack, and sent Morris on his way, too. Before taking his own leave, he reminds Melanie of the upcoming joint interview with the film's leads and Sellerman, slated for August 13 on Venice Beach, and the premier in Beverly Hills scheduled for Labor Day. "Now, please," Adam says, "no more of *this!*" His gesture takes in not only the heat-stunted yard but also the entire 108-degree, sun-beaten valley. His face is blotchy and damp. "We're not coming out here next time. You're driving in, understand? Mel? Dottie?"

"We'll be there," Dottie says. "I promise."

Melanie says, "Fuck off, Adam."

He sends a miffed glance at Dottie before turning and heading to his car.

"She's sorry," Dottie calls out. And then, to her daughter, "You take so much for granted, dear. You've got the world at your fingertips. Everything we've done, you and I, it's been for you."

Often now—several times a day—Melanie feels like she does in this instant, resentful to the point of violence for the way her mom oversees her life, pushing and cajoling, telling her how ungrateful she is. This, on the one hand. On the other, Melanie can't deny the needful wanting that only her mom's voice and sheltering presence can satisfy. It's as if she's become a fetus again, greedy for quiet sanctuary, anonymity, total provision, her acute awareness of which makes her all the more angry. "I hate you, Mom. You know that, don't you?"

"Oh, Melly, you've always been like this. Blowing everything up in your mind like a giant balloon and then letting it all out—poof! Usually in my direction."

In Melanie's room, Dottie helps her off with her shoes and dress then lays her down and covers her with an afghan. "I'll get you a Perc, dear—you earned it. Evolution! That was good."

"And Morris, I hate him too."

"You should. He's a snake in the grass."

"*Two* Percs, Mom."

"Just one, dear. Now sleep for a while. Can you do that for me?"

Melanie watches her mom leave the room. Then listens for the creak of the cupboard door, the twist of the faucet, the stream of water filling up the glass. Pain has inched back into the base of her brain, and she is aware of the trembling in her fingers and also a presence—like an unwelcome, listening shadow—crouching behind the big chair in the corner, or maybe on the other side of the wall, in the bathroom. She thinks of her new film and the threat it conjures of inundating fires, existential terror, annihilation. Maybe it wouldn't be so terrible, that kind of an end. Better, anyway, than the prospect of more days like today, more pain in her head and back, more lies, more plastic smiles, more nights alone, more regrets for everything she has allowed herself to be stripped of.

"Mom," she calls.

As Dottie breezes back into the room, glass of water in one hand, yellow pill resting in the palm of the other, Melanie is overjoyed to see her, and not only because of the pill, which she takes in a quick swallow.

"I need you, Mom," she says, disgusted because she means it so much. "Could you sit with me for a little while? Please?"

AUGUST 7—WEDNESDAY

His son left hours ago to drive out to the farm, and though the hospital is silent now except for sporadic, impersonal beeps and bells, sleep won't come for Enoch. Ribs aching, hands folded on his belly, he notes with quiet amazement the metronomic regularity of his heart.

From birth he was taught by his mother that God selects very few on whom to bestow Truth, and the idea of having been chosen is a creed he has come to embrace with all of his strength. It governs not only his waking thoughts but penetrates to his dreams. He sees everything through this lens: his interactions with others, his perceptions of himself, the basic facts of his physical existence. The minute-by-minute unfolding of his life is a tapestry of infinite complexity being woven, he believes, by the mindful omniscience of the Almighty Himself, no thread out of place.

And now—having been given a burden he never imagined would be his, there is so much to be done! So much to prepare for! Come morning, no matter what the nurses say, or the arrogant young doctor, he means to leave this bed, go down to the radio station, and do his show like he does every Wednesday morning at nine. He will tell his audience what he knows and what he is certain they need to hear, which of course will generate resistance from every quarter: from the Ranchers and Saturday night worshippers, from the local clergy and media, and of course from Sylvie, too. And yet there is something else on Enoch's mind tonight, a memory he cannot seem to purge—an incident from years ago, when he was still farming.

Peter was fourteen or fifteen at the time, and starting to show his willfulness in the wrong ways, presenting a sullen eye at family devotions, shirking his chores, hiding liquor bottles in the barn, this last a particularly troublesome thing for Enoch, whose father had been fond of alcohol. Then one morning that spring—it was early March, birthing season—they found three new calves dead and partially eaten, a bloody carnage in the calf shed. Two loose siding boards had been forced apart, and outside in the damp dirt they found the tracks of a huge cat: a mountain lion, rare in Minnesota, though neighbors of late had been talking about missing stock. Aware that animals of prey return to the site of their kills, Enoch explained to Peter how they would bait the lion with one of the live calves. "And when it comes back," he said, "we'll be waiting for it."

"We?" Peter asked him.

"You and I, yes. I want you to see with your own eyes what we're up against in this world."

It was cold that night, and the pair of them sat bundled in their winter coats behind a low barricade of hay bales inside the back of the shed. From over the top of the bales, they watched the place at the bottom of the wall, some fifteen feet away, where the lion had gained entrance. Enoch had the single-barrel Stevens twelve-gauge, loaded with buckshot. Moonlight to shoot by streamed through the small window behind them. A verse from the apostle Peter's first letter played through Enoch's head on a repeating loop: "Be sober, be vigilant; because your adversary, the devil, like a roaring lion walketh about, seeking whom he may devour."

Sometime past midnight, Enoch heard soft padding steps through the wall at his side. A snuffling sound. He laid a hand on Peter's mouth, nudged him awake, then lifted the shotgun and rested its heavy barrel on the hay. Peter moved closer to him, and Enoch felt the boy's fear like the weak current in a bad electric fence. Twice the lion circled the shed, pausing every so often to sniff or to scratch at the ground. The live calf lay sleeping within arm's reach, and Enoch gave its rump a hard shove with his fist. The animal grunted, struggled to its feet, yanking on its tether. Peter grabbed hold of his dad's arm as the calf let out a long moan, the sound of which Enoch used as cover to thumb back the hammer of the shotgun into cocked position. He slid the gun along the top of the bale to Peter, who brought it to his shoulder as he had been taught. There was a moment of quiet before the creature pushed its big nose between the loose siding boards—only its nose, which by itself filled up the small opening. In the moonlight, its tongue made a swipe across the front of its mouth. Then came a flurry of scrambling motion that revealed the entire animal, crouched and still, a specimen of perfect symmetry just ten feet away and facing them. Enoch willed his son to take a bead on the front of its chest. In the silence, Peter sucked air. The lion hissed and appeared to shrink into itself, then exploded forward as the orange burst from the shotgun left everything in white silence.

They waited until morning to skin out the lion, whose coat was a rich tawny gold, still thick from winter. A mantle for a king. The charge of buckshot had entered the animal's chest and taken out its heart and most of its lungs. As Enoch remembers it now, he and Peter were silent as they worked. He didn't explain to his son what the lion meant, the way it represented with such aptness the nature of sin—how stealthily it approaches and how sleekly it presents itself. How surely it exacts its price, which is death. They used knives to strip the carcass then nailed the lovely skin, seven feet high by five wide, to the sunny south wall of the granary, and in the days to come, as together they tanned the hide with saltpeter and alum, Enoch couldn't help but notice that Peter seemed chastened, humbled.

He sits up in bed now, opens the drawer of the nightstand, and fumbles for his pocket watch, whose glow-in-the-dark hands show 12:37. He lifts the bedside phone, sets it on his chest, and dials his own number. *Let him answer,* he prays, which Peter does on the fourth ring, his voice sounding high and full of something like relief, or maybe hope: "Hello?"

"Peter, it's Dad."

"Ah." Disappointment.

"Who'd you think it was?"

"Is everything all right?" Peter asks.

"I dropped a bomb earlier and thought I should explain things better."

Peter is silent for a moment, then says, "Do you want some advice, Dad? That stuff about August 19th, it makes you sound like a fucking lunatic. Best not to talk about it."

Enoch winces. "You should hear the whole thing before you write me off."

Peter moans, a resigned moan, but it's an opening nonetheless, and Enoch doesn't let it pass. He describes walking out on the porch with his coffee yesterday, new sun lighting up the chrome-steel cross at the top of his barn and touching the tall obelisk of black granite in the Lutheran cemetery to the west, past his neighbor's hog farm. He recounts to Peter the smell of bacon frying and Victor's monotone voice coming to him through the screen, "A couple of minutes," and how he stepped down into the yard to check on the struggling buckeye tree. That's when he felt a vague tickle in his throat, but no pain whatsoever as his heart spiked to four hundred beats a minute, its lower chambers reduced to an ineffectual quiver, this, according to the doctor. First the ground beneath him disappeared, then the buckeye tree, and finally the sky itself, a dark wash rising up on all sides and lifting him—astounded—to a promontory high over the sea. What sea it was he didn't know, but the sun was a blood orange, hanging above it. Then a voice from behind caused him to turn, and he saw a woman, tall as a spruce and wearing a gown of water, her hair a blue flame. "Watch," she said, "and count the days." Which Enoch did, turning in time to see the sun fall like an egg from a table, down into the sea and blacking out the world. *One*, Enoch thought. But it was already roaring up behind him, a bright, booming spotlight, and climbing to its zenith before dropping and disappearing again. *Two*. Then it was back once more, rising and falling, which it did again, and again, and again, until a storm arrived, a wind so terrible the Earth pitched like a great, mad bull. Enoch could feel beneath him the land itself being urged across a wide vastness—until finally he was back at his own place.

"And all of this, Peter, while I was lying on the ground, more or less dead."

"You say she had blue hair, this angel?" His son doesn't even try to hide the scorn in his voice. "Maybe it was your mom. Grandma. Remember that dye she used to use, the way it glowed in the sun? And she always had a thing about the end of the world."

"This was not your grandmother, Peter. Make fun all you like, but you heard what the doctor said, and I know what I saw. Fourteen sunsets. Fourteen days."

"Not fifteen, not thirteen."

"Let me finish, please. The sound I heard then, coming from an opening in the clouds—it was as if all humanity were present, exercising their lungs. I was standing in the pasture behind the house, next to the rock pile, with you beside me, and others, too—a whole crowd of us, looking up at the roiling sky, the noise above us rising to a great shout."

"Today is the sixth, Dad. Six plus fourteen makes twenty, not nineteen. Didn't you say August 19?"

"Yes. Because tonight would have been the first sunset. Not to mention, the nineteenth of August has always been a significant date for me. It was your mother's and my anniversary, of course. But this isn't about me. Look what's happening in the world. The Middle East—my heavens, Armageddon just around the corner. And here at home, what they're doing to Nixon."

"Look what he's done to us."

Enoch tells himself to remain calm. "I will only remind you: 'There is no power but of God, and the powers that be are ordained of God'—that's Saint Paul, from the book of Romans. The president was placed where he is, and we ought to be praying for him, not working against him."

"Bullshit, Dad. You'd rather be deceived than have to think for yourself."

A spur of anger catches in Enoch's throat, but he swallows it.

Peter says, "And because some guy happens along and performs CPR, that makes him an angel. You're just lucky he was driving by."

"I don't believe in luck."

"If you're so sure, put a notice in the local paper asking him to come forward."

"He wasn't local. His car, remember?"

"You don't dare."

"Of course I dare."

"Then put a hundred bucks on it."

"I don't place bets."

"If you want me to believe you, get behind it. Put a notice in the paper. You pay me a hundred bucks if someone responds to it."

"All right. But remember, it was you and I together when it happened. The last thing I saw as I rose was the image of your feet above me. I was following *you.*"

Enoch takes hold of the bridge of his nose and squeezes, trying to put himself back there again—the noise in the sky, the black obelisk in the Lutheran cemetery glowing with an odd, greenish light. Yes, and the bottoms of Peter's feet with their long, splayed toes.

"Are you still planning to check yourself out in the morning and do your radio show?"

"I am."

"And the fact is, I have to head back to New York, like I said."

"What's so important?"

"Career stuff, Dad. Look, I'm sorry. Was there anything else?"

Enoch takes a moment to breathe, wishing he didn't need to pull out his trump card. Except that now he has no choice. "Your son," he says. "I'm going to find a way to bring him here." There is a pause on the other end. Enoch is aware that the two of them have broached this subject only a few times, and neither has ever used the word *son.*

When Peter finally speaks, his voice is tentative: "We don't even know where he lives."

"Let me take care of that."

Peter is quiet, and Enoch waits, recalling the one time he saw the boy. He'd flown out to California when a problem came up between the adopting parents—people Enoch knew—and the agency whose imprimatur he'd negotiated. It was a matter of money, naturally, and Enoch wrote an additional check in the hospital lobby. Then before leaving he took the elevator up to the maternity ward and saw him through the glass: the bald head, Annie Magnussen's curved lips, and the small dent in his chin, which was Peter's. He watched the infant's chubby arms trace patterns in the air. *But this is how it has to be,* he remembers telling himself—for the sake of Peter and Annie, for the sake of the child. It was 1958, after all. People would not have understood.

"It's a legal thing, Dad. *He's* the one who makes contact—I had to sign something."

"*I* didn't sign anything."

"Don't bring him into this." Peter's voice is hard, but Enoch can hear a crack in it now.

"I won't leave this world without him, or without you, for that matter," Enoch says. "Not if I have anything to say about it. And I do."

"Sounds like you're off on some road trip and you think you can drag everybody else along. Look, I have to get going, get some sleep."

"Good night, then."

"What you're saying is nonsense, Dad." And before hanging up: "Don't be a fool."

Enoch replaces the phone on the side table, throws off his covers, and finds the floor with his feet. Careful to keep enough slack in his IV line, he gets down on his knees and begins to pray.

Peter turns and slides his spine down along the wall to the kitchen floor, where he sits with his legs crossed. He presses his palms against the linoleum, which is cool, nearly cold. Summer in the north woods. He's wearing a white T-shirt and threadbare cotton boxers, nothing else, and the chill is comforting after the day's heat. He can feel his testicles drawing away from the floor, up toward his body. His belly, though, is a burning knot, and the veins in his arms pulse with each heartbeat. He reaches for a cigarette from the pack on the counter and lights up, inhales deeply. Holds it, blows it out.

In fact, it's been years since he's given much thought to the boy, the infant he never managed to conjure, the hypothetical child whose gender he didn't learn until months after the birth. For a long while he was vexed by a nagging sense that he should have done more to keep him—keep them both. But what could he have done? Annie didn't tell him she was pregnant until a week before he graduated from high school. And the day after graduation, she left—she and her mother both, the business of their disappearance a conspiracy that Peter learned about after the fact.

"You're eighteen and she's underage" is what Enoch told him. "You're lucky I intervened." Annie's dad, Gerald—their neighbor, the hog farmer—said, "If I had any scruples, I would've had you thrown in jail. And if you try to see her, that's exactly what I'll do." On top of it all, Peter was on his way to Tennessee to play rookie league ball with the Chicago Cubs' affiliate in Morristown. Before leaving, he managed to find out that Annie and her mom had gone to stay with an aunt out west someplace, where Annie would presumably have the baby. But that was the extent of it. No phone number and no address, no information about the aunt, no way to get in touch. Surely, though, Annie would find a way to contact *him*. She knew what his plans were and where he was going. And so he spent the summer learning how to hit a curveball and how to sleep on a jouncing bus and how to fill his stomach on ten bucks a week—all the while waiting for a letter or phone call that never came. By season's end, in September, he was convinced that her declarations of love had been empty and that her brother's words, uttered in a whisper on the night of Peter's graduation in May, were true. It was after the ceremony, and the two ended up in front of adjacent urinals in a restroom at the high school when Skinny—a big-shouldered, big-bellied guy with a dull, squashed face—leaned over to say, "She told me she'd rather kill herself than be with you."

Peter glances at the clock on the wall. One fifteen. He stands up and for the fourth or fifth time tonight dials Freddy's number. Again, no answer. Next he tries Joanie, who doesn't pick up either—out late no doubt with Margie, her friend at work who has the capacity for drinking to excess and still turning up in the office the next morning, fresh. Upstairs, the mountain lion skin covers the wall at the foot of the old single bed. He sets the alarm clock on the bed stand for 5:30, then walks over and puts his face close to the hanging skin, the edge of which is charred from the time he started a fire behind the granary, meaning to destroy it. He takes in the smells—smoke and dust and old leather—and remembers the triumph on his dad's face the morning they skinned it out, as if Peter had no choice now but to yield his will to God.

By six o'clock, wooden-headed, he is dressed and out the door and sliding behind the wheel of his rental car. The end of the driveway is blocked by Victor Stubblefield, perched on a ladder and doing something with the sign—LAST LAKE RANCH—that his dad put up the year he sold the animals, renovated the barn into apartments, and opened them to the most fervent of those who attended his Saturday night meetings. This was after Peter's mom died. The sign is fifteen feet off the ground and spans the width of the gravel drive, its horizontal boards mounted on a pair of old telephone poles. Peter stops the car and gets out. Victor is putting the finishing touches on his edit. He has whited out the word LAKE and with black paint and matching stencils replaced it with DAYS.

"He's not wasting any time, is he?" Peter says.

Victor squints down from the ladder. "No time to waste." Then he descends, paint can, paintbrush, and stencils in hand, and Peter helps him take down the ladder before driving away, south, through a light fog. At the airport in Minneapolis he just misses a nine o'clock nonstop to LaGuardia and buys instead a ticket for a 10:30 flight scheduled to lay over briefly at O'Hare. Then he finds a pay phone.

Freddy answers on the first ring this time. "Where the fuck are you?" He's breathless, close to hyperventilating, as Peter has seen him do at the Morning Bird more than once, Freddy having to lie down on his back on top of the bar, knees lifted, arm thrown over his eyes as he sucks the air for oxygen.

"Minneapolis airport. My dad—it's a long story."

"You've got to be in D.C. an hour ago. I tried reaching you all night."

"I was trying to call *you*. Look, I'm booked for a ten o'clock to New York, but I'll change it to D.C. I should get in just after lunch."

A pause. Peter can see Freddy holding the phone away from himself, trying to catch his breath. Then he's back. "Here's the deal. Trond called yesterday afternoon at five. 'Send your man tonight,' he said. 'Shit's about to hit the fan.' He called again at six this morning, and he's like, 'The general wants him *now*.' I told him you'd be there at noon, one thirty at the latest, and where should he meet you? He says, 'Fine, but if he's not here by two, we're going to plan B.'" Freddy stops for air. "You hear me? And he liked your stuff, too. Hey, I'm way out here on a limb for you, and you're fucking up."

"Plan B?"

"Yeah. Another guy."

"I'll make it in time, I promise, the first flight out of here."

"It's my ass on the line here, Peter. I look like a bloody cretin."

"Where do I meet him?"

"You got a pen? Here." He reads the address and Peter scribbles on his hand.

It's not hard to cancel the New York flight and schedule one for D.C., but this one too lays over in Chicago. It leaves Minneapolis at 9:30 and isn't slotted for Dulles until 1:45. Trond might have to wait a little while— but what's a few minutes? Barring further glitches, everything should be good. In Chicago, he'll call Freddy and fill him in. He buys coffee in a Styrofoam cup, then walks to his gate. Joanie was right, of course. He was an idiot for coming out here in the first place.

The morning fog is gone, sunshine now with a few high, gauzy clouds, and Peter's flight is on time, the airliner's thrust into the sky like the hand of chance pushing against his chest. It's finally going to happen, the breakthrough he's worked and waited for, often blindly and without much hope. And why not? It's no less plausible than sitting inside a giant, howling, aluminum goose that will carry him halfway across the North American continent in less than three hours. Isn't life full of implausible things that happen nonetheless? Like a guy from pee-drip Minnesota whose dad believes he can speak for God, and who at thirty-two has never held a real job, hiring on to shadow the chief of staff for the man who will soon be the first United States President forced from office.

The plane lands in Chicago with a rough bounce that sends it briefly airborne before coming down the second time, gently. Five minutes later he's running toward the gate and looking up at the board for the 11:20 a.m. to D.C.

FLIGHT DELAYED, it says.

He goes up to the counter, butting to the front of the line. "Delayed how long?"

The woman's eyes move past him to the person he stepped in front of. "There's no pilot, and we have to wait for one. We're saying 1:00 p.m. at the earliest."

"Arriving when?"

"Four o'clock."

"Call another pilot. I have to be in D.C. by one thirty."

"Sir, these people are ahead of you. If you get in line, we can help you when it's your turn." Her smile flattens, and Peter steps away, his stomach pitching. He runs down the concourse and past the next few gates until he comes to one without a line, where he asks the attendant if any flights are leaving for D.C. within the hour.

"I have to be there by one thirty."

"Please go down to the main ticket counter, sir. I don't have that information."

Another long run, another line, and it's twenty minutes—11:50—before he's told there are no departures for D.C. until after two. He finds a pay phone and calls Freddy, whose voice is quiet now, serene. "Where are you now?"

"You need to buy me a couple more hours. I can be there at four."

"Look, I'm sorry, but Trond couldn't wait. The other guy is on his way."

"It's not even noon yet. He said by one thirty."

"Right. He's an anally retentive prick."

"Four hours, Freddy! Nothing is going to happen in the next four hours!"

"It's over, man. Take it easy, something else will come up. Something always does. Go get yourself a drink."

And that's it. Freddy's voice is gone.

Peter does not tear the pay phone off the wall or sit down and cry but instead he finds a bar and has that drink, then three more, while smoking half a dozen cigarettes. Finally, he returns to the ticket counter and rebooks with a flight to LaGuardia. Through the wall of windows he watches rain move in and darken the runway and drench the luggage handlers.

Later, aloft, when earth vanishes beneath clouds and the sun emerges unobscured, he will question whether he might be losing Joanie and what it will feel like if he does. He'll wonder if he is meant to spend his life striving for things he cannot achieve, or if he's delusional, like his old man. He'll imagine what it would have been like to write the Haig/Nixon story, describing the great fall from inside the halls of power, and to know the whole country is reading it, including Joanie, who has never really believed in him, and Melanie Magnus—as the world calls her now—who must drop to her knees each night and thank her stars for how fate uprooted her from a hog farm on Last Lake and transplanted her in the sunny hills of California.

"You're wearing that?" Dottie says. She's standing before the mirrored dining room wall, applying bright orange lipstick, her appraisal coming through the glass.

Melanie stops just short of the kitchen, five Tylenol clutched in her fist. "What's wrong with it?"

"Dear, we're going to the doctor."

She joins her mom at the mirror and strikes a pose, arms above her head, a girl in a beauty pageant. She's wearing faded bell-bottom jeans, a Dodgers T-shirt with arms cut off at the shoulders, a pair of flip-flops.

"We need that prescription, don't we?" Dottie says. "Please, just go put on something nice. It's not that hard."

She swallows the Tylenol in the kitchen, sucking water from the faucet stream. In her bedroom she finds a powder-blue jumpsuit with a plunge neckline. Also a pair of silver, high-heeled sandals. For good measure, she brushes on rouge and thickens her lashes. They take the car Morris bought her for Christmas last year, a Chevy Camaro, metallic black with a white stripe down the center, which he liked so much that he rarely let her drive it before the split. Now, of course, as with every other asset the court has awarded her—the Palm Springs house, the apartment in Aspen, and half of all their accounts and investments—the Camaro is in her mom's name, temporarily. After Morris left in January, Melanie exiled herself to her room, refusing to speak, and then in March she fell off the deck in Brentwood, drunk, and broke her back. That's when everybody ganged up on her, claiming she was unfit to handle her affairs. Too brittle to fight, she signed an agreement that granted power of attorney to her mom for one calendar year.

Her doctor sports tortoise-shell glasses and a Ronald Reagan comb-back. Two-tone, wing-tip shoes. He is attentive in a fatherly, annoying way—and always ignores Dottie, a redeeming virtue. "It's a little worse, right here." Melanie reaches back to where two of her discs were fused in March. "It really hurts," she whines.

"You got through your shoot in May with no issues."

Dottie leans forward. "She fell, too, Dr. Rowan, by the pool. She slipped and went down like that"—she smacks a fist against her knee. "I had to help her back up."

For the first time, Melanie notices Dr. Rowan's nose, the sudden, crooked turn halfway down its long shaft, and she imagines him as a boy being smacked by a ball or punched in the face. Thinking about it, tears well in her eyes. How sad for his mother!

"I can't renew the prescription," he says. "You have to understand, it has addictive properties. Have you noticed any mood swings lately? Anxiety? Insomnia?"

Melanie shakes her head.

"Stomach issues? Sweats?"

"No."

"What about paranoia?"

Dottie says, "No, no."

"I'm sorry," he says. "Longtime usage can result in a higher level of pain than one experiences without the drug."

Melanie cries into her hands. A pulsing ache starts at the base of her cranium, and she looks up at Dr. Rowan's poor, ruined nose. "Is your mother still living?" she says.

"Mel?" Dottie says.

The doctor cocks his head at her, removes his glasses. "She is. Why?"

"No reason, I just wondered."

He reaches out and touches her arm. "Tylenol," he says. "I'll have the nurse give you samples. No more than two tablets every six hours. And I will see you in two weeks."

Dottie is silent until they're back in the car, heading west on Tahquitz, its long row of palm trees pointing toward the San Jacintos. She slams her hand against the steering wheel. "The man thinks he's God. Do you see the way he walks, with his shoulders thrown back? And those shoes he wears? I bet he makes his wife polish them every day. That's what I hate about men, always having to call the shots."

"He's right, Mom."

"He's wrong, Mel. He doesn't understand the pressures you're under. He doesn't watch you suffer, day in and day out."

"I didn't fall down by the pool."

"What are you saying? It was last week. You don't remember?"

"No, you're lying. You're the one who fell." She turns and slumps against the window, which is cool against her face. There is not a person she knows who gives a damn about her. Not one. They shuffle and scheme on her behalf, but always with a sharp eye on what she makes possible for *them*—even her mom. Especially her mom.

At Desert Hospital, an institution into which they have never stepped foot, Melanie pays only vague attention as Dottie makes her case: "... my daughter, Melanie Magnus. An accident earlier this year. Surgery. Yes, *that* Melanie Magnus. Chronic pain. No, her doctor's in L.A., but we can't get there till next week."

In the examination room a nurse takes Melanie's blood pressure and sheepishly requests an autograph, which Melanie provides. When the doctor appears—young, athletic, large hands—he gestures toward Dottie, explaining that she must leave the room, and because he has the masculine authority Dottie respects, out she goes. Melanie explains about the accident, the surgery, and her hectic summer. Her upcoming schedule. Her pain. "Please, if you could just prescribe the medication my doctor in L.A. has been giving me."

"Which drug?" His voice is gentle, if not sincere, as though talking to a child in public.

"It starts with a *P*, I think."

"Percodan?"

"That's the one."

"Can't you phone your doctor in L.A.? The one who performed the surgery?"

"I could if he weren't in Europe for two months." And this is a fact. In the meantime, Dr. Rowan is supposed to handle pain control. "Jupiter," she says. "Norman Jupiter. Back and Spine, Pasadena." She offers a weak smile through tears that are mostly real, at the same time conjuring an image of herself, cheeks glistening, eyes vulnerably wide, lips wobbling just a little. It's as if she is watching her dailies after a good shoot.

"All right," he concedes. "But I'll need to do a brief manual exam."

He is gentle and efficient, even if his hands are cold, and soon she is dressed again and clutching the prescription in her fist. At home, she props herself on pillows and listens to her mom move about in the kitchen, opening and closing the fridge, slicing something on the chopping board. When the bedside phone rings, she snatches it up. "Yes?"

"Annie, it's me." A soft, conspiratorial voice. "Is your mom around?"

"There's nobody here by that name," she announces and sets the receiver back in its cradle just as Dottie arrives with the pills and water, also a plate of sliced carrots and celery.

"Who was that?"

"Wrong number." Melanie swallows two pills and takes a carrot. "I'm craving a Dr. Pepper," she says. "I think I'll run over to Stan's."

"Finish your veggies. Then I'll go out and buy you one."

"I need to walk, Mom."

"I'll go with you."

"Mother, for God's sake—I need some air! Leave me the fuck alone!"

It's partly an act and partly not. The truth is, sometimes she has no choice but to get right up in her mom's face, use the power that even Dottie, if she were honest with herself, would have to admit has made their life, such as it is, possible.

Their house is at the edge of the Las Palmas neighborhood—plenty of actors living nearby—and she can usually walk the few blocks to Stan's Quick Stop without attracting attention. It doesn't hurt that Palm Springs cops are good about keeping mercenary cameras in check. She buys her pop from the sullen girl at the counter, then ducks into the phone booth around the corner and places the call to Minnesota.

"Sarah? Sorry about that, earlier. Mom's been all over me."

"No worries. Hey, I saw you on TV last night. You looked great. Are you all right?"

Sarah Levitz, a childhood friend, is the only person back home whom Melanie has contact with anymore. She and her husband and their new baby live at Enoch's farm.

"I'm fine. How's the little guy?"

"He's perfect, you've got to see him. Listen, though, the reason I called. Enoch nearly died yesterday. His heart quit. It happened first thing in the morning, right in front of the house. Most of us were down in the Cities. Victor was the one who called the ambulance. I guess they used those paddle things to bring him back."

The air is suddenly thick and hard to breathe. "Heart attack?" Melanie says.

"Something like that. A bad rhythm. But here's the thing. He goes on his radio show this morning, right? And get this. He announces on air that Jesus is coming back in two weeks. On August 19th."

"What?"

"He says God sent an angel who told him. While he was lying there dead."

"That's not possible, right?"

"They're saying it might be some kind of brain damage. But I don't think so—he seems just fine to me."

Melanie holds her breath, remembering how Enoch always spoke with his eyes closed, long passages of scripture flowing off his tongue, his hair askew. And his prayers, as if he had a hotline to God. Which Melanie has reason to believe he did.

"What do you think, Sarah? I mean, do you believe him?"

"I don't know. But things are gonna get crazy up here, I can tell you that—once people get wind of it. Oh, and Peter's back in town. At least he was yesterday. He hasn't been home more than once or twice since his mom died."

"Peter," Melanie says. *Peter*, she thinks. She leans back against the glass wall of the phone booth and lets the sun bake her, recalling, as the conversation winds down, her last morning in Minnesota, Dottie asking the sorts of questions she never asked, like "Where is my purse?" though it lay as always on the stool next to the door. And her dad, perched on his tractor, watching as they drove out of the yard, unaware that he was losing them both for good. The idea had been Enoch's, with Ruth claiming to see it the same way, and Dottie finding it agreeable, too. Her sister in California had plenty of room, after all. Why expose Melanie to the cruelty and judgment she was in for? And Peter, off within days to play pro ball and completely unaware of the plan. On their way out of town, they'd stopped in Battlepoint to fill up with gas at the Standard station on Main and were just leaving as Peter pulled in, driving his dad's car. When he turned and looked, Melanie lifted a hand to wave, guiltily, her stomach cramping. Her mom stepped on the gas, and Peter waved back, half-smiling, as if he sensed that something wasn't right, those beautiful, sensitive, smart brown eyes of his trying to puzzle things out.

By the time he lands at LaGuardia, it's well past six, and he has the cab driver drop him a few blocks from home at Helen's, a Greek deli with a twenty-four-hour breakfast. He ate nothing on the flight and needs more time to think about the best way to break the news. In a corner booth, he orders what he likes best, gyro on toasted pita with scrambled eggs, feta cheese, tomato. Black coffee. It wouldn't surprise him, the way Joanie's been acting, if she'll want to call it quits, once he tells her what happened.

When he moved here in '72, she was one of the first people he met. He was crashed on a friend's couch in Brooklyn and washing dishes, nights, at an Indian restaurant where Joanie waitressed, and by the time she landed her job at Knopf, a few months later, he'd moved into her flat. At the beginning, she begged to read everything he wrote and exclaimed over it. Gushed. His talent was going to open doors, and they'd spend their winters together in the south of France. Stupid shit. Recently, of course, she's come back to Earth. "If you're going to do journalism, then go after the real thing," she said the other day. "Not this I'm-so-damn-clever, macho bullshit that you and Freddy seem bent on doing for *Rooster.*" From the beginning he ignored her admonitions that she was fickle in matters of love, that she wasn't ready for anything long term. Her praise of his writing made up for that. It was a magic tonic, and he convinced himself that she was not only sincere but possessed a sensibility that could see in him the artist he was growing into. Didn't that suggest a kind of love?

The food arrives, large portions of everything, and Peter takes his time, trying to enjoy it. He doesn't know where he'll go if she kicks him out. Freddy's place maybe, except Freddy isn't that kind of a friend. Or back to the Midwest, a conventional news job of some kind. One of the wire services. A daily. Even a weekly. There'll be something.

When he finally lets himself into the apartment, it's eight thirty, and she looks up from the couch where she's reading the paper. She's lying on her back, wearing her bra and panties, the heel of one tan foot pressed up against her pale ass, long legs scissored together one over the other, a triangle of sky-blue silk covering the place where everything converges.

It must be ninety degrees in here, but Joanie hasn't cracked a window. She lowers the *Times,* her eyes opaque, the beads of an abacus. If she's surprised that he's back so soon, she's not showing it.

"I tried reaching you all night," he says.

"I was out with friends from work. Aren't you going to kiss me?"

He drops his bag and goes to her and leans down. She looks at him hard, eyes narrowed, but when they kiss, her mouth is soft and wet. He wants to squeeze in next to her on the couch but feels too much like an asshole, a fraud—returning like this, with nothing.

"I ended up at Margaret's, actually, and went straight to work from there," she says. She doesn't ask about his dad.

He goes to the window and wrenches open the sash, dry wood squealing in its frame. A tepid breeze floats in. She scoots over to make room for him, uncrossing her legs and letting one fall open, but he drops instead into the stuffed chair next to her.

"What, I'm that gross?" She lifts an elbow and sniffs beneath her arm, then tosses the newspaper to the floor. "I'll go shower," she says and starts to swing off the couch, but he intercepts her, pushing her back and releasing the button of his Levis and unzipping them as she peels free of her underwear, turning to press her ass against him. *This could be the last time,* he thinks, but without regret or sentiment. There is only the blind, hot tunnel they're in, no other considerations at all.

He's nearly finished when she pulls away and spins around and climbs on top of him—her need to make sure he knows she can't be dominated. She centers herself squarely, legs squeezing, as if daring him to move, then leans over and puts her face close to his, her hair a dark curtain around them. She bares her teeth, presses hard against his chest with both palms. He's still wearing the shirt he traveled in.

"What're you doing back so soon?" she says. "He must not've died, huh?"

"He died, all right."

"What?" She straightens up, her face twisting, and he tips her off, then pins her down beneath him, and together they finish what they started, her nails digging into the flesh of his back.

Fifteen minutes later they're still tangled up, Peter halfway through a second cigarette and tracing his finger along the rise and fall of her hip.

He has explained to her about his dad's brush with death and hospital stay, drawing out the story to milk her for sympathy before he drops the bomb. Not that it's going to make any difference.

"The doc wanted to send him on for tests, but he wouldn't listen. Said he felt fine. As far as I know, he checked out of the hospital this morning. That was the plan. Against everybody's advice."

"Do you think he'll be all right?" As if she cares.

Peter shrugs. "It gets worse."

Fanning his smoke away, she crawls over him and off the couch, then disappears into the bedroom. Soon she's back in denim shorts and a halter top, crossing into the kitchen where she takes bell peppers and bok choy from the fridge and starts chopping. He doesn't tell her that he already ate.

"Let's hear it," she says.

He stubs out his cigarette and shakes another from the pack. Lights it. "While he was dead, God told him when the world is going to end."

"Cool."

"*Exactly* when. Two weeks. On August 19th."

"Ah." She makes a sour face, puts down her knife, and sets both hands on the half-wall separating kitchen and living room. "God communicated this to him how?"

Peter can't bear to explain how much he longs for his dad's Empire State Building of self-delusion to implode and come raining down. And how much he dreads it. How much he can't help loving his dad, as eccentric as he is.

"There's something else, too, isn't there? You're not finished."

Shit.

"Your face is yellow. Like you're scared."

"Wouldn't you be?"

"You mean, if *my* dad . . ." Joanie's eyebrows jump. "That's hard to imagine." Her dad is a stockbroker.

"But you're right," Peter says. "Things fell through for me in D.C. Haig wanted me at noon today, and my connecting flight in Chicago was delayed."

Joanie says, "They called in the other guy and told you to screw off?" She seems unsurprised.

"Basically."

She starts chopping again, going after the bok choy with hard cranks of her elbow. "You should have listened when I said don't go."

He agrees, nodding, but something in what she said or didn't say tugs at him. And what the hell was he supposed to do anyway, getting a call like that, his dad in the hospital, dead for all he knew?

"At least you can't blame me—it's not my fault."

"Who's blaming you?"

They eat a silent dinner, vegetable stir-fry over basmati rice, and afterwards watch an episode of *Kojak*, followed by the news: Nixon hiding out while his defenders try explaining yesterday's story about the tape of June 23, 1972, in which he ordered a halt to the Watergate inquiry. There is nothing about Haig, but when the camera offers a live shot of the White House, placid and elegantly lit, Peter imagines himself there, huddled inside some basement bunker with the hawkeyed general and his crew-cut staff, listening as they strategize an endgame to the nation's first-ever peaceful coup. Except it's not a coup. It's a constitutional crisis.

After Joanie goes to bed, he walks east along Sixth through Washington Square Park and another few blocks to an unassuming brownstone with a clock shop and jewelry store on the ground floor. It's nearly midnight and Bird Petrocelli, just arriving, says, "Humid," dabbing at his forehead with a handkerchief. He wears sunglasses, a Fu Manchu, and a dark silk shirt stretched to the limit by his cask of a chest. In the unlit alley, they climb the fire stairs to a second-floor landing where Bird lets them into the warehouse space he rents from his uncle the jeweler.

"How can you see with those glasses on?" Peter says. He's always wanted to ask.

"Better than you think." Bird flips on the lights.

The twenty-foot mahogany bar is from a nineteenth-century saloon, down near the Battery, the mirror too, and leather-covered three-legged stools. Herman Melville drank at this bar and stared into that mirror and sat upon these stools, at least according to the salvage guy who sold them to Bird. The rest of the room is scattered with cast-off tables and unmatched chairs. Brick walls. A divot-covered plank floor. A ceiling laced with pipes and conduit. Except for Sundays, Bird opens at midnight, closes at dawn, and pours from a well-stocked bar to people he likes, cash only. He forbids entry to groups of more than three and shows the door to anyone who causes problems. It's a quiet place favored by plasterers, plumbers, and other journeymen. Also writers and painters. Ever since Freddy found it, a couple of years back, Peter has done most of his writing here at the corner table, which he sits at now, laying out his spiral notebook and pencils, and turning on the lamp that Freddy brought from home. At the moaning of hinges Peter looks up.

"An hour late and a dollar short," Freddy calls from the door. "And I don't mean me." He's tall and lumpy with a bookish face, and he's wearing what he always wears—a fraying corduroy jacket over a wrinkled shirt, baggy trousers. His eyes twinkle behind wire-frame glasses, and his hair stands out from his head, a frizzy halo. He looks like a stand-up comic or a man plotting rebellion. He tosses a worn portfolio on the table and smiles, showing small straight teeth. "It's a bitch."

"Who's the other guy?" Peter says.

"Forget it. Sludge in the pipes." He heads to the bar. "What's your pleasure?"

"Black and Tan."

"Fuck that." Freddy wags a finger, and Bird produces a bottle of Jameson, which Freddy brings back, along with a pair of tumblers. He pours, filling them to the brim. They keep their thoughts to themselves as men filter in from outside, and after the first glassful Peter's stomach and then his arms and fingers start humming silently. Freddy refills their tumblers, then leans across the table. He taps Peter's notebook.

"What's in there?"

"Not much. You?"

Freddy gives his portfolio an angry shove. "Damn thing is breaking my balls." A few months ago Freddy received a small advance to write the biography of the artist Neely Vaughn, who was drafted in '67 and sent to Vietnam, where he painted plein air oils of the raped jungle and published them in *Life*. He was killed in the Tet.

"You want to talk about your old man?"

Peter's brain is wrapped in warm gauze now, and the story comes right out, all of it, the cardiac event and recovery, the female angel and imminent Rapture, while Freddy sits there with his chin propped in his hands, elbows planted on the table, his eyes closed. He might as well be asleep. When Peter is finished, Freddy says, "Who believes that shit, anyway?"

"People who need clarity," Peter says, "who can't deal with paradox."

"Religious people, you mean."

"Some religious people, yeah. There are different kinds, aren't there? I'm talking about the ones who are in it for the uncomplicated answers. Boom, here it is, nice and simple. People who would rather be deceived than have to figure things out for themselves. Who can't imagine Nixon might be lying to them."

"Fuck," Freddy says, and he slaps the table with his hands. "You're right. I mean, your old man's timing is perfect. All the poor dreamers who need a 100 percent guarantee—their little world's gotta be shaking right now. And he's going on air with this?"

"It's not much of a megaphone. He's got maybe a hundred, two hundred people up there who listen. Pious farmers, lonely housewives. And hey, it might be a bridge too far even for them. They'll probably think Enoch needs cash."

"Who cares about folks up there. No, you've gotta go back and write it down—everything you see and hear. I'll sell it for you, we'll have Rusty drooling. I won't take a penny for myself, or a byline either."

"Rusty?" Rusty Rivers is senior editor at *Rooster*.

Freddy refills their tumblers, and Peter takes another warm swallow, watching his friend across the table. Freddy has pushed himself straight in his chair, and his hands are flat on the table, his eyes like June bugs behind his lenses. Fading June bugs.

"You mean it?" Peter asks. Freddy's always messing with him.

"If you don't go, I'll have to go myself. And I guarantee your old man would love me—I'd *make* him love me. Trouble is, that cult he's running, the whole messiah thing, I couldn't translate the language they use. You, on the other hand." He lifts up his hands in a grand gesture. "Agents at your door. Book contract."

"I can't do it," Peter says. "He wants me out there *with* him, on his side. He's my old man."

"And he's going to be a damn spectacle, whether you write it or not.

It's your choice, of course. Stay here and let him self-destruct, or go back out and make people see him the way you want them to see him."

"I'd feel like Judas."

Freddy takes another drink. "Your call, brother."

An idea drifts just beyond Peter's reach, but he can't bring it into focus. He finishes the whiskey, closes his eyes, and tries again, catches a glimpse of feet, their pale, horny soles rising in the air above him, flattened pads of all ten toes, leathery heels.

"Think about it, though—what if he's actually right?" Peter says.

"His crazy-ass dream?"

"Yeah."

"You're drunk."

"Seriously, what if he's right and *we're* the fools? Just think, to be a part of something that big, that transcends everything—you've got to admit, it's appealing. Not the Rapture thing so much, but the idea that there's a God who actually gives a shit."

"Maybe there is," Freddy says. "Go home and sleep, my friend. If you can find your way home."

Peter reaches out and pats his notebook. "I have work to do."

"What work? If you'd stayed here and taken the train to Washington, you might have a career. But now you've got nothing, you just told me."

Peter doesn't like that word, *nothing,* and he doesn't like Freddy's tone either. "I should've listened to Joanie, you're saying."

"I'm saying you ought to be in D.C."

"Joanie told me I shouldn't go home, tried to make me stay."

"Smart girl." Freddy taps his forehead, then gets up and heads for the bar, taking the bottle with him. Soon he's back with two coffees. "Look, I'm sorry," he says. "Just forget about it."

"Fuck you," Peter says. "It's bad enough, everything coming apart on me like it has. But now you're going to rub it in my face? And talk about my girlfriend, as if that's your business?"

"Shut up and drink your coffee."

Peter's coffee is too hot, though, and the first swallow burns his tongue and the roof of his mouth, causing him to lurch backward, spilling, and burning his fingers, too. He sets the cup on the table, pushes back his chair, and leans forward on his knees, gripping his hand with his fist. His head is momentarily clearer for the pain, and it strikes him that Freddy has other things on his mind, gazing as he is toward the far wall and drumming a rhythm on the table, like he's forgotten everything they've just said. But why should he give a fuck, anyway? A man's problems are his own.

Peter says, "The whole thing just stinks, is all," and he gets up to leave.

AUGUST 8—THURSDAY

The barn's upper floor, which Enoch calls the aviary, is shot with brightness, the new sun pouring through skylights, shafts of dust-filled brilliance ending in neat squares on the old plank floor, which for nearly a hundred years bore the weight of countless bales of straw and hay. Barn swallows and pigeons dodge and zip near the rafters. The old mow, insulated and air-conditioned now—it's heated in winter—serves as the meeting place on Saturday nights when Enoch and the Ranchers are joined by twenty to thirty other worshippers, Sarah Levitz finessing the piano and one of the single men, Matt, flailing against his guitar, Elvis Presley style, hair slicked back and stomping his boots. Two hours of Holy noise, the Spirit flowing through Enoch's hands to those he touches, often knocking them to the floor—though of late he wonders if the Spirit is manifesting with reduced power and effect.

He sits on a straight kitchen chair, waiting. The kids got home late from the Cities, and he has called a meeting for 7:30 this morning, before everyone leaves for work. Behind him is the upright piano his wife used to play and beside him the lectern he built. He faces the empty chairs, ten of them, arranged in a half-circle. At the far end of the build-ing Victor pushes his broom, a rag hanging from his back pocket for bird droppings. Enoch gets up and moves the lectern back two feet to catch the sun flooding through an east-facing skylight. He nods at Dave and Sally Drobec as they emerge from the apartments downstairs and take the middle seats. Dave is an accountant, Sally a clerk at the bank in town. Both donate a third of their income to the Ranch, as every resident does. No one pays rent.

Over the next few minutes the rest trail in. Jimmy Levitz, a stout plumber's apprentice, and his tall, lively wife, Sarah, who taught fourth grade at Battlepoint Public until their son was born a few months ago and whom she's holding now, an armful. The single girls, Rainy and Maude, housemaids for a nearby resort and often mistaken for sisters. And fi-nally the three single men in their twenties, whose names Enoch mixes up sometimes, especially Eddie and Ted, who paint houses—and of course Matt, too, aspiring musician and shoe salesman. Normally they'd be crowding him, telling stories about their trip or seeking some permis-sion or other—to make a purchase, date somebody new, change jobs. Enoch tries to shepherd them closely. But this morning they keep their distance. There is no banter. The boys aren't teasing the girls or groom-ing themselves. The girls aren't laughing. Aside from a bit of glancing around, their eyes are fixed on Enoch, who recalls Sylvie's warning last night over the phone: "You better be ready. If you follow through on this, some of those kids won't be sticking around."

"You know why we're here," he begins.

Dave's hand slips into the air. He tips his head deferentially and squints at Enoch through his glasses. "We caught part of your broadcast yesterday, and we had a chance—"

"You got the signal all the way down in the Cities?"

"Sort of. Through the static."

"Ancient of Days!"

Dave nods. "We talked about it on our way home last night. Oh, and thank the Lord you're alive."

A few quiet hallelujahs. Some raised hands and "Praise Gods," though everyone seems restrained, cautious, watching him carefully, faces half-averted.

"And we do have questions," Dave adds. He doesn't look at Enoch straight on.

"Of course you do." Enoch is aware of his arms and hands cooling, the top of his head too, and he drags the lectern back to recenter himself in sunlight. "I have never been tempted to calculate the hour and the day, as many have," he says. "Truth to tell, until now it hasn't been a subject much on my heart. Maybe because of my mother, who talked about it incessantly." He allows himself a self-deprecating laugh. "God's irony, don't you think?" He looks at Dave Drobec, who is fiddling with his necktie. "Please, your questions."

But Sarah Levitz is the one who speaks up: "We heard you say that Christ is coming back on August 19th."

"Yes."

"That verse, the one that goes 'No one knows the hour or the day.' Doesn't your prophecy contradict it?"

Enoch smiles and opens his Bible. The obvious question. He starts flipping pages. "The Gospel of Mark," he says. "Here—and note, Sarah, what comes before the verse you quoted." He gives her a pointed look. "'Heaven and earth shall pass away,'" he reads, "'but my words shall not pass away. But of *that* day'—did you hear that, Sarah? 'But of *that* day and *that* hour knoweth no man, no, not the angels which are in heaven, neither the Son, but the Father.' You see, Christ is referring here not to the Rapture but, rather, to his final return—'that day,' he says, when 'Heaven and earth shall pass away.' You're confusing the Rapture, when he rescues believers, with his final return. Heaven and earth are not going to pass away in the Rapture. And my vision was clearly of the Rapture, which comes before the Tribulation—which, thank God, we won't be around for."

Dave has laid hold of some courage and now raises a hand. "So you believe the Tribulation is about to begin?"

"Don't *you*?" Enoch says. "Bible scholars have been saying as much for years. Look what happened in the Middle East last fall. Do you think Egypt and Syria aren't itching for another shot at Israel? And do you know how close that war brought the world to a nuclear showdown? Not to mention what's happening right now in Washington, D.C. We're about to witness a duly elected United States President being forced out of office. It's shameful. There is no respect. The forces of chaos are in ascendance."

Sarah lifts a hand. "Isn't it possible that God was sending you a personal message?"

The room is silent. The swallows and pigeons have perched on the rafters, and the Ranchers seem to be collectively holding their breath. Yet it's a question that had to be asked, and he can't help but think of Jesus's words from the Gospel of Luke, 'Verily I say unto you, no prophet is accepted in his own country.' Suddenly Enoch is exhausted, spent, and he lowers himself to the chair, giving up his warm spot of light. He rests his elbows on his knees.

"It is personal, Sarah, yes. That's what makes it so clear. If you heard the broadcast, you know what I saw. Fourteen sunsets, then the storm, the clouds parting above me, the liberating weightlessness as I rose to meet Him. But I didn't talk about the significance, for me, of August 19th. That was my dear wife's birthday and our anniversary date as well. Eight-one-nine are the first three digits of my Social Security number. Also this: when I was a child, my father built the house I still live in"—he points toward it—"a kit home from Sears, Roebuck that came on rail to Battlepoint when I was just seven. When it was finished, I insisted on sleeping in the attic. I loved the smell of the wood up there and the view of Last Lake. As you may not know, all of the beams and studs and joists of kit homes were marked with a code to aid in construction, and the sill of the window next to my bed was marked E-eight-one-nine. It's still there. Enoch 819 is how I thought of it. My number."

"Wow," Jimmy Levitz says, nodding.

Dave Drobec narrows his number-crunching eyes. "That angel you saw, the tall woman with the flame on her head? Are there female angels in the Bible?"

Anger flares in Enoch's stomach. First his own son, blaming the dream on Enoch's poor mother and her dyed hair. And now Dave with his cynical questions. "I didn't call her an angel, did I?" he says. "And she wasn't merely tall. She was as tall as a spruce tree. God can take whatever form He chooses, I would imagine."

Dave bites his lip.

Enoch checks his watch. Eight fifteen. "You need to go," he says. "But

I want you to understand—if you're unable to support me in what I am doing, I will not hold it against you. All I ask is that you make your decisions quickly. If you believe I am in error, fine, but in that case you'll want to move on from here. Leave." He scans their faces. "Let's pray."

When he's finished they sit dumbly, like a crowd of strangers who have been told the train they're waiting to board has been canceled. Only Victor seems happy, smiling as he starts to push his broom.

Enoch goes downstairs and crosses the yard to his house and calls Sylvie to let her know he's on his way, then out to the machine shed where he keeps the '67 Mercury Cougar, along with the red Farmall, the McCormick baler, and the old Chevy pickup. The Cougar is seafoam green, with a leather interior and white sidewall tires. Under the hood, a 351 V-8 with twenty-six thousand miles. It's the only vehicle he has ever purchased off the showroom floor, and he drives it only during the warm months, May through October. With a chamois he rubs down the body—doors, hood, fenders, trunk lid—then he gets in and starts the engine, pleased by the vibration that comes into his hands through the leather-wrapped wheel. He backs out and pulls up next to the house, where inside he changes into a clean pair of trousers, a short-sleeved cotton shirt, and his town boots, brown pull-ons with round toes. In the bathroom he smooths down his hair with water. He splashes cologne on his neck.

Axe-Head Lake is twenty minutes away, and he drives with the window down, elbow jutting, the air sharp with pine smell and the ripening pollens of mustard and purple clover. He's been acquainted with Sylvie Young ever since she and her husband, Porter, a medical doctor, moved here from Pennsylvania in the forties. Enoch and his wife knew them only enough to say hi. Then in '66, Porter Young and Ruth Bywater both died, and it was during the following summer that Enoch was trolling an isolated bay on Axe-Head Lake for walleyes when he heard somebody calling from shore—Sylvie, standing on the end of her dock, wrapped in a towel after a cold swim. He went inside, on her insistence, for a cup of coffee and a slice of pumpkin cake, and after an unexpectedly satisfying hour of talk, he stayed on for supper. Since then, they have seen each other nearly every week, except in winter when she spends time in Florida with a daughter. For the sake of the Ranchers and those who attend Saturday night meetings, Enoch characterizes their friendship in Great Commission terms. She is Unitarian, after all, which to most Bible believers—Enoch included—is akin to atheism. And though at times he is still clouded with guilt, aware that to persist in a sin is to undermine the strength it exerts over one's conscience, Sylvie gives him a perspective he has come to value deeply, a naked view of himself and his place in the world, free from the filter to which he wholeheartedly subscribes. It's as if she offers him a second life, untainted by the Fall. Fortunately, he is bolstered by his firm belief that the souls of those who have been saved by Christ are sealed until the day of judgment, their sins notwithstanding.

This morning he finds her in the kitchen, dressed in a loose blouse and baggy shorts, her graying blonde hair pulled back in a braid, rimless glasses perched at the end of her nose. She sets down her rolling pin and spreads her arms. Her eyes are blue-gray, sympathetic, moist, and Enoch knows how much they see. She hugs him, pressing her face into his chest. He runs his hands down to her waist and pulls her close.

"Let me finish this first—please," she says and retreats to the counter.

He called her from the hospital the night he died, and so she's had a chance to acclimate herself to the new dispensation—aware she nearly lost him, and aware too of what he believes is soon going to happen. A preposterous idea, of course, by her lights.

For a quarter of an hour he watches from the kitchen table as she lines a pie plate with dough, fills it with chunks of cooked chicken, sautéed onions and peppers, and then finally a buttermilk roux before sealing it. She is always wanting to feed him. Why? Pie in the oven, she boils water on the stove and pours it over teabags, then comes over and sits next to him at the table, her arm resting against his on the tabletop, steaming mugs of tea before them. Through the living room windows they gaze at the Norway pines at lake's edge and the white-and-black birches whose leaves are already yellowing. A breeze ripples the surface of the water, making of the clouds a pattern of white bones.

"I need to hear again how it happened," she says. "How you didn't die."

"I did die."

"No, you didn't."

He keeps it short, reciting the facts as they were told to him. She listens, her eyes closed. "The Almighty needed to get my attention," he says.

"He already had your attention." Sylvie starts to cry but fights the impulse, her nose shooting little spurts of air. "I should have been there," she says.

"There was nothing you could have done." He wraps her in his arms, and then as she gives in, he breaks too, weeping as he hasn't done at least since Ruth died. He has always envied men who are able to cry and feared what it says about his own character that he cannot, and so the relief that washes over him now is so sweet that he cries all the harder—for Sylvie's hurt and kindness, for her love, for his own life spared, for God stooping low and offering him a picture of what is to come.

"I hate that image in my head of them lifting you into the ambulance," she says. "I want to be rid of that." She gets up and walks into the bathroom, where Enoch can hear water running. Then nothing for a while. When she comes back, they go into the living room together and sit on the couch, facing the lake. "You're pale," she says.

"My arteries are fine and my heart appears undamaged. According to the doctor."

"He didn't want to send you somewhere else? Like Mayo?"

"I have things to do."

"Enoch, please." She turns and looks right into him. She's wearing the pair of earrings he gave her years ago, danglers, black onyx on sterling silver, and he touches one with a finger, starts it swinging.

"Do you remember when you got those?" he says.

Of course she remembers, and her smile tells him she doesn't resent being reminded. It was the morning he drove her to Duluth where a surgeon was scheduled to remove a cancerous tumor in her stomach. Enoch anointed her with oil and prayed. This was five years ago. When they opened her up, they found nothing but a plum-sized husk of benign tissue. Sylvie has never discounted the possibility of a healing from God. But God, to her, as she has tried explaining to Enoch, is a numinous power residing within the collective unconscious—a concept Enoch struggles to understand. It's as if she believes there is some sort of an all-encompassing, spiritual amniotic fluid in which everyone is floating around together, the whole idea disturbing, if not heretical.

Her face is taut, her lips are trembling. "I will never make light of what you say or think, you know that. But this time, Enoch, you're over-reaching." All of her features—nose, eyes, mouth—are symmetrical and large, and he's always thought their size and beauty correspond to her generosity, her willingness to give herself away.

"I love you," he says.

She nods and takes a deep breath. "You've had a trauma, and you're here now because you know that I always tell you what I think. Not what you want to hear."

He says, "I thought maybe this time you might be able to hear what I'm saying."

"No, Enoch, you didn't think that. You wanted someone to tell you the thing that you are afraid to accept but need to hear." She puts her hands on either side of his face and with her thumbs she strokes his lips. "There is a part of yourself, way down deep, that knows what you're meant for, and it's trying to reach you. I believe that's the purpose of our dreams—and you're right to pay attention to them. But this is not about the end of the world, it's about the end of something in you. It's about a change you need to make. A kind of death, I suppose." She plants kisses on the palms of her hands, one and then the other, and then she presses them gently against his chest.

He should have expected something like this. Sylvie is strong-minded and sure of her beliefs, as is he. And yet he can't help the disap-pointment he feels—her inability to grasp what has happened to him. To be kind, he says to her, "A part of me wants another part of me to change, is that what you're saying?"

"The best part of you—God in you, yes. And it wants you to give up a little control, relax. It's okay if there's not a single explanation for every-thing. You're a complicated man, Enoch, with a complicated psyche, and all parts of it need to be attended to."

If Sylvie weren't so kind he would be inclined to argue with her, but she has a way of disagreeing that unmans his defenses. He says, "I've felt this way only a few times in my life. That afternoon in the pasture, with Annie—you remember. And the day you were healed. It's like I'm watch-ing myself from a distance, or from some future point and looking back. It's peaceful, Sylvie, this kind of certainty. You can't imagine."

"You're right, I can't." She smiles, the crow's feet around her eyes darkening. She steps back, in retreat.

"There's something I have to ask you," he says. "When the day comes, I want you there at the Ranch. I am going to take you along. I believe He'll do that for me."

She scowls, then laughs.

"Is that a yes?" He reaches out and touches her. She moves toward him again.

"No."

"I mean it. Will you be there?"

"Of course," she says. And when she puts her arms around him and presses her body against his, he feels the heat rising in a way it hasn't for months. He whispers into her hair, "Let's go upstairs."

"But the pie's nearly ready. Aren't you hungry?"

"Oh, yes," he says.

The picture on their ten-inch black-and-white is pretty good tonight except for an intermittent rolling of the image, which Peter remedies by adjusting a small dial at the back of the console. At 9:00 p.m. sharp there he is, sitting behind a big desk, Stars and Stripes on his right, the flag of the President's Office on his left, a dark drapery—probably royal blue—behind him. He's holding a sheaf of paper in his hands.

"Looks better than he should," Peter says.

"He looks beat up to me."

The truth is, Nixon has a brave smile, and his eyes are clear. His voice sounds good too, probably the man's best quality—a broadcaster's pipes, deep and resonating. If only Peter had been able to cash in his ringside ticket. He'd be there now, watching the show from up close.

"And all for nothing," Joanie says. "Like he had to break into the Democratic offices to win the election—it couldn't have been his idea. He's too smart. I mean, George McGovern?"

"What's wrong with McGovern? I sure the hell voted for him."

"Shhh." She waves her hand.

Nixon is making solid eye contact now, his jowls trembling as he describes his fading support in Congress and his consequent decision to give up the fight. He invokes the Constitution, naturally. Again and again.

"Don't you love the passive voice?" Peter says. "The euphemisms? 'With the disappearance of my base.'"

"Shut up and listen! This is history. He's doing what has to be done. For the good of the country."

"Ah."

"Don't do that! 'Ah.'"

"You're sounding like your dad," he says. Her old man is a lifetime Republican.

"Quiet!"

Peter manages to hold his tongue until Nixon has finished salving his ego and then even longer while Joanie offers a rundown of his contributions to history—the Clean Air Act, the China breakthrough, energy policy. All of which Peter grudgingly absorbs. But why in the world does she feel the need to defend a man she never even voted for?

"You're just bitter because you blew it," she says, "and you're stuck watching it with me. You're so damn naive, Peter. If everybody in D.C. had to pay for their peccadilloes, there'd be no one left to run things."

"It comes down to trust," Peter says. He can't help himself. "Without it, everything falls apart. The same thing with people."

Joanie stands from the couch and stares down at him, her hands in fists at her sides. "Are you trying to make this about us?"

"What are you talking about?"

"You don't *trust* me? God, if someone were going to have trust issues, it ought to be me—watching you blow it like you did this week. How can I trust that you'll ever get anything right?"

Peter watches her face go from hard mask to vulnerable pucker, all in an instant, and then she starts blinking, fast. She turns and marches into their bedroom and slams the door so hard the Van Gogh print falls to the floor, its glass shattering.

"Now look what you've done!" she yells through the door.

For ten minutes he paces, one end of the apartment to the other, before tapping on her door with his fingertips and speaking in a low voice, "Hey, I'm sorry, come on. I know I screwed things up."

In fact, he is sorry. But angry too, and not sure why. In most cases, he can shrug things off, step away from the moment. He likes to think he has a long fuse—though he also knows that when he does blow, it's not a pretty thing. During his final season of ball in Rochester, one of his teammates, a mediocre right fielder, made a habit of telling Peter he was too slow for the big leagues. It was the same thing Peter's dad used to say, and probably true. But then the guy spoke up at the wrong time, on a sweltering night after Peter was thrown out at home, and Peter broke the guy's nose. There was no prelude and no follow-through. Just one punch. The league suspended Peter for ten days.

"Just leave me alone," Joanie pleads, sobbing. "Don't talk to me, you don't know what to say. You never do."

"Try me," he says, hoping she won't.

"Leave me alone."

He turns the knob and she screams, high and piercing, as if she's been impaled by a long blade. The door is locked, lucky for him, and he retreats into the kitchen where he pours himself a glass of wine and takes his time with it, willing himself to calm down. Her reaction to Nixon's plunge is no surprise, he thinks, with her Daddy complex, and it was a mistake to torment her, even if he didn't intend to. What a fuck-up.

After a while he turns on the television, volume low, and watches special coverage on CBS. Bloviating Democrats and sullen Republicans. Triumphant journalists. He switches to NBC, meaning to lighten his mood, but Carson has been bumped in favor of news. He shuts it off and goes to the bedroom and puts his ear to the door. He tries the knob, unlocked now. Okay, good. Her breathing is heavy and slow. Steady. After washing up and brushing his teeth, he eases into bed next to her and then tries not to move as he waits for sleep.

AUGUST 9—FRIDAY

t's as if the perimeter of his brain has been outlined with permanent marker. Before waking, he was dreaming of his conversation with Joanie the night before last, when he confessed that he'd missed his chance, and she said, more or less, "And so they called in the other guy?" her voice in the dream identical to her voice that night, sharp with scorn.

"Are you awake?" he says. The clock radio on the nightstand reads 5:45 a.m.

"No."

"What you said to me after I got back—about Freddy's friend calling that other journalist. How did you know?"

"How did I know what?"

"That Trond called in somebody else?"

"Trond?"

"Freddy's friend."

"You must have said something."

"I couldn't have. I didn't know anything about it till it happened. Freddy told me over the phone when I was stalled in Chicago, at O'Hare."

Joanie flips on her side and looks at him. "What's your point?"

53

"You said to me, 'So he called that other guy.'"

"Yeah. I assumed they had somebody in the wings, in case you couldn't do it. Geez, what are you, a prosecuting attorney? You're watching too much news."

Peter thinks of Joanie's rage only hours ago, and of Freddy's petulance at the Morning Bird, telling Peter he should have listened to her. He remembers trying to reach her all night long in Minnesota.

"You talked to him," he says. "He came over here, looking for me."

She's silent a moment too long.

"Tell me," he says. In the dim light streaming from the window, he can see her throat move up and down as she swallows.

"No. I was with Margaret, like I said, and some of the other girls from work, and I spent the night at her place."

"And you think I'm . . . what? What did you call me—naive?" Peter puts on a laugh. "Did you really think Freddy wouldn't tell me?"

Joanie takes a sharp breath and sits up straight. Then she hits the bed on both sides of her with the flats of her hands. "I can't believe this! That he'd fucking say something."

"I didn't say he did."

"Shit!" She turns and slams Peter's shoulder with her fist. A pretty good pop.

"Just explain it, tell me what happened. Your version."

"My version," she hisses. He makes out the flair of her nostrils, the jagged smile.

"Things are complicated, right?"

"Shut up." She slips from bed and turns on the lamp. She's wearing a sheer nightgown, and the light shows the fork of her legs where they meet. The curve of her waist. She walks from the room. He can hear the stiff creak of the freezer door and the shatter of ice cubes freed from their aluminum tray, the tinkling clank as they land in a tumbler. Then she's back with her whiskey.

"I suppose you want one too. Get it yourself."

"That's okay."

She puts on her flannel robe and sits at the foot of the bed, facing him. Lifts her glass and takes a swallow, thinks for a moment, then drinks some more. "Like I said, I went out with the girls till the bars closed. Then I came back and got ready for bed."

"Tell me the truth."

"Then shut up and listen. I was a little drunk. No, I was pretty damn drunk. A little scared too. When I came back, that creep who lives at the end of the hall was standing in front of his door, watching me. You know his shtick, rubbing his chest sort of, with that look on his face? So I'm a little freaked out. Anyway, I get into bed, and before I even shut off the light—now it's close to three—the buzzer goes off. I thought it was the creep. But it kept buzzing, so I got up and went over and said, 'Who is it?'"

"Freddy," Peter says.

"Shut up. My version. And I say, 'What's going on? Who are you?' And he tells me. Then says he needs to get ahold of you, it's really important. Asks if he can come up. So I buzz him in downstairs, and go to the door and wait till he knocks."

"And you had on what? Your nightie?"

"My robe, idiot, what do you think? When I went to the door, he said, 'Can I come in?' It was raining hard, and he was soaked through, hair dangling like strings across his face. So I go into the bathroom and get a towel, then have him sit down in the kitchen so he doesn't soak one of the stuffed chairs. He told me he needed to call you."

"You didn't call me."

"We tried. I couldn't find your dad's number. We don't have it written down anywhere, and when I called information, I couldn't remember the name of the town."

"Battlepoint," Peter says.

"Fine. I told the operator to find a listing for Enoch Bywater in rural Minnesota. Up north. He came up empty."

"His name is James Enoch Bywater."

"There you go. If *you* had called at that point, everything would've been fine."

"At 3:00 a.m."

"Yeah."

"I stopped trying about twelve thirty, one. I had to sleep."

Peter is sitting cross-legged at the head of the bed, arms folded on his chest, preparing for the worst. It's like the feeling he gets when he's about to vomit, tightness in his jaw, right in front of the ear, and the issue of saliva. On the other end of the bed, Joanie sits half in shadow, her posture slackening from the whiskey—and defeat. The anger she had is gone. Postfight slackness in her face.

She shakes her head. "Freddy had his arms in his armpits, like this, and he was wet and shaking, and I went to the closet and pulled out that quilt and put it over him."

"This was after you tried calling?"

"He was filling me in, saying how he wanted to make it happen for you, but things were going south, and his friend wanted somebody right now, and what was he supposed to do? I apologized on your behalf, damn it."

"Wow, thanks for that."

"I asked if he wanted something to drink. He said no, he had to go. But then lightning struck close by, literally, like a bomb went off, and the wind started up, and rain beating on the windows, and he said, 'Sure, why not? To bide the time.'"

Peter can't look at her anymore. He puts his face in his hands to protect himself and lets her finish unobserved, mercy all around.

"We had a couple drinks apiece. Then heard something out in the hall, this big thud, and he went to the door and looked out. I followed him. That creep again, he was drunk and knocking on every door, moving right up the hall, and shouting. Like 'America's finished, it's all over.' We shut the door and went to the couch and sat waiting for him to knock, which he did, pounding like a lunatic. He'd seen us staring at him and knew we were here. It was scary. I was going to call the cops, but Freddy said, 'No, the guy's got enough problems, let him be.'" Joanie stops and puts her face in her hands.

"Yeah?"

"And that's when it happened. He told me thanks for the drinks and the quilt, and I said I appreciated what he tried doing for you, and he reached out and touched my shoulder, then leaned over to kiss my cheek. But he didn't stop. And I didn't stop him. I was rattled, I guess. And drunk, too."

"What, so you just sleep with somebody like that? I mean, you met him at that book party on Varick Street, right? And maybe one other time?" Peter isn't so much angry as mystified. He's never slept with a woman he barely knows, and it seems crass, though in fact Freddy has talked enough about his own habits that it shouldn't be a surprise. Still, it's like Peter himself counts for nothing—with Joanie or with Freddy, who until now he considered his closest ally.

"It's not like it was planned, Peter. I'm sorry. And Freddy is too, no question. It's like—I don't know—like everything conspired against us, the way it happened."

"Against *me*."

She crawls off the bed and grabs her pillow and goes to the closet for a blanket—the winter quilt—and leaves the room. "I'm not going to sit here any longer and let you stare at me," she says. "It makes me feel like something the cat dragged in."

Peter gets up too and puts on his pants and shirt, socks and shoes. He goes into the bathroom for a piss. As he crosses to the coat rack, she mutters from the nest she's made on the couch, "I can't believe he told you." Then she jumps up and runs to the door—as if she has the power to keep him from leaving. He puts on his windbreaker.

"He didn't tell you, did he? And now you're going over there. Please don't."

He takes her by the shoulders and moves her aside, then opens the door and goes out, locking up behind himself and into a morning that's cool, which he's glad of. It's easier to move fast in this kind of weather, easier to think dark thoughts with a chill on. Two blocks east, the bank sign tells him 56 degrees, the streets wet and shining beneath the glare of the lights. Fewer people out than usual. Washington Square empty. The night doorman at the Maxim, with his neat white beard and gold-braided suit, asks Peter if he's got time for a smoke, but Peter walks on by.

There have been moments in his life when everything changed for the worse, like the day at eighteen when he learned that Annie was gone. Or the night of the mountain lion. Or the afternoon he slid into third base, snapping his ankle and ending his eight-year failed experiment. Or the recent round of universal rejections he endured on behalf of his memoir. And now one more defeat, of the first order, for a top-flight cuckold king.

He sprints up the two flights of fire stairs, feet ringing on the steel treads, but the Morning Bird is locked already, and so he heads east again, six more blocks to Freddy's building where he punches in the number. "Come on, you bastard."

Freddy's voice comes over the intercom, thick with sleep. "Who?"

"Me."

"I just got to bed, asshole."

"Buzz me in."

"Shit." But the door buzzes, and Peter pushes through and takes the stairs to the second floor where Freddy stands in T-shirt and boxers, one bare foot in the hall, one inside his apartment. Eyes bloodshot. Chest hair curling from the top of his V-neck, lending him a vulnerability Peter resents. Freddy steps aside.

It's an open, one-room studio, kitchen on one side, bed on the other, bathroom with partial walls off in a corner. Freddy goes into the kitchen, padding flatfooted across the wood floor, his skinny legs shuffling. He sits at the table, scowling, then gets up and lights a burner and sets the teapot to boil, pulls a pair of mugs from the cupboard. Also a box of tea-bags and a fifth of brandy. Peter stays put, just inside the door. He feels too large for his own body, as if he's outgrown the capacity of his skin somehow and is going to burst open, flooding the room with himself.

"Now that you've got me up, tell me what for."

"Put on some clothes."

"What—this bothers you?" He glances down at himself. Boxers, bare white legs, long feet, sagging T-shirt.

"It bothers me."

"Get over it."

"Put something on, damn it." Peter is aware of being more curious than angry, though. It's as if he's watching himself and taking clues from his own posture in order to see what might come next—his shoulders back and his head erect, hands clasped at the front of his chest. Freddy's watching him, too, and finally disappears into the dimness at the edge of the room, emerging soon in a pair of jeans. Still wearing the same T-shirt.

"This meet your approval?"

The teapot starts singing and Freddy fills two cups, teabags inside, and sets them out. The brandy too. He sits down. Peter comes to the table but remains on his feet, watching as Freddy adds brandy to his own tea and then takes a swallow.

"Ooh, hot. Sit down."

Peter can't, though. He's stuck where he is, an irritating rhythm repeating in his head.

Freddy takes a breath and nods, as if finally coming to see that something is amiss. He frowns, scratches an ear, squints at Peter through his glasses. "Shit."

"Yeah."

"Have a drink, at least. Say something, man. I'm getting nervous here."

As if to see whether he's capable of movement, Peter reaches down and slaps away the mug of tea that Freddy poured for him. It smashes into the side of the cupboard, raining fragments to the floor. Freddy jumps up, overturning his chair, and takes a step back, away from Peter, who feels better now, unfettered, coming around the table, Freddy cringing in front of him, sagging T-shirt stained with a long wet stripe where his tea spilled, his face crumpled like Peter has never seen it before, his mouth saying, "I've done so much for you." Peter buries a fist into Freddy's paunchy middle, then stands back to see where this will go, watching as the man doubles over, wheezing. When he straightens up, there's a pathetic gleam of hope in his eyes, as if the moment has passed. Peter can't help laughing as he steps forward to correct the misunderstanding with a jab that snaps Freddy's head back on his neck. Staggering away, he mumbles, "I'm shhorry."

Peter follows and pins him against the wall, and when Freddy drops his hands from his face and begins to make an appeal—"Please!" he says—Peter is there to punish him: a right hand against the left side of Freddy's face. The term *roundhouse* leaps to mind, and Freddy drops, not like a body in the movies, arms wheeling, but like a tower of children's blocks tumbling in vertical disaster, like a hanged man disappearing through a trapdoor. Peter waits until Freddy, from the floor, looks up through his fingers to say, "You fucker," slurring his words, "Eew vugger."

Peter then turns and leaves. He goes out the door and down the stairs into the foggy, waking street, not sure where he belongs or how to slough off the heavy matter settled inside his skull, and not much giving a shit, either.

But of course he does give a shit.

It matters to him that he's been deceived by Joanie, and by Freddy, too, both of whom he thought he could trust, and it matters to him that he was foolish enough to put his trust in their hands. It matters to him that he was denied his chance for a small part in the drama playing out in Washington, D.C., and he resents his dad's role in that loss. It matters to him that Enoch's self-deception has escalated—my God!—to the point of madness, that his dad's variety of deceit, witting or unwitting, and Nixon's lies prey on the same vulnerability in people, their need to believe in whatever story makes them feel good about things, validates their notion of how the world ought to run and be run: a president who acts always in the best interests of those who elected him, a God who snatches into the clouds all who are righteous.

Enoch is typically up and finished with breakfast at this hour, but today he's in bed when the phone rings, thanks to Sylvie who at midnight pleaded with him to get extra rest when he phoned her. She refused to talk. "You sound exhausted, go to sleep," she instructed. "We'll visit tomorrow. At a reasonable hour."

He picks up on the first ring. "Hi, Sylvie."

"Are you in bed?"

"I am."

"Stay put."

He turns to one side and doubles his thin pillow to prop himself up, then lies back again. His chest where the stranger in the foreign car pounded on it three days ago is sorer than it was yesterday. It feels like a horse kicked him there.

"What's up? Why'd you call last night?" asks Sylvie.

"I just wanted to thank you, that was nice."

"It was. What else?"

"Very nice."

"Tell me why you called, Enoch."

"Skinny paid me a visit after I got home. He said Chaffee sent him."

Skinny Magnussen, Gerald Jr., who took over the hog farm after his dad died, is also deputy sheriff of Fat Lake County and answers to Ron Chaffee, sheriff. Skinny is no easier to get along with than his old man was, and the fact that Annie and their mom never returned from California is a prime source of his bitterness. He holds Enoch responsible.

"What did he want?"

"He asked if I'd considered the kind of fuss I'm going to have on my hands, and he told me I need a permit if I'm going to host a large public gathering."

"Good points."

"There's hardly a fuss here, Sylvie, and I doubt there will be. I was on the radio Wednesday and I've heard nothing from anybody. Not even Art Ulman." Ulman writes and publishes the local paper, *The Scroll*.

"You sound disappointed."

"You make it sound like I'm doing this for attention."

"You don't want the attention?"

"I certainly don't relish the idea of being lampooned. But it's hard to believe God would show me what He did if He didn't want people to know about it."

"Skinny's right, you're going to have a three-ring circus over there." Behind her voice he can hear birdsong, and he pictures her in the chenille robe she favors, sitting in the kitchen next to the sliding glass door and watching the chickadees and sparrows on the feeder.

"Maybe a few stragglers," he allows. "My reach is small."

"It's not too late to back away. Please think about it, Enoch."

In odd moments, like now, it occurs to him that Sylvie's acceptance of him resembles the love of God Himself, and it's terrible to imagine the next world without her. "Don't forget, we have a deal," he says. "You're going to be here with me when the time comes, you promised me."

They hang up before he remembers to tell her the real news—Dave and Sally Drobec, with a couple of relatives in tow, backing up to the barn with a moving van last night, loading their things, and leaving, just like that. Enoch spoke with them briefly, a cordial conversation in which Dave said they'd prayed in vain for the grace to accept Enoch's vision.

It's nearly eight o'clock when Enoch finally moves from his bed to the floor and performs his ritual push-ups, cranking them out, elbows fully straightening, then jutting out till his belly touches the floor, and then straightening again, as many times as he can manage, only twenty-one today, pain stabbing his chest with each extension, sweat coming out on his back and his neck, his old heart thumping in his ears. He can't help but wonder who will bail next. Last night Jimmy and Sarah Levitz asked for permission to drive to Minneapolis Sunday, something about Sarah's brother needing help. It seemed fishy, but at least they asked. As for the single girls, Enoch has a hunch they will leave, since Sally Drobec was their assigned shepherdess, providing guidance for them as Enoch does for the men and the husbands for their wives—monitoring relationships, decisions large and small, recreational activity, not to mention all things monetary.

Freedom in Christ means accountability to others. A Ranch axiom.

Downstairs he sits for breakfast with Victor, who has prepared the same thing for years. Two eggs poached, three slices of bacon, and toast with peanut butter.

"Do you want to get started on the showers and latrines?"

In spite of his caution with Sylvie, Enoch has been reflecting on the number of pilgrims who might arrive and trying to calculate how to provide for them, if and when they do. Victor is eager to get started, though of course there's no sense in getting ahead of themselves.

"We'll just mark things out today, you and I, put in stakes where the slabs should go. In the meantime, the lawn needs cutting. I pulled the blades off the belly mower. Maybe you could take them into town and have Billy put an edge back on."

Victor hasn't been gone five minutes when a black Cadillac turns in at the approach and rumbles pleasantly up the driveway, sun exploding on its long, waxed hood. It belongs to Father Dittmer of St. Jude's, and he's not alone.

Here we go.

From the front porch, sipping coffee, he watches them come across the dewy lawn, lifting their feet to stay dry. Young Father Dittmer is natty in pressed trousers, clerical blouse, and buffed wing tips, everything black except for the small white collar, which flashes like a badge. Pastor Eckstrom from Calvary Lutheran wears a loose Hawaiian shirt and aqua-blue Bermuda shorts. His chunky calves are deeply tanned. The Baptist preacher, Smythe, is tall and straight with a military-style flattop. Powder-blue leisure suit buttoned to the neck. Enoch shakes hands with each in turn as they join him on the porch.

"Make yourselves comfortable, I'll get coffee. Cream or sugar?" Smythe lowers himself to a metal folding chair. "No coffee," he says.

Pastor Eckstrom takes half the love seat, which hangs from the ceiling, and it swings backward with his weight, his sandaled feet kicking into the air. "Whooh!" he says. "Black, thanks."

Father Dittmer settles himself next to Eckstrom. "Both, please, if it's not too much trouble."

In Battlepoint, lines between churches are heavily drawn, and Enoch can't help but smile at being used as an instrument of ecumenism. In the kitchen he pours coffee from the pot he made this morning and places the mugs on a TV tray, along with a carton of half-and-half and a glass sugar shaker. On the porch the men sit quietly, hands in their laps.

"So," Enoch says.

Smythe runs a hand across the top of his cropped head. For years he's made it clear to his parishioners that Enoch's Saturday night meetings are off limits. Those who defy him are asked to leave the congregation, Dave Drobec being one example. "You must know why we're here," he says.

"I'm guessing you've talked to Dave."

"Not yet. But he and Sally have moved out, as I understand." His straight, lipless mouth curves up at one corner.

"And I've had people calling me," Father Dittmer says. "But the thing is, none of us heard your broadcast, and we decided it's not right to rely on hearsay."

Enoch has always liked the young priest and suspects that, of the three, Dittmer is closest to being an ally. Which isn't saying much. "I'm glad you're here," he tells them.

Pastor Eckstrom leans forward. "Are we right in understanding that you, um, have announced the date of the Second Coming?"

"Not exactly."

Eckstrom cocks his head and sits back, glances around at the others.

"But I did learn the date of the Rapture, and that's what I passed along."

"The Rapture," Pastor Eckstrom says.

"When He comes for His saints. For all of us."

"Good coffee." Father Dittmer lifts his mug in salute. "And it's good to see you're looking well. I understand you had a setback."

"That's one way of putting it. Thank you, Father. Truth is, I shouldn't be here. They had to shock me twice to bring me back. But now I'm right as rain, praise God. I left the hospital the next morning."

"Praise God," Father Dittmer says.

"The Lord is good," Pastor Eckstrom adds.

Smythe shifts on his chair. A purple vein pulses on his forehead, and his voice shakes when he speaks: "It's a serious thing, what you're doing. I'm not sure you realize it, sitting here like this, pretending like nothing's going on. No, I don't think you do."

"I've tried to be clear about everything. God struck me down, and while I lay there on the grass—right there, gentlemen, beside that buckeye tree—He let me know that He's coming to rescue us on August 19th. That's ten days away. You can accept it or not, but I am pretending nothing."

Pastor Eckstrom slides forward on the hanging seat and sets his feet on the porch floor, as if to leave. He looks around at the others, smiling. "We came to hear it straight from your mouth, and now we have. Well."

Smythe glares across at Eckstrom, his face like stone. "You don't even believe in the Rapture," he says.

"I'm not a pre-millennialist, if that's what you mean. When it comes to the apocalyptic scriptures, I'm afraid literal interpretations don't interest me. Things like that, we ought to leave plenty of room for mystery."

"Your dismissive attitude, it's spiritual malpractice," Smythe says to Eckstrom. "And you"—he turns to Enoch—"your careless talk is setting up vulnerable people for grave disappointment. Maybe for the loss of their faith. Not to mention exposing the entire Body of Christ to ridicule from the unchurched. Don't you agree, Father Dittmer?"

The young priest is contemplating a dragonfly alight on the sleeve of his jacket, its wings golden, its many-faceted eyes glittering. "I'm not sure about a secret rescue of the Church. But I do believe, as our Lord said, that He will return one day and catch us up. And yes, failed prophecies can be stumbling blocks to vulnerable souls—"

"Exactly." Smythe aims a bony index finger at Enoch's face.

"But I was going to say, too," Father Dittmer adds, "vulnerable souls, at least in my experience, always manage to find *something* to invest their hope in—something less, I mean, than Christ's life-giving sacrifice."

Smythe grunts through his nose. "I think we're finished here."

"The world is full of false idols," Father Dittmer adds.

"And false prophets." Smythe stands from his chair and runs a hand over his head again. He walks to the edge of the porch and turns. "You're playing with fire, Enoch."

"I am not playing."

"You must know what happened to Old Testament prophets whose words proved false."

"Christ came to fulfill the law and liberate us from it," Enoch says.

"They were put to death. Deuteronomy, chapter 18, verse 20."

Enoch swallows the last of his coffee, then sets his mug on the floor beside him. "And Jonah, who refused God, was swallowed by a whale," he says quietly, and can't help the little jump of triumph in his veins. "I appreciate your concern, all of you. And I don't doubt your convictions, not for a minute."

Pastor Eckstrom and Father Dittmer get up from the hanging seat, moving stiffly, and Enoch reaches out and shakes hands with them. Smythe retreats down the steps into the uncut lawn, and the others follow him. As they walk toward the Cadillac, Enoch calls out, "I covet your prayers, men."

Smythe turns in the yard. "If anyone from my congregation shows up here, please remind them that I disapprove."

"I will do that, Reverend Smythe."

The Cadillac's V-8 engine growls to life, and the big sedan makes a turnaround by the granary, rolls past Enoch, where he waves from the porch, then continues up the driveway and onto the township road, heading toward town. Upstairs, he kneels at his bedside. It's a humiliating thing to be counted a fool in matters of the Kingdom, and he finds himself compelled to examine his motives. God forbid that he is too proud to admit that he might be wrong! He thinks of how often he has begged to be used as a vessel for God's power, how often he has prayed for the Ancient of Days to speak directly in his ear, same as He spoke to the First Generation. And yes, he has witnessed answers to these appeals—lives redeemed and healings unquestioned by those who were touched. Yet failures, too, most notably with his own son who can't bring himself to bend a knee. Could there be a more convincing rebuke of Enoch's work?

He prays deep into the morning, till almost noon, and the longer he stays on his knees—which ache, grinding against the floorboards—the more he is drawn back into the moment his fleshly body gave way to confusion, his heart falling into chaos, his mortal self dissolving. But then the sunsets, the whirlwind, and the promise of Rapture. How can he turn from such grace, or deny the revelation entrusted to him? Whom is he obligated to please? Questions for which he has ready answers.

Still, he remains beset by private doubts—about the eternal souls of his son, his grandson, and lovely Annie Magnussen, whose life he saved and whom he fears has wandered from the garden. And so, with all of his strength he intercedes on their behalf, recalling his dream and demanding that God honor the promise He certainly was making in it: to bring them back here, and then to take them home.

The door clicks shut and she slips from bed and watches through the window until her mom's car pulls out on Via Lola. The plan was to spend the day with their realtor, looking at properties in Beverly Hills, since the Brentwood home is going up for sale on September 1, the day the divorce is finalized. But Melanie bailed. Dottie wants to buy a new place with money coming in from the film. Melanie would prefer to rent.

"Renting's like flushing money down the toilet," Dottie likes to say.

During their first years out here they lived in a tiny, fourth-floor apartment in Glendale, just down the street from her mom's sister, a comfortable enough place, except the neighbors were loud and the building was hot. Her mom whined mercilessly. A month or so before the baby came, Melanie's dad showed up to bring them home and Dottie locked the door and called the cops. She had taken a liking to not being yelled at or knocked around. Also by then, she had a bank teller job and was dating a man who ran a talent agency. He was older than she by a decade and wore a toupee that looked like a muskrat. Immediately he'd promised Dottie two things: to marry her, and to make her daughter a star. The first promise fell through after a year, when it came out that he wasn't single, as he'd claimed. The second fell short—though in fairness to the man, he did set things into motion, landing Melanie a shampoo commercial that caught the eye of a director who was scouting roles for a television pilot about a family of Swedish immigrants heading west during the Gold Rush. The pilot never aired, and Dottie ended things with the agent. Nonetheless, through an actor she met on set, Melanie found other representation, and a couple of years later won the female lead for *Boy and Girl*.

She goes to the phone and dials the number. The palms of her hands are clammy. A bead of sweat runs tickling down her side from beneath her arm.

Then his voice—"Hello?"—unchanged, the deep pitch and clear tone, a preacher's voice, but guarded too. "Who is this?"

"It's me."

"Annie? My goodness, how are you?"

How am I? She remembers a doll she had as a little girl, and how it lay naked and broken in the yard after Skinny got hold of it one day. "I'm all right. I talked to Sarah."

"Sarah Levitz? I didn't know you two were in contact."

"She told me what happened. I'm sorry—I mean, I'm so glad you're okay, Enoch. And what you said, she told me about that, too."

He's quiet, and she wonders if he expected this call. He doesn't seem as surprised as he might be. They haven't spoken, after all, since the day she left, fifteen years ago. He says, "It's a weight to carry. I suppose you disapprove, like everyone."

"Not everyone, I'm sure."

"You're right. But it's difficult, Annie. Or should I call you Melanie?"

"I'm Melanie now."

"Are you all right, Melanie?"

"I have a film coming out in September, and it's a good one." It's what she tells people when they ask how she is.

"And your mother?"

"She's fine."

67

"Have you been in touch with your brother?"

That brings a laugh, which she stifles. "No, but you must see him all the time."

"On occasion. Today, in fact. A gorgeous morning—I saw him through the oak grove. We didn't talk."

The images crash into Melanie's brain, and she sits down hard on the carpeted floor. The green pine trees and white birches, the silver-edged leaves of the oaks, and the eternal, lavender-blue color of Last Lake where she fished for sunnies in the shallows and learned how to swim. Another universe entirely, with its heaven-wide space, its smell of cut hay. She remembers the singing and shouting at Enoch's Saturday night meetings and her silly wish that summer day of feeding an apple to the old bull in Enoch's back pasture. What in heaven's name was she thinking?

Enoch says, "Are you coming for a visit?" Nonchalant, as though she lives a few miles away.

She wants to say, *Of course I'm coming!* She dreams of it, doesn't she? Leaving Dottie behind, and Adam too, and Morris who has never loved her, and all the vultures, all the obligations, all the pry-bar eyes that find every seam through which they can squeeze inside of her? *Yes.* And if Enoch has seen the end, Jesus on His way, all the better. She gets to her feet and goes into the bathroom, phone cord trailing behind, and shakes out two pills and bends over to wash them down, drinking from the faucet stream.

"Are you still there?" he asks.

"What Sarah told me you said on the radio—did you mean it?"

Another pause, and Melanie wonders if she has offended him. She remembers that he can be that way sometimes, when people doubt his words.

"Melanie," he says, "are you in the will of God?"

His question draws her closer to the mirror and deep into her own eyes, blood vessels spidering out from the corners. "I want to be."

"That's the best answer one can give. And yes, Christ will return in a matter of days. When He does, you may want to be here with me."

"What if I'm not?"

Enoch laughs. "Oh, He'll catch you up wherever you are—if that's your wish. But I did see you in the dream I had. You were here."

She closes her eyes, sees herself flying into the clouds, her face bright with God.

"You can probably imagine who else is coming," he says.

"Peter?"

"Oh, yes."

"But you never wanted us together."

"I might have been too harsh, Melanie. I'm sorry if I was mistaken."

His voice is tender, and she can feel it in the depth of her belly. She covers the mouthpiece and lets out a groan, tries to swallow the next one but ends up coughing it out. She puts the phone to her ear again.

". . . your son, too," Enoch is saying.

"My son? What about him?"

"I'm working on it."

"You've seen him?" The heat inside of her—it's as if her lungs have filled with blood and she is close to saturation.

"Not yet. But I think he'll be here soon."

"My God."

"It's not easy," Enoch says, "being chosen for great things. We both know this."

She goes to her knees and bows low, her hair spilling like fabric to the floor.

"He knew you from your mother's womb, Melanie. Even now His hand is guiding you, the fact that you called today is evidence of that. You've touched millions in ways you can't imagine, all because He willed it. We have less control than we think we do."

"I have to go," she tells him.

"I know you'll do the right thing."

"And you're going to bring my son there, to be with you?"

"We'll be here together, all of us."

She remembers her night in the Glendale hospital, the infant's wrinkled face, the bloody knot on his stomach, the uncanny strength of his fists as he punched the air, as if to say, *You can't do this to me.* All with the silent couple standing in the corner, watching her, as everyone still does.

"Would you like that, Melanie?"

"I have to go now."

"Think about it. I would love to see you again."

She sets down the phone and takes hold of the pedestal sink to pull herself upright. Who's to say it won't happen like he says? The Rapture is not science fiction. It's in the Bible. Lots of people believe it—maybe most. She read a book last year—no, this spring while she was in the hospital—and its author explained how everything is ripe for the harvest, prophecies of two thousand years ago all checked off, nothing standing in the way. It made sense from every angle but spoke to her personally as well. Every time she opened its cover and started reading, she felt God speaking directly to her.

She dresses in jeans, tennis shoes, and a loose-fitting T-shirt that hangs straight from the shoulders, applies a flesh-tone blemish cover to efface her lips, pulls back her hair into a ponytail, and puts on a Dodgers cap and a pair of huge dark glasses. In the phone book, she finds Pedro's Limousine Service. "I'm here in town and need to be in Brentwood by three," she says. "How much?"

"Round-trip?"

"I'm not sure yet."

"Fifty, round-trip. Thirty, one-way."

"Pedro, this is Melanie Magnus. My husband and I have hired you before."

"Oh yes, ma'am. For you, round-trip forty dollars, twenty one-way. Are you still at the Alejo?" That was the apartment Morris owned when they first married. Their getaway place when they needed a break from L.A.

"No." She gives him her address and then the one she's heading for in the city.

Dottie keeps household cash in an envelope in her underwear drawer, and Melanie raids it now, taking five twenties, most of what there is.

The driver is a tiny man with large ears and thick glasses, and he drives like a kid on a go-cart track, his little head glancing left, right, and over his shoulder, braking and accelerating with no hint of nuance, both hands on the wheel as he jumps from lane to lane. He doesn't talk, though, which counts for a lot, and he pulls in behind Mac's Gym in Brentwood ten minutes early.

"We'll wait here for a bit," she says.

He smacks his lips and punches on the radio. Elton John, "Don't Let the Sun Go Down on Me," that melancholy, euphoric, unrelenting voice of his. The driver hums along, bobbing his head. Out the window, the sky is full of dense, shapely clouds, rare out here, the sort she loved as a child in Minnesota, the kind that offers a parade of human faces. High above a trio of palm trees, a man with a prodigious chin and nose—wise, empathetic—ages a lifetime in a minute, bringing tears to Melanie's eyes, his features widening, wrinkling, sagging, dissolving. And then Morris appears, exiting the gym in black sweats and his slumming hat, a fedora too small for his head. It makes him look like a British rock star, dark curls showing at his neck and winding out behind his ears.

She wiggles two twenties from the front pocket of her jeans and hands them over the seat. "Thanks, you can leave now." She pops open her door and makes a straight line toward Morris, who stops when he sees her coming and tips his hat back with a finger. Behind her, she can hear the car pulling away, the driver stepping on the gas.

"Your ride is leaving," Morris says.

"You're my ride."

He unlocks the black Mercedes and ducks in. Melanie goes around the front, dragging a finger across the hood, then climbs into the passenger seat.

"I need cash."

"We're not going to *my* place." He looks over, his eyes slicing her in half.

"That's right, we're going to the bank."

He turns left on Sunset Boulevard, drives past the shop where she bought her wedding dress, then south on Bundy. Like the limo driver, he turns on the radio. Same station, Top 40—now playing Clapton's nod to reggae. He's a fucking chameleon.

At the intersection of Bundy and San Vicente, she says, "The bank is that way. I mean, if that's the one you're still using."

"Look, Mel, you'll be coming out fine. Jimmy's not pulling anything funny, he has instructions from me. Everything's clean. Fifty-fifty on the shit we own together. You know this." He turns left on Gorham, heading east, palm trees on both sides, elegant fronds undulating above.

"But I need something *now*."

"Didn't Widmer come through?"

"Look." Melanie doesn't want to say anything, but what can she do? "The accounts are in Mom's name," she says. "Temporarily."

"What?" He taps his horn at a woman jaywalking in front of them. She's squeezing a tiny dog, a puff of milkweed, to her chest.

"She was worried someone might take advantage of me, make off with everything—I mean, after the accident. You know the story. She grew up rock poor and always thinks we're going to lose it all. And she thinks I'm in a vulnerable place."

"What do you need it for?"

"Look at me, for God's sake!" She turns toward him, reaches up and touches the top of her head with the tips of her fingers. Her T-shirt hangs from her arms like a rag on a clothesline. "I've got events coming up, and nothing to wear."

"How much?" He signals and pulls into the left turn lane. His expressive mouth is drawn flat, his eyes distracted behind the little pink glasses he's wearing today. His mind has gone somewhere else already.

At the bank she waits in the car. When he comes back, he tosses the envelope into her lap and watches her count the bills. Two thousand dollars in hundreds. She thanks him as graciously as she is able, then persuades him to drive her back to Palm Springs, which in fact he seems happy enough to do. The whole way, two hours, he listens to the tape of a man with an Eastern European accent explaining how success can be achieved through the right sort of meditation. Morris lip-synchs along with the oft-repeated mantra: "Your outer world is a by-product of your inner world."

The fact is, getting along with Morris was never the problem. Making him pay attention in the first place, that was another matter.

At home her mom is still gone, thank God, and Melanie writes a note that says, "Went for a walk," puts five twenties in her mom's underwear drawer, leaves the house, and walks four blocks east and then two south on Palm Canyon Drive to Desert Sun Travel, a business she and her mom have never patronized. The man at the desk recognizes her—she can tell by the double-take, the feigned indifference. After explaining what she wants, she hands him her driver's license and sits back while he calls and books a flight to Minneapolis. She pays him cash.

"Minnesota," he says, allowing himself a strategic glance into her eyes. "Filming, I suppose. Haven't heard about that one yet," he adds.

"You will." She walks out the door and into the heat.

From earliest memory, Peter knew that his dad had a peculiar connection to God, or seemed to. Some people he laid hands on claimed they were healed—he all but brought Annie Magnussen back from the dead. Others swore that Enoch's prayers accounted for a needed check in the mail, a new husband, a sudden indifference to alcohol. And his faith was not so grand that it overlooked his son's moments of childish despair. In the summer of '51—Peter was ten years old—the local Little League organized a trip to watch the Millers play in Minneapolis, where an outfielder named Willie Mays was batting .500 and making headlines in the papers. On the night before the trip, the weather was stormy, wind with heavy rain, forecasters calling for more of the same tomorrow, and Peter was despondent at the prospect of the game being postponed. Enoch brushed away his son's tears with the pads of his fingers, then demanded that God calm the storms, his words so buoyant and sure that Peter knew, in the moment, that the prayer was taking flight and would strike its mark. He woke next day to Enoch nudging his shoulder and pointing at the pine tree outside the window. A bald eagle, imperially tall, was perched on a branch against blue sky, its yellow eyes bright with sun. "His courier," Enoch said. "Sent to remind you whom to thank for this beautiful day."

By the time Peter was fifteen, though, he had grown tired of his father's dazzling certainty about everything. Peter thought of God as unfathomable, incalculable—larger than what any person could imagine. That is what drew him toward faith. Not his dad's ready answers or pious withdrawal from what he regarded to be a sinful world. And so Peter pulled back from Enoch, biding his time, meaning to leave Battlepoint for professional ball at the earliest possible moment, the two of them finding a way, in the interim, to coexist in a semi-peaceable standoff. But then on the night of the mountain lion, something changed. If he had been a year or two older, he might have refused his dad, skipped the whole thing. But he was at an age where he needed to prove he could not be intimidated, and then, when the animal materialized a body's length away—its terrible head and shoulders, its stillness, its carrion breath that Peter inhaled like a poison—he understood the risk Enoch had been willing to take with his own son's safety. Although he couldn't have put it into words, Peter understood that his dad's love for him, an implied extension of the love of God, was provisional.

He has spent the day wandering through Central Park, so angry with Joanie that his brain, like a chunk of wood, feels incapable of clear thought. Not to mention Freddy, the damned traitor! Which of the two is more loathsome, more deserving of hatred? Which of them more at fault? And why can't he stop thinking about the fucking lion, which he still dreams about some nights? Maybe his dad was right, in a perverse way. Maybe the lion was a messenger after all, some kind of flesh-and-blood signal, or spiritual juju, that Peter can't escape no matter what he does. And maybe that's not entirely a bad thing.

As evening falls, hunger drives him into a Chinese restaurant where he sits for a plate of chow mein. Then he walks to the Natural History museum and spends an hour staring at the dinosaurs, which always offer a humbling perspective. He finds it almost impossible to reconcile a society so stout and imposing with the fact of its ultimate demise. And yet here he is, pitying himself, as if the life he has built in New York has any substance at all. By 9:30, as he heads south on Eighth Avenue with the day's remaining light melting into Hell's Kitchen, his mind has cleared. It's obvious that Joanie's love is no less qualified than his dad's, and that her cheating with Freddy was not situational, the stuff of drunken lust as she described it, but a calculated retribution for how he has let her down. He knows, too, where he'll go next and what he will write, and he feels such relief at seeing his way forward that he turns left on Fifty-fifth and walks two blocks to the Jewish deli across from the Wellington Hotel and sits down for one of their chocolate pastries and a coffee.

An hour later, he lets himself into the apartment. She's lying on the couch again, wearing nothing but her underwear, again, and watching him out of the corner of her eye as news blares from the black-and-white set.

He walks over and turns down the volume. "I had some thinking to do."

She puts a finger to her lips and points at Cronkite intoning on Nixon's departure, the screen dominated by the old trickster himself, smiling through his shame, Pat wilting at his side, daughters and son-in-law standing behind—the entire family prisoner to the man's final obligations to the office he has disgraced. Then a clip of the helicopter lifting away.

"And this guy," Joanie says. "What a difference, huh?" A close-up of the swearing-in, the new President all forehead and Midwest earnestness—a pleasant change—his hand on the Bible.

Peter sits down and lets her finish watching. When it's over and she switches to Johnny Carson, he tells her they have to talk.

She gets up and shuts it off. "Good. I have something to say."

"Let me, first."

She settles back, facing him, hands at rest beside her, knees together and feet spread. She waits. Her eyes look softer than normal, her face more relaxed, her smile bland, disinterested, as if she and Peter are two strangers who have passed a forgettable half-hour together in a waiting room. He says, "I think I figured you out."

"Lucky me."

"You're like my dad. It's all about whether I can become the person you want me to be. I can't. And that gives you the right to punish me."

"Which gives you, in turn, the right to punish Freddy, I suppose. God, you're lucky you didn't kill the poor man."

"He's an asshole, he'll be fine."

"Barbaric," Joanie says, but there's nothing in her voice but the weariness he's been hearing whenever she talks about Nixon, politics, all the tiresome crap on TV.

"I'm leaving," he says.

"That's best."

"I'm taking Freddy's advice and going back home. I'm going to document the end of the world."

"Freddy the asshole, you mean. You're taking his advice."

"That's right."

"Perfect. Maybe it's something you can get your teeth into. Seriously, I hope it is." She hops up from the couch, light as a kitten, and Peter watches her glide away, her ass—small, but with a tremulous plasticity—

giving him pause. From the cupboard she takes down a can of peanuts then comes back, curling up and commencing to munch away.

"What happened?" he asks. "What changed?"

"You're so simple, Peter. This hasn't ever been about you and me, not really, though I guess it was fine for you to think so. Not to put myself in a positive light here, which I don't deserve, but I've been your muse. A cliché, okay, right. But that can be a useful advantage for somebody like you, who's had to do it all on his own. You have to understand, my thing has always been for what you might accomplish with *my* help. I'm sorry, but there it is. And if everything had gone a little better, like with your memoir, or with this Haig story in D.C., it might have worked out. Of course, once the cat's out of the bag—right? Believe me, I know. I've been through it before."

Peter feels sick in his stomach. He thinks of the time he ate bad seafood in a dark supper club in the middle of Iowa. "There've been others?"

"Oh, God. I always thought I had some special aptitude for picking winners. You know, some kind of ultra, fine-tuned, universal sensibility?" She laughs. "But who knows, maybe you'll prove me right someday." She tosses a palmful of peanuts in her mouth.

"Who else?"

"Oh, this playwright from Columbia. And a gorgeous poet from Montana. I'm zero for two—zero for three, now. Batting triple-zero." She goes into the kitchen, rummages in the cupboard, and pours two glasses of wine, comes back and hands one to Peter.

He takes a swallow, watching her. If only he hadn't expended his anger on Freddy and spent the whole day walking off his bewilderment. If he felt something besides collapsing sadness right now, he might be able to make a show of his injury, throw his glass of wine against the wall, scream and yell, register the magnitude of what she's done to him. "I was even more right than I thought" is all he can manage.

"Please. Love is complicated, life is complicated. What you and I had, it's actually pretty normal. I mean, you can pretend all you want, but you knew what was going on."

"I won't concede that point."

"Oh, come on."

They sit for a while without speaking, Peter feeling like a child cowed by an adult whose language excludes him. "Will you miss me?" he asks, wishing he could keep his mouth shut.

She rolls her tongue around inside her cheek, not inclined to give an answer.

"I'll miss *you*. Or what I thought we had."

"That doesn't count."

"Sure it does."

"No, Peter. You can't miss what you never had. You might kick yourself for believing something you should have seen through, but that's a different thing. It's pathetic."

"Thanks for that."

"I sound terrible. I probably *am* terrible. And look, I get what you mean. I don't want you hating me or beating yourself up. Or pretending it might have been different. And I *will* miss you. You're fun, and you're sweet, and you're talented, too. It's just"—she lifts her hands, defeated—"I can do it only for so long, till the juice runs out. And then I'm done."

He gets up and kisses her forehead, touches her cheek, then goes into the kitchen, pours his wine into the sink, and rinses away the red before walking past her into their bedroom where he takes down the big canvas duffel bag he used for years, playing ball, and starts filling it.

AUGUST 10—SATURDAY

Fargo is a two-and-a-half-hour drive, first through hills and pine forests—Minnesota lake country—then down onto the wide, implausibly flat valley of the Red River of the North, green with ripening beets. Yesterday he phoned Rick Stuart and arranged to visit the boy—Willie, he's called. For all these years Enoch has kept track of where he is and how he's doing, even while honoring the spirit of the promise made to Ben Riplinger, the lawyer who handled the adoption: no initiating contact with the family or the boy on the part of the biological parents or grandparents. If Willie wants to learn where he comes from, he has the legal right to initiate that process at eighteen. More than two years from now. But like Enoch told Peter, he never signed anything. And now there are mitigating circumstances.

On the outskirts of Moorhead, as he washes dust from the Cougar in a self-serve carwash and applies a quick coat of wax with the chamois, he thinks about Annie at the age her son is now—a girl with ethereal dignity, not part of this world, with lavender eyes that were hard to look away from. Ever since the episode with the bull, when she was seven, Enoch has thought of her like a daughter, even if her parents, after that, forbade her to step foot on Bywater land. Whenever he saw her waiting for the school bus or caught sight of her through the oak grove, she waved at him, light jumping from her face. If they met in a store or on the sidewalk in town, she would touch his arm. She knew and understood his work as few others did. For Enoch, Annie Magnussen's very being was divine validation.

Peter's teenage rebellion, meanwhile—his scornful attitude and cigarette reek—was an embarrassment. It seemed as if the boy's primary drive was to undermine his father's efforts for the Kingdom. And so, in January of '58, when he learned that Peter had taken Annie into Battlepoint for Cokes at Slim's Pool Hall, he pulled him into the barn and pinned him by the throat against a milking stanchion. "Stay away from her," he told his son. A few months later, the four parents—neighbors, adversaries—met to confront the crisis of Annie's pregnancy. It was a job of several hours to talk her father, Gerald Sr., out of bringing rape charges and persuade him that privacy was the best plan for everyone, Gerald included. And that no one in Battlepoint need be the wiser. At that point Dottie suggested her sister's place in California. And then, with almost no discussion, agreement was reached on the matter of adoption. Enoch and Ruth mentioned a young couple of their acquaintance who lived in Fargo, stable, discriminating people, unable to have children of their own.

Enoch parks on First Avenue North across from the bar and grill where Rick suggested they meet. It's dark inside with high ceilings of stamped tin, the place all but empty except for the line of men hunched at the bar. Rick is waiting in a booth at the back of the room, elbows on the table, hands clasped in front of his mouth. Or at least it looks like him.

"Rick?"

"Yup."

Instead of the well-groomed man Enoch remembers, with a face that blushes pink at the cheeks, he is shaggy and watchful. Greasy hair, untrimmed beard, hard lines etched in his forehead. Enoch knew him before the adoption, briefly, when Rick and his wife, Judy, lived for a year or two in Battlepoint and came to Enoch's earliest Saturday night meetings. The couple divorced a few years after they got Willie, and now the boy lives with his mom in Duluth during the school year and with his dad in Fargo, summers.

"I appreciate this." Enoch sits down and the two shake hands across the table. "How is he?"

"Good, good." Rick's voice is the same, thin and trapped in his throat. He doesn't look at Enoch but, rather, at a point beyond Enoch's shoulder. "He's at practice now, Legion ball. This weekend they have their last tournament."

"You've had him all summer?"

"Beginning of July."

"What position does he play?" Enoch tries to recall the positions Peter used to play, but he can't.

"Outfield. Center, mostly. He's got an arm, and he can hit, too. He's a big boy, he got his growth this summer. Bet he shot up four inches."

"He's with you until school starts, I suppose."

"She wants him back early. Says she needs time to buy him some things. What it comes down to, she wants to cut short his time with me." He pulls out cigarettes and shakes one loose from the pack. "Mind?" He lights up with a Zippo.

"What day is he going back?"

"Around the twentieth, twenty-first."

The waitress arrives to take their orders: a burger and fries for Rick, a burger and salad for Enoch. As she leaves, Rick exhales a long stream of smoke.

"I'd like to have Willie out to the farm, spend some time with him."

"Because you believe the world's going to end?" There is nothing in Rick's voice that Enoch can read. No irony, no contempt. He's squinting through smoke, eyes still aiming past Enoch's shoulder. "There are folks in Battlepoint I'm still in touch with. They told me what you said on the radio."

"Ah."

"And I'm guessing you're serious." He leans back as the waitress delivers coffee. "You want your grandson there for the big day, is that it? Or you just want to meet him before you fly off?"

Enoch waits, praying for wisdom. "Both."

"Most people would take offense, somebody wanting to yank their kid into something like that." Rick lifts a hand to silence Enoch, who's opened his mouth to protest. "But I'm not most people. I've been around it—your kind of thinking—as you know. And though it's definitely in my past, I do have a soft spot for high-octane theology. As long as it's not being used to milk people out of their wealth. Which is not to say I'm convinced by your forecasting."

"Let me explain," Enoch says.

"Please, no. I've had plenty." He reaches for his cigarettes, but Enoch flaps a hand at the lingering smoke and shakes his head. Rick shoves them back in his pocket. "Might not hurt Willie, spending time around folks who talk about God like he's real—though in fairness to his mom, she gets him to church. It wouldn't hurt him either to get acquainted with his grandpa. Thanks," he says as the waitress sets plates in front of them.

After a few bites, Rick pulls out his cigarettes again and starts to shake one loose before remembering and putting them back. "What I don't know is whether he'll want to go. I floated the idea a couple days ago, after you called. He didn't seem excited."

"It'll be up to the boy, naturally," Enoch says. "What have you told him?"

"About himself? Where he comes from?"

"Yes."

"Most everything. I mean, who he is, who his mom and dad are. You. Figured why not. The kid's been asking for years. Your call was an excuse to fill him in a little more than I had. Don't worry, though. He knows better than to let his mom know anything. She wouldn't be pleased." Rick smiles for the first time.

"Did you say anything about, um, my dream?"

"No. Didn't want to put you behind the eight ball. I did mention the commune arrangement at your farm and told him you're pretty religious." Rick picks up his burger but sets it down without taking a bite. He folds his hands on the table. "You were saying something on the phone about money."

All right, then.

Enoch pushes his plate to the side. He says, "Until now I've stayed out of Willie's life and yours, which hasn't been easy for me. Now, though, my obligation is to a higher authority, and because I'm asking you to make a kind of exception to the rules, I'm prepared to offer compensation. If you like, we can call it a loan—though we're not going to be around long enough for you to pay me back."

"So you say. How much?"

"What's your situation?" Enoch's funds are limited, and he knows that what he has might be drawn on heavily over the next week or so. In particular, excavation, concrete, and building materials for the latrine and shower facility, which will be necessary if and when people start showing up. This morning, as an act of faith, he called an order in at Great North Lumber in Battlepoint.

"You want the long version or the quick and dirty?"

"How much time do we have?"

"He's done about two." Rick checks his watch. "We've got half an hour." He takes a couple of bites from his burger and washes it down with coffee. "Trouble is, I'm out of work right now and burning through my savings. Plus I've got some lawyer fees." He looks up from his food and glances briefly into Enoch's eyes. "Last guy I worked for, he gave me some tools. 'They're yours,' he told me. A drum sander and some other stuff. Then a month after he let me go, he came and said he wanted it back."

"Give it back."

"I sold it."

"Pay him."

Rick takes the last of his burger and talks with a bulging cheek. "That's what I said I'd do, soon as I got the money, but he pressed charges. I ended up in jail overnight, a friend had to post bail. This was in June. I've got a lawyer who tells me it'll be okay, but I'm already five hundred deep with him. Not to mention, I'm late on my August rent. Two hundred bucks." He sighs, pats his chest pocket where the cigarettes are, then places his hands flat on the table.

Enoch fishes his wallet from his back pocket and lays it down between them. It's fat with bills and falls open of its own accord. He counts out ten hundreds and ten fifties, and he pushes the pile across the table. "This might help," he says.

"Whoa. Yeah." Rick shoves his plate aside, scoops up bills with both hands, and rolls them into a tight cylinder. He shoves them into the front pocket of his shirt, alongside the pack of cigarettes, then takes the last of his coffee.

"Are we good?" Enoch says.

Rick strokes his mustache, squinting at Enoch's chin now. "If you want him to visit for a few days, I don't see a problem. Once his tournament's over, I mean, and depending on whether he wants to do it. Tell me again—or maybe you didn't say. When's this supposed to happen?"

"The Rapture? The nineteenth of this month."

"Holy shit—sorry." He holds up his hands. "Seriously, it's a lot to ask of people, isn't it?"

"No one is obliged to listen."

"All the same. But hey, we need to blast off here. Ballpark's a ten-minute drive."

Enoch follows Rick's old GMC truck to the ballpark on the Red River, which flows indolently on the other side of the left-field fence. They park and walk into the small grandstand. "That's him, see?" Rick's finger tracks a boy loping back toward the fence in deep right center. He reaches up for an over-the-shoulder catch, turns, and rifles the ball back to the infield. He's rangy, big feet and hands, but there is a grace about him, too, an instantly apparent self-possession.

"Ancient of Days," Enoch says. Tears well in his eyes, and he blinks them away.

Rick nods, his chin lifting a notch. "He's a good one."

After practice, Willie joins them behind the chain-link fence, a bit of swagger in his stride, hands on his hips, worn glove tucked beneath an arm. He's wide-shouldered and skinny-strong, and he looks Enoch up and down, his face turned to one side.

"This is Willie. Willie, your grandpa."

They shake hands, Enoch resisting the urge to wrap his arms around the kid. The fitting together of their palms is comfortable, precise. Willie's lips twitch a little, and he says "Hey"—his voice shaking in a way that causes Enoch to tear up again.

"Let's go, then, we'll have lemonade and coffee." Rick points to the west. "We're a dozen blocks that way." He reaches up and puts an arm around the boy's shoulders—Willie is a head taller than his dad—and steers him toward the truck.

"I was thinking he might want to ride with me," Enoch says. "Take a little drive, talk for a bit. If that's all right. Fifteen minutes or so?"

Rick glances up at Willie, who shrugs and nods.

The freshly waxed Cougar is sizzling in the bright sun, and he gestures for Willie to climb in. The boy frowns at his dad, then swings open the passenger door and eases his long frame into the low-riding bucket seat. Enoch climbs in, too, holding the roof with his left hand as he lowers himself behind the wheel. "Won't be long," he tells Rick and gives a three-finger tug on the door, which closes with a satisfying thump. The dashboard and instrument panel gleam, hardly a speck of dust anywhere. Willie runs a hand along the dash, pops the glove box, clicks it shut.

They head north, the tree-canopied streets of Fargo soon giving way to flat prairie, and out of town Enoch turns left on the first road heading west. The only thing in every direction is cropland, to the right a blazing field of sunflowers, their big heads turned in worship of the sun, to the left a vast stretch of beets. "Fasten your seat belt," he tells Willie. The boy glances over, and Enoch, one hand resting on the top of the leather-wrapped wheel, scowls at him. "Do it," he says, and Willie obeys. Enoch looks in the rearview mirror, nothing there, scans ahead to the right and left. All clear. Then he swallows hard and jams the accelerator to the floorboard. The V-8 kicks and howls, pausing for the briefest instant before yielding up its power, and then the vehicle lunges ahead, seeming to rise up off the hardtop, the world a disappearing blur on either side. At ninety-five, he glances over at Willie, who looks back, eyes bulging, as if the old man he's stuck here next to has disappeared and materialized again. Enoch lets the needle touch 115 before backing off. Heart knocking against his ribs, he keeps an easy smile on his face.

"Best not to tell your dad about this." He does a U-turn and heads back toward Fargo. "Plenty of life, wouldn't you say?" He taps the dashboard.

Willie rubs his face, a single motion, palm of his hand moving from the forehead down, a family gesture.

"Open the glove box. Yes. See that envelope? The car's title. If you come to my place next week after your baseball tournament, I'm going to sign it over to you."

"What?"

"You're fifteen, aren't you? Do you have a learner's permit?"

"Next year. But Dad let me drive his truck this summer. He said I did a good job."

"This is going to be your car."

"Why?"

"Because you're my grandson. Because I've gone all these years without seeing you, without getting to know you like I wanted to."

"All I have to do is come and visit?"

Enoch laughs. "That's right." He can feel the boy's eyes like heat against the side of his face.

"There's more to it, isn't there."

"What do you mean?"

"Dad says you're a preacher. That you've got your own church, and that people live out there on the farm with you. And other stuff."

"That's all true," Enoch says.

The boy leans back in his seat and turns to the passenger window. They're driving through a sparsely settled development at the edge of town, ranch-style homes and staked trees, brownish lawns. Willie reaches out and sets a fist against the dashboard. "What about my dad—is he going to be there? My first dad, I mean."

"I hope he will."

"You're not sure?"

"No."

"What about my mom?"

"I think so. I'm pretty sure."

"I know who she is," he says. "But I can't tell anybody, Dad made me promise." He cranks down his window, pushes his head into the rush of wind like a dog might do, hair streaming behind him, and Enoch tries to imagine what he's thinking, if things are moving too fast for him. Willie pulls his head back in and cranks the window closed. "I saw one of her movies. This girl falls in love with a soldier who gets his legs blown off in Vietnam."

Enoch has seen the film, too, all of her films, and each time he's surprised at how transparent she is, how easily he can see the girl she was in the woman she is.

"What did you think?"

"Wow." A red blotch grows on the boy's smooth cheek. "She seemed so nice—kind, I mean. Like she wasn't even acting."

"That's how she is, your mom. And I know one thing for sure. It was hard on her, giving you up. Down this street up here?" They've passed beneath the Burlington Northern tracks, the river on their left.

"Turn at the light." Willie gestures with his right hand. "Then one more block and go right again. We're across from the old depot."

The building is a wreck: brown bricks painted white but flaking through, a tilting porch that extends along the entire wide front. Four units in a line, rowhouse style. The door second from the left swings open and Rick leans out and waves them in. Enoch lowers his window, lifts a hand over the roof of the car, and waves back.

"Tell your dad I can't stay this time, I need to get back. But I'll give you a call on Monday. Meanwhile, you think about it. If you're game, I'll come and pick you up."

Willie releases the handle but doesn't push open the door. He says, "Dad told me you've got a lake at your farm."

"Last Lake, it's called. Beautiful. Ten miles long."

"He's always saying we'll go fishing over in lake country, but we don't have a boat."

"I've got one."

"Sometimes I walk down to the Red with my pole. I've caught a few catfish."

"Last Lake," Enoch says. "Oh my gosh, you'll love it—walleyes, northern pike, sunfish, crappies, bass, you name it. If you come next week, you'll get a chance to try your hand."

Willie nods, reaching for the glove box and releasing the catch, dropping it open. He snaps it closed. "Okay." He slips from the car, goes up the sidewalk, and mounts the steps two at a time. He turns and offers a kind of salute, a little half-wave, hand next to his face. Enoch manages to navigate half a dozen blocks before he has to pull over and regather himself. He closes his eyes, his hands resting on the wheel, and summons the image of Willie on the outfield grass, reaching up to make that catch, so easily. He pictures the shape of the boy's head, the squared-off jaw and bony cheeks, the slight cleft in his chin, the long straight nose, and those eyes—everything about him so familiar that a surge of feeling rises in Enoch like a storm. Fists against forehead, elbows jammed into his belly, he fights it off, every muscle tensed and burning, until finally the wave breaks inside, leaving him high and dry, ready for the next thing. He takes a breath and holds it, counting to thirty before letting it out.

There is no time to lose, no time to remove his focus from the single end on which he is bent. No time.

At the Northern Pacific tracks, he stops for a coal train to pass and waiting there can't help but notice how flat his wallet feels beneath him. Handing Rick Stuart a sizable chunk of his savings account was hard. And of course this morning he ordered lumber, a few hundred dollars' worth, for the showers and latrines. But what if they aren't needed? What if he has anticipated too much in the way of a public response? It has been three full days since the radio show and there's been no reaction, except for the visit from the pastors—and yes, Dave and Sally's decision to leave. No stream of pilgrims, as he imagined there would be, and nothing from the media. Yesterday he called Art Ulman at *The Scroll* to place a notice for the stranger who stopped and administered CPR—Enoch's concession to Peter—and Art had no questions at all.

In a phone booth at the edge of town he calls Great North Lumber in Battlepoint, where he gets a busy signal. He hangs up and dials again, this time his own number, and Victor comes on the line. "I need you to call and cancel my lumber order. Can you do that for me?"

Victor is silent for a moment. "Rainy's dad came with a truck this morning and moved them out. I'm sorry."

"Both girls? Maude, too?"

"Yes."

"I expected as much. Look, I'll be home by six. Be sure to make that call."

Clouds have been gathering in the west, heavy purple ones that occupy the entire half-dome behind him, their bulbous tops promising rain, if not something worse, and Enoch reminds himself that people in their frailty have the choice of believing or not believing the hope offered them. He drives faster as he goes and arrives in advance of the weather, barely. Parked in the approach to his driveway, its right front wheel jammed half in the ditch as if to leave the way open for other cars, is a yellow Pontiac Bonneville, model year about 1963, two heads visible in the front seat. Both turn to watch him as he climbs out and walks up to the driver's-side window. He lays a hand on its roof and bends to look inside. A young man, wild hair and plastic glasses, and a peach-skinned girl snuggled up next to him, an open jar of peanut butter sitting on the dash, its smell emanating in the heat.

"Enoch Bywater?" The young man puts out a thin hand.

Enoch takes it and receives a quick, hard pump.

"I'm Felix Roper, and this here is Connie Dopp, my girl." His accent is Missouri or Arkansas, maybe Tennessee. *Ahm Felix Ropa.* The button-up shirt he wears is open at the front, showing a concave chest and washboard ribs. A nose like Groucho Marx.

Connie scoots forward to see around him. Platinum hair, brown eyes shocking inside the pale girlishness of her face. "Hi," she says. It comes out in two syllables.

"Do I know you?"

"Nope." Felix shakes his head. "But we know you, in a roundabout sorta manner. We drove up here, Mister Bywater, for the Rapture of the Saints."

"That's right," Connie says. She looks seventeen or eighteen, as ample in shape as Felix is bony, the scoop of her blouse hiding nothing as she leans forward. Her smile is a miniature sun.

A dime-size raindrop whacks the roof of the Bonneville, and thunder booms from the clouds, which have massed around them. Enoch says, "Follow me," and climbs into his car, rain starting in heavily now. He goes up the driveway past his house and stops at the door of the machine shed, where he jumps out to slide open the door. He's soaked in an instant. After waving Felix inside, he follows with the Cougar. Rain hammers the steel roof so hard they have to shout.

"Appears like you used to farm. Maybe still do?" Felix is looking around at the tractor and bailer, the hayrack.

Connie lifts her nose in the air. "Smells nice. Like my granddaddy's garage."

Enoch ushers them over to the hayrack, which the two kids climb onto by way of its steel tongue. They sit down along one side, legs hanging.

"How far have you come?" he says.

"Kentucky. Brambleburg. A tiny little town."

"And you heard my show way down there? The signal has a funny way of carrying sometimes—I've gotten letters and calls from as far away as Michigan and Iowa. But Kentucky, that's a new one."

"It's a God thing," Connie says. "And here's what's sweet. We were down in my parents' basement, listening to *Superstar* for the first time." It comes off her tongue as *Supastaawa*. "Felix finally bought the album, and he brought it over that morning and we sat right down at my dad's bar and listened straight through. You've heard it, right?"

The girl is so vivid and bright, her voice so nice on the ear, that Enoch wants to say yes. "No."

"*Jesus Christ Superstar*? Really?"

"I've heard of it. Listened to a couple of the songs." One of the young men has it, Matt the guitar player, and Enoch isn't impressed. It strikes him as vulgar secularization of the Word—Jesus as man instead of as God-man.

Connie says, "No matter. Music's how we came to the Lord, Felix and me. We got saved at an Andraé Crouch concert in Lexington. You've heard of *him*, right? That's where we met. You know that song Andraé does, "Soon and Very Soon"?"

"I do."

"Anyway, we finished *Superstar* the other day, and we're sittin' there dumbfounded—I mean, clubbed by the Spirit—and that's when your voice comes on. We looked at each other, and Felix says, 'We gotta find that guy.'" The rain stops so abruptly it strands Connie's voice, loud and high, in the dusty air of the shed. She slaps a hand to her mouth, blush spreading across the top of her chest.

"How old are you kids?"

"Seventeen—well, sixteen. Felix, he's eighteen."

"Almost nineteen," he says.

"So you're done with school."

"Yeah," Felix says. "Never finished, though—which I'm glad of now. What's the point?"

"Do your parents know you're here?"

"Oh, they don't worry much," Connie says. "Mom's out of the picture, and Daddy, when I told him, he says, 'Make sure you call me every other day or so.' He's just glad it's God I'm into, and not drugs or things like that."

Enoch looks at Felix.

"My folks are in Missouri, but I called and told them—about the Rapture, I mean, what day it's going to happen, and how I'm coming up here for it, and they said, 'Fine and dandy, put a good word in for us when you see Him.' *Him* meaning God, like it's a big joke. They don't take things serious, as they ought to."

"Well, you're welcome to stay here, though I hope you know it's not necessary. God will catch you up wherever you might be."

"We know that, sir." Felix is holding tight to Connie's hand. "We could even sleep on this hayrack," he says.

"There's space for camping outside and a couple of vacancies in the barn—we have apartments there." Enoch points east.

Felix loops a skinny arm around Connie's shoulder and pulls her close. "We brung a tent to sleep in."

"You won't be staying together, of course."

"Sure we can," Felix says. "We won't *do* anything."

"If you stay here, it'll have to be in separate quarters."

Felix smiles, his dark eyes rolling to the top of his head. Connie jumps down from the wagon, runs to the door, and throws her body against the edge of it, sliding it open. The hard, post-storm sun engulfs her. "Wow!" She improvises a pirouette.

Enoch has Victor prepare liverwurst sandwiches, which Felix and Connie fall on like scavenging bears, and then before the meeting begins and while the light is good, he takes them out to the oak grove and helps find a camping spot. Until a few years ago this four-acre grove was part of the grazing pasture for Enoch's milk cows. It's large enough for at least a hundred tents, and Felix's, a small red triangle of nylon, goes up in minutes.

"Now let's get *you* situated," Enoch says, turning to Connie.

They're heading across the yard toward the barn when a vehicle with a bad muffler pulls into the driveway and stops in front of the house. A rusty white Volkswagen van that Enoch hasn't seen before. Behind the wheel is a craggy, bald man with arm hair as thick as wool and beside him a woman less than half his age, blonde, waif-like. A couple of towheaded children in the back. Wisconsin plates on the vehicle.

"Mr. Bywater?"

"That's me." He walks up to his open window.

"Heard you on my transistor radio. And what you said was something I dreamed myself. I was caught in a storm, gale force, and a voice spoke from the wind. I believe you will know the passage." The old man's eyes are as ice-blue, as pure as Last Lake in December. "'For they have sown the wind, and they shall reap the whirlwind.'"

The meeting that night is heavy with the Spirit, the singing full-throated, the reception of Enoch's message from Hosea gratifying to witness, people nodding and crying, or rocking quietly in their chairs. The group is larger than usual, despite the Ranchers who have fled. Enoch counts thirty-five worshippers, most of whom have attended before at one time or another, plus of course the pilgrims who arrived today, Felix and Connie right up front, clapping, raising their hands to God. When the Spirit finally lifts, it's midnight, and Enoch, spent, sits on the chair beside his lectern and watches them leave, offering a prayer for each one. Then, his entire body prickly with fatigue, he walks alone across the yard, past the little buckeye tree, and climbs to the porch of his house where he stands for a moment. There is enough moonlight to see the two tents pitched in the oak grove—no, three, and a third vehicle parked now in the pasture south of the grove.

Ancient of Days.

AUGUST 11—SUNDAY

Yesterday he disposed of the books he's collected over the past two years, hauling them one box at a time to the used bookstore at the end of the block, nine boxes in all, for which he received two dollars a box. He also collected on an old debt from an editor of a quarterly who had promised him twenty bucks for a book review. Finally, he called an old U of M buddy with sway at the Minnesota bureau of the Associated Press in Minneapolis and asked if there was any work to be had. He must support himself, after all, while documenting the world's end.

"Maybe," Al told him.

He was ready to leave by five but waited until Joanie walked down to the corner store to buy orange juice. Then with fifty-five bucks in his pocket he strapped the duffel to his back and left. He had no appetite for the kind of goodbye it would have been, and he certainly didn't want to give her the satisfaction of watching him go. By six, he was riding the subway, and by seven he was standing on I-78 with his thumb out.

Now it's Sunday morning and he's sitting in a truck stop in northwest Indiana, having passed most of the night with a hardware sales rep from Oregon who buried his mother in Philadelphia yesterday and has to be back at work Monday. The guy would have driven Peter all the way to Minneapolis, but he was poor company, whining about the people in his life who have let him down: toxic mother, unfaithful wife, ungrateful kids. And his driving was so erratic, seesawing between sixty and ninety miles an hour, that Peter made up a story about having to visit an uncle in South Bend.

Sleep is all he can think of. That, and his empty stomach. He sips on coffee as he waits for his order of hash and eggs and reads the morning paper. According to a story from the AP wire, a crowd of two thousand greeted Nixon's plane when it landed in California yesterday afternoon. "Having completed one task," Nixon is quoted as saying, "does not mean that we will sit in this marvelous California sun and do nothing."

"And what task was that?" Peter asks, aloud.

The man in the booth ahead of him turns around. He's wearing a White Sox cap and a gold chain around his neck. "You talkin' to me?"

"Nope."

Out the window and across the freeway is a heavily treed park—aspen, cedar, cottonwood—with a picnic area and a river flowing through. Peter's plan, once he's finished eating, is to walk over and find a quiet place to nap for a while, down along the grassy riverbank or underneath a picnic table. Then he'll walk back over here and lobby a trucker for a lift to Minneapolis, which can't be more than eight or nine hours away.

He's flipping through the paper when a full-page ad takes his breath. It's not that she doesn't look her age but, rather, that she still has those sweet eyes whose uncanny effect is to make you feel as if she knows who you are but loves you anyway. There is a close-up of her face, and just behind and next to her the face of a steely-jawed man, presumably the male lead, wearing a pair of dark glasses, the ghost image of a mushroom cloud visible in both lenses. At the top of the page is the film's tagline: *With the world in the balance, whom will you trust?*

Peter knows if you haven't had your heart ripped out and stomped on, you haven't paid your dues to the fate-monger. Still, he'd be lying to himself if he didn't admit that she left an ache in his chest that lingered all through his twenties, a decade in which he went through girlfriends like some men go through cars, falling for their shine and their nice lines. Trouble is, every one of them had some quirk that burgeoned in his mind into a deal-breaker. And in any case, she is no longer the girl she was but somebody else, having traded Peter's attention for the adoration of the whole damn country.

No, his job is to remain fixed on telling the story in front of him, about the grandiose, apocalyptic psyche of America—and just maybe, if he's lucky, tell it well enough to make himself a new life.

H er flight is early by design, allowing her to slip out of the house be-fore her mother is awake and leave by way of the sliding glass door of her bedroom. The note in the kitchen says: *Flew to Minnesota to help Sarah with her new baby. Sorry to sneak off, didn't want to argue. Back in time for the premier.* Adam will have a coronary, but Thursday's photo shoot is not contractual, and he'll deal with it. Mom will, too. And there's no way she'll come chasing. Every day for the past fifteen years, she's said, "You couldn't drag me back there with a John Deere tractor and a logging chain."

It's an easy flight to Denver. Then a two-hour layover.

In the restroom she stands before a mirror, adjusting the brunette wig whose full bang rests on top of her eyebrows. She takes flesh-colored lipstick from her purse and applies it generously, then dulls her cheeks with a pale foundation. Finally a pair of round, blue-tinted sunglasses, which along with her recent weight loss brings a soaring sense of ano-nymity. She takes out her pills and swallows two, enough to stop the ache at the base of her neck and dry the film of sweat on her back and chest. She lifts the curtain of her hair from either side of her face and lets it drop to her shoulders. Then smiles at herself—the Annie smile with its naive sparkle and apologetic plumping of the cheeks. The Midwest sincerity that worked so well in her first few films.

A woman arrives at the adjoining sink, clears her throat noisily, and says, "You're not Melanie Magnus, are you?"

Melanie looks at her sideways. "I'll have to tell my husband, he's such a fan."

"Mine, too. You're really not her?"

"I'm sorry."

Three hours later she pulls her luggage from the carousel—a pair of jumbo, hard-sided cases, thirty or forty pounds each—and struggles from the airport into the humid Minnesota afternoon. The first person she sees is Sarah, *thank God,* waving from a blue Impala, then jumping out and running toward her, long arms spread wide. Melanie lets herself dissolve into them. It's been years since they've seen each other, since before Sarah got married, when she flew out over Christmas and spent a week in L.A. Melanie doesn't protest as her friend commandeers both suitcases and without apparent effort tosses them into the trunk.

They embrace again. "You've got to see him," Sarah says and pulls Melanie around to the side of the car and swings open the front passenger door. There, stout and sober-faced, and perched on a rumpled blanket like a small Buddha, is her infant son. He lifts his arms, fat-creases like bracelets on his wrists. He grunts. Sarah plucks him up, gestures for Melanie to sit, then hands him into her lap. The boy is naked except for a diaper.

"Meet Jimmy Junior."

"How can he be this big?" Melanie clutches his fat little body against her breasts and starts to cry. "What is he, six months?"

Sarah goes around the front and climbs in behind the wheel. "Yeah. Isn't he gorgeous?" She blushes, as if she knows she shouldn't take credit.

"He's such a stud, I'm never giving him back."

The boy twists on her lap, trying to get a look at the woman holding on to him so fiercely, then back at his mom.

Sarah tells him, "It's okay, it's okay."

Tears streaming, Melanie loosens her hold, but the little fellow starts crying, too—a whimper, really, except that his voice is deep, almost guttural.

"He always does that."

"Does what?"

"Cries every time someone else does. He understands."

I'm so pathetic that babies feel sorry for me, Melanie thinks, and she stops even trying to restrain herself. She and Jimmy Junior cry and whimper together until Sarah pulls into the driveway of a stucco bungalow on a shaded street, her brother Nate's place.

"We'll stay the night and drive up tomorrow," she says.

Inside, they settle themselves with glasses of sun tea, and Sarah squeezes Jimmy Junior into the canvas seat of a windup swing whose motion puts him immediately to sleep. Every five minutes or so the spring winds down and one of them has to get up and crank it before Jimmy starts fussing. Sarah's husband and her brother are out buying shingles, a recent storm having dropped an old red maple on top of Nate's garage, which needs a new roof.

"Did Enoch give you any grief about coming down here?" Melanie asks. She's heard from her friend how Enoch keeps track of where everybody is and what they're doing.

"Not really. He's been easier lately—ever since the vision he had. Distracted. Bigger stuff on his mind. And people are leaving, too, moving out. Half of us so far, or almost. Dave and Sally Drobec, a couple days ago—but you don't know them. And the two single girls, they left yesterday."

"What about you and Jimmy?"

"We're talking about it. Mom thinks we should. But look at us—I mean you and me. Where would we be without Enoch?"

Years ago Melanie explained to Sarah all there is to say about the day at age seven when she was stomped by the bull in Enoch's pasture, and how his prayers brought her back. And though Sarah's story might be less dramatic, it's remarkable in its own way. After high school, she and her boyfriend moved to the Cities, where she went to college and then started teaching. Eight years they lived together, Sarah waiting all that time for him to follow through on his promise to marry her, and then one day the cops showed up and took him away in handcuffs. He was charged with, then convicted of, molesting multiple children in his job with the Minneapolis Parks department and sent to prison. Sarah retreated to Battlepoint, depressed and distraught. For several years she lived with her mom and dad, watching daytime TV and working the night desk at the Westview Motel. Then one evening Enoch came to see her. He said she ought to come to worship on Saturday night, that God had told him there was someone she needed to meet. And though Sarah had been to some of Enoch's gatherings when she was younger, she had no intention of going. She felt betrayed by everything and everybody, God especially.

And yet she went. "I don't know how it happened," she'd told Melanie. "Saturday night came and there I was, sitting in my car in front of his barn. I didn't plan it. I didn't make a decision. I don't know how I got there. It was like I'd been transported."

In any case, she got out of her car, climbed the stairs into the old haymow, and there was Jimmy, "standing off in the corner, shyly," she'd say later, "like an overgrown hobbit." His round face, his solid body, an aura of kindness surrounding him. Three months later they married. Melanie has yet to meet him.

"Jimmy's on board?" she says, cranking the swing. "With Enoch's dream?"

"Sort of."

"Same here. I know it's absurd. But when you told me on the phone last week, I felt this little click inside"—she touches her breast—"like something flipping over. It's like when you get a piece of good news. Like when I heard about my Oscar nomination. I mean, maybe he's wrong, he's probably wrong. It's too wild to be true, isn't it? And yet I can't help believing it."

"Did you call him, or did he call you?" Sarah asks. On the drive from the airport Melanie explained how Enoch suggested she make the trip and told her that Willie might be coming.

"I called him. It was the first we've talked since I left home. Fifteen years."

"Do you feel manipulated?"

Melanie points at Jimmy Junior, asleep in the swing. "I've never seen *my* boy, Sarah."

"I know. And I was the one to put the idea in your head in the first place. But now I'm not so sure. Enoch must have his own reasons for wanting you here."

"Such as?" Melanie's headache is back, and also the sense of someone close by, listening. She thinks, *Where is my purse?* picturing the bottle of pills inside. A little help is all she needs. Half a pill would take care of everything, make her feel fine again.

"You'd be great publicity, Mel."

"That's what you think it's about?"

"Enoch wants to get out the word. People ought to know, right? You go up there, the papers catch wind of it, the TV news—problem solved."

Melanie rises from her chair and pulls the front of her blouse away from her damp skin. There is a tremble in her fingers that she doesn't want her friend to see. She kneels next to Jimmy Junior's swing and gazes into his face, which in repose looks like Sarah's after all, the slant of his eyes and the fine bones of his cheeks. "Such a lovely boy," she says and gets up and goes into the living room, where she finds her purse on the couch and takes it into the bathroom where she swallows another pill, just one, before returning to the kitchen.

"I don't want to be used for that," she says. "I don't want to drag my craziness up there. That's what I'm leaving behind."

"Tell him that. Do it on your terms, if you're going to do it."

"I will," Melanie says. But then immediately recalls how people laughed at Enoch for the claims he made after she was healed, how angry it made her that nobody could simply look at what happened and say, "Yeah—thank God!" Not even her mom. And now, God bless him, Enoch has climbed out on yet another limb, and she's in a position to give him a hand. "I don't want to be selfish," she says.

"And I don't want to see you hurt."

"Hey, what do I have to lose? I can go up there and make myself the butt of every joke from Burbank to Broadway, and I won't be worse off than I am now. Because there's not a soul out there who gives an actual fuck about me, Sarah. Not one. Enoch might be off his chain, but he saved me once and he would save me again if he had the chance. Besides, what if I get to see my son?"

There's a rattle and thump as the front door opens, and Sarah leans across the table. "Promise me you'll give it more thought," she says before the men walk in.

Her brother Nate, whom Melanie remembers as a boy, is still pale and shy. He waves and ducks his head. Jimmy, a larger version of the infant he helped to make, has a broad, honest face and blue eyes that sparkle beneath the high dome of his forehead. Sarah gets up and gives him a hug, then hauls him by an arm to the table where Melanie waits.

"See? I told you she was coming. Melanie, my husband, Jimmy."

She can't help but stand up, wrap her arms around the solid trunk of him, and press an ear against his steady, thumping heart. He feels like such a sure thing—such a guarantee—that it makes her cry again, her tears coming fast and warm.

"Things are going to be okay," she whispers to herself. "I'm going home."

When Enoch woke this morning, the phrase *splendid isolation* was fixed in his mind, and though he can't recall who said it or where it's from, it's the perfect term to describe a prophet's place in the world: no one to confide in, no one but God to offer validation. He thinks of Saint John at the end of his life, banished to the island of Patmos by Roman authorities and living in a cave, alone, driven by need toward intimacy with the Ancient of Days, yet human too, and no doubt in anguish. How did he keep his wits about him? How, with everything in the balance, was he able to marshal such terrible, gorgeous language to translate the revelation he was given?

Only six days into carrying his own burden, and Enoch is already drained. Also he's begun to regret that he didn't put his vision to paper. He could have done so on the first day, as he lay in the hospital. It was all so vivid then—but of course there was no need to preserve what he had seen for subsequent generations. Now, though, the edges of the dream are blurring. He can still see the heavenly messenger with her gown of water and the fourteen sunsets occurring in fast succession. He can feel the titanic storm and the release of gravity, the sensation of rising. He can hear the triumphal shout. But the rest is less clear. Was it Peter, in fact, ascending above him into the clouds? Victor? Enoch can see the feet, pale and long, but whose are they? And wasn't Melanie among the crowd, surrounding him in the pasture? He thinks so—he can picture her there when he closes his eyes. And Willie, too. Yes, he's quite certain of it. And what about the black granite obelisk that stands in the cemetery beyond the Magnussen farm and that he can see from his porch through a gap in the grove? In the moments before ascent, wasn't it glowing a strange green color?

A couple of years ago Enoch was out fishing and ended up anchored off Baily's Point, explaining to the man in the next boat how to rig his line for walleyes. The fellow turned out to be a preacher from Texas named Mize, a pilot with an itinerant ministry. After receiving a tour of the Ranch and staying for Saturday night worship, Mize offered to fly Enoch down to Galveston to serve as co-preacher in a three-day revival slated for later that year, in October. A good trip, as it happened, one of the few times in the past thirty years Enoch has escaped Minnesota. Mize took him to an Oilers game in Houston's new marvel of a stadium, and the meetings the two men led in Galveston were well attended. But the thing he remembers best is something Mize liked to say in his free-form sermons: "If you promise something in our God's name, He'll make darn sure that you're good for it. God will never make you eat crow."

It's an idea that resonated with Enoch then, and still does.

"He's pretty good, isn't he?" Victor says.

"Huh? Yes, yes."

It's early evening, and they're watching Felix, the skinny kid from Kentucky, as he navigates an excavator that Enoch borrowed from a neighbor who runs a gravel pit. This morning Felix came up to the house to use the bathroom and found Enoch and Victor at the kitchen table, tinkering with their plans for the latrine and shower. "I can dig those trenches y'all need," he said, scanning Enoch's sketches. "I can help put up the structures, too." His father is a contractor, he explained, and Felix has tagged along with him from the time he could walk.

It's Sunday, of course, and normally everybody would be resting and praying. Honoring the Sabbath. But two more campers arrived overnight, and who knows how many will show up this evening? How many more by the nineteenth? It would be imprudent to wait longer. This morning after his neighbor unloaded the excavator, Enoch wrote out verses five and six from the fourteenth chapter of Luke and tacked it to the notice board in the barn: "And He answered them, saying, Which of you shall have an ass or an ox fallen into a pit, and will not straightway pull him out on the Sabbath day? And they could not answer him again to these things."

The single boys, Eddie, Ted, and Matt, all of whom Enoch has placed at Felix's disposal, are raking out piles of dirt produced by the newly dug trenches. Hunched over and sweating, they cast resentful glances at Felix, who manhandles the boom and bucket while simultaneously pointing out the spots they've missed and shouting directions above the engine noise.

"The Rapture is turning out to be more than they bargained for," Enoch says.

Victor rubs the tip of his nose. "I'm surprised they're still here."

"Why do you say that?"

"Saw them making eyes at each other while the girls were moving out. Like they wished they were leaving, too."

A car comes rolling up the driveway, and Enoch turns to look. A brown Chevy Biscayne—Dave Drobec, who parks in front of the house and steps out from behind the wheel but then remains inside the angle formed by the driver's door, as if unwilling to leave the safety of his car. He shakes his head when Enoch waves him forward.

"Everything all right, Dave?"

The man nods, chewing his bottom lip. Enoch and Victor walk over to him.

"Come inside, we'll talk."

"I can't stay." He's gripping the top of the driver's door with one hand. The other is planted on the car's roof.

Enoch turns to Victor. "Maybe you should go and check on the trench work."

As soon as he's out of earshot, Dave says, "We want it back."

"You want what back?"

"The money we put in when we moved here."

"Was that our agreement? That if you left, you'd get it back?"

"It was twenty-five hundred dollars, for heaven's sake! The payoff from our house sale. It's only fair."

"How long were you here, Dave?"

"You know how long."

"Three and a half years. And in all that time I never asked you for rent."

Dave lifts his hand from the door and puts an index finger in Enoch's face. Enoch looks right at it, straightening himself to full height. Dave drops the hand, and it occurs to Enoch that he has never had much respect for the man.

"I was giving a third of my income. Sally, too."

"Same as everybody else. And when you were laid off two years ago, I don't remember anybody saying anything to make you uncomfortable. How long did it take until you found another position?"

"Seven, eight months?"

"It was more than that, Dave. And I remember you telling me how blessed you were, not having to meet your mortgage obligations."

"All the same, I think Sally and I deposited more into the Ranch fund, up front, than anyone else. Rainy, for one, put in nothing at all. She told me as much. And Ted, I believe, put in fifty bucks."

"There's never been a policy, no minimum amount. You know that. It's a New Testament arrangement."

"But you *own* the place, don't you? We all contribute to its upkeep, and you don't distribute shares."

Enoch stares him down. The land has been in his family for a century, ever since his great-grandfather came from Massachusetts to homestead. Enoch himself tilled, sowed, and harvested its fields for most of his work years, and until World War II he did so with draft horses. Bone-breaking work.

"I take it, then," Dave says, "that you're willing to let money come between us." He looks off toward the barn, squinting, and his face hardens, jaw flexing. Then he takes a long breath and exhales. "All I'm asking for is what Sally and I put in. It would give us the chance for a new start, a down payment on another place. Which doesn't seem like a big request. And I make it in good faith, having given my best effort during our time here."

People see Dave as a steady, phlegmatic sort, on account of his unexpressive face and his measured way of speaking. But he has a lazy eye that gives away his mood, either drifting listlessly or locking tight in its socket, and now it's so unmoored that Enoch can't help the rush of sympathy in his chest.

"Look around," Enoch says and gestures toward the campers in the oak grove and the commotion of the excavator. "More expenses than ever. Think for a minute of the charge I've been given, and which I am bound to honor."

Dave's eye is struggling back toward true. He clears his throat. "What good will this farm be to you? After the nineteenth, I mean. You could make an allowance for me, out of your estate."

"Allowance?"

"Have an attorney draw up a quitclaim deed, which on August 20th—at your disappearance—allows the farm to be turned over to the individual you designate." Dave is serious. He is always serious, and now he seems to have found his courage, both eyes fastened hard on Enoch's face.

"If I chose to do something like that," Enoch says, "you're not the one I'd pick."

"So you've already made legal provision?"

"That's my business."

"Your son's getting it."

"Look. When I'm taken up on the nineteenth, you'll be taken too, along with the entire remnant. And believe me, at that point neither of us will have any need of this farm or any fleck of worldly wealth."

The man rubs a hand over the bristly top of his head and looks straight up into the sky, an odd smile on his face, as if waiting for a voice. "You're going to make me do this, aren't you? Sally told me you would."

"You don't have to do anything."

"You have no idea how loyal I've been."

"What are you talking about?"

Dave makes fists of both hands and brings them close against his chest, like an actor in a melodrama. Behind him, Victor rounds the southeast corner of the house and comes forward in the grass, behind Dave, silent. Victor stands there, his bland face alert.

"What, Dave?" Enoch says.

"Your secret. I've known about it for a long time, and I haven't spoken a word. Except to Sally."

"What secret would that be?"

"Sylvie Young. I know what's going on between the two of you."

Exhaustion falls on Enoch like a weight, and it's all he can do to keep from turning and walking off. Why the fastidiousness about sex—a fixation he himself has been party to? Who has been hurt by the love he and Sylvie have shared? "She and I have been friends a long time," Enoch says.

"I don't like to do this, I don't." Dave sighs and looks at the ground. Directly behind him, on the other side of the car, Victor stands on the lawn, listening. He lifts a hand as if asking permission to speak, but Enoch shakes his head. Dave looks up. "You know that weekend a couple summers ago when you sent us all to Wisconsin for the Kathryn Kuhlman crusade?"

Enoch doesn't respond.

"We left on a Friday afternoon—it was a two-hour drive—and after the service that night, Sally realized she'd forgotten her mother's birthday gift, it was something she'd spent weeks sewing. Her mom, you see, lives in a little town near Chippewa Falls, and we were planning to see her on Saturday. So I got up at three-thirty that morning and drove back here." A smile sneaks into the corner of Dave's mouth. "You never knew, did you?"

"Nope."

"There was a strange car in the driveway, parked right here where I'm parked, and I figured I better check to see if everything was all right. So I went up to the front door, where I saw you through the window— both of you, in the kitchen. Wearing your, um, nightclothes. I left by way of the back drive, past the marsh. I didn't tell anyone except Sally. Like I said."

"And I should be grateful?"

"Yes, actually. And ashamed."

"Whatever shame I might have has nothing to do with you or with what you think you know."

"Here's the deal, Enoch—and I hate to do this. But if you won't write me a check for twenty-five hundred dollars or put my name on a quitclaim deed for this farm, I'm going to tell the Ranchers about Sylvie Young."

"The ones that are still here, you mean? Do you think they'll care?"

"I'll tell the whole town. I'll tell the folks camping in the oak grove."

"I took you for a bigger man, Dave."

"Ditto," he says. He turns then, as if sensing Victor's presence, and seeing him, flinches, one hand jumping to protect his face. He puts his arm back down and breathes. "Think about it for a day or two," he says, and then he climbs in behind the wheel. "I'll be in touch." He slams the door, starts the car, and backs up fast, nearly hitting the buckeye tree before jamming the car into drive and gunning past Enoch toward the township road, tires throwing gravel.

Watching Dave's retreat, Victor says, "You've got a phone call."

"Who?"

Victor shakes his head.

Inside, the kitchen phone is off the hook and lying on the counter. Before picking up, Enoch drinks a full glass of water from the tap. It's close to ninety degrees today, and humid. Minnesota's dog days.

"Enoch Bywater."

"Did I catch you at a bad time?" The voice is hers, good news offsetting the bad. Or at least he dares to hope so.

"I'm sorry I kept you waiting. Are you coming up, Melanie?"

She's quiet for a few moments. Too long. "There's something I have to know. Before I can feel right about it."

He can almost hear the labor of her thinking and sense the sharpness of whatever devil has trapped her in its corner. He pictures the girl she was in 1950, scrawny and towheaded, and recalls the weightless burden in his arms as he lifted her that day and carried her to the house and laid her on the kitchen table, her chest indented by the hoof of Enoch's breeding bull, a deep concave impression as neat as a handprint in fresh cement, her face the color of blue clay, no breath in her mouth, her eyes showing only white.

"I'm afraid of all the attention. I want it to be just me, not the person they think I am. Do you understand?"

"Yes," he whispers.

"Is that possible?"

"I'll do what I can, Melanie. I'll be discreet. I'll try to protect your privacy." He has hoped and prayed she would decide to come—not least because of the cameras her presence would bring. Now, though, he sets his disappointment aside. He thinks of Christ in Gethsemane: *Not my will, but Thine, be done.*

"And my son?" Her voice nearly inaudible.

"I expect he'll be here, Melanie. But I can't promise."

"Please don't say anything to Skinny."

"I won't. Are you coming soon?"

"A few days, I think. But I have to go now, I have to go."

"All right."

"Thank you," she says, and the line clicks. She's gone.

In the living room, he kneels at the couch and prays, asking God to clear the path before her. He also begs forgiveness for the doubt that led him to his lawyer's office yesterday, where he willed over the farm to Peter, in the event that Enoch is Raptured and Peter is left back. As if God weren't capable of answering a father's lifelong petitions on behalf of his son! He prays for nearly an hour, and by 8:00 p.m. he's driving north as the pumpkin-orange sun slips into clouds the color of ripening sumac—an autumn evening despite the heat—and it occurs to him that he might never see a sunset this lovely again, his life on this spinning, God-made ball nearly finished.

She's watering her geraniums from a galvanized pail, her gray hair pulled up with a yellow scarf. He goes to her and folds her in his arms, then pulls back and looks at her. The generous but elegant nose and the well-shaped lips. The specks of yellow-gold in her green irises.

"Have you finally come to your senses?" She notches her cheek into the hollow of his breastbone.

"Don't you wish."

She takes his hand and leads him inside where she brews a pot of swamp tea out of leaves she gathers from a nearby tamarack bog, and Enoch settles himself on the sofa. He tells her about Dave's visit and the newly arrived pilgrims in the oak grove. He doesn't mention Melanie's phone call, not yet.

"I should have seen it coming. Dave's a money guy. But he's always been solid, too, the one I can count on. When somebody needs prayer, Dave is willing. When somebody's in trouble, he's the one who steps up. Remember when Victor got into it that night with those kids who showed up drunk at the meeting? I was down in Texas. Dave's the one who dragged him out of that squabble and set him straight. No easy thing, either. You know how Victor can get."

She sets their tea on the coffee table and curls in next to him. "Maybe you ought to listen to him."

"And give him the money?"

"I mean *listen* to him. He's distressed for good reason."

In the cage of his ribs, Enoch's heart performs a double flip. He takes a breath and holds it until his beat steadies. This beautiful woman whom he loves, and she's taking up with Dave! *Splendid isolation.* "I should listen to everybody, I suppose—you, the pastors who came to visit, Dave. You're all saying the same thing, after all, trying to save me from myself. Well, Dave isn't."

Sylvie is shaking her head. "All you really have to do is listen to your-self. God is talking to *you*, from the center of your being, it couldn't be more personal. He's not talking to the world out there."

"You say God, and I say God," Enoch says. "Same word, two differ-ent ideas."

"Not so different as you think." She touches his hand, and her fin-gers are warm, moist, they feel almost hot. He looks at her mouth, and though his impulse is to kiss her, he doesn't want her to think he agrees with what she's saying.

"God is an entity," he says—and the vibration starts up in his chest, the need to set things straight—"who existed long before us, from the beginning. He is the spirit of creation and benevolence. And also of judgment."

"*Spirit*—I like that word," she says. "Spirit has no boundaries."

"God comes to dwell within those who acknowledge who He is, Sylvie."

She smiles, not agreeing, but not contending with him, either—a position that Enoch has learned to accept as satisfactory. There is no use in pushing harder. "Oh," he says, "and I didn't mention, the girls moved out yesterday, both of them. Rainy and Maude. Less than a week now, and half my people are gone."

"Your people?"

"I thought it would be a thrill for them, being at the dead center of God's plan. Of course, you warned me."

"Are you worried about Dave . . . telling about us?"

Enoch swats at the air. "I'm a nutjob, already. Why not be a nutjob with a mistress?"

"You're ashamed, though."

He turns to look at her, the scattering of freckles across her nose and cheeks a mark of her vulnerability. "I understand shame. I grew up with a dad who would disappear without notice to go drinking for a week. And I suppose I'm ashamed of my own hypocrisy. But ashamed of us? No, Syl-vie. Never. Tell me, why have you bothered with me for all these years?"

She smiles, thinking. "Maybe I thought I could change you."

"Seriously. You must have asked yourself a thousand times."

"It's not just one thing, Enoch. Don't make me explain."

"Your daughter knows about us, doesn't she? What do you tell her?"

She rubs her eyes. "For starters, that no one in my life has treated me better than you have. That you demand little. That you offer love and accept whatever of mine I'm able to give. But there's more. Sometimes I feel like what you believe is what I want to believe but can't, in a god who is an actual—What did you say? Entity?—who is aware of my presence, in a benign way."

"It's more than benign awareness, Sylvie. He knows everything about you, down to the number of hairs on your head."

She touches his lips to quiet him. "Please, it's just you, and that's plenty."

They sit on the sofa, leaning into each other and watching the sky darken, and then the lake, which holds the light longer than seems possible.

"Why don't I make you some cookies?" she says. "Do you have time?"

"Please, don't move." He takes both her hands in his and holds them.

"When do you expect the starlet?" she asks.

"She called this afternoon. I was going to tell you. It wouldn't surprise me if she's here by Friday, maybe sooner. But she's worried about the attention. She doesn't want a spectacle. That's what she called about."

"It won't be a secret for long. You know small towns. You're going to get all the publicity you want, Enoch."

"For Melanie's sake, I'm not sure I want it anymore."

"Of course you want it. I suppose you told her that Willie will be here."

"I did."

"And I imagine Peter is on his way, too."

"I haven't heard a thing since he went back. He was upset that I didn't die."

Sylvie groans. "Spare me the pity party. He'll be here soon, mark my words."

"How can you be so sure?"

"He'll get wind of Annie—Melanie—once she arrives. And don't pretend you're not planning on telling him." She laughs, putting her hands together. "But you've already done it, haven't you?"

"No." He feigns offense. "I haven't mentioned her."

"You will, though, and I have to say, I'm glad of it. For my own reasons."

"And what are those?"

"I'm glad you're finally making things right. Those two shouldn't have been separated in the first place."

Enoch sits up straight and studies her. She's never spoken like this about Peter and Melanie, and he didn't know she had an opinion. "What do you mean? They were kids, and way over their heads. Peter was on his way to the rookie league, for heaven's sake. It would have been a disaster. Her father and I actually agreed on that."

"Come on. You and Gerald Sr. agreed on one thing, that you didn't want to be relatives. He didn't want to send her away. Or send his wife away, for that matter. Look, it's permissible to make mistakes, and that was one of yours."

Enoch's stomach gives a turn, and the air constricts at the top of his lungs. "Mistake or not, Ruth and I did what we thought was best."

She touches him, her hand pressing against his heart.

"It felt necessary," Enoch says.

"Forget it," she whispers. "Please." She slides close and puts her arms around him. "You know what I'm going to do on the nineteenth?"

"You're coming to my place."

"I've got this chain hanging in the garage that Porter used for hauling in the dock every fall, and when I come over there, I'm going to padlock the pair of us to something unmovable—I don't know, like that old concrete hitching post by your barn, with the cast-iron ring on it. And then God won't be able to take you."

The darkness is nearly complete—sky and lake both gone—and though he can barely see her face, he can tell that it's open to him, warm, her lips suggesting the comedy of who they are together. He finds himself wishing, as he did earlier, that time was not so short, and remembers what it was like as a boy when his mother spoke with excitement about the Last Days, how swindled that made him feel, enslaved to his mortal body as boys are. As men are, too, even old ones, in the right moments.

AUGUST 12—MONDAY

ast night, late, a station wagon full of hippies, Jesus freaks, drove in from California, saying they'd heard about Enoch's vision from friends in Minnesota. He helped them put up their tents in the dark and sat with them for a while, then long after he went to bed he listened as they sang and played, somebody on guitar, another sawing away on a mouth harp. His neighbor, Skinny Magnussen, Gerald Jr., must have heard them too, his bedroom no more than a hundred yards from the oak grove, his window likely open, as warm as it was. And so his visit this morning comes as no surprise.

It's nine o'clock and he's standing on Enoch's front porch, a reincarnation of his father: large head and wide shoulders, big torso, spindle legs. His face redder and fuller than usual. He's wearing his uniform, service revolver parked in a holster at his side. "How am I gonna sleep with that noise? Smelly, long-haired fools." He wipes sweat from his forehead with the back of his hand. Behind him the driveway is empty. He must have walked over.

"I'm sorry. I'll talk to them."

"It wouldn't be so bad if they could sing, but they sound like a flock of geese."

"Please come in for a minute." Enoch waves him forward, and Skinny steps inside, apparently too surprised to do otherwise. He allows himself to be led into the living room, where he takes the stuffed chair offered to him.

"Did you get that permission you need to stage an outdoor event?" He's perched uncomfortably on the edge of the chair, his belly slung forward.

"I checked the county code, as I'm sure you did, too. As long as the number of people on my property remains below 250, I'm within my rights. Can I get you some coffee? Or how about tea? Victor made a batch of sun tea yesterday, and I could pour it over ice."

Skinny blinks and looks at his watch. "Sure, um, the tea."

"Give me a minute."

In the kitchen Enoch remembers the last time he saw Skinny's dad. It was 1970, when Gerald Sr. was dying of cancer. For years Enoch had been half-expecting him to show up at the door with a shotgun—payback for Enoch's role in the loss of his wife and daughter. Instead, Gerald swallowed his rage and found ways to parse it out. He built a new hog barn, the kind with a stench-producing liquid manure pit, as close to Enoch's property line as legally permitted. He went after Enoch's reputation, telling folks that Enoch made a habit of sleeping with the single women at the Ranch. And often, during Saturday night meetings, he would go down to the pasture adjoining the two properties and blast away at tin cans with his shotgun. The two men spoke just once during the final years of Gerald's life—on the morning he showed up on the front porch, like his son now. He had dropped half his weight and had to lean against the door frame to support himself, the skin of his face stretched tight against his skull. "I'm on my way out," he said. "Doc told me it's all over." Enoch asked if there was anything he could do to help, and Gerald told him yes, he could tell his wife and daughter to come back and visit, and he could ask God to heal him—requests that Enoch acceded to, both of them. Dottie, when he phoned her, laughed in his ear. God, for His part, kept His own counsel.

The tea is a combination of Darjeeling and herbal cinnamon, and Enoch fills two large tumblers, then adds ice cubes and slices of lemon. Skinny drains his glass immediately. He wipes his mouth with a forearm.

"Those latrines you're putting in. I'm not sure if they line up with regulations."

"More tea?"

"Sure."

Enoch returns to the kitchen, refills the glass, and comes back. "Actually, they're fine, Skinny, but I appreciate your concern. The ground is plenty high above lake level and the drainage field exceeds the minimum distance from the shoreline. I checked."

Skinny takes a long swallow and then one more before sighing and placing the tumbler on the coffee stand next to him. "Hogs got out this morning and I had to chase them down. Found their way into the goddamn cemetery. Rooting around that big Hansen stone." He takes out a handkerchief from his pocket and wipes at his face. "There's also noise regulations."

"Not to worry. I'll talk with the folks who kept you up last night."

The porch door creaks, and Victor walks in. He looks from Enoch to Skinny and back again. His hands ball up into large, bony fists.

"Hey, Spud." Skinny shifts in his chair and lays a hand on his sidearm. "You're just in time to watch me arrest an old man."

"He's only kidding," Enoch says.

Victor's eyes are like pinholes into his brain, and right now they're boring into Skinny. "Don't call me that." His voice is shaking. The two were in the same class at school until Victor dropped out at thirteen or so. Minnesota law required attendance till sixteen, but in Victor's case nobody bothered to follow up. He didn't learn easily, and Battlepoint's teachers were happy to be rid of the extra work.

"Shit, man—don't be a pussy." Skinny has drained his second glass and he points with the empty tumbler toward the kitchen. "Mind?"

"Be my guest. It's in the fridge." Enoch turns to Victor. "He came by to ask about the campers. Was there something you needed?"

"That order from the lumber yard. They're supposed to drop it off at ten-thirty. Where should I have them unload?"

Enoch tells him, and as the porch door closes, Skinny comes back from the kitchen with his tea.

"Why do you call him Spud?" Enoch says.

"Everybody did, back in school."

"I know that. But why?"

"Look at him, for God's sake. That face and those eyes. What else are you going to call him?"

In the window behind Skinny's head, a car pulls up and stops in front of the barn, the Levitzes' brown Impala. Jimmy's at the wheel and Sarah's in the passenger seat with the baby. But there is someone in back, too, a woman Enoch recognizes even at fifty yards and in spite of the brown wig she's wearing. That unmistakable profile—celestial nose, full lips, pouty chin.

Enoch jumps to his feet. "Hey, I've got to show you something. Come on." As Skinny rises from his chair, Enoch catches sight—behind Skinny—of Victor stepping to the car, bending and flapping his hand, at the same time glancing back toward the house. Enoch hustles Skinny into the kitchen.

"What, what?" Skinny asks.

Enoch points. Through the west window above the sink is the excavation work that Felix completed yesterday: a shallow rectangle for the concrete slab and a trench for the latrine. In the oak grove beyond, the half-dozen or so tents, green, blue, yellow, red. Four people are sitting on camp stools around a wood fire, though it's hard to tell from here which are men and which are women. Lots of hair, in any case. Enoch puts a hand on Skinny's big shoulder. "See? Look, it's all right here in front of me. I'll keep tabs on things, you don't have to worry. Now go on home and figure out a way to arrest me." He takes Skinny by the arm and escorts him to the back door, which lets out to the north, beyond eyeshot of the Levitz Impala, and sends him on his way. Then he runs back through the house, across the porch, and into the yard in time to see the door of the granary swing shut.

Inside the dimly lit first floor of the old building he finds them standing together uncomfortably, Victor with his arms at his sides and staring at the floor, Sarah trying to settle the baby who's fussing in her arms, and Jimmy with his hands on his hips and glaring across at Victor. All of them looking off balance. Melanie has moved to the rear of the room next to the old mohair couch in storage there, and she's leaning against its high back, arms crossed in front of her, face troubled. She's drowning in an oversized sweatshirt, and the orange toenails of her sandaled feet remind

Enoch of the M&M candies she was always eating as a child. It seems to take a moment before she realizes that he's entered the room, but then she comes straight to him and allows him to wrap her in his arms. *So small,* he thinks—smaller than when she left all those years ago. There's a slight but unmistakable tremble in her body.

"Are you crying?"

She pulls back to let him see her face, which is taut, composed.

By way of explanation he says, "Your brother was here when you drove in. He was in the house with me. That's why Victor hustled you all in here."

Jimmy Junior starts squalling and Sarah hands him off to his dad, who sniffs at his bottom, makes a face, then takes him outside, holding him at arm's length.

"Let's get your things from the car. You'll be staying right here— there's an apartment upstairs now. Victor, you'd best go out and wait for the lumber. And if you get a chance, would you throw together some of that cinnamon coffee cake?"

Upstairs it's bright and tidy, with original planking on the floors and varnished pine boards on the walls and ceiling. An eat-in kitchen, a living room with a view to the south, and a bedroom at the back that looks out over the pasture and hayfield toward Last Lake. When Melanie disappears into the bathroom, Sarah puts a hand on Enoch's forearm and draws him into the kitchen.

"I'm worried." She speaks close to his ear. "She doesn't seem well. I'm not sure it's the best thing for her, being here."

"It's God's will, Sarah. She flew into Minneapolis?" He can't help the pang of envy in his gut, knowing Sarah's the one Melanie sought out for passage home.

"Sort of a last-minute thing. We happened to be down there, helping Nate."

He scrutinizes Sarah's face, the quick smile and wrinkled forehead— contrition or evasiveness, he can't tell which.

"I need to go," she says. "Jimmy Junior's hungry."

Enoch takes Melanie downstairs and into the house, where he brews a fresh pot of coffee in the kitchen, and then up to his study on the second floor, which faces north, its window offering the same view as the granary apartment—lake and pasture, and of course the rock pile next to which Melanie was stomped by the bull. It's not long before Victor comes upstairs with a hot pan of coffee cake, pieces of which he plates for them before leaving. Melanie has the same ethereal presence she had when she was a girl—that strange depth in her eyes, as if there is no end to what she can see. But her face seems clouded, the easy joy it used to hold deadened somehow. And her flesh animated by a nervous vulnerability. She's seated in a small plush chair, her fists planted on her thighs, and her right foot hasn't stopped shaking.

"Your son and I have spoken on the phone, and I'll probably be going to pick him up on Wednesday. He's looking forward to seeing you."

Her mouth falls open.

"Yes," Enoch says.

She closes her eyes, and Enoch listens to the passage of air into and out of her lungs. She has spoken no more than a few dozen words.

"I don't know yet if Peter is coming. He thinks I'm unhinged."

She nods and then shakes her head.

"I've been told it was a grave mistake, keeping you and Peter apart. That your father and I did it out of hatred for each other. In any case, I've spent the past fifteen years telling myself I did the right thing—that all of us did."

"He never loved me," Melanie says.

"How do you know that?"

"He would have come for me. No matter where they hid me."

"Your dad threatened him. Told him he'd have him arrested if he tried seeing you. And he could have had it done, you were only fifteen. Peter was a legal adult."

"Oh," she says, her face so plastic and variable. "But he didn't answer my letters."

Enoch looks away. *Forgive me—please forgive me.* He stands and goes to the window, where at the edge of his view he can see the campers in the oaks. Someone has strung a clothesline, and it's hung with jeans and shirts and underwear, the garments so wet and heavy they're touching the grass. They must have done their wash in the lake. "Peter couldn't answer your letters because he did not receive them. I made sure of that. I got hold of his manager, and he took care of it."

Behind him she's silent, and at first Enoch can't bring himself to turn around. Finally, he does. She has lifted her feet off the floor and tucked them up against herself, and she's hugging her knees, her face hidden behind them, nothing of her head visible except for the dark hair of her wig.

She's remembering her last time with Peter—in the abandoned sand-pit north of the lake, their bodies woven together on the wide seat of Enoch's old pickup truck, the sun blasting through the cracked windshield. Late May, first real heat of the year, and she'd stolen out of choir practice, met Peter behind the bus barn, and gone off with him for a ride around Last Lake. It was the day after they told their parents, who forbade them to see each other again. A murder of crows squawked from the stand of birches to the east, and inside the hot cab they inhaled each other, Peter in his white T-shirt, sleeves rolled up over the muscles of his arms and smelling of cigarettes and the grease he used in his hair. His face—smooth except for bristles on his chin—burrowed into her neck. His hands were gentle, worshipful, resolute. He told her how beautiful she was, how pure and how kind. She let him take off her bra and hike her skirt, knowing this was wrong but not caring because he meant what he said, she was certain of it, every word, and she wanted to believe it was true. She unbuttoned his Levis and pushed them down over his narrow hips and allowed him to do it again—it was the fourth time and the best, even if he lasted only as long as it took her to say, "Be careful," which he was, pulling out and emptying himself on her chest and her stomach, same as he'd always done, or tried to. No one since has made her feel like Peter did in those moments. It was as if she were giving him the only love he would ever need, deprived of which he might as well lie down and die.

But what did she know at fifteen?

She looks up from behind her knees into Enoch's face—no longer full and lineless, the way she remembers it. His cheeks are washed-out gullies beneath the high bones that frame his countersunk eyes, which are shining with regret but also with certainty. Through the window behind him the sun is crushing the green pasture, and off to the west she can see the southern edge of the burr oaks, the pattern of their branches like jittery puzzles. She wonders about the people in the tents and where they've come from. She wonders if the single pill she swallowed will dull the pain rising into her skull from the top of her spine. She wonders if Enoch can hear what she's thinking, if he's noticing the sweat breaking out on her neck and arms. She has the sense of somebody outside the door, trying to listen in.

"Forgive me," he says. Or maybe he's asking a question: *Forgive me?* He raises his left brow, the left side of his mouth.

"I forgive you."

"I don't deserve it, Melanie."

But she insists, "I forgive you," knowing that if they had been allowed to stay together, she would have watched Peter turn into the self-pleasing creature that men become. Her mistake has always been, early on, to confuse their single-mindedness with a need to share their love. She puts her feet on the floor and straightens in the chair. "Please, let's not talk about it anymore. That's not why I'm here."

He comes away from the window and sits across from her. "Why *are* you here?"

"My son, I suppose. That's part of it."

He waits, as still as a lion. "What else?"

"I've always believed it would happen," she says, "and the more I've lived, the more I've wanted it to happen. But I didn't think I'd be around to see it. How can you be sure, though? How can you take the risk, telling everybody the way you've done? God never talks to me, though I've prayed and prayed."

"Of course He does."

"No. Or if I thought so, I couldn't be sure."

"It's not often that He speaks like this to me, directly."

"But how can you know?"

He clamps his lips in a tight line and squints past her. "It's a matter of practice, I suppose, like other things. You make mistakes, which result in harm to yourself and others. Or you make the right call and see the fruits of the Spirit." He smiles, warming to his subject. "Over the years, I have learned to tell the difference. Does it line up with Scripture? If not, it comes from the Tempter. Is it feeding the image you have of yourself? That's a dangerous thing. Will it require dependence on Him to see it through? If not, you're doing it for yourself."

She's feeling better now, her neck and face cooling. "You don't need to convince me," she says.

He sits back and raises his hands in the air. "So here we are," he says and looks out the window.

She looks, too, recalling the color of the sun as she lay there next to the rock pile. Yellow-blue, like aluminum. She remembers how the black hoof punched through her ribs and sternum, the awful sound of it, like a dry branch breaking. And the immense pressure. How the bull's hoof lifted then and came down again, beside her face this time, the ground shaking beneath her. She remembers the sweet, rich scent of manure, so different from the smell of hog shit. As she reached out to push the hoof away, the pulsing in her chest flourished into an orange flame that absorbed the rest of her body into it, the entire world distilled by the blaze, which burned for only moments before going white. Then a pleasant, saving breeze. She knew she was dead but knew also that she was being lifted and carried and then laid out on a hard surface—learning only later that Enoch was the one who found her, reknitting her bones and flesh with prayer, and demanding that God bring her back, which God did. This is what she believes. This is what she is certain of, regardless of what her father may have said, or Dr. Young, or anybody else.

"Did he ever admit to you what he knew?" Melanie asks. "What he must have known?"

"Your dad?"

"Dr. Young."

"In his way, yes."

"When? What did he say?"

"It was the year he died, the same year I lost Ruth. He said there was something more in the X-ray that he didn't tell us at the time. You remember about your heart being misplaced."

"Yes." She can even recall the name Dr. Young had for it, *dextacardia*, when the heart points right instead of left and sits on the wrong side of the chest. A congenital condition, he explained, something he discovered in the X-ray he took that day. It had nothing to do with the accident, he said, and it was nothing they needed to worry about. As for the rib cage and lungs, they were fine. She'd simply had the breath knocked out of her. A little bruising was all.

Enoch gets up and goes to his desk and takes something from the bottom drawer, a piece of yellowed notebook paper, folded several times. He comes back and sits again and opens the paper. His eyes pass down across the page. He wets his lips. "I had him write it down for me. Here." He clears his throat and then reads it to her. "'Costal cartilage of the fifth rib, left side, detached from the sternum and oddly *fused* to costal cartilage of the sixth rib below it, leaving a wider than normal gap between fifth and sixth ribs.' He underlined the word *fused*."

"That's it?"

"That's what he wrote. Here, look. He told me it was the only time he'd seen such a thing. That it was an irregularity that might have been caused by extreme pressure, maybe a heavy blow. *Might* have. Although a fusing of two ribs would require time. Months."

"Wow." She presses her fingers into the little gap in her chest, the place where the hoof came down. "He admitted it, then. He believed it."

"I wouldn't go that far."

"But the X-ray. It was taken that day, and the detached rib was already healed. How could he not believe it?"

Enoch's laugh is quiet. "There's always more than one explanation, is what he said. He believed it was congenital."

"But if he thought I was born with my ribs like that, why didn't he tell me at the time? Why keep it a secret?"

"I asked him that. He said because he couldn't explain it to his own satisfaction. The odd fusion of those ribs was a bridge too far, I suppose. At least he came clean to me, which he didn't have to do."

There's a stab in her bowel and Melanie leans forward, hands on her belly. Probably grease from the diner where they stopped for breakfast this morning, though sometimes the pills have this effect, too. "Something I ate," she says.

"Can I get you something?"

"No, please."

He sits, patient. Then reaches out and touches her knee, a parental gesture. He says, "God took me and then sent me back again, for a reason. Like he did you, Melanie."

The nausea hits again, and this time it brings a sense of guilt. "If you hadn't said anything about Willie, I might not have come. I would have been tempted, but it's such a hard thing to believe, as much as I want to."

"Wanting to believe is the same as believing."

"I want to see my son, and if God comes back for us, all the better. But I don't want interviews. I don't want photographers. I don't want people looking at me. I don't want people coming up to me. I don't need it. I didn't come here for that."

"Nobody here knows anything—except for Sarah and Jimmy. And Victor. And I won't tell anyone else. But I can't promise that you won't be recognized. You can spend as much time in the apartment as you like. And maybe you should wear what you're wearing—the glasses, the hair."

"I don't want my brother to know. I don't want to see him. Or Adam, my agent."

"What about your mother?"

"She knows where I am, but she'll stay put. I'm not worried about her."

"We'll do our best." He folds his large, crooked hands in front of his chest.

She pushes up from the chair, her body impossibly heavy. Sleep is what she needs, and she imagines it like a black, windless forest. "I have to go now," she says.

"Can I walk you back?"

"I'm fine." She takes his offered hands and squeezes them. They're warm and dry. She turns and leaves the room, but then comes back. "When did you say Willie gets here?"

"Day after tomorrow. Wednesday."

"And what about Peter? You said he's coming too, right?"

"I said I didn't know."

"But you think he will? I'd like to see him again."

"I'm sure he feels the same."

They regard each other for a moment, and Melanie is aware of the connection between them, like a cable running from a socket in her bones to a socket in his. She makes herself turn and go down the creaking stairs and through the house and across the lawn to the granary, doubting if Peter even thinks about her anymore.

Yesterday was an out-and-out loss. After breakfast in the diner outside South Bend, he found a nice spot in the park down by the river—too nice, as it turned out—a quiet hollow inside a little stand of boxwoods where fatigue caught up to him. He fell asleep midmorning and didn't wake until late afternoon. Then he walked back to the diner for a burger before spending fifteen of his last thirty dollars for a room at the motel next door.

Today—it's Monday night, right?—a succession of rides has carried him across Illinois and Wisconsin and finally into Minnesota, his current benefactor a middle-aged man piloting a rusted-out Chevy van with a front end in need of realignment. He calls himself Rutherford and has to grip the steering wheel with both hands to keep the vehicle between the centerline and the highway's shoulder. Still, the van keeps drifting left, then right. It doesn't help that Rutherford reaches for can after can of Hamm's beer from the cooler next to him and never stops talking. He's angry with the press for getting rid of Nixon, who would have "won the goddamn war if the wimps in Congress hadn't tied his hands behind his back." Rutherford's girlfriend, about twenty years old and sitting in a BarcaLounger behind him, nods along to what he says and tosses his empties out the window. Peter chooses to agree with the man—the hitchhiker's obligation. It's been a long day: traveling salesmen in need of a sounding board, a young woman in flight from her husband who vowed to kill her, and now this political know-it-all who claims to be a veteran. He seems confused about the location of Vietnam, though, going on about his weekend furloughs to Argentina and boasting about secret raids into Madagascar, where the mission was to find and destroy a Russian nuclear missile factory. He's well launched into his plot to infiltrate the CIA and reinstate Nixon when, at the exit to Fort Snelling, Peter shouts, "Here—this is mine!"

Rutherford is able to muscle the van onto the ramp and bring it to a stop. Peter hops out, thanking him. "And good luck with the Nixon thing," he says. The clouds are close and ragged. It's getting late, eleven-thirty or so, and a growl of thunder disturbs the air. He hasn't walked half a dozen steps when he hears the voice behind him.

"Looks like you might get wet."

Peter turns. A guy in an orange Volkswagen Fastback is leaning out his window and waving him forward. He must have followed Rutherford up the ramp.

"You heading into the city?"

"That was the idea."

"Toss your bag in the back and give me an address."

Fifteen minutes later he's standing in a steady rain in front of a modest bungalow on a South Minneapolis avenue overhung with elms. He had hoped to have enough money for a night in a motel once he got here—a chance to clean himself up a little before going to see Al about a job at the AP, present himself as a competent professional—but all he has left in his wallet are ten bucks, and he's too tired to start hunting for a dry place to sleep. He rings the doorbell. The rain is coming harder, and he lifts the duffel and rests it on his head. No lights inside. No sounds. He rings the bell again, then he skirts the side of the house and crosses a small back-yard to the garage, which is set against the narrow alley. Locked—both the overhead and side doors. It's nearly midnight. He sets down the big duffel and tries lifting a small side window, but it doesn't yield.

The city center lies forty-some blocks to the north, and he knows he could find a dry place there, one of the university's twenty-four-hour libraries, an apartment building or rooming house vestibule, an all-night laundromat. And between here and there he'd come across churches, bars, and who knows how many other sorts of shelter—but he has no appetite right now for a walk in the rain. He moves to the lee side of the garage, edges up close to it, unzips his duffel, and digs for his waterproof jacket. As he straightens to put it on, a car swings into the alley from the street, its lights bearing down upon him. He lifts a hand to shield his eyes and steps toward the front of the garage, out of the car's path. It swerves, though, jamming on its brakes, and Peter freezes, caught be-tween the car's bumper, half a dozen feet away, and the garage door. Be-hind the windshield the driver's mouth opens wide, and the man laughs, then glances over at a woman in the passenger seat. He cranks down his window.

"You might have called ahead," he says.

AUGUST 13—TUESDAY

nside and out of the rain, Al introduces Peter to his wife, whose expression is not encouraging, then takes him downstairs and installs him in a basement bedroom. Al hasn't changed a lot. His eyes and mouth still telegraph his general belief that off somewhere behind the big curtain they're plotting a cruel joke. He shows Peter a roughed-in bathroom and pulls a clean towel out of the dryer.

"Keep the volume down, if you tune in," he says, pointing at the TV in the corner. "Linda's a light sleeper."

"When did you get married?"

"Last winter."

"Do you think you'll have some work for me?"

"We'll talk in the morning. Hey, maybe you want a shower—you could really use one." He throws him the towel and goes upstairs.

The stream of water is weak and smells like rotten eggs, but at least it's warm, and once Peter's head hits the pillow, he's gone. Next thing he knows, the sun is slipping in through the room's high, small window. He finds Al upstairs at the kitchen table in a T-shirt and boxers, going over copy with a pencil. It's seven o'clock.

"Where's your wife?"

"Starts early. Nurse." He doesn't look up.

"You don't work today?"

"I'm working."

Peter and Al roomed together for a few months at the U in 1970, and Peter knows what he's like in the morning. Good for a nod or a shake of the head, but not much else.

There is coffee on the stove, and the first cupboard door Peter tries produces cups. He pours for himself, then sits at the other side of the table and spends half an hour going through the Minneapolis paper. A story about the Nixon endgame and Haig's role in it, which makes Peter wonder how things turned out for the guy who stepped in. A piece on Ford's address to Congress, in which the new president called inflation the nation's number-one problem. Another on Ma Bell's 21 percent rate hike. And finally, Nolan Ryan's single-game strikeout record, nineteen, in a game from yesterday.

Al sets down his pencil and stabs his big black glasses higher on his nose. "Are you going to sit there and read all morning?"

"Maybe."

"Hey, Linda's fine with you staying downstairs till you get your own place. I mean, if you don't mind the shitty bathroom. It'll probably take a day or two, let's say a week before I can get you started, and then a couple more till your first paycheck."

"That would be perfect. Thank you."

"Better wait before you say that." He takes a sip from his cup, then looks back down at his copy.

"Mind if I use your phone? Long distance?"

Al points toward the dining room, where Peter dials the number, direct, then ducks into a closet, stretching the phone cord to full length. Shuts himself in. Joanie picks up on the second ring, her voice high and taut—probably on her way to work, it's that time.

"It's just me," he says.

"Where *are* you?"

"Minneapolis. At a friend's place."

"Did you take the bus?"

"I hitched."

"Smart."

"The thing is, I forgot my typewriter and I need you to send it, if that's okay. It'll take some work to pack it up." He'd found the Olivetti at a junk shop in the Village, and it has a light, sweet action. "Put some padding around it, if you can, and write 'Handle with Care' on the outside. Could you please do that for me?"

She doesn't respond, but there's another voice behind her, a low-pitched murmur. "Sure, yeah," she says, "if you give me the address. Who is it you're staying with?"

He tells her. "Is Freddy there?"

"Okay, I'm ready."

"Well?"

"No, he's not. Give me the address."

"Actually, you should send it to my dad's place in Battlepoint. I'm heading up there for a few days."

"Careful he doesn't take you off with him."

He gives her the address.

"Oh, and he called here for you last night, your father. He needs to reach you but didn't say why. Said it was important."

"I just told you, that's where I'm heading. Today."

"Give him a call, Peter," she says. There's noise in the background, a shoe sliding along the floor, or a zipper, and Joanie stifles a laugh. "Look, I've really gotta go. I'll be late for work."

"Tell Freddy hi for me," Peter tells her. He leaves the closet, hangs up the phone, and for a minute he stands with his eyes closed, doing what it takes to keep the past where it belongs, bringing to mind instead the next thing, his trip north and the complications it holds—his dad, of course, and the fiasco he's orchestrating, and the son Peter has never met. Who knows what else? When he picks up the phone again and dials his dad's place, Victor is the one who answers, in that flat, nasally voice of his.

"Last Days Ranch."

Peter ducks back into the closet. "Is Dad around? It's me."

There's a clacking sound, Victor setting the phone down, and a minute or two passes before Enoch comes on, out of breath. "Thank the Lord! Joanie must've got hold of you."

"What's going on?"

"Melanie's here. Annie."

"Oh," Peter says. *Of course, that too.* "Why?"

"Maybe you can ask her."

"Doesn't she have a film coming out? Is she alone?"

"All by herself. I think she's AWOL. On the lam."

"You baited her? Geez, Dad."

"She came of her own volition. Peter? Please come home." His dad sounds uncharacteristically small and weak. "Where are you? What's going on with you and Joanie?"

"It's a long story. I'm in Minneapolis, about to start a new job."

"You're between things, then."

"And I'm broke, too. I don't have a way up there."

"What if I wire you something? You could buy a bus ticket."

Peter can't help smiling. "Thanks, but it's not going to work right now."

A pause as Enoch draws a breath. "How about if I wire a thousand bucks? It's all I can scrape together. You can go out and buy a car, a decent one—a few years old—and have something left besides." He coughs. "Melanie would love to see you."

Peter covers the mouthpiece and calls to Al in the kitchen. "Nearest Western Union?"

"Forty-third and Chicago. A mile from here."

"Dad?" Peter is careful to modulate his voice. "Yeah, that might work."

"You'll drive up?"

"I might be able to come for a few days. Until this new job starts."

"Good. Is there a Western Union close by?"

"In fact, I think there is."

In the kitchen, he pours himself another cup of coffee and drinks it on his feet, leaning against the cupboard. He can't even guess what it's going to be like, seeing Annie again, though he knows whatever they might have seen in each other has been worn down to nothing. That's what life does. Why has she come back, though? Surely not for the end of the world. It must be to see their son—though with her resources, she could arrange such a thing on her own, couldn't she? But of course it doesn't matter, because if she's actually there—if Enoch isn't pulling a stunt—then Peter's luck has changed again.

Hollywood meets the American apocalypse.

Al looks up from his work. "You look pleased with yourself."

"There's this story I need to get started on. This week."

"Fill me in."

"No, I don't want to jinx myself." In fact, he doesn't want to say too much and risk that Al insist on coming along. There is no one with fewer scruples than a writer with ambition.

"I'm the one giving you a job, man. Tell me what you've got."

"How about if I give you the general idea, see what you think." Peter sits down across from him at the table. "Let's say there's a guy who runs a religious commune and he believes that Christ is coming back."

"Half the country believes that. Is this somebody people have heard of?"

"Nope."

"He's a nobody."

"That's right. But let's say that he claims to know the date."

"How far out?"

"August 19th. Next Monday."

"You know this character?"

"Sort of. Yes."

"It's thin." Al flaps his lips like a horse and shakes his head. "There was this wing nut down in Oklahoma a few years back. My first posting with the AP. Same sort of deal, and one of our guys did a little piece on him. A few regional dailies ran it, but mostly it got buried. And none of the networks followed up—not even with the pics we took. Prophet beard, crazy eyes. Think John Brown. No. Too much big shit in the news right now, no chance of breaking through."

"I think you're wrong," Peter says. "Think about it. Two years of deception and dissembling at the highest levels—people's trust in the system gone to hell—and here's a guy who says God's coming back to put an end to it all. The timing is perfect."

"Nobody's going to listen, Peter." Al takes off his glasses and squints across the table, he's at the end of his patience.

Peter says, "Best-selling book of the year so far—you know what it is?"

"Nope."

"*The Late Great Planet Earth.* Millions of copies. People are going to listen, trust me."

Al lifts his hands in surrender. "Okay, fine, give it a try."

"There's more," Peter says.

Al rocks his head to one side, touching an ear to his shoulder. His spine crackles. His mouth stretches into a bland, tolerant smile.

"Let's say a Hollywood actress, first rank, has flown in to be here with the prophet, waiting for the end. Academy Award winner. Young and gorgeous."

Al blinks. "Now you're yanking my chain. Who?"

"I can't tell you that."

"Why not?"

"I promised my source I wouldn't say a word."

"And nobody else knows?"

"That's right."

"So this girl, this actress, she's all by herself? Without her entourage? She's not waiting for the right moment to let her publicist turn on the lights? Doesn't sound legit."

"She's alone. Her agent and her publicist, the film's director and producers, her manager—apparently none of them knows where she is. As far as I know, she's prepping herself for the Rapture."

"Where's this happening?"

"I can't say."

"How long does it take to get there?"

"A few hours."

"Maybe I should drive you."

"No. There's a guy inside who can wiggle me in. But only if I'm alone."

"You need a vehicle? Money?"

"I'm working that out."

"You need a lift someplace?"

"I will in a couple hours."

"Okay, then," Al says.

In the other room Peter dials Joanie's number once more, then ducks into the closet as Freddy's voice comes on the line. A plain "Hello?"

"Joanie left for work already?" Peter says.

"Look, man, it's not like you think."

"Here's the deal," Peter says. "Over the next forty-eight hours I want you to watch the AP wire. Carefully." He exits the closet, returns the receiver to its cradle, and goes down in the basement to put his things together. *Here I come, Dad,* he thinks—and without any guilt, or at least not much. Because it's clear that his old man is using Melanie to reel Peter in, willing fish that he is.

t's the human problem in miniature, a metaphor of the divide between God and man, soul and body. Jesus is on his way, almost here, and Enoch—light-bearer, herald of the New Day—is managing sewage.

He's been outside working since Peter's phone call, helping Felix, Victor, and the bald man from Wisconsin, Jed, rough up walls for the showers and latrines. Now they're hanging corrugated-steel siding on the studs, and though the air is still cool—it's only 9:30—the men are down to their T-shirts and sweating. Yesterday they poured the concrete slab, ran a waterline from the house and a line of clay tile in the trench that connects the new latrines to the existing septic field. Felix's idea. "Long term, might be a problem with overload," he said. "We'd have to expand your system. But we're looking at less than a week, so I don't see an issue." The boy is smart. By evening, everything should be operational.

The number of tents in the oak grove has grown since last night, and people have been bathing in the lake, soap suds now staining the shoreline white. This morning, early, Enoch spotted a man ducking behind a clutch of red willows with a roll of toilet paper in his hand. The smell of the Magnussen hogs is constant, of course, and Enoch has adapted to it. But last night in bed, his window open, he couldn't help but notice another, spinier scent in the air.

"Did you make a count this morning?" he asks Victor.

"Yes. Two more since yesterday. Old couple from South Dakota. They're sleeping in the back of their truck. That red GMC with the topper."

"What've we got then? Thirty?"

"Twenty-eight."

"When you get a chance, let everybody know we're going to meet for worship tonight. Seven thirty in the aviary. And put a notice on the board, too." He leans over and says into Victor's ear, "You haven't seen Melanie, have you?"

Victor glances toward the granary and shakes his head.

"She'd rather people don't know she's here. You understand, right?"

Victor straightens and frowns, his expression saying, *What do you take me for?*

As Enoch heads toward the house to fetch ice water, the boy Felix follows after him and takes hold of his arm. "Can we talk, you and me?" He looks serious, a deep crease in his forehead. They settle in the porch chairs, and Enoch waits as Felix crosses his skinny arms and glares at the floor, the sun catching the sparse whiskers that sprout from his chin. Apparently, he has never thought to apply a razor to himself.

"I better just come out and say it," he says, finally. "Connie—well, me and her have been sleeping together in my tent."

"I figured as much." Enoch knows he ought to be more interested than he is—in the transgression, in Felix's remorse—but he finds it hard to summon the called-for moral authority. "What do you want to say about it?" he asks.

"I'm sorry?" Felix shrugs, lifts his palms in a gesture of helplessness.

"Are you?"

"I mean, what if me and Connie don't get Raptured? She says we're going to be stuck here for the seven years of tribulation when the Devil rules the earth."

"Yes, well, Satan will have a free hand, once we're taken up."

The boy's eyes are like targets at a shooting range. "That's what'll happen to us?"

Enoch looks out across his long front yard to the woods on the other side of the township road where the aspens are still in full leaf, most of the birch trees, too. The straight trunks of the Norway pines offer a pattern of vertical red bars against the green. The skies are clear, nothing up there now except a few high, floating clouds in the blue. Such a gorgeous world! Enoch has never seen the Lord's coming as a means of escape, the way some do. Even now it's difficult to think of leaving—and more difficult to reckon with the idea of Hell: eternal, unquenchable fire. It's always been this way for him. He has rarely preached on the subject. Nonetheless, he accepts the words of scripture as Truth, and they promise that in God's absence the powers of darkness will have free reign. *And there shall be a time of trouble, such as never was.*

"Sir?"

He should let Felix wriggle and twist, but with the beauty of life pressing hard, the boy's sin seems like a paltry thing. "Felix, do you believe what you're doing is wrong?"

A heavy sigh. "I guess so."

"How do you justify yourself?"

"How do I what?"

"Why are you doing it?"

Something passes through the boy's face, making it harder. He sets his teeth together. "It makes me a little angry, Christ coming back before I have much of a chance to, you know, do that sorta thing."

"Yes, I'd feel the same if I were eighteen. But what about Connie?"

"What do you mean?"

"This isn't only about you, is it?"

"We love each other."

"Now listen. Here's what I think. You and Connie should repent for what you've done, then ask God if He will consider the two of you married in His sight. If you do that, I believe He will honor your request."

It takes a moment for the words to fix in the boy's brain, but then a smile grows on his face, and he jumps up from his chair. "I'll go tell her," he says, and he runs to the steps and leaps to the ground below. Then he stops, turns, and comes back up, walking now, deliberate. He puts out his long, narrow hand to shake.

A quarter of an hour later Enoch, after balancing his accounts, is backing the Cougar out of the machine shed as Sarah crosses from barn to granary with a covered plate. He stops and leans across the seat to crank down the passenger window and flag her down. "Is she doing all right this morning?" he asks.

Sarah comes over and bends down. "I'm about to find out."

"Keep an eye on her, please."

As he watches Sarah disappear inside, he remembers his dream last night, sparked no doubt by his conversation with Melanie yesterday, the details and images strange, as if part of some other man's life. Everyone involved, of course, with the exception of Melanie, has been gone for years: Ruth, whose face lost all color as he carried Annie's body into the kitchen, and who wouldn't stop saying, "The hospital, the hospital." Gerald Magnussen, who charged in having witnessed the stomping from the top of his silo, and took one look at the crater in his daughter's chest before sweeping her up and running for his car. And Dr. Young, Sylvie's husband, who after more than an hour materialized from the emergency room, explaining that Annie was fine, she had sustained no injury, that the bull's hoof had merely given her a "thump in the solar plexus." The doctor's words struck Gerald like a hammer, and he fell to his knees.

Enoch heads down the driveway and turns onto the township road toward Battlepoint, where he needs to pick up more sheet metal screws to hang the steel. As he drives, he can't help but wonder how much Melanie really wants to be here, and why. Or how much she simply wants to be gone from the place she left.

The quiche is airy and jam-packed with healthy things like broccoli and peppers and mushrooms and spinach. Sarah sits close by, making small talk—sweet Sarah, her presence comforting—and after she leaves, Melanie remains in bed, eyes closed, face exposed to window light, hardly daring to breathe out of hope she has been cured, rewarded for the strength she mustered last night, the first night in months that she didn't break down and give in to her need. The cadence of pain is absent from the base of her skull, her body's temperature stable, the crouching man gone from behind the walls and doors. She holds herself still, hands upon her heart, aware of a pleasant buzzing in the soles of her feet.

She sleeps again.

When she wakes, the sun is low and God has fled. Her limbs feel thick, swollen, sore, as if filled with mercury. Her back and breasts are damp, her throat as dry as gravel. The old knot of grief has lodged in the place her spine meets her brain, and the little man is hunkered in the bathroom, or possibly lying in wait beneath the bed, sucking energy from her mind for his good pleasure. When she finally musters the courage to haul herself into the bathroom, she swallows two pills, climbs into the bathtub, and fills it to her neck, inhaling steam and wondering what it would be like to slide under the surface and breathe water. Is there any pain in drowning? She read somewhere there is not, though in fact she doesn't want to die, not really—at least not by her own hand. She thinks about her son, imagining what sort of boy he's grown into and picturing his dear face: squarish, with a fine brow like her own, Peter's straight long nose, and the molded lips of a thinker.

Tomorrow—think of it! Is she going to recognize him? Will he recognize her? Have his parents explained things to him? Does he have the capacity to forgive? The idea of her son's censure is enough to make her lungs shrivel in her chest, and she covers her face with her hands and allows herself to cry, ashamed of the self-indulgence she hears in her sobs. "What am I doing?" she asks.

The room is nearly dark, and the bathwater has cooled. The pain at the back of her head all but gone. She reaches forward to open the drain, rises, and wraps herself in a towel. As she steps from the tub, a sound penetrates the walls—an orchestra of undisciplined voices and the strident chords of an upright piano, a hymn she remembers from childhood, before the accident, when she went to Enoch's meetings with her mom. It starts slowly then rises in volume and tempo, urged ahead by the beat of a single drum. The effect is stirring, the voices loud enough now that she can make out the lyrics of the chorus: *There is power, power, wonder-working power in the precious Blood of the Lamb.*

Again and again.

She pulls on a pair of Levis, drapes herself in a baggy, lightweight sweater, then wrestles the dark wig into place, pulling lanks of it forward to obscure her forehead and cheeks. In the bathroom, she effaces the color and shape of her lips with light foundation, then applies a heavy liner to her eyes. Finished, she regards herself in the mirror. A gloomy, innocent girl-witch.

"Who are you?" she asks.

In the haymow of the old barn, twenty-five or thirty holy revelers, some jumping or dancing, others lying on the plank floor, some reaching in the air, clutching for heaven. Sarah's hands leap and fall above the keyboard, while next to her a kid in a pageboy cut alternately slaps and strokes his guitar. Someone, somewhere, is beating on a bongo drum. At the front, Enoch worships as if alone, arms at his sides, and at the rear, apart from the others, Victor Stubblefield shuffle-dances in a tight pattern, back and forth, like an addled child. Melanie can't help but lift her hands and add her own voice to the choir. Then Sarah shifts into a minor key, launching into something urgent and strange, a melody that brings to mind the Magi on camels, a soundtrack for the arrival of a new age. Melanie works her way into the middle of the hairy, denim-clad worshippers, giving herself up to the Spirit as pigeons and swallows arc and loop through the air above. She sings and whirls, intermittently remembering to put a hand on her head to hold her hair in place. She struts and cries and laughs, she marches in step with the saints around her. And when she's used up, her insides as clean as polished glass, she slips to the floor and waits for the end—for stillness and silence, which, when it comes, Enoch fills up with his voice. He talks about Daniel and Jonah, and then about old King Nebuchadnezzar, struck down and munching on grass. He warns of the coming whirlwind.

Melanie remains in place long after he has finished, sitting hunched on the floor, face in her hands, dead to every touch and query until all have drifted away. When Enoch bends close to ask if she is all right, she simply nods.

He leaves, too.

The floor is cool beneath her. She can hear crickets. The pigeons in the rafters are quiet now, settled. A breeze enters through the big front mow door, which is propped open and through which she can see the moon, nearly full. She swivels her head, testing for pain, works a hand beneath her sweater and lays it on her chest, which is dry. Her palms are dry too, her fingers steady. She looks all around, searching the edges of the room, but with no sense of anyone crouching there, trying to pry into her mind. Finally, she gets up from the floor and goes down the stairs and outside, where the grass in the pasture is already moist with dew.

She walks past the rock pile and down along the lake, its surface rippled and moving. A small wind blows in from the south. She goes all the way to the board-and-wire fence at her brother's property line, then follows it uphill into the oak grove, the closest tents just twenty or thirty yards to her left. She hears voices, but they're quiet, someone humming a tuneless melody. To the west, her old place. A low-slung hog barn, new since she left here, and the white clapboard farmhouse, still in need of paint. The reek of pigs. She remembers the clothes her dad always left in the mudroom on his way in from the barn, which in turn makes her think of the way he ruled the house, shouting orders from his arm chair, or from his place at the head of the table: *Get me some coffee. Grab me a beer. Clean your plate. Go feed the piggies. Shut your goddamn pie-holes, I'm trying to think.* Every morning after barn chores she bathed herself and dressed in clothes that she sprayed with perfume from the Battle-point dime store, then rode the bus to school with children from other farms, barn stink clinging to their bodies. She swore that she would never smell like they did, never be mocked by the town kids. And she never was.

As she starts back across the oak grove, giving the tents a wide berth, she spots someone leaving Enoch's house from the back door and moving north across the pasture. She can't help but recognize the even stride, head gliding like a balloon above the tall body. He stops next to the old Farmall tractor, which is parked near the rock pile, and leans against a big rear tire, where he stretches, lifting an arm and latching it over the top of his skull, elbow pointing at the sky. Melanie pauses to watch him. A match flares. Then the orange dot of light. Soon she catches the faint acrid smell. He's gazing off toward the water, meditative, and though Melanie wants to withdraw, hunch down, hide, instead she finds herself moving toward him—*What am I doing?*—and stopping short just yards away. Holding her breath.

And now she's caught by the light of his face, turning. His alertness like a force field, so familiar. He shakes his head.

"What?" she says.

"Hi, Annie."

"It's Melanie."

"I know." His voice is low and raw, less buoyant than she remembers. He's had a hard time of things, and too many cigarettes.

"Why did you come, Peter?"

He drops his smoke and steps on it, moving toward her. She accepts the embrace he offers without returning it and without allowing herself to feel it. "Good question. How about you?"

Seeing him finally, being in his presence, she knows she hasn't come here to recover the part of her life he took away from her. She doesn't even want to think about it, not when she might be close to breaking free of her cage, close to letting God back in. "Maybe it's better if we wait till morning," she says. "I'm beat."

He shakes a cigarette from the pack, lights up, and offers it, same as he used to do. It smells different from the Gitanes Morris always smokes, stronger. She puts it to her lips and draws tentatively, watching Peter watch her. She hasn't smoked in years, except for pot sometimes. He lights one for himself, eyes squinting in the match flame, then, as if time never passed, he touches her arm and leads her around the back of the tractor to the rock pile, which rises to five or six feet at its peak. He goes over and plucks the cushion from the tractor seat and places it on a flat stone halfway up and helps her navigate the climb, then takes his own perch beside her.

"You always had a certain way of smoking," he says.

"What way was that?"

"You held it right here"—he presses a finger to the center of his lips— "and puckered up, like you were kissing it. See? You're doing it now. And you never inhaled."

"Sure I did."

Peter looks back toward the house, and she does too, in time to see a light blink off in a second-floor window.

"I tried reaching you, all that first summer," he tells her. "I called your friends. Becky, Julianne, Sarah. None of them knew a thing. I called Dad and Mom, too, and sent letters, asked them to forward them on. I even called your dad, who hung up on me. If I'd had any idea where you were, I would've left my team and come there straight away. I would have made my case." He stops to exhale a long stream.

She wants to blame him, hold him responsible. Doesn't she have that right? Wasn't he the older one, the one who should have known better? Isn't he the man? "But you didn't," she says.

"No, and I shouldn't have given up." He takes a long pull from the cigarette wedged into the *V* of his fingers and holds it for a long time before saying, "I'm sorry," through a cloud of smoke. His mouth is flat and troubled, with significant lines on either side. The creases in his forehead make him look older than he is.

"I wrote you, too," she says.

"What?" His eyes snap.

"It wasn't hard, I knew where you were. I found the address."

"I never got them."

"I know you didn't. Your dad asked your manager to destroy them. He told me yesterday."

"Son of a bitch!" Peter gets up from the rock he's on and steps down into the grass, tosses away his cigarette. "Shit." He drops to the ground and folds up, knees out, ankles crossed, elbows tucked into his stomach.

"I know." In spite of herself, she climbs down and sits at the edge of the pile and puts a hand on his hair, lightly. It's warm to the touch, and thick. It's like petting a cat.

He says, "The thing is, it always made such perfect sense to me."

"What did?"

"The way you left, without saying anything. And Skinny telling me you wanted nothing to do with me. It seemed right, exactly what I had coming."

"Why?" she says.

"Because what I did was wrong, and you were right to leave, put me and everything else behind you."

"Nothing's ever behind us, Peter. Isn't that half the problem?"

He lights two more cigarettes and hands one up to her. "You were going to tell me what you're doing out here. Don't you have a film coming out? Shouldn't you be taking care of business?"

"I suppose I should be." She thinks of her mom in Palm Springs and wonders if she's tried making contact. Dottie would have given it a few days, then run out of patience and tried to reach Sarah, whose number is unlisted. A couple of phone calls to old acquaintances would be enough to let her know that Sarah doesn't live in Minneapolis, as Melanie's been telling her. At that point Dottie would hand off to Adam. "Your problem," she'd say, and Adam would book a flight to Minnesota. Which is fine, because Melanie can deal with Adam.

"If you don't want to talk about it, that's okay," Peter says.

She has to take a breath, get some oxygen.

"You all right?" he asks.

"Nobody's going to drag me back out there and turn my bones to mush."

Peter says nothing—a strength of his. A weakness, too.

"I got a call from Sarah last week. Sarah Petersen, you remember her. Sarah Levitz now. She and Jimmy are living in one of the apartments here. She's the one who told me what's going on, what Enoch said on the radio."

Peter shakes his head.

"You think he's lost his mind."

"It's more complicated than that."

Melanie says, "Don't most people think it's going to happen anyway? So why not now? It's in the Bible, after all. Christ Himself spoke of it."

"And my old man speaks for Christ? No, he's joining a long line of fools."

Melanie tosses away her cigarette, orange flecks of light in the darkness. "Or making fools of us all. I don't care what people say, not after what Enoch did for me. And I don't care if it makes me a fool."

Peter tips back his head and blows a perfect smoke ring, then looks over quickly, like a boy hoping for praise.

She says, "Don't you believe any longer?"

He watches her for a moment. "I really can't say. I only know that when I think of trying to pray, something closes like a door inside me. A door made out of lead. It's the same feeling I get around my dad."

"I'm sorry" is all she can say, though she wishes there were more.

"It's okay," he tells her, and they're quiet for a while.

"I'm here too because of our son," she says, watching his face. "As soon as Sarah told me, that's what I thought of. Didn't you?"

"Not till Dad said something."

"But aren't you curious? Even a little?"

"I'm not ready."

"It's been fifteen years."

"I was planning on eighteen. That's what I was told."

She is aware of the nicotine quickening her senses, rousing her, the stars above so sharp she has to shield her eyes, the crickets deafening, their trilling drone crashing in her ears. Her hands are steady, too, and when Peter holds out his pack of smokes and she takes another, her thumb and index finger connect on the first try. He lights it for her.

"Don't you wonder what he looks like?" she asks.

Peter waits before responding. "Sort of. In my mind, though, his face is always a blank, like he's wearing a nylon stocking over his head. I can't see him." He knocks a fist against his skull, something he would have done when he was a boy. "What if he hates me?"

"Yeah. I worry it's too much to lay on a kid that age. 'Hey, we're your *real* mom and dad.'"

From the west, where the tents are pitched, comes a muffled, ecstatic groan then another, followed by a voice: "Shh, quiet." Melanie looks down, as if the crack in propriety is her own fault.

Peter says, "All this waiting, what are they supposed to do with themselves?"

"You still haven't told me why *you're* here," she says.

He pushes up from the ground, goes to one knee, and reaches past her to snub out his cigarette on a rock. Then he puts a hand on her shoulder and rises to sit beside her, close, his warmth comforting—that old trick of his, using his body as an excuse for not saying what he doesn't want to say, as cover for what makes him uncomfortable.

"This new movie of yours. You're playing the same role again, right? The girl who married the soldier."

Smooth, she thinks, pivoting to a subject she can't resist—though she's beyond cynical when it comes to those who yank her strings and the system that yanks theirs. "It's not a bad film. You don't want to hear about it."

"I do."

"Okay. It's set eight years after the first one. My character has earned a degree in international relations, and she's working for this U.N.-like group. Her husband is still in the Army, a desk job at the Pentagon. But this one's not about duty, honor, and country. No flag waving. The Soviet Union takes out an American jet over Poland, and the U.S. President throws down the nuclear gauntlet. It looks like World War III—except Mandy has this friend in the Russian embassy who lets her know the public story is miles from the truth, and she has to work through Pentagon back channels to avert war."

"And it's called what—*World's End*?"

She laughs.

"Unbelievable. Your folks in the studio are going to love this, aren't they?" He gestures toward the tents.

"They don't know a thing."

"Seriously."

"If they get wind of it, which they might, fine. But that's not what I'm doing here, Peter. And you still haven't answered my question." She looks at him straight on, his face a foot away. "I saw a couple of stories in the paper when you were playing in the coast league. And Sarah told me you went to college for a while, then out to New York. I totally believed you were going to be a big-league star."

He lifts his shoulders and drops them.

"What happened?"

"It's what never happened. I never had the talent. I could hit the ball, but my glove-work sucked. And I was slow. If the designated hitter rule had come along six years ago, I might've had a chance."

She hears the disgust in his voice, the self-loathing, and can't help wishing that she had been around to help him. A silly impulse, as if she hasn't matured since she was fifteen.

"I went to the U of M and studied journalism. Figured I would learn how to write, make some kind of mark that way. I have to make a mark, right? But it turns out writing takes longer to learn than baseball. Or at least it's harder. I've got a knack for picking things I'm not cut out for."

"You're still at it?"

"I guess so."

"And living in New York?"

"Minneapolis. I just moved."

"What are you working on?"

"It doesn't matter." He stands, apparently finished, then reaches out and pulls her to her feet. His hands are sure of themselves.

"Our lives have been so different," Melanie says. "I didn't have to do a thing. Mom hauled me around to auditions, and I read what they told me to read. It all fell at my feet. People look at me and see what they need to see, whatever they're hoping for, and it makes them feel better. But it's a curse, too. Because I'm a million people, not myself at all."

They stand facing each other, the pressure of Peter's eyes deflecting hers toward the lake, the moon trembling there on the black, rippled surface. If only she could tell him more about herself—not that he would understand. She understands him, though, with his longings so unlike her own. He's a lamp, trying to shine a light even as the wind keeps blowing out its flame. She's a wide, clean window through which the sun pours light on those in need of it. She presses a hand on his stomach, and he steps close and puts his arms around her. He smells like sweat and stale clothes.

"I feel like I did on the day Mom took me away from here," she says. "The day after you graduated, remember? She hadn't told me anything, I didn't know we were leaving. But when I woke up that morning and looked around my room, I knew I wouldn't see it again."

"How?"

"I don't know. And your dad? He's right, I'm quite certain of it."

Peter shakes his head but doesn't argue, God bless him. He says, "I wouldn't do anything to hurt you, Melanie."

"Anything that isn't necessary, you mean."

"No," he says. "Anything."

He's afraid he won't do the right thing in the morning, that with a night's rest and a clear head his self-interest will be too strong. That's why he goes straight to the phone in his dad's kitchen and dials the number. As it rings, he pulls a chair from the table and sits, receiver pressed against one ear, the scent of her hair and skin still in his nose. He's trying not to lose it—the orangey smell of her fragrance, whatever it is, and beneath that, something earthier, like a sand beach in a hot sun.

"Hello?" Al's voice is quiet, anticipating trouble.

"I know it's late. Sorry."

"Peter? What the hell?"

A freshwater beach.

"Things aren't working out like I planned."

"Okay."

"I got some bad information."

"Meaning what, your actress didn't show up?"

Peter makes a sound with his throat between a cough and a yes.

"And she isn't going to?"

"It's unlikely, no."

"Unlikely, or no?"

"No."

"No story, then."

"Probably not one you'd be interested in."

"Come back, then. I'll get you started on something else."

"Will do."

Instead of going up to bed, Peter goes outside, climbs into the car he bought this morning at a car lot in South Minneapolis, a '66 Ford Galaxie 500, and drives into Battlepoint where he buys a fifth of Jameson at the off-sale counter at the back of the Valhalla, the only action in town this time of night. The woman who waits on him looks familiar. Pipe-cleaner arms, hollow eyes, dyed-black hair, white at the roots. The mother of a high school friend, Larry Bottineau, who played left field on the baseball team. She always brought snacks to their practices. Potato chips, Rice Krispie bars. She doesn't recognize him.

In his old room he opens the whiskey, fills the tumbler he brought from the kitchen, and climbs into bed. What was it Melanie said tonight? *Nobody's going to drag me back out there and turn my bones to mush.*

After that, what was he supposed to do?

AUGUST 14—WEDNESDAY

noch's last time behind the microphone, his last chance to reach
an audience beyond the few locals who attend his meetings. He's
sitting in the glass-walled sound studio of KROW–Battlepoint,
crimson *live* bulb glowing above the door, and yet he finds himself only
half-focused on his message. He narrates the vision again: female envoy
and fourteen sunsets, the great wind and bodies rising. He recalls the
pointless rebellion of Jonah. He reads from First Thessalonians: "And the
dead in Christ shall rise first: then we which are alive and remain shall be
caught up together with them in the clouds." And from Revelation about
the great tribulation to follow: "And I stood upon the sand of the sea,
and saw a beast rise up out of the sea, having seven heads and ten horns,"
reminding those listening not to forget the unprecedented upheaval occurring even now in the nation's capital, a duly elected president forced
from office. Not to mention the recent Mideast wars. Or the godless, de-
structive will of nuclear Russia. Gog and Magog.

As he speaks, though, Enoch can't help thinking of Willie, waiting
to be picked up this afternoon, and excoriating himself for the promise
of a car he made to the boy, an artless bribe that Willie will no doubt see

for what it is, once he arrives at the ranch. *Here's a car to drive—until next Monday when we're all enveloped by the Whirlwind.* How foolish! Puny. An act of cowardice and deceit, an insult to Providence. What was he thinking? And who's to say Willie wouldn't have wanted to come anyway, without the ruse of a gift? Of course, the only thing to do now is level with him immediately, give him the chance to back out.

He gathers up his notes and Bible and takes his leave, brushing past station manager Ernie Hobert as he goes. The Cougar, freshly waxed and gleaming, is parked out front—and standing in front of it, hands folded as if making a plea, face as white as rotting fish, is Dave Drobec.

The money, Enoch thinks.

The thousand dollars he wired Peter yesterday wiped out most of his savings, and the four hundred and change he owes the lumberyard will do the same to his checking account. His Social Security payment isn't due for another week. Moot point. And how much was it Dave asked for? Twenty-five hundred?

"How are you, Dave?"

"I'm good, good," he says, nodding fast, moistening his lips, his eyes blinking behind the heavy lenses.

"You look like you swallowed a nail."

"I just wanted to touch base about our conversation the other day. Sunday."

"When you tried blackmailing me?"

"That's not how I meant it. I'm sorry."

"You don't want the money?"

"No, and I shouldn't have asked. I'm here to say I'm sorry. I'm not interested in the money or the farm."

"You're not?"

"Just forget about it." Dave's eyes are wide, too much white showing around the irises.

"What changed your mind?"

He shakes his head and backs away, arms raised. "Nothing."

"Tell me."

"Please, forget about it." Dave turns and half-runs, half-walks toward his car, which is parked a block up the street. He trips on his own feet, stumbles, and catches himself. Enoch remembers the look on Dave's face on Sunday—his slackening mouth and popping eyes when he sensed Victor's presence behind him and turned.

"Dave!" Enoch shouts, and the man stops.

Enoch walks up to him. Dave has taken off his wire-rim glasses, and he's polishing the lenses with a handkerchief. He squints.

"Did Victor talk to you?"

"No, no."

"Really?"

"I have to go." Dave turns again and heads for his car.

"What did he say?"

Without slowing, Dave lifts a hand and swats at the air.

Enoch walks back to the Cougar, falls into the deep bucket seat, and sits there, hands resting on the leather-wrapped wheel. He doesn't know if he should praise God or plead clemency on behalf of Victor, whose cast-iron sense of right and wrong occasionally puts him at odds with civil behavior. He can't help but remember last year when a boy from a neighboring farm came calling on a single girl who lived briefly in one of the apartments, a pretty one named Becky on whom Victor had imprinted himself, unrequitedly. When the boy stepped out of his car that night, Victor intercepted him, stuck the barrel of his .22 varmint gun in his face, and told him to leave. The next day Skinny Magnussen showed up in his role as deputy sheriff, and Enoch found himself bearing false witness, something he had never done before.

"There was no rifle," Enoch told Skinny. "The boy is mistaken."

God forgive me.

He checks his watch, making a mental note to talk with Victor. Loyalty is one thing, and Enoch is aware that he takes Victor's for granted. But threatening somebody—and God only knows how and with what— that's something entirely different. When Enoch finally turns the ignition key, nothing happens. No grinding of the starter, not even a solenoid click. He removes the key, reinserts it, and turns it again. Silence. If he's going to make it to Fargo by noon, as he promised Willie, he needs to leave now. "Get thee behind me, Satan," he says, before trying once more.

The Cougar has never failed to start, and Enoch has been meticulous about maintenance, preemptively replacing components that tend to fail: water pump, belts and hoses, spark plug wires, brake shoes. In the spring, for good measure, he had Toby install a new battery, even though the old one had a year left in it. One part he has not replaced, though, is the starter. He gets out and pops the hood and leans over the engine, running his fingers along the battery cables, tugging to make sure the connectors are tight on their posts. Just to be sure, he gets a crescent wrench from the trunk and snugs them up. Then he follows the wire down to the starter and checks that connection, too. After laying his hands on the motor and offering a prayer, he tries again, without success.

Deluxe Auto is three blocks east, and he finds Toby Trask in the repair bay, hunched beneath a filthy pickup truck and knocking away on the transmission housing with a large spanner. Enoch has to shout to get his attention, and Toby stoops out from under the truck. He reaches under his leather skullcap to scratch at his scalp, grins. "You're supposed to be hunkered down, waiting for God."

"That's not till next week. Meantime I've got things to do. Not to mention a little problem I need your help with." He explains about the Cougar and tells him he needs to drive to Fargo.

"The starter, you think?"

"Best guess."

"Any clicking sound when you turn the key?"

"Nope."

"This one I've gotta finish." He jerks his thumb at the hoisted truck. "But you're next. And if it's like you say, it oughta be a snap. Dick should have the part, and I can get her in after lunch, have her done by two, three o'clock. Then you can be on your way."

"What'll it set me back?"

"Let's see." Toby rubs his beard with a grease-blackened hand. "Parts and labor, ninety-five bucks. Assuming, of course, it's the starter. Tow, another fifteen." He raises his brow. "Are we good?"

"You wouldn't have a loaner I could use—right now? I've got an errand to run."

Toby points at a rusty AMC Matador parked out front beside the gas pumps. "I mean, if you don't mind driving that shit heap. Pardon my French."

They go into the office for the key to the loaner, but Toby moves to block the door before Enoch can leave. "I saw those tents in your pasture, under the trees. Lots of folks getting their hopes up, and probably more on the way. Coming from all over, I take it."

"They are."

"Can't help wondering, though. Let's say nothing happens next week. Then what?"

"It's going to happen next week, Toby."

"But if it doesn't."

"I'd have to apologize."

"That's it?" He screws up his face in a way that gives Enoch pause. None of the pushback so far has struck him like Toby's simple question.

"No," Enoch says, "that's not it, not by a long shot. It would be the end of me. I don't know how I would go on."

"But you would." Toby winks, steps out of the way, and suddenly there's a catch in Enoch's lungs, as if he's taken on water, inhaled a bug. He gags, slaps at his own chest. Toby gets behind him and clubs his back with a fist, nearly knocking Enoch to the floor.

"You okay?"

Enoch is bent over, supporting himself with an arm against the wall. "Doing the best . . . I can," he says, between hacks. A true-enough thing. The room is blurry with his tears.

"Are you sure?"

"It's nothing." He straightens, clears his throat, and fills up his lungs, which seem fine now, a little gravelly. "I'm good."

"Hey, I heard about your trip to the hospital. Glad it turned out the way it did." He takes Enoch's arm, like he would an old man's, and walks him out to the loaner. Carefully, he places the key in Enoch's palm. "See you this afternoon," he says.

The Matador is balky, the transmission slow to engage, the engine hesitant when he touches the gas, but he makes it in one piece to Sylvie's place, where he has to ring the bell three times. She's wearing her chenille bathrobe and her hair is up in a towel. She looks past him at the strange car in her driveway, then back into his eyes.

"Are you on the run? You look terrible."

"You look wet."

"A swim and then a shower. What's wrong?"

Enoch touches his face. "I look that bad?"

"You do. I was going to make some cookies. Can you stay?"

"I'm sorry, I can't."

She takes his arm and pulls him into the living room and deposits him in a stuffed chair. Then walks into her bedroom, shedding her robe as she goes and hanging it on the bedpost. "You're troubled," she says. He watches through the open door as she dresses, all the while facing him—bra and panties, jeans, short-sleeved blouse, sandals—not the least bit shy about herself. "You're not going to tell me?"

He says nothing, and she crosses her eyes at him.

"Aren't you picking up Willie today? And what are you doing with that ugly car out there?"

"Mine's getting fixed. Toby says he'll be done by two or three, and then I'm leaving."

"What's bothering you?"

"Once I bring him back here, and he sees what's going on, he's going to feel manipulated."

"Duh. Didn't I tell you that? The Cougar is the least of it. Think for a minute—a fifteen-year-old boy walking into a situation like you've got. Not to mention meeting his biological parents for the first time. But you'll figure it out, I have no doubt. That's your specialty."

"*What* is?"

She circles around behind his chair and starts massaging his scalp. "Convincing people that you're not trying to manipulate them."

"Whoa." He smiles, though—he and Sylvie have been through this before. "If there's a fire," he says, "and somebody screams fire, what do you call that? Manipulation?"

"Don't play dumb. I mean the part where you're not telling the whole truth."

"Sometimes you can't."

"The ends justify the means?"

"In this case, yes."

She sighs, then comes around and sits in the chair next to him. "How's Melanie?"

"She doesn't seem very well."

"And Peter—is he back?"

"Yesterday."

"And I suppose they've taken up where they left off."

"I can only guess. They spent a long while talking last night."

"How do you do it, Enoch? Get everybody to jump when you say jump?"

"It isn't me."

"There's one thing I don't get, though," she says. "Why is it so important that everybody comes back here? Why do they need to be here with you? Isn't it supposed to come down to what a person believes?"

"Yes, but in my dream they were here. At least Peter was. All of them, I think."

"And what about me?"

He takes her hand and looks in her eyes. "I remember the feeling of being surrounded by the people I love. And I love you."

She makes a sad face. "That's not much to go on."

"Just be there," he says, aware that he sounds irritable and short. He glances at his watch.

"So serious today." She scowls at him. "What are you here for, anyway?"

"Money," he says, and quickly explains about the thousand dollars to Peter, the cost of installing the showers and latrines, and now the hundred and ten it'll take to get the Cougar running again. He doesn't like to be in this position, and he's not blind to its irony. But if he has to be indebted to somebody, Sylvie's the one.

"Won't that make me a culpable party?" she asks.

He leans over and gives her a kiss. "You're in way over your head already."

"Oh, God," she says.

When Peter wakes, a high sun is lighting the room and making the lion skin glow like a mythic fleece where it hangs on the wall. The hammering Armageddon inside his brain has given way to a small, pulsing nuisance. The bottle of Jameson on the nightstand is nearly half-empty. Earlier, he got up and swallowed half a dozen aspirin tablets, the only painkillers he could find in the old man's medicine chest.

He gets out of bed and brushes his fingers against the coarse hair of the skin, remembering the summer night at seventeen he was home by himself and started a fire behind the machine shed with deadfall and old boards. The lion skin for years had been hanging on the inside wall of the porch, right next to the front door, and Enoch, coming and going, often pointed at it, catching Peter's eye as he did so—his way of saying *Don't forget who you belong to.* He fed the fire until the flames rose five or six feet in the air. Then he went up and tore the skin off the porch wall. When he tossed it on the fire, though, the big hide extinguished the flames. He was pulling it away to try again—sparks flying, flames huffing and breathing—when Enoch came around the corner of the granary, snatched it from Peter's hands, and shook it like someone airing out a dirty rug. "Get the hose," he said and walked away.

Downstairs in the kitchen he fills the reservoir of the two-tiered stainless percolator and spoons coffee grounds into the top. There's a note on the table: *Went to Fargo to pick up Willie. Back this ~~afternoon~~ evening.* The word *evening* is written in someone else's hand. Crude, blocky letters. Victor. Although Peter had planned to confront his dad this morning about the intercepted letters, he can see now what little there would be to gain. Maybe an apology of some kind—dutiful, calculated—but for Peter only the hollowest of pleasures, because Enoch is congenitally unable to understand that his own actions might be anything but God-directed.

Through the window above the sink he looks out at the tents in the oak grove, more than a dozen now, in all colors. Three boys are kicking a soccer ball in the pasture. There's a girl heading down toward the lake in a yellow string bikini and another, wrapped in a towel, entering the new shower building. Half a dozen bodies on blankets, sunning themselves. A biker sort with a beard reaching to his belly, sprawled in a chaise lounge, reading. If their mortal lives are all but finished, they're certainly not behaving like it. The journalist in Peter would like to go out and talk with them, ask what brought them here—curiosity, boredom, conviction— find out what they've left behind, what they're running from, what they plan to do once it all blows over. Their stories would make for a good piece, whether Al thinks so or not.

He pours himself coffee, lights a cigarette, and goes out on the front porch where he takes a wicker chair that faces east, toward the granary and barn, beyond which he can see Victor on his knees in the vegetable garden. Peter knows that Melanie's presence won't go unreported for long—which is not to say that Battlepoint is much interested in their native daughter. It hasn't laid claim to her, as small towns do with celebrities who have local ties. For one thing, she's never come back to visit. For another, her dad, while he lived, pretended like she'd never existed. After the Academy Award—this, according to Enoch—a guy from the *Los Angeles Times* made the trek to the Magnussen hog farm, only to be turned away at the door. Neither Gerald Sr. nor Skinny would talk to him, and the writer had to settle for a couple of photographs and some tepid quotes from townspeople. Of course, that's years ago, and in Battlepoint since then an intentional forgetfulness has settled in, a civic amnesia born of being snubbed.

Nonetheless, Peter knows in a day or two there will be a leak, one of the pilgrims, maybe a Rancher, possibly Enoch himself, and the floodgates will open. And some other lucky bastard will get to write the story, because Peter is leaving. As much as he would love to spend some time with Melanie, as much as he'd like to meet his son, it all feels wrong. The thing to do is wish her well and drive back to the Cities, forget about her. Try to move on. Again. Find some honest work.

He puts out his cigarette, lifts his cup, and drains it. Then as he stands from his chair, she emerges from the front of the granary and comes striding across the grass, still wearing that ridiculous wig and a pair of huge dark glasses. He lifts a hand in greeting.

"We have to talk," she tells him. "But not here." She glances over her shoulder at Victor, who is on his feet in the garden and looking their way. "Come on." She turns and floats back in the direction from which she came, glancing around to make sure he's following, which in truth is about the easiest thing in the world to do. Inside, she takes the stairs to the second-floor apartment two at a time. Following, he climbs deliberately, stunned by the choreography of her movements, her presence inside him so powerful that he has to stifle a sneeze.

"Remember this?" she asks.

She's standing in the galley kitchen, holding up a yellowed news clipping. He walks over and takes it from her hand. It's cut from the

Minneapolis Tribune, April 1958, after Peter signed a minor league contract with the Chicago Cubs to play for their rookie league team.

"Where did you find it?"

Her head tips toward the cardboard box on the counter. In his mother's messy hand, Peter's name is written in wax pencil on the side. "Downstairs, behind that couch we used to use. I couldn't resist."

There is a small photograph of Peter, hopelessly skinny and posing with a bat on his shoulder. The story includes a quote from his high school coach as well as one from Peter himself, who claimed that playing ball was the only thing he could imagine doing. He remembers the morning Melanie showed up at school with the newspaper, and how she showed the piece to her friends, then folded it up and kept it in her purse. This copy doesn't have any fold marks.

"How long did you carry it?"

"As long as it took me to give up on you." She takes it back. "I know why you're here, Peter. It's not about your dad, and it's not about me. Or about our son."

"It's been great, seeing you again," he manages to say. And he means it—more than he'd like to admit to himself.

"Remember how it was between us? We knew things about each other."

Peter doesn't dare speak. She's the one person, after all, who has the power to hurt him deeply.

"It's okay," she says.

"What is it that you think you know about me?"

"Go ahead and write it," she tells him. "I'm the one that makes it something valuable, something you can sell. Isn't that true? So I should have some say. And I say, do it. Write it down, the whole thing. Please. That's what I want."

Peter feels dizzy, disoriented, as if he's been spinning on a merry-go-round, one of those little ones that go so fast you lose your balance getting off and have to grip the earth on all fours till your head clears. He's not sure if he's angry for his selfishness being exposed or humiliated by Melanie's kindness. He moves past her into the tiny living room and sits down on the sofa. She joins him there.

"Where will you publish it?" she asks.

"I already cancelled it. I made the phone call this morning."

"Call the person back, whoever it is. Look, I have to come clean. Nobody out there knows the first thing about me, Mom's always made sure of that. Nobody, anywhere. They don't know I lived on a hog farm till I was fifteen, we leave that out of the bio, or that I had a baby I haven't seen since the day he was born. They don't know that a bull stepped on me when I was seven years old and killed me, or that your dad put oil on my head and prayed me back to life. They don't know that my mom dragged me to auditions against my will, saying if I got this commercial or that little part she'd take me back home for a visit, which she never did, or that we'd go and visit my son, which we never did. They don't know I've lived other people's lives, not my own. Or that my back hurts so bad I can't get through a day without pills I get from whatever doctor I can charm into writing a prescription. Or that nights I sleep alone because my husband and I have been living apart for eight months, and that he never loved me in the first place."

Peter wants to reach out and pull her close, but he can't move.

"Write the story, Peter. Grant me the dignity of my convictions. I *want* the world to end. I *want* Jesus to catch me up. And even if Enoch's wrong, at least I'm acting according to my own instincts, not someone else's. I'm doing something *I* care about, something *I* believe in—as naive and foolish as it might look to the whole smug world. For once in my life, I'm not acting out someone else's fantasies."

Peter wants to say, *Of course you are.* But then it occurs to him that he was the first to use Melanie's beauty and soulfulness for the slaking of his own need. "I understand," he says. "And I'm sorry. I'm sorry."

Her lovely face comes undone, symmetry giving way to a cubist dream, and he slides over next to her and holds her, gingerly, afraid of the damage he might do. And when she says, "No one has ever told me that," tears push like pins at the back of his eyeballs.

He lets them come. "I wish I'd done things differently," he says, knowing it would have been possible, somehow—even at eighteen, and more selfish than he is now.

"Just write the story. Tell me you will."

"If I do, it'll be nuts around here. More than it is already."

"In five days it will all be over. Please." She pulls away. Her eyes are wet, but her face is back in place, and her smile is one he has seen her use in her films. A pledge.

"Okay, then," he says.

She stands up from the couch. "Now go and write. Get it done. Go on." She pushes him toward the door.

In his old bedroom, he takes a spiral-bound notebook from his duffel—Joanie probably won't bother sending the Olivetti—and a number-two pencil, which he sharpens with the jackknife he always carries, directing the shavings into the wastebasket next to the desk. It's half past noon. Often, he struggles to work his way into something, but this time it's different. He brings to mind the professor who taught reporting at the U, and how he drove the idea of putting essential facts up front then following with material in a declining order of significance. No fluff, no pretty sentences, no posturing:

> *A seventy-three-year-old man who heads a religious commune in rural Battlepoint, Minnesota, has announced that Jesus Christ will arrive on Earth next week, on August 19, to snatch up all true believers. Among those who have joined him at his farm to wait for their translation into heaven is Melanie Magnus, one of Hollywood's most loved and admired young actresses.*

The story writes itself: Enoch Bywater's vision, which comes on the heels of a near-death experience, his prediction of an imminent Rapture announced on his weekly radio program, the appearance at Last Lake Ranch two nights ago of Battlepoint native Melanie Magnus, a thumbnail history of the Ranch. And finally, a brief account of the incident with the bull and Melanie's claim of being healed after Enoch's prayers. Nothing about her pregnancy, or leaving Minnesota at age fifteen with her mom. That will come in due time, as part of the magazine piece or the book. This is a teaser.

Finished, the story is twelve hundred words but could easily be cut to a few column inches for placement in a news-roundup section. He walks it over to the granary and lets Melanie have a look. She reads it in bed, holding the notebook close above her face, and when she's done— "It's just right, you're good," she says—he convinces her to ditch the black wig and the glasses and follow him outside, where he uses an entire roll of film on her. She poses beneath the Last Days Ranch sign, with the sad-looking tent city as her backdrop. And standing on the front porch of the big house. And finally, perched on top of the rock pile, Last Lake glinting in the distance.

By four o'clock he's ready to phone the story in, which he does in Melanie's apartment. Al sounds irritable this time. "Now what's going on? Where are you?"

"What I said earlier was wrong, I'm sorry. In fact, she's here. And I've got the story written."

"Slow down, man, you're all over the map. Last night you've got nothing. And now the story is finished?"

"That's right."

"Who is she?"

"Melanie Magnus. I'll put her on. She'll talk to you. Right now."

"What?"

"Here." He hands her the phone.

"Hi, Al," Melanie says. "I think you're going to like what he wrote. Every word is true. Here he is again." She hands it back to Peter.

"This is fucking real?" Al says. "And she believes this end-of-the-world stuff?"

"Enough to make the trip from L.A."

"You got pictures?"

"Plenty."

"Where are you?"

"A farm outside of Battlepoint."

"North of Bemidji, right? Wait, isn't that where you grew up? This prophet you've got. What's your connection to him?"

"He's my dad."

"Thanks for telling me. And you plan to break this thing with your name on the byline?"

"The story's legit, Al."

"That's for me to decide. Look, I've got a guy in Bemidji today. I'll put you two in touch, and you can give him the film you've exposed. We'll get it processed tonight. You can dictate the story now—I'll hand over to Maggie. When it goes out on the wire tonight—*if* I green-light it—there will have to be two bylines. Yours first, then mine. That's the way it is."

"Fine," Peter says, knowing it won't make any difference to Freddy or *Rooster*. They're going to love the father–son angle. They'll get down on their knees and lap it up.

He reads the story to Maggie as she transcribes—it takes twenty minutes—and then he tries Freddy. When he gets no answer, he calls Joanie, who picks up right away, home from work already. It's a quarter to six, New York time. "Yeah, he's here," she says.

Half an hour later Peter is dialing *Rooster*'s executive editor, the man Freddy speaks of with such reverence and who has just been given a heads-up. Rusty Rivers. As Peter explains what he has, Rusty listens, breathing hard. He sounds like a boxer between rounds.

"Deadline for the next issue is a week from today, Wednesday the twenty-first," he says when Peter is finished. "What've you got for photos?" Rusty's voice, befitting of his name, is smoky and raw.

Peter tells him.

"Put her into something sexy. Halter top, shorts up to her ass. And let's have a look at her praying, holding a Bible. Get it?"

"She won't do that," Peter says.

"Huh? And we'll want some Holy Roller types, too, preferably in the same frame with Ms. Magnus, okay? Hollywood and the Bible Belt, juxtaposed. And a few shots of the old man, as well. *Your* old man, right? Eight thousand words, and they better be good ones. Can you have it by Wednesday? On second thought, I'll fly a photographer out there tomorrow."

"That won't work," Peter tells him, and it feels good saying no to the man.

"Where are you again?"

"Minnesota."

"Is that in Colorado?"

"No. How much for the piece, Mr. Rivers?"

"What did you say your name was?"

"I'm Peter Bywater."

"And your question again?"

"How much for the piece?"

"Pe-ter By-water," Rusty says, each syllable an enunciated growl. "Well, Mr. Bywater, I suspect it'll be more than *you're* used to getting.

Oh, and one more thing. Freddy didn't really explain. How in the hell does a Hollywood siren get involved with a religious kook in Montana?"

"Minnesota."

"Whatever. How?"

"That's the story I'll be writing," Peter says. "Stay tuned."

Before Morris, before *Boy and Girl*, before everything changed, there was Howard, whom she met on the set of a commercial she did for Prell shampoo, her first real break. She was seventeen. He was three years older, a Hollywood native with Hollywood looks and more charm than talent. The two didn't marry, though Melanie assumed they would, and with her mom's encouragement she moved, at age eighteen, into Howard's Beverly Hills apartment, which was financed by Howard's father, a B-film producer that everybody knew and pretended to love.

Melanie has been thinking of Howard all afternoon. More to the point, she's been thinking of the day he left her. The night before, there had been a party at his parents' estate for Howard, who had just won a role in Annette Funicello's new beach movie. He and Melanie went home drunk, a little high too, and the next morning when Melanie woke Howard was gone and the phone was ringing. It was him, calling from his new girlfriend's place with instructions. Those were his words: *My new girlfriend's place. Instructions.* A moving van, he explained, would come by that afternoon to haul Melanie's things—*all your shit,* he said—back to Dottie's apartment in Glendale.

No explanations. It was over.

In retrospect, the split and its timing were no surprise. They'd been reasonably compatible, and Melanie was fond of him, but she also knew it wasn't love that drew her into his circle and kept her there. It was Dottie's conviction that Howard and his father were going to be Melanie's path to success. So when Howard got his own first taste of success, it made sense that he would put an end to things. Karma. And now that Peter is about to launch himself with a breakthrough story, he will disappear as well, she is certain of it. Not that he owes her anything. And not that it matters anyway, with the end so close. Five more days. Before driving off this afternoon, purportedly to meet an AP guy in Bemidji,

Peter kissed her forehead and told her, "See you tonight." But she knows better. He won't be back—at least not until he needs more information, interviews, or photographs.

She opens the bottle and tips two of the little yellow pills into her palm. It's seven thirty, and she needs to be in a good place in her head when she first lays eyes on Willie. At the sink, she fills a glass with water and swallows them, then takes half of one more for good measure before walking into the bathroom and turning on the water to fill the tub. Except for the brief time she spent with Peter and a visit with Sarah this morning, it's been another day spent in hiding, though at least she's abandoned the disguise. Whoever sees her now will see her for who she is. Except she still doesn't want to see her brother. That's what she dreads most. Skinny was cruel, like her dad. And always so jealous.

After a long soak, she dresses in jeans and a lightweight cotton sweater and pulls back her hair. No makeup. No lipstick. She smiles into the mirror, noting the faintest soft lines around her mouth. What is Willie going to think of her? Will it be too much to absorb, meeting his mom for the first time and discovering she's someone he's seen before, someone whose face everybody knows? How bizarre is that? Probably no more bizarre than being told Jesus is coming back in five days. Maybe Peter was right in leaving, in wanting nothing more to do with this spectacle. Maybe she should leave, too.

But I'm here. And I want to be here.

It's near dark, past nine o'clock when she leaves the granary, walks to the house, and takes a chair on the front porch to wait. There is no pain in her head. Her skin is soft and dry. The tightness of fear is gone from her chest, in its place a soft vibration, like a quiet motor, humming. Victor sticks his head out the door and gives her a long look. He withdraws, and the door clicks shut. An odd man.

She's been sitting less than ten minutes when a car approaches on the township road and turns in, headlights sweeping her brother's farm then flashing and glancing through the oaks and the tents. Her stomach rises in her throat. It's not the car Enoch drives, but a larger one, green, a sedan that rolls past her and pulls right up to the machine shed. The driver cuts the engine, steps out, and comes across the lawn. He mounts the steps and takes the chair next to her.

"You came back."

"Surprised?"

She looks away, unwilling to give him the satisfaction.

"I take it they're not here yet."

"No."

"The story will be out on the wires tonight," Peter says. "There'll be papers that run it tomorrow. At least we think so. I hope you're ready."

She hopes so, too. But whatever might happen tomorrow, or the next day, or the day after that, it all seems irrelevant tonight. From the west comes the sound of a guitar, a few bars of a song she recalls but can't name, and then a half-dozen voices joining in.

"Feels weird, huh," Peter says. "Waiting like this for him. Why don't you tell me what it was like?" He leans forward, leaning on his knees. From the side, in dim light, he looks careworn, old, the lines and shadows of his face complicated, a man on the verge of some trial.

"His birth?"

"If you'd rather not, I understand."

"It was December, three days before Christmas," she starts. "I was at the apartment with my mom. My aunt's place, actually. That's where we lived that first year. We didn't move till Mom found her job at Universal. We were watching television when my water broke, and they got me into Hazel's old Studebaker and drove me to the hospital. Here's the thing, though. It was nothing like any of the births I've heard about or seen in the movies, nothing like Mom told me it would be. She'd tried to prepare me for it. The pain and the duration of it. The cramping and contractions. The pushing. But none of what she said touched me. I wasn't scared. I was enjoying my time with him, rubbing his bottom through my belly—I could feel it there. He'd wiggle and press against my hand, and I would talk to him. I knew it was a boy, I called him Zach, I don't know why. I told him I loved him and wished things were different. I told him you and I had fallen in love too soon and weren't ready to take care of him. All the talking, the closeness between us—somehow it made the birth seem like a part of what we had together, and not something to dread. He was making his way through me into the world, and that was something to be desired, if that makes any sense. And when the moment finally came, I didn't want the pain to end because I knew our time was short. I wanted to *feel* him there, I wanted him to know the friction and struggle of birth was part of my love for him. If I'd known I was going to keep him, I guess I would have suffered, but that's not how it was. In fact, for a little while I even stopped pushing, to keep him longer. But the doctor—this old man, he had a face like one of those wrinkly dogs, skin hanging from his skull in big folds—he said, 'Okay dear, the little fellow needs some air if he's going to make it.' So then I pushed, and he came right through. And the doctor laid him in my arms, and he stopped crying and started to nurse. He knew what to do."

Peter reaches for her, and she takes his hand. His skin is dry, and his fingers are large and strong.

"Turns out the adoptive parents had car trouble that night and didn't make it to the hospital on time, so I had him to myself for nine or ten hours. Well, not quite. I fell asleep once, and they took him to the nursery—but then I woke up and demanded that they bring him back to me, which they did. At some point in the night the people finally showed up, and I ignored them as long as I could, pretended they weren't there, refused to acknowledge them. It was a terrible situation. I was planning on how I could sneak out of there, get away. But I was so tired I could barely keep my eyes open. I'd forced myself to stay awake most of the night, and I had nothing left. You can't imagine. So I kissed him goodbye and looked into his face, which I had memorized. I can still see it. He didn't smile or probably even see me—but there was this solemnness about him, and the sound he made when they lifted him away was low and guttural, and he moved his head from side to side. I didn't cry or hang on to him because I didn't want him to feel that something awful was happening."

"What did he look like?"

She laughs. "He had a strong nose, for a baby. Like yours."

"Big?"

"Yeah. And lots of dark hair. And my lips—at least that's what I thought. Well-shaped, the top one with a sharp double point at the center. My eyes, too. And he was long, the nurse said twenty-three inches, very long for a newborn. And thin, too. Seven and a half pounds, which is plenty heavy, but not for that length. He was quiet and thoughtful. And frowning, like he knew everything."

"Holy shit," Peter says, squeezing her hand. "I think that's them."

Headlights ricochet through the oak trees, then flash over the porch as the car enters the drive from the west and comes on. Tires crunch on gravel, the engine drones.

"Oh, God." Something inside Melanie starts unraveling. "Should we be sitting here like this? Let's wait till tomorrow."

"Why? It's us he's here to see."

"I'm not ready." She rises and steps past Peter, whose arm encircles her waist and holds her fast.

"Now is the time. Tomorrow's going to be crazy. We'll do this together."

She stands, watching, Peter seated in the chair beside her, his arm around her waist as the car pulls up next to Peter's sedan, lights glaring against the corrugated steel of the shed door. They blink off. For a moment there is nothing, Melanie holding her breath. Then both doors swing open at once and Willie emerges—*He's so tall!*—from the driver's side. He bends over to flip the bucket seat forward and reaches into the back for a suitcase, barking a laugh at some remark from Enoch. In a deep voice Melanie can't believe, he says, "Not if you put it that way!"

The yard light throws shadows in their path, Melanie noticing how similarly they move—their long, certain strides—and how they both cock their heads to the right. They have the same wide, squared-off shoulders. And though she feared she would cry, she does not, not yet, her happiness safely contained, and within her rights to accept. He mounts the porch steps, light from windows bringing his face into view—the face of her dreams, but more rugged than she would have guessed, hard and soft at the same time, a man inside the boy. Next to her, Peter stands from his chair as Enoch, mounting the steps behind his grandson, says, "This is Willie Stuart. Willie—Melanie Magnus, Peter Bywater."

But the utterance of names is not adequate for the moment, and no one moves or speaks. Enoch lifts his hands, grandiose, like an orchestra conductor. "Willie's not uninformed," he says. "His dad has filled him in, and so did I, on the drive over. He's eager to meet you both."

Melanie can't hold herself back, and when she steps forward, her son does too, allowing her to slip inside his arms, which open just enough to let her in—*Don't hold him too tightly!*—his heart like a mallet between them, pounding. Or maybe it's hers. And before they part, he gives her a brief squeeze. When Peter hugs him next, their arms collide, and they both laugh, breaking the tension. Willie is taller than Peter by a couple of inches. And yes, their noses are alike, long and a little hooked, Roman-style.

Inside, they gather round the kitchen table, Melanie sitting across from Willie, Peter to her right, Enoch at the stove, making hot chocolate. For a long minute there is nothing to say, not even for Enoch, whose movements are fast and tentative. He pours milk into a pan, drops a spoon on the floor, spills chocolate powder on the counter. Melanie glances over at Peter, as if to ask why he's so quiet, and sees panic in his eyes. But then he shrugs, almost violently, like someone jerking in his sleep, and turns to Willie.

"So, which of her movies do you like best?" He gestures toward Melanie, then sits back in his chair and folds his arms on his chest.

She sits back as well, horrified—and relieved, too. Why be ashamed of what she does? She's meeting her son for the first time. Why pretend to be anyone other than herself?

Willie straightens in his chair and sets his hands on the table in front of him. "That last one, *Married Men*," he says, and looks right at her, then across at Peter and back again.

Oh, please! She tries to remember if her scene with Terence Stamp on the beach at Big Sur made the final cut. She hopes not.

"What did you like about it?" Peter asks.

"That part near the end." Willie smiles right at her. "When you were in the car with that guy and he said something about your mom and lit a cigarette, and you grabbed it out of his mouth and shoved him out of the car and got behind the wheel and drove away. That was cool."

"I liked that part, too," Peter says.

"It was a terrible picture. I shouldn't have made it."

"Here you go." Enoch sets mugs of hot chocolate in front of Melanie and Willie. Then goes back for two more and joins them, sitting down between Willie and her. He looks all around the table and brings his hands together and rubs his palms. "I want to thank God for bringing you all here. The people I love most. All praise. Now drink up."

A few moments of awkward silence, everyone sipping from their mugs, then Peter nods across the table at Willie. "How do you like the car?"

"Nice—and he's giving it to me." The boy tips his head toward Enoch, who looks chastened, a hand covering his mouth.

"Wow." Peter glares at his dad, the challenge on his face all too clear to Melanie, who thinks, *Nothing has changed.*

"Once you turn sixteen, you can start driving to school," Peter says. He hasn't taken his eyes from Enoch.

"Sure, I guess so."

For twenty minutes the conversation skims along the surface, its focus on Willie: the baseball tournament in which his team took second place, his life in Duluth with his mom. He speaks with a nonchalance that takes Melanie by surprise, though she understands that it's the way of adolescent boys not to let on that anything matters too much. What a burden it must be! But then Peter asks him what he does for fun, besides baseball, and Willie's enthusiasm betrays him.

"I like to fish," he says, coming alive.

"He goes for catfish in the Red," Enoch says, and he gives the boy a thumbs-up. "He's caught some big ones. A twelve-pounder this summer."

Peter says, "Dad, do you still have your fishing rods?"

"Of course. In the basement, I think. I'll have a look."

"Well, then." Peter turns to Willie. "Let's try our luck tomorrow. What do you say? We'll launch the boat and see if we can hook a walleye."

"For sure."

"Melanie?"

"Why not?" she says, thinking, *Yes, yes, I'll have him all to myself—* though next to her, Enoch is shaking his head.

"I've got other plans. I was going to show him around, take him to town with me."

"That can wait." The face Peter turns toward his dad is a blunt instrument, and Enoch only narrows his eyes in response.

Then finally: "Maybe you could have him back by noon."

Peter finishes his cocoa, sets down the mug, and pushes his sandy hair behind his ears. Beneath the fluorescent ring-bulb on the ceiling, silver-gray strands are visible in the gold and blond. Melanie watches the line of his mouth, hard, unforgiving. "Nope, we're not going to be on a timetable," he says.

Enoch bounces his knotted fists on the table. "How about some toast before bed?" he says, peering at Willie. Then he stands and goes to the cupboard, where he takes down a loaf of bread and starts slicing. Melanie can't help but notice the steel in his smile and the ruthlessness of his hands as he drops two slices in the toaster and levers them down with a knobby thumb.

AUGUST 15—THURSDAY

ive-thirty a.m. and his mind is racing down too many tracks at once. How many papers are running the AP story this morning, and how many readers will see it? Did the *Minneapolis Tribune* get it off the wires in time to carry it in their outstate edition? If so, what page is it on? Enoch is going to be thrilled by the coverage, but what about Melanie—how does she really feel? And who's going to show up here looking for her, once word is out? Her agent? Her mom? The director of the new film? Peter is worried about her. The shaking in her hands, and the way she's sweating and biting her lip. Her distracted eyes. And what about Willie? What's he thinking behind that Steve McQueen facade?

Peter rises, dresses, and goes down the hall to the next room. When he touches Willie's shoulder to wake him, the boy swings out of bed automatically, even before his eyes are open. He's still wearing his clothes from yesterday.

"I'm awake, I'm ready," he says, blinking.

"So it seems."

In the granary, at the top of the stairs, he knocks then waits for a minute before it opens. She's holding up a pill bottle, her face behind it sunken and red-eyed. And lovely.

"I have to stop taking these."

He plucks the bottle from her hand. "What's your dosage? How many and how often?"

"As many as I need."

"Once a day? Twice? More?"

"Twice, usually."

"And how many?"

She holds up one finger, adds a second.

He walks past her to the kitchen counter, finds a knife, and cuts a pill in two, drops half into her palm, then shakes out one more from the bottle and gives that to her also. She swallows them down with a glass of water. While she dresses in the bedroom, he looks out at the lake in the distance, its surface trembling, glimmering like foil. The sun is rising. By 6:30, Peter is piloting the eighteen-foot Crestliner north, the far shore barely visible. He's seated behind the steering console and its Plexiglas windshield, the forty-horse outboard going at full throttle. Melanie is next to him, hair streaming behind her, arms crossed in front of her, hands gripping her own shoulders. It's chilly out here. He reaches for a sweatshirt from the bag he brought and puts it around her. Willie on the bench seat one back from the bow is leaning forward into the wind. He's wearing a Twins cap, its brim pulled low and bent like a funnel over his eyes.

They head straight up the lake for a couple of miles, then Peter angles toward the eastern shoreline, navigates around Griffin Point, and heads into a pine-crowded bay where he cuts the throttle and floats up to a long dock, the land end of which abuts a log building that for as long as Peter can remember has been a bait-and-breakfast run by a tiny man named Buck Vandermeer who was already well past middle age when Peter first knew him. Last night, after gathering up the fishing rods, tackle box, bait pail, and fishnet, he searched the phone book for Buck's Bait. Sure enough, it was there.

Inside they find Buck himself, unchanged though even smaller, if that's possible, his bristly white hair starting to yellow, his prominent mouthful of coffee-stained teeth looking capable of any job one might need a pliers for. "Ain't seen you in a while," he says, but seems otherwise uninterested as he rings up two dozen shiners and a box each of leeches and nightcrawlers. A pair of teenage girls in halter tops and tight bell-bottom jeans preside over the fry surface, cracking eggs and turning bacon. Peter, Melanie, and Willie take stools at the counter, Willie in the middle. They place their orders for the Whitecap Special: eggs, pancakes, bacon, and toast. Coffee, too.

What to talk about?

Peter watches the girls work—one of them with cropped red hair, the other with a swinging blonde ponytail, both glancing back at Willie every now and again to make sure he's paying attention, which he is. Melanie is somber, possibly afraid, as she has a right to be, and in any case not seeming able, this morning, to enjoy her son or bridge the space between them. Peter for his part has no idea what role he is supposed to play. He's ashamed that what he's thinking about more than anything is the story he wrote and the events it will set into motion, the opportunities and successes it will usher in.

No one speaks until one of the girls, the freckle-nose redhead, turns to Willie and says, "You got a cabin around here, or what?"

"Just here for a visit."

The other girl saunters over and checks the salt and pepper shakers that sit next to Willie's folded hands, lifting each in turn and giving it a shake next to her ear. "Who're you visiting?"

Willie turns to Peter.

"We're over at the Bywater place," Peter says.

The girl glances back at her friend, whose mouth twitches at the corner. A small knowing smile. "You mean the Ranch?" the blonde says. She looks at Willie, as if he were the one who spoke. Her eyes are merry.

Willie nods, his smooth cheeks crimson. Last night Peter asked him what he knew about the grand revelation and learned that Enoch had already given him the lowdown. The boy seemed skeptical, but unfazed.

"So I guess you're . . ." She points at the ceiling, toward heaven. "Next week, right?"

"Hope not," Willie says.

The girl spins back to the fry surface, a little twitch in her rear, and flips pancakes, tossing them a foot and a half in the air. With a pair of tongs she turns slabs of thick bacon. The redhead arrives with a pot of coffee and refills their cups, watchful.

"Who do you know over there?" she asks Willie.

He doesn't shy from the question. "My grandpa," he says, the strength in his voice confronting the girl. Pride swells in Peter's chest.

And now it's the girl who blushes, though she manages to say, "The radio guy? The preacher?"

Willie tells her yes.

Melanie leans forward. "Do you girls plan on getting Raptured Monday?"

The redhead seems to notice Melanie for the first time, her tongue showing between her lips. She's pensive for a moment. Peter half-expects her to say, "Do I know you?" but she shrugs and turns away. The blonde pipes up from the grill, where she's plating food: "My pastor said there is no such thing. He said there's nothing to worry about."

"And you're taking his word for it?" Melanie speaks in a tone that Peter recognizes from her films, the little girl voice but with a rough edge that makes you wonder if she's angry.

Drop it, Peter thinks.

The blonde doesn't back down. "Makes no sense to *me.*"

Peter claps his hands on the counter and says, "Not to me, either," as the girl brings two plates, Melanie's and his, the steaming food pungent with fry grease and bacon. She brings Willie's next and sets it before him with both hands, leaning forward enough to allow a view of her cleavage, what little of it there is. Smiling, she moves along to the next arrivals, a party of men whose boisterous talk eclipses all other conversation in the room. Peter doesn't mind their noise, devoting himself to his food, Melanie and Willie doing likewise.

When they're passing through the bait room on their way out and Peter asks for a *Minneapolis Tribune,* Buck points outside, toward the dock. "Heard 'em drop off the stack just now. Grab one. That'll be thirty cents."

Peter lays a quarter and a nickel on the counter and outside finds the bale of newspapers still bound by twine, which he cuts with his jack-knife. He finds the story in the bottom right-hand corner. Front page. The photo of Melanie is not one he took but a publicity shot he recognizes from an old piece in *People* magazine—her hair pulled up in a tight bun, her eyes bright behind a pair of wire-rimmed glasses. No smile. The story's headline reads *Minnesota-born actress home for Apocalypse.*

Willie has run ahead to untie the boat, and Peter holds up the paper for Melanie.

"Oh boy," she says.

"Good day for fishing." He tucks the paper inside a rolled-up raincoat and stuffs it beneath the steering console.

The lake has some chop now, and he aims the boat northwest toward the three-mile bar, glancing past the pines on Griffin Point toward the Ranch. It's too far away to see anything. He imagines his dad's euphoria when the reporters arrive, and the television crews with their cameras, pictures how he'll greet them—regally, slightly bemused, monarch of an empire they do not understand. Peter can see the lightness in his dad's step and hear the timbre in that Johnny Cash voice of his, made for telling people how things work and what they mean, a voice Enoch wields like a weapon.

Melanie slides close to Peter on the bench seat and speaks in his ear. "I need another one. You brought them, right? Just that half-pill."

"After lunch," he tells her, then throttles down and signals to Willie, who has swung round on his seat as the boat settles flat on the water. "Toss the anchor," he calls, ignoring Melanie's scowl. "Let's set up and see if we can hook a walleye."

He rigs tackle for all three lines—heavy sinkers, six-foot leaders, leeches for bait—explaining as he goes, Willie watching with his whole body as Peter describes how they'll troll at low speed, allowing the leeches to bounce and drag along the lake bottom, where the walleyes prefer to lie in the heat of summer. "When you feel something hit your bait, count to three and do this." He yanks the end of his rod straight up. "That will set the hook firmly in its jaw. I'm sure it's the same with catfish." Willie gives him a look that says *I think I know that much,* and Peter wonders when it's really going to set in, the idea that he played a part in making this kid happen.

As he hands out the rods, Melanie says, "I haven't used one of these since I was a girl."

"Here." He takes it back and gives her a quick lesson on the spin-cast reel, how to let out line by pressing the thumb bar and adjust tension with the drag lever. "See? Nothing to it." She's watching him hard, and he can't tell if she's upset or simply bearing down to gut out the pain. He lays a finger on the side of her face.

"Anchor," he says then and starts the engine.

He runs his own line off the stern, Willie off starboard, and Melanie off port as they troll in reverse above the underwater rock bar, a spot where Peter often caught walleyes as a boy. The air has warmed, and the lake smell, though not unpleasant, isn't as clean as he recalls. A flock of white gulls wheels above them. There's no hint of clouds in the blue sky. The fish aren't biting.

"What those girls were saying," Willie says. "Does everybody know about it?"

"Everybody around here, I guess."

"And those campers in the trees. They believe it's going to happen?"

"I've stayed out of their way," Peter says. "Some of them must. Otherwise, why are they here?"

"What do *you* think?" The brim of Willie's ball cap is so close above his eyes he has to tip his head back to get a level view of Peter.

"What did Enoch tell you?"

"Stuff about the Rapture. All that. And he felt guilty about giving me the car."

"Yeah?"

"Because he thinks I won't be around to drive it."

Peter laughs. One good thing, anyway: his old man's lunacy is overshadowing the strangeness of being out here with Melanie and the son they have never seen before. "And what do *you* think?" he asks Willie.

"It's a great car." He glances from Peter to Melanie, who's frowning at the place her line enters the water. "But I don't want to see him hurt," Willie adds. "I mean, he's sure putting it all out there."

"Whatever happens next week," Peter says, "he has it coming. There's no reasoning with him, and there never has been. He knows what he knows."

"And what if he's right?" Melanie says.

They both turn. "You think he is?" Willie asks.

"I want to think so."

Peter can tell that she's fighting something off. The unhealthy luster in her eyes and the sheen of sweat standing out above her lip. He puts a hand on her shoulder and she moves away.

"But *do* you?" Willie says.

"I think so, yes," she responds.

Willie shakes his head. "I went to this church with my parents when I was little, before the divorce. And they were always talking about it, like it was this great thing. It sounded terrible, I used to have nightmares. I didn't want to die, and I still don't."

"It won't be like death," Melanie tells him.

"The end of this life, though."

She nods. Then "Oh!" and swings to her left, where the tip of her rod is bent clear to the water. She yanks it up and leans back, the rod curving 180 degrees, then starts cranking in line, the reel's drag whirring. "Help!" she cries. Peter cuts the engine, and Willie scrambles over and straddles the bench, leans into her back and puts his arms around her, stabilizing the rod as she works the fish.

"Perfect, keep it coming," Willie says. "You've got a big one on."

Peter gets up from behind the console and fetches the landing net and moves to the gunwale. He turns and sneaks a look at Melanie, her eyes streaming tears, her face full of color now, and right beside it Willie's, his chin notched into her left shoulder.

"There, right there," Willie says.

Peter turns and sees the swirl of silver-green. He lowers the net until his hand meets the water, then he sweeps up and forward, catching the fish into the air and over the gunwale, a single movement that ends with the fish on the floor of the boat, free of the net's webbing. It flips over once then lies at rest across the aluminum ribs, its gills working for air, exhausted from the fight.

"Walleye," Willie says. "And big, yeah?"

"Five, six pounds. Not bad at all."

Peter goes to one knee and takes a grip on its body, careful not to let the spiny dorsal fin pierce his hand. He eases the hook from the translucent mouth. The scales on its body—gold, olive, black—shine like polished metal.

"Do we keep it?" she asks.

"I brought my cleaning knife and a fry pan."

Her tears haven't stopped, and she makes no effort to wipe them away.

"What?" Willie says.

"I've never seen anyone so beautiful in my whole life." She reaches up and lays a hand against his cheek.

Beneath the brim of his cap Willie's eyes look alarmed, but he takes the rod from her hand and sets it aside and encloses her in a hug, his long arms encircling her completely, only the top of her head visible. A large gull drops down close as if to see what's happening and makes a strange cry, like an old deaf man saying, *Huh, huh?* Crouched on the floor of the boat, Peter leans back and tries to relax his shoulders, the muscles of his belly. His life until now has been small, he realizes, and he is aware of being caught in a moment he'll wish he had been able to absorb, fully—Melanie vanished within Willie's hug, the sound of the cranking reel, and the smell of fish, barking gull overhead. Then Melanie and Willie separate, light showing between them, and they both turn to face him.

He swallows hard, says, "How about shore lunch?"

The spit of land he's thinking of is clear across on the northwest side of the lake and owned by out-of-staters, a banking family from Massachusetts—or used to be. By now it's probably been sold and developed. A gorgeous spot in any case, and according to local legend the place where an Ojibwe chief is buried. The wind is up from the northeast, slowing their progress, but when they get there, it looks unchanged—the narrow strip of sand giving way to a rise of land with outcroppings of granite, then a heavy stand of trees on higher ground. Peter beaches the boat and then leads them twenty yards to a spot where a hummock of grass has formed a half-circle around a sandy floor.

"We'll have the fire here. I'll clean the fish and gather wood."

Willie says, "I'll get the wood."

"Why don't you put a spoon on your line and try casting for pike in the shallows? We're in no hurry." He looks at his watch. "It's only eleven."

Willie runs back for his rod, and Melanie sits on the grass, leaning back and giving her face to the sun as Peter starts on the fish she caught, taking off the head and gutting the belly, then guiding his knife down along the backbone to separate meat from carcass, one side and then the other. Firm, white filets. When the boy comes back with his rod and tackle, Melanie says, "I'm sorry, Willie." She's wearing her dark glasses. A wobble on her lips. "You need to know that."

Willie is tying a swivel at the end of his leader, and Peter can't tell if he heard what she said.

"I was fifteen, and Peter was eighteen," she continues. "Our parents decided for us. We shouldn't have listened. I don't expect you to understand."

The boy turns toward the water, brings back the rod, and with a snap of his elbow performs a straight overhead cast, the spoon sailing thirty yards out before splashing down. He starts reeling in his line.

"You probably know this, but I grew up on the farm next to Enoch's. We were neighbors. When I got pregnant, Mom and I went out west to her sister's in California, where I had you."

Without turning, Willie says, "You didn't want anyone to know?"

"It's awful, isn't it?"

"You were ashamed?"

"More scared than ashamed."

"You were in tenth grade?"

"How did you know?"

"Enoch told me. Said you were the same age as me."

"Yes." She glances at Peter over the top of her dark glasses. *That half-pill,* he thinks, but she tips her head and curves a finger, wanting him next to her. He finishes skinning the two big filets and lays them out in the grass, white as paint and threaded with tiny dark veins. He joins her.

Willie turns around finally, his eyes solemn. He's looking at Peter. "You were out of school, right?"

"I graduated the spring we found out. I was on my way to Tennessee to play ball. That's what I thought I was going to be. A ballplayer."

"You didn't make it?"

"Uh-uh. Big dreams, is all."

Willie casts again, far out into the lake, his wrist snapping forward so hard that he grunts. As he reels in, Peter rises to his knees, thinking of wood for the fire, but Melanie puts a hand on his arm.

"Didn't you miss each other?" Willie says.

Melanie groans. "Terribly."

Peter says, "Of course we did." What he doesn't say is that he turned toward baseball with a single-mindedness that mitigated his loss and from that experience learned how even the most insistent needs can be suppressed—trampled flat, for that matter. At least for a time.

"But the reason you're here is Enoch, right? The vision he had." Willie glances back at them before making another cast. "Not because of me."

Melanie pushes herself up straight and squares her shoulders. "No, no, that's not true. If it weren't for you, I wouldn't be here."

"You said you believed what he's saying."

"All right—but whether it happens next week or in a hundred years, I'm here now because of you."

Willie comes ashore and kicks off his wet shoes and rolls up his pant legs to the knees, lays down his fishing rod. He says, "When I was about twelve, me and Dad were watching TV one night, and suddenly he goes, 'Look—your mom!' It was the movie about you and the soldier, and Dad pointed right at you when he said it, kind of laughing. Big joke, see? And I went, 'What are you doing? That's not right,' because he'd already told me I was adopted. He laughed and waved his hand at me, told me to forget about it. Then later I saw another movie of yours, the one where you're going on this trip to Europe with a few other girls, and you get in trouble with the police and end up dying. And it felt so weird, watching that. I mean, after what Dad said before. What's that one called?"

"*Final Chances.* It's set in Paris."

Peter can't see Melanie's eyes behind her dark glasses, but he can tell she's having trouble keeping her face together.

The boy laughs nervously. "I think about that Paris movie a lot, and how I felt when the girl was dying. It seemed so real."

Melanie takes off the glasses. She looks naked without them, her beauty so complete, so fragile. She gets up from the grass and goes over to Willie and hugs him, but only for a moment, because he pulls away, his hands gripping her shoulders and holding her at arm's length.

"I better get some wood," he says, and he lets go of her and starts up the slope toward the trees.

Without intending to, Peter sits down hard, his palms jamming into the hot sand. He feels stunned, as though he's been clubbed. He looks up and squints at the bright sky.

"Did I say something wrong?" Melanie says and drops down next to him. "I think he hates me."

"Shhh." Peter pulls her close and strokes her scalp with his fingertips.

"Did you see his ears?" she asks. "They're as big as yours, almost." She reaches up and takes hold of his earlobe and tugs on it. He parts her hair at the back of her head and puts his lips on the tender skin of her neck. He can feel her tension ease, but only for a moment.

"Yeah," he says and pushes to his feet. "I'll get the fry pan and picnic stuff from the boat."

"I need that Perc now. You've got them, don't you?"

He takes the bottle from his pocket, searches out the half-pill from morning, and sets it in her palm, then watches her dry-swallow, eyes closed. She takes a couple of deep breaths. When he gets back from the boat, she's standing at the edge of the water, bare toes working the sand, her arms crossed in front of her, holding herself.

"Are you all right?"

She nods. "What do you think is happening at your dad's?"

"He's getting some calls. People have read it by now, maybe seen it on the tube. Twin Cities media are heading this way, for sure."

"Oh, God. What I'm dreading, though, is my brother. Skinny puts it all on me—Mom leaving and never coming home again. As if our parents had anything close to a marriage."

Peter touches her arm and tips his head toward Willie, who's on his way down the hill, leaning backward to keep his scavenged pile of firewood from spilling.

"Don't you just love him?" she whispers. "And he's ours."

"Dump it here," Peter tells him, and Willie lets it tumble, then kneels and starts building a teepee of kindling, Melanie dropping down to help. Peter, taken as he is by the picture of the two of them, their matching foreheads nearly touching as they work, allows himself to do something he never does, a dangerous thing: he imagines what his life might have been like if he had made choices other than the ones he made.

t's past eleven when Victor pulls into the drive in the Chevy pickup. He left this morning in search of a replacement coil for the Farmall, which stalled last night when he started mowing the oak grove. Now he rolls past, lifting a finger off the wheel in greeting. When he emerges from the machine shed, Enoch waves him over to the porch.

"There's something we need to talk about."

Victor frowns through his heavily lidded eyes. "I better put on the soup I made yesterday," he says and hurries into the house.

Enoch drops into one of the wicker chairs. He spent the morning in a blue funk, paying bills, balancing his checkbook, and reading from the Book of Psalms to calm himself. He can't help feeling ignored, wronged, disrespected. Here it is, first full day that his son and grandson are home, not to mention Melanie, and instead of enjoying their presence and having the chance to prepare them for what's coming, he's stuck here by himself while they're off fishing. Not to mention this business with Victor and Dave Drobec.

"Had to drive all the way to Bemidji," Victor says, closing the screen door behind him. He takes a chair and sits with his hands folded, knees together. He stares at the floor. "Lyle's was sold out, and tractor repair in Roofing was closed up. Sign on the door said Rocky's sick in the hospital."

"But you got it?"

"Yup. I'll put it in after lunch. Mow this afternoon."

"That would be good."

"Oh, let me get you some coffee." Victor pops up and retreats once more into the house.

Enoch would prefer not to say anything, pretend like nothing happened, but he's accountable for the man, responsible for him. Victor's dad ran off before Victor was born, leaving his mom to raise him, then she disappeared too, with a traveling carnival, people said. Victor left school with eight or nine grades under his belt and moved into Mrs. Shippenberg's rooming house, supporting himself with a job at the Red Owl grocery. From the very beginning, he attended Enoch's meetings, pedaling the four miles out from town and back again on his fat-wheeled bicycle, no matter the wind, cold, or snow, and he was the first to move into the converted barn after Ruth's death. Enoch is aware of Victor's limitations, such as they are, but more so of his zeal for God, which is rare. The truth is, nobody that Enoch knows has a purer heart. No one is happier than Victor to live a life in service of the Kingdom.

Now he backs out the door, coffee in both hands, and gives one to Enoch. He sits again. Looks at the floor. He knows what's coming.

"I saw Dave in town yesterday, and he mentioned that conversation last week. You were here, remember? I think you overheard most of it."

Victor glances over at the driveway, the place where it happened.

"Dave told me he was sorry. He told me to forget what he said about the money."

Victor clamps his lips tight, then thrusts them forward in a pucker. He does this several times in rapid succession, a habit of his when he's nervous.

"What do you think about that?"

"Good?" Victor says.

"I was pleased, yes. I'm strapped for cash, for one thing. And giving it back wasn't part of the agreement, as Dave knows."

Victor's lips clench and pucker.

"But I can't help wondering what made him change his mind. Any ideas?"

Victor turns his hands over and examines his palms.

"Did you go and talk to him?"

One of Victor's shoulders tips up, barely, then drops again.

"Dave was scared. Really scared. Why, Victor?"

The man lifts his face a degree or two, the slimmest line of black light shining behind the slits of his narrowed lids.

"What did you say to him, Victor?"

"I said he shouldn't ask you for money."

"You went to his apartment?"

Victor blinks.

"When?"

"Night before last."

"That's all you said to him?"

"No."

"What else? Did you threaten him?"

Victor squints past Enoch toward the oaks, then down at his lap again. "I didn't say I'd hurt Sally," he mutters, his voice mostly air.

"You said you'd hurt *him*?"

"No." Victor breathes. He glances at Enoch then down again. "Kill him."

"You said you would *kill* him?" Enoch looks at the man's outsized, bony hands, the unrefined blandness of his face, and thinks of the time a few high school boys drove out from town and interrupted the Saturday night meeting, drunk. And how Victor took hold of the biggest one, a lineman on the football team, and pushed his head through a window—cutting only the top of his scalp, thank God—and then grabbed the other two by the neck, one with each hand, and choked them until their eyes all but popped from their heads. Enoch was out of town, and it was Dave who convinced Victor to let the boys go.

"You would never do that, I'm sure of it. You would never kill a man."

"Dave took it all back. Said he was wrong. I knew he would."

"But what if he hadn't?"

"I knew that he would."

"But you wouldn't have done anything to hurt him, not really—would you? No, I don't believe you would." Enoch shakes his head back and forth, several times, waiting for Victor to mimic the motion and thereby deny the possibility of such a thing. "I know you wouldn't have done such a thing because I know *you*. Am I right?"

"I think so," Victor says, meekly.

Enoch reaches out and puts a hand on his shoulder. "Christ came in fulfillment of the law, one of those laws being 'Thou shalt not kill.' I don't have to tell you this. Any loyalty you have to me is nothing compared to your obligation to Christ. Do you understand?"

Victor's gaze is fastened on Enoch's mouth.

"You'll need to apologize to Dave, tell him you meant him no harm, that you were only trying to frighten him. Can you do that?"

"Uh-huh."

"On second thought, no. It's best if you leave him well enough alone."

Inside, the phone rings, the sound like a trigger releasing a coiled spring in Victor's body. He bolts up and sweeps past Enoch and through the screen door. Seconds later he's back. "It's for you."

"Who is it?"

"The man says it's important."

When Enoch puts the phone to his ear, he makes out only a high-pitched, urgent tone, and he fears some kind of bad news. "Can you please repeat that?"

"This is Robert Blaze with the *Minneapolis Tribune*. I'm trying to reach Enoch Bywater. Is this he?"

"This is."

Enoch thinks, *Who spilled the beans?*

"Reverend Bywater, would you have time to talk with me?"

"I'm not a reverend. Who says I am?"

"Um, maybe I read into it. Would you have time to talk?"

"We're talking right now, aren't we?"

"I mean in person."

"I'm happy to visit on the phone."

"Mr. Bywater, I read the AP story this morning, and I'd like to ask you some follow-up questions. Our readers want to know more. About Miss Magnus, naturally—but about you, as well. I want to get your take on things. And we'll want more photos."

"AP story?"

"Associated Press. The one we ran this morning, yes. Haven't you read it? Haven't you gotten other calls?"

"I don't subscribe to a newspaper. Can I ask who wrote the story?"

"Let's see. There are two names on the byline. Peter Bywater and Al McCarthy. You and Peter wouldn't be related, would you?"

Actually, Enoch is no more surprised than he was by his son's willingness to take the thousand dollars. Until people grasp the full truth of Christ's redemption, they follow their own nose and interests. But at least it's out in the open now. In fact, Enoch isn't the least bit troubled—and he can't help but wonder if Melanie herself might be culpable in some way.

"Look, I'm a few miles down the road but I can be there inside the hour. I need forty-five minutes of your time, Mr. Bywater, and a sit-down with Miss Magnus, if you can arrange it. We don't want to put anybody in a negative light, of course. We simply want depth. I believe there is a lot of curiosity out there."

"I'll be here," Enoch says.

"And Miss Magnus?"

"I speak only for myself."

"But she's there on site, correct?"

"Do you need directions, Mr. Blaze?"

"That would help."

Minutes later on the porch, Enoch sends a prayer of thanks, one hand reaching toward heaven, the other planted on his heart. Of course Melanie ought to be told what is happening, given the promise she extracted from him, but who knows what bay they're in, angling for pan fish, or which trough or bar they're trolling for walleyes. It will have to be a surprise to her—of the sort she must be half-expecting, even if she is not complicit. He moves to the southeast corner of the porch, from which he can see Victor at work on the Farmall, then hears somebody coming fast across the lawn and turns around just as Skinny Magnussen mounts the steps, his face as dark as a thunderhead. He shakes the newspaper in his hand.

"Where is she?"

"She's not here."

"Bullshit. You tell the world about her, and you don't tell me?"

"I didn't tell anybody."

"Why is she here?"

"What does the story say? I haven't seen it yet."

Skinny tosses the paper on a chair. "When did she come?"

"Day before yesterday. Look, I'm sorry. She said she wasn't ready to see you."

Skinny levels a finger at Enoch. There is a dot of white foam at the corner of his lips. "You've fucked over a lot of people, haven't you, and all in the name of God Almighty. But now you're working overtime. Outdoing yourself."

"Are you here on business, Skinny? Last I counted, there were thirty campers in the oaks, give or take, well within the legal number. And I've been reminding them to keep it quiet."

"Where is she?"

"She had to go someplace. I can't tell you."

"When is she back?"

"Sometime tonight."

"Who's she with?"

Enoch shakes his head.

Nodding, Skinny taps himself on the front of his skull as if pointing out a brand-new thought. "Shit. He's here too, isn't he?"

"He is."

"Couldn't keep his hands to himself—that's where it all started. You tell my sister I want to see her. That I don't mean any harm, I only want to talk. It's my right."

"I'll do that."

"You've got things figured out, don't you, everything going according to your fucking plan."

"It's not my plan, Skinny."

"Go to hell." He descends the porch steps into the yard, then turns around. "Somebody's going to bring you down," he says, then heads past the showers and latrines and across the oak grove toward home.

Enoch doesn't even have a chance to look at the newspaper before a car turns off the township road and heads up the drive—*The words and the strength*, he prays—a foreign job, likely Japanese, red, smaller than any car he's ever seen, not much bigger than a golf cart. It stops in front of the porch, and a young man steps out. Tall, good-looking, with a serious face that would look just right on the Greek statues in picture books. Faded jeans, a white T-shirt that shows off his muscles and tan skin. He crosses toward Enoch, surveying the place, smiling with half his mouth, confident.

"Mr. Bywater?"

Enoch stays where he is. The young man stops short of the porch steps. "And you must be Mr. Blaze from the Minneapolis paper."

"Nope." He shakes his head. "You won't remember me, but I was here a week and a half ago. I stayed till the ambulance arrived and their guys took over." He glances at the buckeye tree.

"My God in heaven." Enoch stands from his chair. He lays a hand on his sternum, which is still sore. The young man's face is so clean, his skin so clear and smooth that it might be glowing. It's as if there's a light bulb burning inside of him. Enoch wants to come down off the porch and touch him to see if he's real.

"Are you all right?" the young man says. "Hope I wasn't too hard on you."

"You gave me a good pounding, but I'm fine, thank God. What's your name?"

"Forman. Michael Forman."

Michael. Of course.

Michael Forman climbs the steps to the porch. His face on closer inspection is unshaven, several days of blondish red stubble, and he smells like cigarettes and cologne. When he extends an arm, Enoch hesitates. Then complies. A solid grip, warm and calloused. A man who works with his hands and his back.

"You must have seen my ad in the paper," Enoch says.

"What? No, I read this morning's story and thought I better check it out."

"And I've wanted to say thank you but had no idea who you were. So—thank you, Michael. I had you figured for an angel. In fact, I've got a hundred dollars riding on it. I guess I'll have to pay up."

"Sorry to disappoint."

"Can you come in and sit down? I'll make coffee."

"I have to go. But you're okay, though, seriously? I thought you were dead."

Enoch laughs. "I *was* dead—but God had other plans, of which you were clearly a part."

Michael looks west toward the oaks, where a new tent is going up, a big square one, gray with bright aluminum poles. A young couple with a pair of kids. South of the grove, where the cars are parked, a gray-bearded man is sunning himself on the roof of his RV. Michael smiles. "I didn't know what I was getting involved in."

"We're all involved, Michael, whether we want to be or not. How did you happen to drive by so early?"

"I work in Bemidji but try to help my dad up in Black River whenever I have the time. He builds stuff. Houses, barns. I was on my way up there, just like I am now."

"This is off the beaten track, isn't it?"

"I like the scenic route. Last Lake, you know? That beautiful shade of purple? Or whatever color it is."

"Are you ready?" Enoch asks him.

"Ready for what?"

"For Monday."

Michael smiles again, and a laugh escapes his throat. "I'll figure that out for myself," he says, then turns to leave. He has to bend low to climb into his tiny red car, and before starting the engine he lights a cigarette and takes a long pull. When he leans toward the windshield, the engine kicks to life. "Gorgeous spot you've got here," he says, exhaling, pulling away. "Why in the world would you want to leave?"

Why, indeed.

After a full day on the water—a lovely hiatus—she has returned to her personal limbo, suspended between a life she cannot sustain and one she can't imagine. Together with Peter and Willie, she is standing at the front window of the granary apartment, the three of them having docked the boat and entered the building from the rear, unspotted. They're watching the clutch of reporters gathered on Enoch's front porch, the corner of which is visible to them. The circular gravel drive is filled with cars, and there is a white van that says WCCO-TV MINNEAPOLIS. It is early evening, five thirty.

"This is it, then," Melanie says and enters the tiny bathroom for a shower, and from there into the bedroom where she prepares herself before a full-length mirror. The yellow knit top is open to the third button. The snug white pants flare out at the bottom, but not too much. Wooden-soled sandals. At the end of the bed she sits to paint her nails and toenails red, then she parts her hair straight down the middle. It falls loosely around her shoulders.

"Beautiful," Peter says, when she emerges. He goes into the kitchen, waving for Melanie to join him, and fills a glass of water at the tap. He hands it to her and slides her a pill on the countertop.

"Pray for me, please, both of you," she says and leaves.

The yard surrounding the house is dotted with onlookers, some of them campers, surely, and up on the porch the knot of journalists has closed around Enoch, who stands in the doorway, a step above them, his mane of white hair swept back, his face notched and angled—it might have been hacked out of oak. He is the first to spot her, and he pauses, closing his mouth, smiling with his eyes. She moves with practiced dignity through the grass. People start turning. A TV cameraman, standing on a chair for height, grabs his partner's shoulder, jumps down, slices through the crowded porch, and leaps into the yard. He comes running, his eyes locked on Melanie. Her instinct is to turn and run. Instead, next to the buckeye tree she holds her ground.

The reporter catches up to his cameraman, then surges past him and shoves the microphone in her face. "Miss Magnus, was this your director's idea? Or maybe your publicist?"

"They don't know where I am. Or maybe they do now."

"This has to be great for the new film, yes?"

She smiles, turning on the high beams. "I'm here for my own reasons, if you can imagine that."

"What reasons are those?"

"Yes, what are you here for?" The rest of them have joined the fray, the single microphone turning into half a dozen, all pushing toward her, and behind them a mosaic of flesh and hair and eyes and mouths.

The stream of questions:

"Are you ready for the Rapture?"

"What do you have to say to your fans?"

"Why didn't you tell your agent you were leaving?"

"Do you believe in the old man's dream?"

"His name is Enoch Bywater," she says.

"Do you believe what he's saying?"

She smells their sweat and the stink of what they've eaten today. Hot dogs, Cheetos, onion rings. She tries to remember if she has ever spoken a word of truth to the writers and cameras. No, she's said what she has been told to say, every time. And she always knows how she's going to look on the screen when they play it back again, just as she knows now: feet planted well apart to prove she owns the moment, breeze lifting her stray blonde hairs, yellow top form-fitted to her breasts—and her lips, painted to match the classic red barn behind her.

"Yes, I believe him."

"You think Christ is coming back next week?"

"I have always believed He was coming back. And I've always believed what Enoch says."

"Why?"

"I trust him."

"He was your neighbor, growing up, wasn't he? Isn't that your old farm over there? The hog farm?"

"It is."

"But you never come back here, do you?"

"I'm here now."

"And your brother still lives there?"

"He does."

"Why won't he talk with us?"

"That's his business."

"Have you seen him yet?"

"Not yet."

"Why not?"

"That's my business."

"Is your being here a message to your fans? Do you want them to believe the same way you do?"

She looks down at her feet, painted nails peeking out beneath the cuffs of her bell-bottom pants—her feet, Morris used to say, the sexiest thing about her, their congress with earth a promise of intimacy. Always such high-toned crap from him, and why she thinks of it now makes no sense at all.

"People should believe what they want to believe," she says.

"What about the bull that stomped you, and the healing? It was in the story this morning. Do you want to say something about that?"

I do, she thinks and peers into the face of the man who spoke. Straight nose and cool eyes. "Who are you?"

"Robert Blaze, *Minneapolis Tribune.*"

"That's a lovely name. Thank you for the question."

"Well?"

"It happened," she says.

"Were you dead?"

"I believe I was."

"What did the doctors have to say?"

She tries to focus on the man's face in the tumble of faces, wants to think he might listen and understand. She sees him, now loses sight of him. She tries to hear his voice among the crowd of voices but can't make it out.

"Was this in the local hospital?"

"What was the doctor's name, Miss Magnus?"

"Have you and Enoch stayed in contact all these years?"

"What does he think of your movie career?"

The sun is low and it's coming through the trees, blinding her. She can feel the heat spreading across her face and chest, sweat running beneath her arms. She's burning up. The ground heaves beneath her, and she throws out a hand to grab hold of the small tree beside her, and then Peter has joined her, his arm encircling her shoulder, the tall length of him pressing close, his presence like a full-body splint.

"She's done with your questions," she hears him say, and she allows him to begin moving her back and away.

"Are you the brother?"

"Please, a few more minutes."

"Come on, we waited all afternoon."

Peter stops and turns. She can feel the pressure like an engine running inside him. He gulps air, and then he shouts at them: "She's done, do you hear me? Now get the fuck out of her face!" He guides, drags, and finally carries her across the grass and into the granary, and then upstairs, where he lays her down and brings a cool washcloth and applies it to her head. When she's comfortable, he brings milk and graham crackers, a treat they shared when they were young, then he watches as she dips them and eats them, one after another, a whole package, until she's satisfied.

"Try to sleep, you've been up since five thirty. It's a crazy day."

"Where's Willie?"

"In the house. He's fine."

He stays next to her as the light fades, both of them comfortable with silence, and when she wakes, he's gone and it's dark outside. She is tucked into cool sheets, the stem of her brain throbbing, her hands and breasts damp with sweat, and though she knows the little man is crouching behind the wall, she summons enough strength to push the image away. She gets up and looks out the window facing south. Someone has fashioned a barricade out of stakes and rope to keep them away from the house and granary, but a few holdouts, half a dozen, are hunched on lawn chairs and stools in a cluster near the porch, where Victor sits in a brooding pose, his chin propped on his fist, watching them.

Half of one small, lovely pill sits on the kitchen counter beside a glass of water, and she swallows it. Then she dresses in jeans and the Dodgers sweatshirt she got from Steve Garvey when she threw out the pitch on opening day—was it last year?—and goes down the stairs and out the back door. For a minute or two she stands in the dark, her eyes adjusting, then walks down through the hayfield to the lake and along the shoreline north of the grove with its tents and campers and night fires. She stops at the fence that marks the boundary between farms, the fence her dad put up when she was nine or ten and which she painted all by herself. It hasn't been painted since, by the looks of it. She ducks between the top and bottom boards and steps onto her brother's land.

The rancid, nostalgic smell of the hog lot. She feels like crying, puking as she skirts the edge of it, hogs snorting and bumping against the boards on the other side. Maybe he's changed from the boy who made her life miserable, breaking her dolls and stealing food from her plate and talking at night through the wall that separated their rooms, telling her she was ugly, threatening to pull up her dress on the school bus to show her skinny ass. She lived in fear of him, yet pitied him, too, for how he was bullied by the older boys. When he was in ninth grade they caught him one day and threw him down into the outhouse hole behind the ball field.

Maybe he's better now. Being sheriff's deputy may have given him confidence. Maybe he's grown up and shed his bitterness. In truth, it was not right that he had to stay here and live with their dad. And why wouldn't he blame her for losing Mom, who had sometimes managed to protect him from her husband's rages?

She reaches the back door, the same old screen with the pull-spring. She draws it open. When she knocks, he is there instantly, bloated face, swollen eyelids. His lips, though, are shapely and fine. An artist's mouth.

He says, "Come in," holding the door wide.

She slips past his jutting belly, thinking *What am I doing?* and moves into the front room whose windows look out on the oak grove and the Bywater farm beyond it. They both sit, Skinny in their dad's easy chair, a mohair relic from the forties, she in the rocker that her mom used when they were babies.

"How is she?" Skinny asks.

"No different."

"Does she ever mention me?" His small eyes widen, and it takes her aback.

"Of course," she says. A lie. Dottie resides in a state of continual denial, as if someone else, not she, lived the first thirty-eight years of her life. Any mention of her dead husband, of her son, or even of Minnesota causes her to swivel and run like a hare chased by hounds.

"What does she say?"

Oh God. "Not much, you know. Sometimes she talks about when we were little. That kind of thing."

"Do you think she'd like to see me? Do you think I should go out and visit?"

"Well, sure. But you'd need to give her fair warning."

He looks at his hands, which Melanie still dreams about. Even when he was small they were big, and he used to grab her by the arm or the leg, or sometimes by the neck, and squeeze so hard that she would bruise. "She thinks I'm a bad person, a bad man, like our dad," he says.

Melanie can't think of what to say.

"She hated us, I know that," Skinny says. "And he was bad. When he died, I didn't feel a thing."

"I didn't either."

"You were out *there*."

"Yes."

"You didn't see him lying in the barn, his face in the slop. I got there before anything happened, I mean before they got a chance to tear into him. The pigs. It could have been worse."

"My God."

"And you didn't come back for the funeral."

"We should have. I'm sorry."

"I had to do everything myself. I had to find a church and cemetery."

"Where is he?" Their father had never stepped foot inside a church, and he mocked anyone who did.

"Lakeside, in Battlepoint. The funeral was at the Lutheran church there. He was the only pastor willing."

She wonders who, if anyone, showed up for the service but can't bring herself to ask.

"And I had to pay for it all. You wouldn't believe what caskets cost. And gravestones. What a goddamn scam."

"I'm sorry, Gerald. Is there anything I can do?"

He laughs, an ugly smile crimping his lip. "You're six years late, Annie. No. But it forced me to get a job—and I like what I'm doing, people respect me. They listen to me."

"And you're good at it, I'm sure."

Her brother almost smiles, and for a moment she allows herself to think they're coming to a kind of understanding, a reconciliation. Her head isn't hurting as badly, and her stomach is calm. Skinny's face has gone slack. His eyes are closed. Then he straightens in his chair, leans forward, and sets his fists like hammers on his knees.

"I was cruel, Annie, I know that. But I was only doing what I learned. I was a kid." He breathes in and out, then points a finger at her, his face swollen. "But you're an adult—and look at you. That was Peter, wasn't it, the one you went out with in the boat? What are you doing with him?"

"I didn't know he'd be here."

"Bullshit. He doesn't deserve a minute of your time. And what about that boy, that's gotta be the one the two of you had. Right?" Skinny's lips are quaking.

"Yes."

"How does *that* work? You gave him up. That's against the law, bringing him here."

"I'm not allowed to go and find him, if that's what you mean. If he finds me, that's something else."

"Enoch's quite the operator."

"He believes in what he's doing."

"Come on, Annie. Don't be a sucker."

"You know what Enoch did for me."

"I know what you think he did."

"Dad knew it, too, but he couldn't acknowledge it. He saw me that day—in Enoch's kitchen. You've heard the story."

"He said there wasn't any damage, that you weren't hurt at all. It only looked bad. Lots of blood."

"There was hardly any blood, Gerald. At the hospital they gave me the blouse I was wearing, which had only a small stain on the front. No bigger than a feather. I wasn't even wearing a bandage when they sent me home—two hours after it happened."

"Enoch lied. He told people you weren't breathing, that your lips were purple. He wanted everyone to think he could raise the dead."

"There's no point in arguing," she says.

"And now you're a fool for God. Isn't that nice—maybe it'll get you into heaven." Skinny rubs a hand on his lips. Then laughs. "You know what bothers me most? After Dad died, I figured you and Mom would come back, at least to visit—because he was gone and I was still here. And that when you did, I'd tell you I was sorry and things would be okay again. But now here you are, and it's got nothing to do with me. You're here for Enoch and Peter. And the kid. I don't matter—I never have, not to anybody."

She looks away, out the window, and just then a flash of silver blinds her. Then another flash, which she feels more than sees, causing her to recoil and shield her face. Skinny flies across the room and slams through the door and charges outside. By the time she steps into the yard, Skinny has a man by the neck—a short man, very stout, who's wriggling and shuffling and tossing his elbows, all to no effect.

"I have my press badge," he whines.

As if neutralizing an unruly dog, Skinny forces him to the ground and jams a knee on his chest. He pries the camera from his hands, examines it, and hands it back.

"Take out the film."

"Screw you."

"I have a sign at the end of my driveway that says 'No Trespassing.' I am also deputy sheriff of this county. Remove the film."

The photographer groans but submits. He hands the little cylinder to Skinny, who stands and watches the man struggle to his feet, wheezing.

"My camera," the photographer says between breaths.

"Where are you parked?"

"Back there," pointing, "along that gravel road."

Skinny hefts the camera with its flash attachment. "Very nice. What is it, a Canon?"

"Nikon."

Skinny tosses it back and forth, one hand to the other, and then he brings back his arm like a quarterback and tosses the camera far into the darkness. The sound it makes, landing in the grass, reminds Melanie of the time their mom undercooked a chicken dinner, and their dad, after a couple of bites, picked up the serving dish, collected the chicken from everyone's plates, then walked to the door and hurled the whole thing into the yard.

"I have to go," she says. "I'm not feeling well."

As the photographer stumbles off in search of his camera, Skinny turns to look at her, his face old and young at the same time—outsized, misshapen, angry, vulnerable.

"No need to thank me," he mutters.

"Then I won't," she says and walks away, east toward the campfires.

AUGUST 16—FRIDAY

Wakened by a quiet knocking sound, she squints at the lighted dial of her travel alarm. One fifteen. She listens and waits. When it comes again, she leaves her bed and steps lightly through the kitchen to the apartment door, where she deliberates for a moment before unlocking it and peeking through the crack. The bulb on the landing is dim, but she can make out Victor, retreating down the stairwell. And there's someone else, too. They both stop and turn.

"What is it? Adam?"

"Mel!" He slides past Victor, charges up the steps, and smothers her in a hard squeeze. Then kisses her on both cheeks before stepping back to have a look. She's wearing a nightgown with a scoop collar, and her hands go automatically to her neck. "Lovely Mel."

"Victor, we're good," she says and takes Adam by the arm and leads him inside, where she pulls the shades on the windows, then turns on the lights. "Here." She takes the couch and he sits, too, in the small stuffed chair opposite. She goes into the bedroom and puts on a robe and slippers.

"You're even more clever than I thought," Adam says, and he laughs, gold showing in his back molars. He's impeccably dressed in powder blue bell-bottoms and a matching shirt with ruffled collar. Blunt-toed, high-heeled, zip boots. His glasses are round, with translucent, red plastic frames.

"It's not what you think, Adam."

"Widmer's dancing on the ceiling. Sellerman even answered the phone when I called. They're loving it. And today before my flight, two new offers came in—just today. Good projects, good roles, better than you've seen in years."

"What I'm doing here has nothing to do with my career."

"Don't kid yourself, Mel, it has everything to do with your career. And authentic? God bless you! That sign above the driveway—Last Days Ranch? Made to order. Those tents in the woods, hippies singing round the fire. And the smell. Is it pigs? And my God, the cross on top of the barn with the spotlights on it. And the AP story! Three days from now there won't be a sentient being in the country who doesn't know about this. And the timing—holy shit. Release date's two weeks off! It's bloody genius."

"You're talking like it's not real, Adam. It's real."

"Ah, yes. Far be it from me to question anyone's sincerity. But you can't convince me it didn't occur to you how perfect this is."

Melanie gets up from the couch and goes in the kitchen. In fact, she's hardly given it a thought. "Do you want coffee? You must be exhausted."

"I grabbed the first flight I could get after seeing the story. Actually, your mom saw it and called me. I got routed through Chicago and landed in Minneapolis a little after nine. It's a long drive up here. Yes—coffee. Please."

"How is she doing?"

"Not happy, as you can imagine, but she'll be fine. She said to tell you she's sorry."

"For what?"

"For being such a bitch, I guess. She said to let you know she's ready to put your name back on the bank account and the deeds. She said to say you're clearly ready."

"How generous of her."

"Also to tell you she feels hurt, your sneaking off like you did."

"Poor Dottie."

"And that it's time to think about hiring a manager, and moving into separate places, the two of you."

"I'm not going back," Melanie says.

"To your mom?"

"To California."

"You mean—" and he points at the ceiling, then flaps his elbows like a pair of wings.

"Well, yes." She's filled the pot and scoops coffee into the top of the percolator.

"I don't know what you expect me to say about that."

"You could tell me I'm out of my mind."

"Please, Mel."

"You would believe, too, if you knew him like I did."

"Whom?"

"Enoch."

He chuckles, fans himself with his fingers. "I thought you were going to say God."

"Seriously, you wouldn't be able to ignore what he's saying. You'd know that something's going to happen."

He gives her a big, happy smile. "Are you going to try and convert me now?"

"I don't have the faith for that."

"Just as well."

She pours two cups of coffee and takes a spot on the couch across from him. He closes his eyes, sniffs it, sips, and shakes his head. "I love you, Mel, always. Which is not to say I think you've got all your shit together right now." He sets his cup on the table beside him, takes off his glasses, and rubs his eyes with the heels of his hands. "I'm wasted," he says. "Look, there's got to be more going on here than what I've heard. I mean, who's that weird guy that brought me up here?"

"Victor? He's one of the Ranchers—part of Enoch's community. Sort of like his personal assistant."

"When I drove in, he came out of the house and collared me, said to come back in the morning. I told him I'm here from L.A., and I was goddamned if I'd leave without seeing you tonight. So he brought me into the house and then took me out the back and through the yard and into this place by the rear door. I mean, there's an army of writers out front! But he said something strange, Mel. He said, 'She isn't going back with you.' And I said, 'Why's that?' And he said, 'She'll never leave her son behind.'"

"Shit." Melanie drains her coffee, then goes into the kitchen and pours herself another cup, the last thing she needs. Willie isn't a part of the story that people have to know. But Adam, for God's sake—he's a friend, isn't he? She can trust him.

"What did he mean?"

"My son, Willie," she says.

Adam sets three fingers against his forehead and groans. "Do tell."

They talk for another hour, or Melanie does—the whole backstory, and for once Adam holds his peace. The few words he offers are kind without being patronizing. Behind the lenses of his glasses, his eyes absorb everything. When she's finished, it's 2:45 a.m., and he gets up from the couch and kneels on the floor in front of her and puts his arms around her. "You're a marvel," he says.

"And I need to sleep."

"Me, too."

"You can have the couch."

"Oh, no." He stands and fishes out the keys for his rental car. "I came through a little city on the way up, maybe fifty miles in that direction"—he points—"and it's got a Holiday Inn. I'm going back there and I'm renting the best room they have, and tomorrow I'm going to sleep all day. Because obviously I'm no good to you here. At least not till after Monday. The nineteenth, right? And if you're still here after that—well, I will be too."

"You're a prince, Adam."

"I won't be far away."

He leans over, gives her a kiss on the cheek, and leaves. No sooner is he gone than she is hit by a wave of fatigue, gravity intensified. She can hardly bear her own weight. What she wants is to sneak over to the house and go up to Peter's room. She wants the pills he's keeping for her—but more than that, she wants him. Except she's too tired to put her body in motion, too tired even to think about it. So instead, she lays her head at the end of the couch, stretches out her legs, and gives herself up.

The voice arrives before the hand that grips his shoulder—his dad's voice, his dad's hand. "Peter, you've got a phone call."

"What time is it?"

"Just after eight."

He pulls on his pants while Enoch stands before the lion skin, arms crossed on his chest. Downstairs in the kitchen, the receiver is lying on the counter. It's Freddy.

"How'd you get this number?" Peter asks him.

"That's a hell of a piece you had on the wire yesterday." Freddy is practically shouting. "Look, I've got a sweet deal for you. Surreal. And don't let what happened between Joanie and me make you a fool, don't think with your tool. Ha ha."

"What've you got?"

"I talked to Rusty yesterday, and he—"

"I already talked to Rusty. We have an agreement. I'm sending him something next week. He wants it by Wednesday."

"Shut up and listen, numb-nuts. I know that. But I got you a better deal. A full-length feature on the whole nutty thing going on out there. We're talking lead article, cover story, art included, for September fifteenth. Or the eighteenth, I can't remember. The End-Times issue, they're calling it, and they're coming at it from every angle you can think of—religious, cultural, scientific, ancient prophecy. Nostradamus and shit. And yeah, the new Melanie Magnus film, natch. Gorgeous, right? Rusty wants copy by the *end* of the week. Not Wednesday but Friday. Ten thousand words."

Peter is trying to focus, but his mind keeps snapping to Willie, who has no business being here, things are too strange. And Melanie—the way she nearly collapsed in front of the cameras. He needs to go and check on her.

"Peter, are you hearing me?"

"I am."

"This is your launch pad, man. And it gets better."

"How much money?"

"'How much money?' You're loving this, aren't you?"

Peter looks out the kitchen window, where a bald man and a young woman in a halter top are walking hand in hand toward the showers.

"Eight grand. What was he giving you before?"

"He didn't say. Why isn't Rusty calling?"

"Because he asked *me* to call. I told him we go way back, you and I. But listen. Rusty wants to make sure this thing works out for him. I mean, *Rooster*'s audience is coastal, and you're out there in the middle of Fuckville. So here's the deal. He's scheduled a tentative date with the *Today Show* for Monday. That's your T minus zero, correct?"

"What do you mean?"

"I mean Barbara Walters and that new guy, Jim what's-his-face—they'll want a heart-to-heart with your old man, and of course with Cleopatra, too, before the trumpet sounds."

"They're coming out *here*? On Monday?"

"It puts you on the radar, preps the market. Some footage of the prophet and the Hollywood queen, zealots watching the skies and counting down to blastoff."

Ear to the phone, Peter nods at his dad and Victor as they settle with their coffee at the table, heads almost touching, hands wrapped around their mugs, muttering together.

"Have we got a deal, then? Monday shoot, Friday delivery."

"Friday, yeah," Peter says. "I can't promise Monday."

"Not good enough, pal. Crank it up. Eyes on the prize, for God's sake."

"Okay," Peter says. "I'll make it happen."

"Perfect! We'll be in touch, then. And you're more than welcome."

Minutes later in the dank basement, Peter finds his dad wrestling with a big green canvas tarp that is rolled in a fat cylinder. Enoch is on his hands and knees, trying to unroll it. "Give me a hand, will you? I need to see if it's still any good, if the grommets hold. I've still got all the poles and guy lines." He points into a dark corner.

Peter bends over and hefts it off the floor—the canvas has to weigh a hundred pounds—then walks backward with it, unspooling as he goes. It's the canopy they used for the reception that followed his mom's funeral.

"Reporters and TV crews need some shade. I'll have Victor put it up."

"I've got good news and bad news, Dad."

Enoch kneels to examine the tarp. "I don't see any rot, do you?"

"Good news is, you're about to be famous."

When Peter tells him about the phone call from Freddy, and plans for the *Today Show* on Monday morning, Enoch seems only mildly pleased. He looks up from the floor with a barbed smile and shakes his head. "And the bad?"

"Willie has to go home," Peter says. "We talked last night. He's running cross-country this fall and their practices start first thing Monday. He shouldn't miss them."

"Rick, his dad, he didn't say anything about that. He told me Willie could stay till Tuesday and didn't have to be in Duluth till Wednesday."

In fact, Peter is exaggerating. It's true that cross-country practices start Monday, but Willie didn't insist on leaving—Peter brought up the idea. The boy is fifteen, after all, and it can't be good for a kid his age, all this chaos. Not to mention, Peter has a story to write.

Enoch says, "We're spending the day together, he and I. Going for a drive."

"His mom doesn't even know he's here. That's messed up."

"It wasn't a problem for Rick."

"And why was that? Did you pay him?"

"He needed some help." Enoch looks up from the musty-smelling tarp, his eyes so bright that Peter has to steel himself against them. "Listen—Rick and I have an agreement, and I'm sticking to it. If Willie's uncomfortable, fine. There are worse things than being uncomfortable. And remember, I saw you rising ahead of me. Your long feet in the air. Come on now, give me a hand."

"Get up, Dad. I'll do it."

Enoch moves aside, and Peter rolls the tarp, puts it over his shoulder. He carries it up the stairs, out the back, and around to the front, where a white van from WDAY TV, Fargo, is parked in the circle drive. The reporters gathered here last night have wandered away, but the cluster of cars to the west, where the campers are parked, seems to have grown by half. Even now a Rambler station wagon with a pile of luggage strapped on top is pulling in off the township road. Peter steps over the rope and looks at Victor, still sitting on the porch, poor devil, then tosses the tarp to the ground.

noch's plan had been to leave this morning, right away, but he had no choice but to visit with the TV people from Fargo. Then a crew from a station in Duluth showed up, followed by a writer from a newspaper in Chicago. They all wanted Melanie, of course, who finally came down about ten o'clock in a mid-length hippie skirt and a sleeveless sweater—a chaste but sensual vision in creamy white. After which Enoch made his daily sweep through the grove, greeting the overnight arrivals, among them a lady falconer who told of her best two birds disappearing on the very day she heard Enoch's radio talk.

"They know," she said. "They always do."

Now he and Willie are driving the Cougar past an old sandpit with a rusted steam shovel adrift in the center of it. "Peter tells me you want to go home," Enoch says.

The boy lifts a shoulder and drops it.

"What's going on?"

"Nothing. I'm fine."

"Is something wrong?"

Willie punches the button on the glove box, and it falls open. He flips it shut then drops it open again. He snaps it closed. "Why did God tell you and nobody else?"

Enoch laughs. "That's hardly the case. Seems to me he's been telling people for years. Centuries. The way I see it, I'm only following up on warnings we've been getting for a long time, and mostly ignoring. And don't think for a minute that I'm the only one who knows. You can bet there are dozens of others, hundreds—thousands, probably. But most don't say anything, out of fear. And how can you blame them?"

Willie opens the glove box again and this time takes out the brown envelope with the car's title. He opens it and takes a look. "If nothing happens, do I still get the car?"

Enoch laughs. "It's yours," he says. He pulls off onto a dirt trail, goes another hundred yards, and parks in a clearing the size of a schoolyard. "Time for a walk, I want to show you something." He pops his door and steps from the car. They set off on a narrow path through birch and aspen, Enoch setting the pace and aware of Willie's displeasure at being taken on this little jaunt. "This is part of a nineteenth-century trail between the trading post on Crow Lake, where Battlepoint is now, and a French fort a few miles north of here. It was used by fur traders. Much later, it was built up into a road for the earliest cars."

"How much farther?" Willie asks.

"The road was closed and rerouted fifty years ago, and of course the trees have taken over again."

The pitch of the ground steepens, and the forest is suddenly lighter, as if they're about to break through into meadow. Enoch motions Willie forward and together they step out of the woods, then scramble side by side to the top of a grassy rise. Enoch has been here a dozen times. Nonetheless, the floor of his stomach drops away at the view. Willie, next to him, gulps his lungs full.

In front of them the ground disappears into a yawning gulf. It's as if the land has been sucked away by some prodigious force toward the center of the earth, or blasted by a meteor. Two hundred feet below and stretching for a mile in every direction is a vast marsh—hundreds of acres of cattails and bulrushes alive with red-wing and yellow-headed blackbirds, their scratchy voices filling the void with a dim cacophony. In the hazy distance a line of wooded hills seems to hang in the sky, nothing between here and there but some rags of cloud.

"It's called Illusion Ridge," Enoch says. "I don't know who gave it the name." He does not tell Willie that they're standing at the death site of his own father, who in 1920 when Enoch was nineteen drove off the road one spring night, drunk, and wasn't found until fall, by duck hunters down in the marsh. He doesn't tell Willie that from that time on, Enoch was responsible for running the farm, and that his plans for college and seminary were put on hold for good.

"It comes out of nowhere," Willie says. "If you're not paying attention, you could walk right off the edge."

Enoch allows the boy's words to hang in the air for a moment. "And that's how God works in our lives," he says, finally. "We're going along just fine, then bam, he brings something new."

Willie looks over, scowling. He opens his mouth as if to make an argument, then turns abruptly and heads back along the trail, moving so fast that Enoch, in order to keep up, must put his head down and concentrate on the ground to avoid tripping on deadfall or an exposed tree root. It's no easy thing, coming to the end of oneself—but there is no other way to prepare for God. If the boy means to leave, so be it. If the truth is too hard for him, fine. At least he's been offered a glimpse of the reckoning to come.

Back home, a woman with a notebook and camera is talking with Victor at the rope line. Black hair, black jacket, black slacks, black boots. Enoch has Willie drive straight into the shed, then walks over, the reporter watching him carefully as he comes. "Lucy Moon, *People Weekly*," she says. "And you're Enoch Bywater? I was asking Mr. Stubblefield if he knows whether Melanie Magnus is here."

"Where have you come from, Lucy?"

"We're based in New York, of course."

"She's here someplace, yes. Have you had a chance to visit with the pilgrims?" He nods toward the tents.

"I only just arrived."

"Let me take you for a walk. Then we'll see about Melanie."

More tents have gone up since morning, at least a dozen, and as Lucy snaps pictures, Enoch takes the opportunity to tell the new arrivals about the meeting tonight. He woke with the idea this morning and asked Victor to let everybody know. Next to Felix and Connie a pair of boys who rode in on bicycles have pitched a pup tent, and they're stooped over a pot of beans bubbling on a wood fire. Shaggy-looking boys, one blond, the other dark and curly-haired. Their bikes, sleek and loaded with packs, lean against a tree.

"We're having a service tonight in the barn." Enoch aims his thumb over his shoulder. "There'll be music and a message. Seven thirty."

"Where are you from?" Lucy asks the cyclists.

Wisconsin, they tell her, and explain how they're on the last lap of a cross-country ride. They read the story in yesterday's paper. "Figured we better not miss out," says the one with curly hair, stirring the beans.

"Just curious?" she says.

"I guess. I read this book last year that said the world's supposed to end before 1980."

"What if nothing happens?" Lucy asks.

He laughs. "We ride on. No offense," he adds, glancing at Enoch.

"None taken. I only hope you're ready."

"Oh, he's ready," Felix pipes up from the stool in front of his tent. "Both these guys are. I asked 'em if they got saved, and they said they did. Hey, Doug"—he looks over at the blond one—"show Enoch what you made."

Doug rises from his crouch and squeezes into the tiny tent, then returns with a square of cardboard about two by two, which he holds in front of his chest. "We were thinking a sign like this, a big one, for people driving by. If you've got boards and paint." There's a large bull's-eye at the center of the cardboard, with the words GROUND JESUS written in a circle around it. The lettering is executed in a stylish, antique font. "You know," he says, "like Ground Zero, in a nuclear war?"

The reporter says "Ha" and lifts her camera.

Enoch can picture the front page of a newspaper, a photograph of the boy's sign with oaks and tents beyond. "Go ahead," he tells them. "There's lumber behind the barn and tools in the steel shed—paint, too. Help yourself. And make sure it's large enough to see from the road."

That evening Enoch presides over the largest meeting there has ever been in the aviary, a hundred in attendance, including journalists and a number of locals who have never set foot in the place. Absent are Peter, Melanie, and Willie, and it's hard not to wonder if they've left to drive Willie home. When it's time to speak, Enoch finds himself expounding on his Old Testament namesake, who in light of his intimacy with God was spared physical death and translated straight to heaven. "And I used to resent my parents for giving me such an odd name," he says. Then he launches into Nebuchadnezzar again, whom Enoch can't stop thinking of these days: the king too proud to humble himself before the one sovereign God. "Don't follow his example. Don't set yourself up as a God unto yourself. Please, you don't want to be chewing on grass like a beast of the field!"

Shouts from the congregation of "Amen!" and "Yes, Lord!"

Hands reaching to heaven.

Swallows and pigeons darting and swooping like correlatives of the Spirit.

After, he follows the pilgrims to their tents, the sky clear, the stars popping out one after another like holes punched in a black screen. The lady falconer produces a fiddle and sets about finding her way haphazardly into an old hymn, *Blessed assurance, Jesus is mine / Oh what a foretaste of glory divine.* It's a moment unlike any Enoch can remember, the woman perched on a tri-legged stool, wayfarers of all ages singing, Felix and Connie, the two cyclists, the bald man with his wife and two babies, the sunbathers in their skimpy dress, an iron-haired grandma keeping time with a wooden spoon against the trunk of a burr oak. Dozens of people. And the Ranchers, too. Jimmy and Sarah. Matt, Eddie, and Ted. Not to mention Victor, who watches from the edge of the house, his head cocked to one side as if listening to something no one else can hear. And out on the periphery, sitting on the rock pile in the back pasture, Enoch spots Melanie, her arm draped around Willie and leaning against his shoulder. And beyond them, Peter too, standing on the dock with the reporter from *People Weekly.*

Enoch closes his eyes, better to hear what these good folks must sound like to people driving past and fishermen floating on the lake and to the sovereign God who even now, Enoch knows, is preparing their mansions in heaven. He thinks of Sylvie, who has given her word to join him here Monday, and prays that when the clouds part and gravity fails, her body too will rise, even if she waits until the instant of revelation to bend her knee.

A disturbance in the earth causes Enoch to look around, toward the township road—no cars or trucks—and then west where he sees nothing in the trees or the cemetery. The sky in that direction is still full of pink light. A high squeal brings to mind the word *pig,* and Enoch clambers up on the wide, low stump of an oak taken by last year's big storm. Below him, people are craning their necks, trying to place the sound, which comes again, coarse and high-pitched, followed by a staccato pounding that rises up through the stump on which Enoch stands. Somebody yells, "Hogs!" then someone else, "What the hell?" and Enoch from his perch sees ten or a dozen of them come stuttering through the trees, herky-jerky but fast, lumberingly a-skitter on the forest floor, pink and tan and mud-flecked in the day's last light. The singing stops, the woman's fiddling too, and the people scatter before the charge—more than a dozen animals coming now, twenty or thirty hogs in a halting, chaotic rush. A brass-colored boar takes out a yellow tent, spearing it with his tusked snout, then careening on, caped and flapping through the dusk, behind him a pink, round sow prancing on her toes, udders wagging fiercely. A man goes down before a sleek hog that doesn't slow at all as it runs him over, then executes a spinning turn and snatches a bite from Felix's pant leg.

Enoch on his stump catches movement at the house, Victor jumping from the porch, a .22 rifle clutched in his hand. *Oh, God.* Victor wades straight into the maelstrom of hogs and panicked campers, jamming shells into the magazine of his rifle. Animals and pilgrims part to make way for him, flow past him like water round a rock, Victor holding the rifle at his chest and watching as the field clears—all except for the caped boar, hobbled and blinded by the yellow tent he wears, the poor mad beast circling back to the center of camp, shrieking and hopping and snapping his head, thrashing and flailing, his apron of canvas drawn tight between tusk and hoof.

The other animals have passed through, some milling now on the lawn in front of the barn, one rooting beneath the porch, another bumping its nose against the wall of the new latrine and grunting. The panic over, people start back toward the grove, drawn by the spectacle of the frenzied boar. They form a wide circle around him, beguiled by his hapless dance—the animal all but obscured by the tent he wears. He whirls and kicks, a demon-child dressed for Halloween. Victor shoulders his way to the front of the crowd.

"Kill the pig!" someone shouts.

"Yes, kill the pig!"

Somebody starts to clap, then everyone joins in, shouting and clapping in rhythm. "Kill the pig, kill the pig."

Victor catches Enoch's eye, looking for a signal, which Enoch does not give. He would like to shake his head, put an end to it, but there's a will here larger than his own. As if to settle the matter himself, the crazed boar takes two steps back, whirls, and performs a pirouette, a twisting, vertical leap that sends the yellow tent flying. The boar comes to ground free, brassy and glistening, his legs like four short pegs fastened to the earth. Everyone goes silent, watching. His mouth is a foaming, bloody slash below his square snout. His eyes are hateful slits. He lowers his tusks, thrusts them into the ground, and tosses a clump of sod that lands on a young woman's bare arm. She screams and ducks behind one of the bicyclists. Victor levers a shell into the chamber of his rifle, and the hog turns at the sound and faces him.

"Kill the pig," Felix says.

Victor sets the rifle to his shoulder and takes aim. Those in the line of fire draw back and away. Then a flame bursts from the barrel and there is a simultaneous crack, and the boar's left eye is a bloody hole. The animal shakes his head, as if to insist that all is fine. He remains steady on his feet, hooves planted. Victor chambers another round and aims once more—except that now the boar lifts his snout, utters a short cry that sounds like *Oww!* then tips over dead, managing only a few weak stutter-kicks before going still.

Hours later in the quiet dark, her body aching, Melanie tries to imagine the Earth falling away beneath her and wonders if she will rise naked, her clothes left behind in a pile on the ground. She remembers the terrible upheaval of the hogs, and afterward, Skinny on his three-wheeler, laughing as he rounded them up. But there is something else, too, isn't there? Her beautiful son with his boy smell, the firmness of his cheek against her shoulder. And Peter, promising to come by later, once he and Willie have dug some baitworms.

"Peter?" she calls. "Peter?"

But he's forgotten, just like God is going to do—like God *must* do, undeserving as she is for giving away her son, abandoning her brother, failing in marriage. For marrying at all, knowing she didn't love him. And for sleeping with Peter against her better nature when she was fifteen years old.

Except that he hasn't forgotten. He's kneeling beside her now, his presence startling but welcome. She sits up straight on the couch and takes hold of his shoulder.

"Did you bring them?"

He stands and reaches down, and she takes his hands, allowing him to pull her from the couch and hold her against him, close. She can feel his head shaking.

"What?"

"I didn't bring them."

"But I need them. It's been since morning—and what time is it? I should have had one hours ago. What time is it?"

"Nearly midnight."

Aware of being wronged, she begins to cry. "My mom never forgets," she says. "Never. And my doctors make sure I have what I need." She can hear the whine in her voice and knows exactly how it sounds to anyone listening. It's a gift she has, projecting whatever she wills: need, rage, sweetness, bitter love, hope, vulnerability, or, as now, self-pity. She can make him understand. Make him feel what she feels. Make him regret that he has let her down so utterly.

"I'm not your mother," he whispers, right up close in her ear, even as he laces his fingers into hers, as if to make up for his cruelty. "And I'm not going to do what she would do. No pill tonight. You don't need it. I'll give you one in the morning."

She drops his hands and pulls away and folds herself in a feral crouch on the floor, watching herself from the edit room in her brain—the way she grips the shag carpeting with her fingers, chin set against her right knee, left leg curled beneath her, lips spread tightly across her teeth and cheeks hollowed, an expression of incredulity. "Go and get them," she tells Peter.

"No." His face shows nothing.

"Get them!" Louder this time, higher-pitched.

He bends close. "There's a reporter down there, within listening range. The best thing is to go to bed and sleep this off." He turns to walk away.

"Don't go," she says, hating the way she sounds. "Peter, please."

He stops but doesn't turn, his back to her, hands at his sides, fingers loose.

"Don't leave me."

He stands there, two steps from the door.

"I won't scream. Please stay."

He brings her into the kitchen and sits her down and finds milk in the fridge and heats it on the stove. She doesn't like the taste, but the warmth is pleasant, and soon her blood and muscles are humming with it, all her inner parts. She closes her eyes and wraps her fingers around the mug.

"You need to sleep," he tells her.

"Don't leave."

"I won't."

Eyes closed, she can feel him across from her like a large, sun-warmed rock. She listens to his breathing. He rises and comes around the table and leads her into the bedroom, where he turns down the bedspread and sheet. Before leaving the room, he tells her to get undressed.

The cotton sweater she's wearing is damp, and she peels it over her head and drops it on the floor. Her bra, too. Then she unbuttons her Levis and wiggles out of them, her underwear too, and steps away from the pile. She threads her arms and head into a short cotton nightgown from the closet, kicks her clothes against the wall, and falls into bed. The effects of the warm milk have dissipated. She pulls the sheet and thread-bare quilt to her chin. She feels chilled.

"Peter?"

But he's already here, his face hovering in the space above her like a planet. She can't tell if he's smiling, probably not, his eyes deep inside his skull, just two holes there, and his mouth a straight line.

"My head hurts, the pain is awful. And I'm freezing. And I'm afraid someone else can hear me." She has the sense of her body turning inside out, every nerve and tender fiber exposed. She is aware of the man behind the wall, crouching, listening, waiting.

"There's no one else but me."

"That's what you're saying. That's what you think. But there's someone else, and I need a Perc now. At least half of one. You can do that for me, Peter. Can't you? If you love me, please, it's all right. Just this one time."

His head moves back and forth as he undresses, his body going from dark to light, clothed to naked. Then he's in bed beside her, holding her, saying, "You don't need it tonight. Quiet now. Sleep." She moves so that her back is pressed against his chest and stomach, her breasts encircled by his arms, his knees wedged into the backs of her knees, and though she still hurts, the discomfort is more tolerable. She breathes, allowing herself a soft, easeful moan with each exhalation, and he remains where he is, encompassing her all around, not moving, his skin like an airtight seal to keep what is left of her from leaking out.

For a time, she forces herself to stay awake, aware of Peter's nakedness and heat. Then her head and body take on a comforting heaviness, as if they're being filled with warm flour, and before long she's gone, dreaming of a long stairway descending into the earth, no light at all, each step she takes—and she can't help taking them—bringing her closer to some rich, damp, fertile smell emanating from below, a subterranean lake or river.

AUGUST 17—SATURDAY

nstead of the old ache, there is something inside her head that feels like a rubbery scar, like a plug in the conduit through which her thinking flows. There is no pain. She fills her lungs with air, fuel for the hurt, ready for the bright surge at the back of her head. But it doesn't come. There is only a dull thickness. Peter is still holding her, his body pressed against her back, his knees tucked into hers, his breathing measured and quiet in her ear.

She whispers, "Is it gone?"

"You won't need them much longer." A morning rumble in his voice. She can feel him hard against her back, pulsing. "Sorry, I've gotta take a leak."

"Don't leave," she says, but not because she wants that. She doesn't. Not now, not yet. She's afraid if he gets up and leaves, the pain will return. He gives her a squeeze before drawing away, his arm sliding out from beneath her, and then he's out of bed and padding toward the bathroom. As she listens to his urine splashing in the toilet, she readies herself, clenching her teeth and her stomach. The pain does return, but it's quiet, uninsistent, almost apologetic. Peter comes back and sits next to her, bending close, looking into her eyes. His own are bloodshot, bags sagging beneath them, his hair spiked and tangled, like a crazy bird that's come through a storm.

"You didn't sleep," she says.

"Of course I slept. Best night of my life." The wrinkles deepen around his mouth when he smiles. She can't help thinking that he is old for his years, and something rises inside her, a feeling she hasn't had for a long time. Pity? Love? She doesn't know, but it makes her think better of herself.

He has a glass of water and also half a pill, which she accepts from him and swallows, but not with urgency. She does it out of duty, knowing that she has crossed over a line and won't be going back again.

"It's like my brain is mud. But it doesn't hurt anymore, or not much. It's just—I feel dumb, like I can't think."

"Because you're thinking on your own. Everything is starting to clear out. All that's left is going to be you."

"I forgot how stupid I am."

"You're brilliant, Melanie."

"You don't know me."

"Maybe I'm the only one who does."

"I've changed since I was fifteen."

He shakes his head. "You're the same. You're kind and you're full of love. But you're nobody's fool. You take in all the beauty that comes your way—it lives in you. But you can also see bullshit for what it is."

"Really?" she says, wanting to believe him. Wanting to think she can reclaim her life. "I'm all those things?"

"Damn right you are."

She throws off the covers and scrambles out of bed and past Peter to the window, where she sweeps open the curtains. The sun is well above the treetops, flooding the farmyard and pummeling the world—the heavy green of the spruces, the yellowing green of the still-dewy grass, the creamy house, the liver-red barn. And the August sky, barely blue, like skim milk. Every single thing radiating life, bursting out of itself.

She shakes her head. "I didn't see it till now."

"Didn't see what?"

"When I woke up, it was clear to me. Lying there next to you, and the smell of your skin, and the feel of you up against my back. And the sun against the curtains. Everything so real that I could finally see it: this prophecy of your dad's? What he's telling everybody? It's only what they wanted to hear. What I wanted to hear."

"You were looking for a way out," Peter says.

"I needed a way out." She covers her face with her hands and sees the massive shape of Enoch's bull, blotting out the sky, its hoof lifting away, feels the choking absence of air in her lungs. She pushes the memory aside and looks at Peter, his tired, lovely face. She sucks air, breathes. "I feel like an idiot," she says.

"Forget it."

"God *has* used him sometimes, right? We both know that."

Peter laughs. "He's off the deep end now, that's for sure."

"He's overextended himself, he's trying to give more than he's able to give."

"A nice way to put it."

She closes her eyes and tilts her head back and lets the sun pour against her, touching her gloriously through the cotton nightgown. Peter drapes an arm around her and they stand together at the window, though not as close as she would like, not jointed together and merging. That will come later—she can feel as much in the warm place where his arm rests on her neck and shoulder.

Then he says, "Oh, shit," and she opens her eyes.

Her brother has parked the sheriff's cruiser in front of the house and he's climbing the steps to Enoch's porch, black holster jutting from his hip, his chest and belly thrust forward in a way that reminds Melanie of when he was a boy, trying to mimic their dad. Peter runs into the bedroom and she follows. He starts yanking on his clothes.

"Please, don't go over there. Enoch can handle Skinny."

"If he tries arresting Victor, things will get ugly."

"What?"

"The pig."

"He doesn't care about the pig. Don't go over there!"

Peter stands from tying his shoes, lays a palm against her cheek. When he leans down to kiss her forehead, the lines on his face and the deep clarity of his irises—they're like little greenish-blue worlds—

make her want to cry. "Stay right here, promise?" he says. Then he turns and leaves.

Through the window she watches him cross to the front of the house and go inside.

What he sees first is Skinny's wide back filling the archway that separates dining room from kitchen. The big man turns. Behind him, Enoch sits smiling at the table with a cup of coffee. Victor stands off in the corner next to the fridge, arms crossed, watching. Peter shoulders past Skinny and takes a chair at the table with his dad.

"He's upset about his hog," Enoch says. "I was just telling him, we're the ones who ought to be complaining. Somebody could've gotten hurt."

Skinny points at Victor. "I could take you to civil court."

"Leave him out of it," Enoch says and turns in his chair. "Go out and move that rope line farther from the house," he tells Victor. "Past the driveway and the perennial beds. This morning someone trampled the tiger lilies. Go now."

As Victor leaves by the rear door, Skinny says, "Later, Spud," and helps himself to a chair at the table, across from Peter. It groans under his weight.

"That was a risky move last night," Enoch says, sipping his coffee.

"You can't prove a thing."

"I'd be glad to pay fair price for the animal."

"I don't want your money. I want them gone from the grove. I want the smell of them gone, I want their noise gone. It sounds like a tribe of witch doctors."

Everybody turns at the yelp of the screen door, and then Melanie walks in, dressed in baggy jeans and a loose sweatshirt, her hair pulled up and hidden inside a Dodgers cap. She points at her brother, who shrinks back in his chair. "What are you doing?" she says.

He swallows, his Adam's apple pumping.

"Don't be a bully, Gerald."

Skinny pushes back in his chair, which squeals against the floor. "I'm the one getting pushed around, living next door to a stinking circus. Then somebody shoots one of my animals." Skinny's voice is rising. "Not to mention, you coming back here and not even telling me. And what's the deal with you and"—he clamps his lips and waves a hand at Peter, who slides his feet back, centering them squarely beneath his weight. Whatever is about to happen, he's itching for it.

Enoch lifts a hand in the air. "Let's wrap this up now."

"No, she's my sister, and there's shit she needs to hear." Skinny brings both fists down hard on the table, making Enoch's coffee jump. "Dad was right, what he said about you and Mom. Nothing was ever good enough, clean enough, pretty enough. Gotta go to California. Gotta be in the movies. Gotta strut around and say all those smart-ass lines they give you to say."

"Shut up," Peter says. The blood is throbbing in his ears.

Melanie reaches out and lays a hand on one of her brother's fists. "Gerald, I'm sorry. Please." Her voice is silk, but Peter knows it won't make any difference, not now.

Skinny looks across the table at Peter, his eyes small and pink. "You think I'm some dumbass farmer. A goon. Okay, but at least I didn't waste my life trying to be something I'm not. And at least my dad never walked around like he had God on the intercom."

Enoch says, "Time for you to leave," and pushes back his chair, standing.

"And one more thing. I don't sleep with married women, and my dad didn't either."

"We aren't sleeping together," Melanie says, quietly. "And you don't know a thing about my marriage."

"Oh, that's right. You're as pure as snow. And you didn't get pregnant and have to leave town. And you don't take off your clothes for the cameras. Hell, you might as well go out on Main Street and lie down naked."

Peter goes right over the table for him, and he's so fast Skinny can't defend against the first blow, which catches him straight on, nose and mouth, something giving way beneath Peter's knuckles like an egg breaking, Skinny going backward and crashing to the kitchen floor, Peter on top of him, grinding a forearm into Skinny's neck. He can hear his dad shouting, and then he's yanked to his feet by the armpits, his dad's strength astonishing. Melanie darts forward and crouches next to her brother, but he pushes her off and scrambles to his feet. Blood pours from his nose, which is bent to one side. He paws at it, then comes forward. Peter tries to wrestle out of his dad's grip, but Enoch holds on tight, wrenching him to one side as Skinny throws a right hand that catches Enoch, not Peter, the sound of the blow like a mallet on sod. Enoch goes down and Peter pivots, driving his shoulder into Skinny's chest and smashing him into the cupboard. Then something at the edge of the room catches Peter's eye. Willie in the doorway, his mouth open.

"We're done," Peter says and drops into the nearest chair. He surveys the room: Enoch still parked on the green linoleum, Melanie crossing the floor to Willie, Skinny at the sink, twisting on the faucet and lifting a dishrag from its hook to dabble at his nose, then turning to squint at the nephew he has never seen, the room so quiet the two-note song of a chickadee makes everyone turn toward the open window.

"Well." Enoch gets to his feet and begins to make order of the kitchen, righting the two flipped chairs and putting the table straight. He stoops to retrieve a fallen saltshaker. At the sink, he takes the dishcloth away from Skinny's face for a better look. "We should get you into the clinic," he says, but Skinny shrugs him off, then takes the shaft of his nose with thumb and forefinger and cranks it more or less back in line. Blood runs from his nostrils. He aims a finger at Peter and taps the handcuffs that dangle from his belt.

"You'll need to go with me."

"I know," Peter says. "Let's go out the back way. We don't need to make a scene."

"What? Gerald, please," Melanie says.

Skinny spins a finger in the air, and Peter turns around and allows himself to be cuffed behind his back.

"Peter, what's he doing?" Willie says. "That guy was fighting, too."

"I went after him first. It'll be okay."

He allows Skinny to guide him into the back entry, where he waits for a couple of minutes until the big hood of the cruiser, a white Lincoln, noses into view. Skinny jumps out and opens the door, and Peter stoops into the cavernous rear seat and leans back against his forearms. The car's interior smells like cigarettes and urine. Instead of driving out past the rope line, Skinny heads north into the pasture, then close along the rear of the granary and barn into the hayfield, the edge of which he follows to

Mackey's slough where a rutted trail separates Bywater property from a wetland preserve. Peter hasn't been back here in years.

Skinny swerves to avoid a sapling that has grown up between the ruts, then he guns the engine through a muddy washout, the car's chassis rattling and squeaking beneath them. He drives with his left hand on the wheel, his right holding the rag on his broken nose. The trail goes on for a quarter of a mile before intersecting with the township road, and as they approach the steep grade, Skinny hits the gas instead of slowing. "Hang on," he says—and then Peter is staring up at the car's long hood taking flight. His head bangs on the roof before they come down hard on the gravel roadbed, the big sedan rocking on its springs.

"I think you broke my neck," Peter says.

"That was the plan." Skinny takes the rag from his face, rolls down the window, and tosses it. He turns and gives Peter a look, his nose like a plum gone bad, then he leans out and hawks into the wind. In Battlepoint, they pull in behind the courthouse and jail. Skinny leads him into a small office with a framed portrait of Nixon on the wall, and down an unlit hall past three cells, steel bars at the front and cinder block walls at the back, cots bolted to the floor, stainless steel sinks and toilets, everything open to view. Concrete floors. "Looks like we've got our pick." He turns Peter around and unlocks the cuffs, opens the door of the last cell, and nudges him inside.

"You haven't charged me."

"No? How about assaulting a peace officer. That's got a ring to it."

"Aren't you going to read me my rights?"

"I guess you weren't listening." Skinny shuts the barred door and turns the lock. Then instead of leaving, he leans back against the wall and runs an exploratory finger along his nose. "The judge will have to decide on bail. That'll be Monday morning. You've got some time to kill."

Peter thinks about the *Today Show,* reporters flying in thirty-six hours from now. "I've got to be out tomorrow," he says.

Skinny heads down the hall toward his office. "Good luck with that."

The bed is a stained mattress over plywood, and Peter lies down and stares up at the single bulb set inside a cage. It's not such a terrible thing, being here—away from the Ranch and the whole cooked-up mess his dad has managed to make of things, though he already misses Melanie.

And Willie too. In any case, he'll be out of here in a day and a half, in time to witness the collapse of the great charade. What's it going to look like? What will happen when nothing happens? What is Enoch's fallback stance? Does he have a speech ready to go? A revised interpretation of the dream? Peter has never seen his dad concede that his claims for God have fallen short, not even when Peter's mom died of cancer after a long struggle, Enoch praying every day for a miracle. He chalked up that loss as God's way of teaching him single-minded devotion—as if Ruth had been the Almighty's competition and existed for Enoch's purposes only. Then of course Sylvie came along, and the old man had no trouble justifying the association they established with each other. One weekend when Peter was home, he happened to overhear the two of them talking on the party line—speaking intimately, something about a sweater of his she had washed for him. Next day he asked his dad about it. "Who was that, anyway?" And Enoch, guardian of everyone else's purity, explained, nonchalant and apparently without remorse: "God isn't bound by the law, Peter. He's larger than anyone can imagine. And He always meets my needs."

The door at the end of the hallway rattles, the light goes on, and Skinny comes walking with a chair hanging from the hook of his finger. He sets it down and lowers himself onto it. Carefully. "I think you cracked my tailbone, too," he says and leans forward, elbows on knees.

"I think you'll live."

"If I could have it over again, you know what I'd do? I mean, if I had the guts."

"What are we talking about here?"

"I would have stopped him."

"Who?" Peter says.

"My dad. Do you think it was easy, after they left? Me and him alone in the house?"

Peter waits. Apparently, he's about to become a repository for the man's regrets and lamentations, or maybe his confessions. Okay, why not?

"A good hard beating of the sort he liked to give me," Skinny says. "I would've waited in the barn with a two-by-four. Then, *bang*. And a few good shots to the ribs. He would've respected that. Have you got any cigarettes?"

Peter takes out his pack and shakes one free, leans forward with it and lights it for him through the bars, then lights one for himself.

"There was this friend of my dad by the name of Van," Skinny says. "Lived in Warroad, and one time we went up there duck hunting. Dad agreed with everything Van said, that's what got me. This was 1960, a year or two after Mom and Annie left, and I remember Van saying, 'I hope you're voting for Kennedy,' and Dad saying, 'Yup,' which made no sense, he was always telling me what a pussy Kennedy was, that hair and his smile, and how Nixon—now there was a man. Later when they're both drinking, Van starts talking cars. He says, 'Which would you buy, Buick or Olds, if you had to buy one?' Dad was drunk, but he got this dead sober look on his face, like he was in a trap. He waits for a minute, then says—he was almost whispering—'I always drive a Chevy, you know that.' And Van's leaning into him, shaking his head. He says, 'Yeah, but which would you buy if you *had* to buy one. Buick or Olds?' He was fucking serious, and Dad took a breath before he said, 'Buick?' like he's asking a question. Van was real quiet, staring. Then he belched and laughed, and he said, 'If you told me Olds, I would've kicked your ass into your throat.' And Dad laughed too—but I'm telling you, he was scared."

Skinny squints at Peter through the steel bars, his head tipped to one side, drawing deeply, blowing it out. "Yeah," he says, "that's what I should've done."

A voice—Melanie's—calls from down the hall, "Gerald?" and Skinny launches to his feet. "Annie?" And he lumbers off toward the office, his fingers pressed to his lower spine. Soon he's back, shaking his head, Melanie and Willie both in tow.

"Guess they want to see you," he says, obviously disappointed. But Melanie corrects him: "Willie does," and she aims a look at Peter that's hard to figure—her eyes drilling him. He thinks of the time she told him she was pregnant, a similar look. They were sitting in his dad's truck that day, parked in the gravel pit again, and what surprised him more than what she said was her calm demeanor. She didn't seem the least bit afraid, only frighteningly solemn, as if she'd been given a glimpse of the whole rest of her life.

"Come with me." She takes Skinny by the arm and leads him back toward his office.

At first Willie says nothing. He doesn't take the chair Skinny left behind or step closer to the wall of bars. He just stands there in his bell-bottom jeans, his wavy brown hair falling in his eyes, his young face looking too old, angular and strong-boned. He seems puzzled, indignant, nose wrinkled and eyes screwed tight.

"I'm sorry you saw that," Peter says. He's balanced on the very edge of the bunk. "I lost control of myself."

"What's wrong with you?" Willie shakes his head, pushes his hair out of his eyes. "Why are you letting all this happen?"

"Letting what happen?"

"Everything. At the Ranch, with Enoch. All those people in the woods, and the ones with cameras. What good is it doing anybody?"

"I'm not the one making it happen."

"You don't believe what he's saying, do you? The end of the world?"

"You know I don't."

"Then why are you letting it go on? Melanie said something about a story you're writing, and about a TV show on Monday."

"It doesn't matter what I'm writing. Dad is going to do what he wants to do. He always has."

"Not if you stop him." Willie steps forward and takes hold of the bars with both fists. His eyes in the dim hallway are burning—it's as if they're generating their own light. "He's an old man," Willie says. "How hard can it be? Put him in a car and drive him someplace, for God's sake. Tell the idiots in their tents to get off your land and go back home, party's over."

Peter stands from the hard bed, then he sits again. He would not feel any more disoriented if Willie had pulled out a magic wand and made the steel bars evaporate. He grasps his own head like a basketball, fingers spread wide, and he squeezes, trying to make his brain work better. "Drive him where?" he asks. It's an idea Peter has never considered—and so simple.

"Does it matter? Figure it out."

"Wow," Peter says but then finds himself adding, "but who am I to stand in his way? This is what he wants. It's what he's always wanted."

"Okay. I guess you could sit there and watch him make an ass of himself in front of the whole world," Willie says.

The boy is a mind reader. In fact, Peter has been daydreaming about his dad's fall, the moment of Enoch's public humiliation. The end of his reign. The happy occasion of his admittance to the human club.

"He'd thank you later," Willie says. "I'll bet you anything."

Peter shakes his head. "And that's where you'd be wrong."

"But you're his son. Doesn't that make it your job to save him, if you can?"

Peter rises from the cot and stands as close to Willie as he can, only steel bars separating them, and looks into his face, amazed at the strength he sees there. "Did Melanie put you up to this?" he asks.

Willie shakes his head, unequivocal. "No." Then he turns at the sound of the door opening, followed by Melanie's voice. "Are you guys finished?"

"Yup," Willie says.

She comes down the hall and hooks her son's arm with her own, saying nothing to Peter, only giving him that glare again, deadly serious, before she leads the boy away.

He's always been a pacer, a walker, someone who puts his body in motion in order to let his mind figure things out. And now, before he's moved from one end of his ten-foot cell to the other, a dream comes back from last night, a dream he has had many times before. The setting might change, but the situation is always the same: he is trying to get someplace—to the end of a hallway, through a door, into an elevator, to the other side of a field—when he comes face to face with the lion he killed in the calf shed. It's a terrifying dream, the animal's muscled thighs rippling, its eyes like small, dusky tunnels into hell, and without exception it ends with Peter in retreat, cautiously back-stepping, or else turning around to sprint for his life, heart running amok in his chest. But last night was different. He was on a high mountainside, trying to navigate a treacherous switchback on his way to a green valley below. That's when the lion materialized before him, perched on a rock not six feet away. Peter's instinct was to turn and run. He did not run, however, because he saw on the lion's face an expression of human care—this was a surprise to Peter—a moistness in the beast's eye, the smallest curve of smile on the terrible mouth. Also, he could hear water running in the valley below and imagined what it would taste like, cold on his tongue. And so he stepped forward, toward the animal, no longer afraid, not caring in the least if it meant his life. And that's when he woke.

"Skinny!" he shouts. "I need you!"

A groan from behind the office door. Then Skinny pushes through and comes down the hall, his boots dragging on the floor.

"What did she tell you?" Peter asks.

"Not much. To give you what you asked for."

"If I promise you that I will clear out the oak grove tomorrow, make them all go away, and put an end to this nonsense, will you drop the charges and let me out of here?"

"How can I trust that you'll do like you say?"

"Look, I have to call somebody first. Then I'll explain."

Skinny sighs, unlocks the door, and leads Peter back down the hall. In the office he points at the desk phone. "Dial 9 to get out. Long distance?"

"No, but I'll need a phone book."

Sylvie Young has a public listing, thank God, and Peter spins her number in, hoping she's home. She picks up on the fourth ring, her voice guarded, as if expecting bad news. Peter covers his eyes, trying to picture her face, of which he has no memory, and trying to understand how she has managed to tolerate Enoch's grandiose convictions.

"This is Peter Bywater."

A pause. "Peter? Is your dad all right?"

"He's fine, Mrs. Young, but I have an odd request to make of you."

On the other end, she is silent for a few moments, and Peter wonders if this woman really loves his father, and if she does, whether it's the kind of love that Enoch needs right now, the kind that could save him. He wonders, too, about his own capacity for love. Is it strong enough to carry the people he's been given over this rough patch of road? Is that even his job? And he hopes it is deep enough to convince Melanie that what they had together, those years ago, was more than a youthful indulgence.

Since getting back from town this afternoon, she has avoided Enoch, afraid that he will see through her, divine her secret. Except for Willie, she has spoken only to Sarah Levitz, who came over and confessed that she and Jimmy are planning to leave the Ranch tomorrow—they've got a friend coming with a truck. Now it's closing in on five o'clock, and she is in the boat with Peter and Willie, anchored a quarter-mile offshore. Peter has cut a deal with Skinny, and he's been setting out the plan, which makes sense to Melanie's head if not her heart.

"It's so cold-blooded," she says.

The sky is clear, with a small breeze out of the south. On shore, campers are tossing Frisbees and playing volleyball and sunning themselves, some moving between the oak grove and the latrines and showers. Some are speaking with journalists, whom Enoch has allowed past the rope line. Enoch himself is perched on the red Farmall, pulling the baler over windrows of cut alfalfa. Astride the hayrack behind is Victor, receiving and stacking bales. A perfect photo op, with a camera crew filming.

Peter says, "Try to imagine what'll happen Tuesday if we do nothing. Seriously. Think about it."

"And this woman, Sylvie. She's going to pick him up and drive him to *her* place?"

Peter nods. "First thing tomorrow morning."

"Why her?"

"Who else is there?"

"And she's certain he'll go along with her?"

"That's what she says. Then we'll join them before he figures out what's going on. You and I—not Willie. We're taking him home tonight."

Melanie glances over at her son, who's staring at the floor of the boat, elbows on his knees. He hasn't said a word as Peter explains how things are going to work. She points toward shore. "And what do we tell the pilgrims?"

"We let them know it's over. We say, 'Scram, get the hell off our land.'"

"They'll want to know what happened."

"We'll tell them Enoch has given it up."

"That would be a lie."

"Fine. We tell them he's not well, which is true."

"What if they won't leave?"

"Your brother's agreed to help with that part." Peter smiles, showing his teeth—happy, she thinks, sure of himself. It reminds her of the boy she fell in love with.

"And who exactly is Sylvie?"

"A friend of his. You remember Dr. Young." Peter looks into Melanie's face. "Sylvie's his widow."

It takes a moment to sink in. Then, "Oh, my," she says. There is an odd kind of sense about it, though. Synchronicity.

Willie perks up. "Enoch's got a girlfriend?"

Peter laughs. "You could call her that, sure. What she wants to do is something called an intervention. It's for people with addiction problems. Drug addicts. Alcoholics. You bring together the significant people in their life, and all together you confront them. In Dad's case, it's not so much addiction as a habit of mind. Messianic delusions. And she thinks it's worth a try."

"Sounds too easy," Melanie says.

"Bottom line, she's got a place we can keep him for a couple days till things blow over. Nobody'll know where he is."

"But what do we *do*?" Melanie says. She imagines Enoch tied to a kitchen chair, a black hood covering his face.

"We sit him down and explain how his actions have hurt us. That won't be hard, at least for me. We tell him what we're going to do if he refuses to confront the problem. And how we expect him to change."

"If he believes in what he's doing, why would he want to change?" Melanie says. "That's the catch, isn't it? And how do we keep him there if he refuses to be kept?"

"That's not hard," Willie says. "You don't let him leave."

"That's kidnapping. It's illegal. I mean, are you ready for this, Peter?"

He points at the prow of the boat where the anchor rope is holding them steady against the breeze and nods at Willie, who scissors over the bench seat and starts winding the crank handle. "I'm past ready," he says. "Let's go. I told Dad we'd have an early meal with him, and I don't want him thinking something's going on."

"Should we tell him we're taking Willie back to Fargo?"

As the anchor breaks water, Peter reaches to the console and jams his thumb on the ignition button. The outboard engine jumps to life. "We tell him nothing," he shouts.

An hour later, at supper, talk is sparse. Enoch seems troubled, his arms lax on the table, his head hanging, as if he senses mutiny. Or maybe he's simply exhausted. Peter has explained that Skinny released him as a favor to Melanie, and Enoch only shrugged. His long white hair comes out from behind an ear and falls alongside his face, but he doesn't bother to push it back.

"Are you all right?" Melanie says.

He leans back as Victor refills his glass from a sweating pitcher of tea.

"Maybe you overdid it today, on the tractor. Too much sun."

He straightens in his chair and rubs his eyes. "Being the one who knows, the one who has to carry it all—the weight of that, I think it's catching up to me. I'll be glad when it's over."

"You should lie down." Melanie's lungs feel empty, crushed. Before supper she took her second half-pill of the day, but she doesn't feel any better. *I'm such a shit,* she tells herself. Doesn't it come down to a choice, after all? Hasn't she *chosen* to turn away from Enoch's dream? And couldn't she just as easily turn back again? Yet she knows that she cannot turn back, even though nothing has really changed since yesterday. The idea of Christ's arrival in the clouds, so epically satisfying, so complete in its answer to every need and question, cannot possibly happen on one man's guarantee or one man's timetable. Not even Enoch's. As if reading her mind, he reaches out and covers her hands with a big warm paw, pins it on the table. She looks into his face, not sure how to read the hard creases there. She can't tell if he is angry or broken.

Enoch turns to Peter. He says, "For years I have prayed without ceasing that you would simply accept His love. What makes you so proud?"

"I'm here, Dad, aren't I?"

"Yes, to write the story of my failure."

Peter leans across the table, his eyes fierce. "You said I rose along with you."

"So I did."

"You don't believe it?"

"Faith is a challenge, it's not a feeling." He squints off into the corner. "On the night before his death, Christ asked his friends to stay with him, but they fell asleep. Then he prayed to his Father that the cup of suffering might pass from him. Until now, I have struggled with that scripture. I haven't known what it means to be alone."

"Look out the window, Dad. They're here because of you. What more do you want?"

Enoch looks up at the ceiling and groans. "What more? I want the people I love to share my hope." He looks around the table, blinking, then he turns to Melanie. "You're still with me, aren't you?"

She opens her mouth to speak but cannot. It's as if she has swallowed a thimbleful of dirt. She wants to say, *Yes, I'm with you—but no, you're asking too much this time.* She wants to say, *No, it's not going to happen.*

"I'm always with you," she says. "And I believe in your dream. But it's *your* dream, Enoch. It's yours alone."

"Well, then." He stands and rakes a hand through his forest of hair, then sweeps the table with cold eyes and strides from the room.

Peter and Willie head upstairs, presumably to pack Willie's things, and Melanie helps Victor with the dishes before returning to the granary, where she spends the next two hours lying on the couch, fighting an urge to go find Peter and ask for a Perc. But she's had her quota for the day and knows what he would say. Besides, the pain isn't bad—it's an annoyance more than anything.

The plan is to leave with Willie about nine, while worship in the barn is still in full swing, and though she doesn't mean to go over there, the sounds from the aviary tempt her through the walls, violin, harmonica, trumpet, and piano of course, along with the assembly of voices, and about eight o'clock she finds herself drawn downstairs and across the lawn to the barn. She is concerned about attracting attention, but when she climbs to the loft, it's apparent that her presence won't matter. There must be a hundred and fifty people, maybe two hundred, all of them swaying, hands lifted. A mingling of smells. Wood smoke and grilled meat, oily hair, unbathed bodies. A thin, skunky trace of pot. The air so close and thick it's hard to breathe. Sweat breaks out on her back and trickles down between her breasts. The only person who seems to notice she's here is Enoch on his high stool, off to one side. He's not singing but scanning the crowd, wiping his face with a handkerchief, eyes sparkling. He smiles at her, tipping his head.

The worship is of such a magnitude—people weeping and shouting, some falling to the floor—that Melanie all but slips into believing again. There is a twitching pulse at the back of her tongue, a warm current flowing through her belly. Then a voice, whispering, *I'm here with you, like I have always been.* She listens to the voices around her, waiting for the whisper to come again, which it does, once the singing begins to fade: *Go. Now.*

She peeks at her watch—eight forty—and begins to weave toward the edge of the crowd, those on the floor rousing themselves and sitting up, the violinist lowering her instrument, Sarah leaning back from the keyboard. Enoch moves to center stage as Melanie starts down the steps. Descending, she hears his voice, soft and urgent:

"There is no time left for anything but the nurturing of your soul. Ask yourself: where will you spend eternity?"

In the apartment, she strips out of her damp clothes and steps into the shower, turning the faucet on cold, then lukewarm, standing with her forearms against the wall, the stream of water massaging her. When she hears the knocking on her door, she turns off the water and wraps herself in a towel and lets them in, Peter and Willie, the two of them looking uncannily alike, their faces square and solemn, all planes and angles, as if slapped together by rough carpentry.

"We gotta go before he wraps things up," Peter says. "I don't want a scene."

"And we shouldn't tell him we're leaving?"

"I left a note on his table. That you and I are returning tonight, late."

She dresses in lightweight jeans, loose T-shirt, and sneakers and leaves her hair to air-dry. Downstairs, Peter leads them past his car, parked in the driveway, and into the machine shed where he flips on the light, beneath which sits the Cougar, freshly waxed.

"I don't think he's transferred the title yet," Willie says.

"There'll be time for that. Here." Peter flips him the keys.

Melanie and Willie follow Peter in his Galaxie, its square taillights leading them west through forests and farmland, the occasional lake glowing beneath a wash of stars. Willie drives with a hand slung over the top of the wheel, as if he's been doing it for years, and Melanie marvels at his self-possession, his strength at such a young age to make things happen. He is a match for his grandpa. More than.

"Why let him ruin everything he's got?" Willie says, as if arguing with himself, doubting himself. He glances over, and she sees the whites of his eyes. "He's in too deep to pull out, don't you think? Someone's got to do it for him."

Melanie hopes Willie is right. "It's going to be hard," she says.

"Yeah." Willie rolls down his window a crack to let in air. Ahead of them, Peter's taillights briefly dip below a hill.

"You must wish you hadn't come," Melanie says.

"No, I don't wish that. It's been a strange few days, though. Of course my whole life has been strange."

She wants him to pull over on the shoulder and wrap him in her arms. She wants to go back fifteen years and live that day over again. This time she wouldn't let anyone take him away from her. She would tell them to leave. She would keep her son, find a way to raise him by herself, without her mom. Melanie cries for a while, the tears hot behind her eyes and warm on her cheeks. Finally, she says, "I wish I could have given you the life you deserve."

"My life has been fine."

"But strange, you said."

He reaches out and flips on the radio and fiddles with the tuner, producing a few seconds of Steely Dan before turning it off. "My dad is good, and my mom is too. They've always been good to me. I don't want you to think they haven't."

"I don't think that."

He turns on the radio again, Top 40, and for half an hour, maybe an hour, they listen without talking. Dumb songs mostly. Paul Anka, Bachman Turner Overdrive, Three Dog Night, Helen Reddy. She wishes the trip were longer, that she could sit here beside him all night. She wonders when they'll see each other again, whether he's anxious to be rid of her, whether it's been a disappointment for him, meeting her. But she stays quiet, out of fear she'll make him say something he doesn't mean. They drive out of the woods into flat prairie, the pulse of heat lightning flashing in the north, patterns against the darkness—there, and there. Then nothing for a while. And there. Gone, then back again, like a coded message, an arrhythmic heart.

"Wow," she says.

"Yeah."

They roll through a small town whose only bar has a large, pink, neon cat perched on its roof, winking and flicking its long tail. They drive past a farmhouse lit up like Christmas, cars overflowing in the yard, and then, farther west, a giant tractor pulling who-knows-what-kind-of-implement along the road. For a time, they pace a westbound train with its mile-long string of empty coal cars. Willie turns and looks at her. "What are you going to do?" he says.

It takes her by surprise. To think he cares enough to ask! In fact, she's given almost no thought to what comes next. Adam came to see her yesterday—he's staying close by, in Bemidji, minding his assets—and pestered her about the Labor Day premier, as if she didn't remember. She told him no, she couldn't promise she'd be there, and he left without arguing, as sober-faced as she has seen him.

"I don't know what I'll do."

"Keep acting," Willie says, and his voice cracks, making her love him all the more, if that's possible. She reaches over and takes his hand.

"I don't know about that."

"Think about it."

"Okay," she says.

"Promise?"

"Yes."

They follow Peter's taillights into Fargo and through its dark streets and park behind his car at the rowhouse apartments a block from the river. It's a minute or two before midnight. Willie steps from the car and she does too, and they meet at the trunk, where he takes out his suitcase and sets it on the boulevard grass, then stands there looking vulnerable but also confident with his outsize shoulders and hands. She reaches up to give him a hug, which he returns. Stepping back, she bumps into Peter, who has come up behind her.

Son and father shake hands, embrace, separate.

Willie looks at her, his eyes like her own, his face like Peter's. "I'll be watching for you," he says. Then he turns and walks up the sidewalk and takes the stairs to his front door, pulling a key from his pocket as he goes. He glances back before letting himself in.

AUGUST 18—SUNDAY

As a boy he trapped muskrats in the small lodges that dotted Last Lake, fur season beginning in November when surface ice was just starting to form. There were times it sagged beneath him as he walked, sustaining his weight, barely, as a thousand cracks snaked away like spokes of a wheel, the ice snapping and creaking and tinging around him. All he could do was head for shore, stepping fast and praying for the best. Just once did he break through, the water only chest deep when it happened.

That's what Enoch is feeling now, things giving way beneath him. The boy wanting to go back home, Peter steadfast in his cynicism, Melanie's lovely face last night at supper, cloudy with doubt. Not to mention the Ranchers, all of whom have fled except for Jimmy, Sarah, and one of the single men, Matt. Of course the pilgrims are here, many of them steadfast in hope—at least if their zeal last night counts for anything. And thanks to Melanie, word is getting out. Has gotten out. Already this morning, a call from the *New York Times,* asking for clarification on the dream and fishing for a memorable quote, which Enoch was happy to provide. And tomorrow before dawn the crew from NBC arrives.

Still, for the first time since his brief death, the conviction in his bones has gone missing. "Help Thou mine unbelief," he says.

Outside, the tents are sagging from last night's storm, the oaks a dull, silvery green beneath a leaden sky. No wind at all, though some branches are down from the cottonwoods behind the house and also from the oaks in the grove. A man is lifting a four-foot, leafy limb from the roof of his tent, and a woman is crossing to the showers with a towel on her shoulder. Otherwise it's quiet. On his way downstairs, Enoch looked into Peter's room, where the bed was empty. Did they drive into bad weather and have to stop someplace? Maybe it got late and they pulled over to sleep on their way back. Unless they slept together in the granary. Enoch hasn't checked yet to see if Peter's car is in the shed.

Bacon is frying, and Victor is making the toast. He turns, his face somber as usual. "We've got cleanup to do. Oh, a hundred and twenty this morning."

"Have you seen Peter?"

Victor shakes his head.

Enoch crosses to the front of the house and goes out on the porch. The journalists who were here last night are gone, and none has arrived to replace them. The weather, no doubt. He stoops to grab an empty fast-food sack from the floor and as he straightens, a car turns into the driveway, a car he knows. It pulls into the circle and stops. Sylvie steps out and waves, awkwardly, elbow close to her body. He looks at his watch—6:40—then moves from the porch in a half-run and goes to her open window. The air is still heavy from the storm, and it makes filling his lungs a conscious act.

"You're a day early, aren't you?" He glances back at the house, then over at the barn, wondering who might be watching. She hasn't been here for years, though it's too late to matter now. "Are you all right?" From the west comes a growl of thunder, and he thinks, *We're in for another round.*

"How many people?" she asks, pointing at the tents.

"A hundred and twenty. Victor's morning count."

"I need time with you, alone, before the carnival starts. I'm taking you home with me for a few hours." She grabs his hand, her fingers are moist and cold.

"Come in for breakfast." He opens her door and pulls her to her feet.

"No, let's go. Please. I'll make you something at my place."

"Then I should tell Victor." As he heads for the house, lightning crashes behind him, the impact like a blow to his back, and he turns in time to see a virgin white pine in the woods across the road fall away in two parts, east and west.

Sylvie has turned too, hands covering her mouth. He comes back to her. Then two snaps of thunder draw his eyes to the cemetery, where the tall black Hansen stone is shimmering, green. Enoch touches Sylvie's shoulder. "It's happening."

"It's a storm, Enoch."

He points at the glowing obelisk. "That was in my dream."

Drops of rain fall like marbles—and from the west comes a revving engine, Skinny's white cruiser, lights spinning as it crashes through the fence at his property line and bounces into the oak grove. Skinny brakes hard and jumps out, arms waving. "Get up!" he shouts. "Tornado! Go to the house! Tornado!"

Enoch grabs Sylvie's arm and he sets off running toward the grove, from which the campers are emerging half-dressed, some in their underwear, one man buck naked, his chest and belly as white as a winter carp, his penis jutting orangey red like a carrot, stiff from sleep. Thunder booms, this time from the depths of the earth. The sky has gone black. *And the sun shall be darkened*, Enoch thinks, *and then shall appear the sign of the Son of man in heaven.*

Skinny races through the grove, whacking tents, yelling, herding the pilgrims like hogs. "No, no!" Enoch shouts. He stops and lifts his arms. "Can't you see? This is it, praise God!"

But they surge around and past him, Sylvie turning to help a woman and her babies, taking one up in her own arms and sprinting east toward the house. A man collides with Enoch, knocking him flat, the young curly-haired cyclist, who keeps on going. Enoch pushes to his knees, then finds himself whisked to his feet by the armpits.

Victor, his slit-eyes cranked wide.

"Peter, Melanie," Enoch says. "Where are they?"

Victor turns and runs.

Skinny grabs Enoch's shoulders and yells into his face, "Funnel in

Kesler at six thirty—do you hear me?—and heading this way." He shakes Enoch hard, as if he were a misbehaving child. Then he's gone.

Funnel, Kesler. The words streak through his brain but evaporate in the next flash, which leaves an image in Enoch's mind of bodies breaking free of the soil and rising like so many doves from a cage. He recalls the sensation from his dream, gravity losing its grip, and he knows that even now the dead in Christ are quickening, their dry bones locking into place, new eyes burgeoning in their skulls. Turning, he sees Sylvie coming forward at a dead run, and shouting, though he can't make out her words. She takes him by the arm and starts to drag him toward the house. Then Victor rounds the front porch, gasping.

"Peter? Melanie?" Enoch says.

"Not here."

"This is it!" Enoch shouts, and Victor's face blooms with unspoiled light. Sylvie, though, has him by the arm, hanging on, and somehow Skinny has the other, and there's no resisting as they pull him onto the porch and through the house and down the stairs into the basement, which is crammed full, every inch of floor occupied, pilgrims squatting on their haunches or huddled in fleshy knots, some standing against the walls, rigid, as if awaiting execution. No bare floor to be seen. A baby shrieks, as if being jabbed with a needle, and a woman chants, "Jesus, Jesus," her voice a two-note wail. Next to Enoch, a man on his knees, fists pressing against his forehead, mutters the Lord's Prayer. In the corner by the furnace a pair of men start fighting, and Skinny lets go of Enoch's arm to break them up.

"Ain't this what we're here for?" a voice says.

Enoch turns.

Felix in a sleeveless T-shirt, pointing at the ceiling, toward heaven.

"It is," Enoch says.

"Then what are y'all doing down here in this rat hole?"

"Yes! Ancient of Days!" Laughing, Enoch pulls free of Sylvie's grip and pushes his way to the stairs, which he mounts two at a time, alighting on the main floor where the air is so thick he has to lean against the wall to keep his feet. He throws himself forward—through the kitchen and back porch then out into the backyard, glancing behind to see Felix and Victor close on his heels.

To the north, a black, anvil-shaped cloud the size of an office building. It hangs above Last Lake, dropping rain like a wall of nails, the sound deafening. As Enoch watches, a bolt of sun pierces it, touching the dark water with a spot of daylight. "Here I am!" Victor shouts and he breaks out in his halting lope toward the water. Enoch follows, heart burning in his chest. They stop, winded, at the rock pile next to which Melanie was stomped by the bull, and together, scrambling on all fours, they climb, Enoch reaching for the elderberry bush that grows from the top of the pile. He pushes to his feet, and holding to the bush he peers straight up into the cloud, which is massed above them, an icy rain pelting his face, Victor right next to him. The sky opens in a spinning vortex that drops toward them like the end of an elephant's trunk, its shaggy opening at least fifty feet across, a dance of lightning inside, arcing blue and yellow and green. Enoch smells gas and dirt and vegetable rot, the essence of the earth. He hears obliterating shrieks, and the white noise of a world in free fall. There is no breath in Enoch's lungs, but if there were, he would say, *Is this the path to glory?*

Victor shouts, "Take me, take me!" as a leaded-glass window zips past his reaching arms. Then a flying sow with two lavender pigs hanging from its teats, followed by a tumbling sofa and a large green wall tent, upright and taut. Somebody grabs Enoch's leg, midcalf, and he looks down at Felix, hunched small and wedged between rocks. At the sound of a hundred trees breaking, Enoch turns and watches the second and attic floors of his house twist and lift away from the floor below, one gable freeing itself and coming toward him in a wobbly line, a wingless plane. And then his dream moment, the end of gravity, the rocks beside him lifting, and Victor lifting, too, the yellow soles of his boots the last things Enoch sees, even as he himself holds tight to the elderberry bush, which nonetheless slips from his grasp. He rises ass first into the air like a child snatched by the waistband—only to collide with something hard and heavy, which compels him to the earth.

For the second time in two weeks, he's gone from himself.

No dreaming this time.

And then he returns, in darkness.

The smell of shattered wood. The taste of grass and dirt. The whine of wind receding. Enoch is lying on his stomach, his arms and legs spread wide, his fingers gripping the sod, his mouth full of cut hay. He recalls a picture from Sunday school: a man in royal attire, purple robes, grazing in a meadow like an ox. When he tries to swallow, he chokes on a lump of soil. He wretches, stomach bile sour in his mouth. The same old body, he's still trapped inside of it. It can't be so, and yet it must be so. He gathers his strength and begins crawling toward a wedge of daylight, and before long emerges from the broken gable of his house, which has come to rest only yards from the rock pile. What he sees first is Felix, lying on his back, wrists crossed on his chest, a chunk of chimney brick jutting from the middle of his forehead. Beside him on the ground, a baby bottle with a rubber nipple, still half full of milk. The poor boy's face guileless, his blue lips parted as if to speak.

Enoch creeps over and puts fingers on Felix's thin neck, which is warm and still, and though he wants to pray, there is no use in it. He knows this. *And how is it possible that I am still breathing?* he thinks. He struggles to his feet and stands to look around. Shattered oaks to the west, and past them Skinny's farm, ruined, flattened barn and missing house, silo still standing. Beyond, the cemetery's black obelisk is untouched. He surveys his own place. The house his father built from a Sears kit reduced to a single story. The machine shed a jumbled pile of steel. The granary roofless. The barn whole, incredibly.

The lake's surface is troubled but shining beneath a sun just now breaking through green-yellow clouds, the dark sky and its rumblings receding northeast. He considers the hundred or so paces between himself and the water, knowing how much easier it would be to wade in among the bulrushes and inundate his lungs than to face what he can feel approaching even now from behind. He has the kind of courage such a thing would require, the animal kind. But he also has the other sort, which can be willed into being—something he does now, automatically, as they begin to emerge from the basement, a woman extending her hand as if to touch Enoch across the space between them. A comforting gesture, but to what purpose? It's Sylvie, he realizes. She might be someone from long ago, an old acquaintance, vaguely familiar.

She draws him down next to her at the edge of the rock pile, the gable jutting next to them and Felix lying there for all to see, a ladybug crawling across his right eyeball. Enoch wills Felix to blink, to reach up and take the brick from his forehead. Instead, Connie Dopp falls beside him on her knees, arms hanging at her sides like ropes. The clean, pretty lines of her face dissolve, her lips open and close like those of a fish pulled from water. She looks up and fastens her eyes on Enoch, launches to her feet, and throws herself against him, pounding his shoulders and chest with sharp fists, Enoch tucking his face into an elbow, not to protect himself but to hide from God and everyone. He welcomes what little pain Connie's fists can deliver, and when she's gone, they all stand and look at him, their faces bland and quizzical, like the faces of cattle being fattened on grain and molasses. *You poor fools.* Those are the words that rush into his mind, surprising him, and he would utter them aloud except that his tongue is locked in his throat.

Soon they all wander off in ones and twos toward the grove, where scraps of their gaudy tents wink and flash in the wreckage of trees.

In the coming days, if he can find the strength, Enoch will have to search out the places inside him that harbored and fed his arrogance. But for now, like a stroke victim, whole planets of his universe careening off course or simply gone, he must absorb the doubt he has always kept at bay and which is settling already like a cold stone at the center of his chest. Sylvie puts her arms around him. She presses her cheek against his neck. "You were so close to right," she whispers, with a tenderness that makes his stomach lurch. "So close."

The sheriff's cruiser, a big cleft in its roof, comes to rest half a dozen feet from Felix's body, and Skinny steps out and kneels down to make sure. Then he climbs back in behind the wheel and speaks for a minute on his radio before getting out again. "Listen up, everybody! I need you over here. Come on, hurry up. We have to do a count."

Enoch wants to say, *A hundred and twenty-six,* but he doesn't speak—can't speak, undeserving as he is.

"There's a hundred and twenty campers," Sylvie says. "Enoch told me."

"Plus six Ranchers, counting Enoch and Jimmy Junior." It's Sarah, from a ragged huddle off to Enoch's right. She's hugging her baby boy to her breast.

Skinny starts herding again, shouting, bringing everyone together in the open space between the shower building, which still stands, and what little is left of the house.

"I have to know who's missing. Listen to me, damn it! Put yourselves in groups according to the tents you're sleeping in. Except for those who live here full-time—I want you over here. Come on, get with it." He claps his hands. "Quick! We have to account for everybody." Soon he starts counting aloud, "One, two, three—good, stay right there, don't move, don't move. Four, five—stay where you are! Six, seven, eight. Thank you."

As Enoch listens, the name twitches on his tongue like an electrical pulse—*Victor, Victor.* He tries to open his lips, free his tongue, but everything is frozen, his jaw like a vice.

"A hundred twenty-four, a hundred twenty-five," Skinny says, wrapping up. "One short. Now stay put, I'm doing it again. Listen to me! Stay where you are!" Once more he moves from group to group, calling out the count and touching each person as he goes, and when he comes to the end for a second time, he says, "Who's missing somebody?"

Enoch's tongue jumps in his mouth, and with the fingers of both hands he manages to pry open his jaw. "Victor," he says. "Victor! Victor!"—shouting now, picturing in his mind's eye the yellow boot soles, rising.

From ten miles to the west, the storm looks massive, a hell-dark cloud in the shape of a dinosaur, its long neck reaching to the ground. Melanie jams a finger into the windshield, pointing. She imagines her brother in his ruined farmhouse, crushed by a fallen wall, and Enoch lifted by the wind and dropped into Last Lake.

"We shouldn't have stopped," she says.

Peter, driving, fiddles with the radio, trying to sharpen the crackling broadcast from a local station.

"Watch the road!" Melanie shouts.

". . . village of Kesler . . . ," the announcer says, but the popping, whirring static cuts him off. ". . . quarter-mile swath . . ."

Peter slams his hand on the dashboard then touches the dial again, and the voice says, ". . . heading east now, northeast, into Spruce Township."

"It's already passed through, it's over," she says. "We should've been there."

"Things are probably fine."

"They're not fine. Shit—I knew he was right."

"It's a storm, Melanie. Not Jesus."

"What's the difference," she says. She pictures the oaks and tents in a whirlwind and presses her fists into the sockets of her eyes, pushing the image away. Last night after dropping Willie in Fargo they stopped at a diner for a midnight breakfast, then drove for maybe an hour before Peter started nodding off. She was in no shape at all to take over, and so they pulled into an empty farmstead for a short nap—only to wake at 5:15 to the sound of thunder.

Peter keeps both hands on the wheel, speedometer needle trembling between eighty-five and ninety, the car rocking and shaking on the old, patched road. She wants him to push harder, faster, but knows it wouldn't be safe.

"I've got a bad feeling," she says.

As they get closer, though, her hopes lift. There is no real damage to trees or buildings, just small branches down and evidence of a hard rain, water standing in ditches. Then they turn off Highway 2, heading south on the township road, and her stomach falls. First the cemetery on their right, where the entire row of blue spruce has been sheared off, as if by the sweep of a giant axe. Then on their left a hole in the landscape where the house in which she grew up used to stand. The entire east wall, picture window intact, leans against the silo. "Skinny," she says.

The oak grove is a decimated field of limbs and shattered stumps, and beyond it a squat building Melanie doesn't recognize. In the pasture, north of what used to be the Bywater house, she sees the ragtag crowd, Skinny standing at the front, his arms moving like a conductor's, his white cruiser parked off to the side. Peter drives beneath the sign that says *Last Days Ranch*, which is canted to one side but still erect. He goes halfway up the driveway then stops, peering into the rearview mirror. Melanie turns in her seat. A white television van has swung in behind them, and its driver lays on the horn. Peter pops his door and strides to the driver's side of the van, reaches in and grabs the man by the collar. Melanie jumps from the car, too, and runs toward her brother, nearly tripping on the splayed body of a hog, abdomen torn open, intestines uncoiled in the grass like a pink garden hose.

Skinny is wearing a brown sheriff's shirt, untucked and too small for him, its tails barely reaching his belt and waistband. When she hugs him from behind, her ear against his back, he turns to embrace her. "You're all right," she says. Underneath the morning cologne and male sweat, she catches a sour hint of barn chores.

"And Enoch?" she asks.

"He's okay."

Skinny goes on with his job, his arm around her shoulders, addressing the barefoot assembly in front of them. People staring ahead or at the ground, eyes hollow. Some wrapped in blankets, a few wearing only their underwear. Melanie may as well be invisible for the lack of recognition on their faces.

"The storm was moving like this." With his free arm Skinny indicates a path from the cemetery to Last Lake, cutting through the Magnussen farm, the oak grove, Enoch's house. "We have to assume he was carried in that direction." He points northeast. "Spread out and cover the area between here and the lake, do you hear? Also the land along the shore— that field and the swamp beyond it. We need to cover the lakeshore up past my place too, just to be sure. Go in groups of five or six, and stay ten feet apart. Walk slow—listen to me!—and when you've gone a quarter-mile or so, turn around and do the same thing coming back. Give a shout if you find something."

The Battlepoint ambulance rolls up next to Skinny's cruiser, lights going but no siren, and two men climb out and walk over behind the rock pile. They bend down. Melanie steps away from her brother for a better look and sees a pair of feet, toes pointing straight up. Enoch is there, too, sitting on a rock beside a thin, gray-haired woman, both of them hunched over, elbows on their knees. Enoch looks ancient, his shoulders like broken sticks, his face a death mask.

The pilgrims begin forming lines, and Melanie says, "Who are they looking for?"

"Victor," Skinny says. "They'll find him."

She gestures toward the body. "And who's that?"

"Some kid." He looks into her face. "I have to get hold of Ron now, he'll need me somewhere else, I'm guessing. People worse off than we are. You okay?"

She nods, and Skinny heads for his car. "Hey," she says.

He stops and turns around.

She gives him a little wave, and he waves back.

"I love you."

He smiles.

As she takes the smooth red rock beside Enoch, the ambulance crew is loading the covered body. One arm falls limp from the gurney. Enoch doesn't acknowledge Melanie. Nor does the woman beside him, whose small hands are clenched in front of her and clutching a candy bar, which she passes to Enoch. Sylvie.

"I should have been here," Melanie says.

He's staring past the devastation into a sky more benign than seems possible, a thin line of white clouds off to the west, but otherwise clear. The sun already warming the air. She lays a hand on his bony back. His long white hair curls over his ears and down over the collar of his shirt. The stubble on his chin and cheeks sparkles. She conjures the sensation of being lifted in his arms and carried across the pasture. The blinding sun on her face, the earth in her nostrils, the kindness and power in Enoch's voice as he prays.

"Thank you for my life," Melanie says.

He turns, jowls sagging. He says, "Do you think they'll find him?"

"Enoch, did you hear me? Thank you."

He looks away and coughs, then back at Melanie, veins bulging in his temple. Thirty feet away a clutch of reporters, including a couple of cameramen, watch from their huddle. Enoch gestures toward them, showing an index finger as if to say, *One moment.* Then he shrugs Melanie's hand from his back and turns to Sylvie. "It's time," he says, standing.

"Please, no. What can you tell them?"

He glances at Melanie, his dark eyes like small, dull stones. "About the taste of grass," he says and moves off toward the cameras.

Melanie considers joining a line of searchers inching toward the lake, but someone calls her name, a familiar voice, and looking around she sees Adam navigating the yard full of debris, not running—impossible in the heels he's wearing—but speed-walking, his eyes huge behind his big glasses.

She rushes toward him and they meet beside a mattress still dressed in its bedclothes, a bale of hay resting at the center of it. He puts her in a death hug and lifts her off her feet, nearly breaking her ribs. "I heard it on the radio and knew you were gone," he says, then sets her down and covers his face with his hands and starts to sob, his body quaking.

He allows himself to be led to the barn, the one building still intact, and in the cool silence she cradles his head and strokes his face. "It's okay," she tells him, remembering the last time she consoled someone— two years ago, maybe three, on a film set where one of the actors, a little boy, slammed his finger in a door. He was six or seven years old and howled like the end of the world, his breath coming in panicked gulps. Melanie picked him up and went off in a corner and held him in her lap until he was done crying.

But Adam isn't done yet, and she is in no hurry, because even if her head and stomach are in a tumult, and even if he needs to be held for the rest of the day, she is glad to be the one offering comfort this time, the one, for once, who is strong.

In Battlepoint he parks in front of the Red Owl grocery and ducks into the same phone booth he often called his dad from after baseball practice, needing a ride home. He dials the number and it starts ringing. "Pick up, you son of a bitch." He looks at his watch.

Seven thirty-five—an hour later in New York. At home, he'd held off the writers as long as he could.

Freddy's voice comes on. "Yes?"

"It's me."

"My man! Are you ready for the limelight?"

"Tell your friends at NBC to cancel their flights."

"Whoa. What? Jesus came and left already?"

"Pretty much, yeah."

"What's going on?"

"I'm calling it off."

"We've got a deal, man."

"It's over."

"Slow down here. Tell me what happened."

"If they show up, fine, but there's nothing to see. Everybody's gone home."

"You're shitting me. Someone else is getting the story, right?"

"The story is mine, Freddy, and I'm guessing Rusty will still want it."

"Peter, listen—it's about money, isn't it? Look, I know what a tight-ass he is. I'll talk to him."

"Just call off the TV people, that's all I'm asking. I'll talk to Rusty, explain everything."

"You can't fuck with me like this. After all I did for you?"

"I'm not fucking with you, Freddy. And I'll have the story in by Friday, as agreed."

"I oughtta sue you. I could make sure you never publish another thing in this town."

"Just tell them it won't work tomorrow. And if you can get ahold of Rusty, let him know I'll be in touch. Will you do that?"

He can see the man's face, his glasses slipping down to the top of his nose, his lips drawn back from his neat little teeth like they do when he's angry.

"Okay?" Peter says.

"Okay, fuck, yeah."

He hangs up, then drives back home where he spends the rest of the day assisting in the search for Victor, who Peter can't help but think is hiding someplace—pleased to be getting the last laugh. They cover every square foot of the country within half a mile north of the Ranch, and the sheriff's department rounds up a dozen boat owners to drag the lake with hooks. At suppertime one of the crews blows its whistle—but it's only a deer, a twelve-point buck, drowned in deep water off the two-mile bar. At dusk Sheriff Chaffee calls a halt to the search till morning, and by full dark most of the pilgrims have taken their leave, driving off in their station wagons, trucks, and sedans, most of the vehicles still functional after the storm, parked as they were in open pasture. Even the boys who cycled in have found their bikes and made them rideable, though one sustained damage to a wheel that Peter was able to replace with one from his old three-speed Raleigh, sitting rusty in the basement. The dead boy's girlfriend has been taken away by a woman from County Social Services.

All the while, Peter's mind is grinding away on the story he has to write. He should be worrying about his dad, he tells himself, and focused on finding Victor, but in fact he's making mental notes of everything he sees. The chair from his childhood desk, wedged into the high fork of a surviving elm tree. The GROUND JESUS sign floating in the bulrushes. A tent pole with a rag of white nylon impaled like a flag of surrender in a muskrat lodge. He takes it all in, composing sentences in his mind, guiltily, and rehearsing them. He also listens to the pilgrims talk among themselves, not with bitterness, most of them—though some are angry, and one comes right up to Peter and says, "I hope that Roper boy's family sues your dad for everything he has." Still, the general mood is stunned relief. With quiet fear, their heads shaking, they whisper about God's mysteries and God's power, cowed, it seems, by the awful, slanted pre-science of Enoch's dream.

At dusk, the electricity is still off, and Peter starts the gas generator and hooks it up to the electrical system of the barn. With two empty apartments—three, actually, since Jimmy and Sarah seem to have fled—there is plenty of room for Enoch, and also for Peter and Melanie, if they decide to stay. Which Peter has, for long enough to help with cleanup, though Melanie wants him along with her in L.A. on Labor Day week-end for the premier of *World's End.*

In the meantime, he can't help wondering if his dad will live through the night. His face is sallow, his mouth hanging, his eyes flat and gray. They're sitting together in the aviary at a makeshift table, planks on sawhorses—Peter and Melanie, Enoch and Sylvie. It's 10 p.m., and Sylvie is just back from Battlepoint with a bag of hamburgers, the first food any of them has eaten all day. "Come on, just a bite," she says, and she lifts a burger to Enoch's mouth. He looks away. He's been silent since morning, when he spoke to media for fifteen minutes, sparing himself nothing, as-suming full blame for the death of Felix Roper and the disappearance and apparent loss of Victor Stubblefield. His face distorted by shame, misshapen, like a boxer's after a brawl, he apologized not only to Felix's family and Victor's, too, wherever they might be, but also to everyone he misled. "Everyone," he said, "whose fears I stoked." He made no effort to recast his vision in a new light. He made no plea to be forgiven.

Peter couldn't tell, as he watched, if this might be the end of his father, or if he had simply never seen before the man his father is. In any case, he looks ill, sitting there across the table, and Peter wonders if he should drive him into town, admit him to the hospital. But then suddenly Enoch cocks his head, as if he's heard a noise. He straightens in his chair and pushes his hair behind his ears.

"Peter, would you take a walk with me? Please?" He looks over at Sylvie. "It won't be long."

She puts a hand on his arm. "Whatever it is can wait. Stay here."

"No, let them go," Melanie says, and Enoch's dark eyes acknowledge her, lingering for a moment.

"All right, then," Peter says.

Sylvie throws up her hands and shoos them away.

He follows his dad down the stairs and across the yard to the dark, truncated house, the upper walls and windows of which Peter saw scattered through the pasture and swamp this afternoon. "Please wait here," Enoch says, and he goes up on the porch and inside. In a minute he's back with an electric torch, and they set off up the driveway, light bouncing in front of them, past the dead hog and a small, lime-green transistor radio—Skinny's?—and a pitchfork spiked into the ground. At the end of the driveway Enoch turns right and they follow the township road as it curves north past the Magnussen place, the Lutheran cemetery approaching on their left, Enoch walking briskly now, their feet against the gravel the only sound except for an owl calling from the woods.

"Where are we going, Dad?"

"Trying to follow the storm track, backwards."

"Why?"

"I thought of something. It should have hit me earlier. This morning when the funnel passed over me, this sow and her brood flew by like they were jet-powered. But they were heading *that* way." He stops and aims the beam of light toward the cemetery. "Against the storm. Just like the radio—did you see it back there? That was from the attic, your mom had it when she was sick. Everybody searched the area to the north, but I'm thinking we should have been searching in this direction, too."

"Makes sense," Peter says. "A twisting wind, after all."

Enoch leads them into the cemetery, aiming his flashlight at the line of spruce trees snapped off clean about twenty feet up. "We'll just walk through and have a look. Hey, see that?" His light catches a paperback book splayed open on top of a gravestone. "Bet it's from our place."

And it is. A novel Peter read one summer, riding a bus between ballparks. *Alas, Babylon.* He slides it into his back pocket.

The deeper they go, the more damage to the trees and the harder it is to walk, branches down everywhere. It looks like a giant game of pick-up-sticks, some of the aspens and birch yanked out by the roots and lying flat. Peter half-expects to stumble on Victor's body, Enoch worked up as he is, kicking deadfall aside, scrambling over fallen trunks, and stooping low to peer through bramble or into clutches of red willow.

"Take it easy," Peter tells him.

Enoch stops and leans against a headstone. He's breathing hard, a hand on his chest. "I always prayed God would crack you open and fill you up with Himself," he says. He gulps air and shines the torch on his own face, which lit from below is a skull, his eyes like empty holes. "But I didn't see till now that I was the one doing all the cracking. I had the hammer, and I was swinging it myself." He pauses to breathe. "I am so tired. So tired. You said to me once—you were sixteen, maybe—'Why should I bother with a god I can't see when I've got one I *can* see right in front of me?'"

"Yeah," Peter says, without thinking. "I'm glad you're out of the way."

Enoch takes the light and shines it all around. "We're not going to find him, are we?" He jams his knuckles into his eyes, and his shoulders move in a single, wrenching shudder. "I'm so sorry," he says. "I hope you can forgive me someday."

Peter wants to say, *Of course I forgive you*—just to perk him up a little, slouched against the stone as he is, head sagging between his shoulders. Just to convince himself to feel pity for the old man—pity it's too soon to feel and that his father does not deserve. "I hope I can, too," he says.

"I suppose you'll get it all down in that story you're writing. Oh, and your typewriter was delivered yesterday, I forgot to tell you. It's in the main floor closet—or at least I hope it's still there." Enoch shifts the flashlight from one hand to the other, its beam jumping in the trees.

"Hey," Peter says, "what's that?" He takes the light from his dad and aims it high into a pine tree, some twenty yards away. There's something up there—flesh-colored, and not small. More than a hundred feet off the ground, maybe a hundred and fifty, close to the tree's crown. Peter walks over for a better look.

"We'll go back and call Skinny, get some guys out here to help," Enoch says. "You can't climb up there."

It's a virgin white pine, well over a century old, here since before the first graves were laid in the 1860s, the cemetery likely responsible for saving it from the loggers. Peter hands the torch to his dad. "I'll need both hands," he says and pushes aside a big, sweeping bough that rests on the ground.

"That's not a good idea."

Inside the tree's reach, Peter sets his palms against the trunk, its bark rough and sticky with pitch, the smell almost enough to make him sick. He takes hold of a branch at eye level, pulls himself up, and begins his ascent mostly by feel, the light from his dad's torch barely penetrating the heavily needled limbs. After a few minutes of steady climbing, he stops to breathe. It's been twenty years since he went up a tree, and never this high. He remembers it being easier than it is.

"I can't see you," Enoch calls.

In fact, he's right up next to the trunk, but now he eases himself away from it, holding tight to the branch above him and carefully working himself toward the outside. He sticks his head as far out as he can, and he looks down at his dad, right into the flashlight's beam. He must be a hundred feet in the air.

"Trying to get a feel for where I am," he says.

"You're over halfway. Well over. It's another twenty or thirty feet, and you'll need to move clockwise as you go. Say you're at twelve o'clock now, you have to be at about three. Be careful."

Peter takes a minute to rest, looking back toward the Ranch and the lit windows of the barn where Melanie and Sylvie are no doubt starting to worry, and beyond them to Last Lake, inky dark beneath a pane of clouds, the night quiet beneath him and silent above. Although he's damp with sweat from climbing, the breeze from the north is cool enough at this height to make him shiver. He wonders, once he has helped his dad square things away, if he will ever spend time here again. He wonders if he'll be comfortable in L.A., and whether he and Melanie will be as good together as it feels like they might be. "Help us," he says, offering the prayer before realizing what he has done—it simply rushes out of him, like a breath held too long, like the forgotten chorus of an old song. Like a cry of joy or pain. "Please," he adds and begins to ease himself back to the main trunk before continuing his climb.

Peter wishes he didn't have to stop, that he could keep on going, rising into air so thin it would burn his lungs with a purifying fire, rising until the entire lovely world is spread out beneath him, every single inch and mile, all of it revealed, nothing hidden any longer. And now the moon breaks through, granting a clear view of the thing he is looking for—not more than six feet away and hanging from the same branch he's holding on to with his right hand.

"Is it him?" Enoch calls.

Peter edges toward it. At this height, the tree's limbs are smaller, the one on which he is standing no bigger around than his wrist.

"Can you see? Is it Victor?"

"Just a minute."

"What is it, Peter? Tell me."

He runs his fingers along the coarse fur, remembering the night in the calf shed, and the next day, skinning it out and nailing its hide to the granary's south wall. He remembers the lion's impassive face as it entered the shed, and the dangerous grace of its movements. The beauty of its symmetry. A creature in full possession of its purpose for being, and for that reason to be envied. He remembers his finger on the cold trigger, the empty space inside his chest, the force of the shotgun's kick against his shoulder. And of course his dad's efforts to frighten him, control him. Peter considers leaving the skin here and being rid of it for good, of calling out to his dad, *It's nothing, only a piece of cardboard.* Except that he doesn't want to leave it here, a realization that takes him by surprise. Because the lion is his—he killed it and made it so. Yes, he means to keep it. He has paid for it dearly.

Or was it a gift?

He reaches out and pulls it free and hugs it to his chest. It smells like his bedroom, growing up. It smells like dust and flesh. It smells like fire.

"What is it?" Enoch calls.

A chilling gust of wind disturbs the tree, which sways now like a great giant unsure of his footing. At the top, Peter holds on, waiting for stillness. When it comes, he drapes the hide across his back and ties the two front legs in a loose knot at the front of his neck, the warmth along his shoulders reassuring. Thus robed, he begins his descent.

LIN ENGER is the author of two previous novels, *Undiscovered Country* (Minnesota, 2020) and *The High Divide*. His short fiction has been published in *Glimmer Train, Ascent, Great River Review, American Fiction,* and other literary journals. He holds an MFA from the Iowa Writers' Workshop and has taught English for more than two decades at Minnesota State University Moorhead.